Helen Stevenson

Helen Stevenson grew up in South Yorkshire, studied Modern Languages at Somerville College, Oxford and spent some time living in the south of France, between the Mediterranean and the Pyrenees. Her first novel was *Pierrot Lunaire*. She now lives in South London and is a full-time writer.

SCEPTRE

Also by Helen Stevenson

Pierrot Lunaire

Praise for Helen Stevenson

'Funny and a touch sad . . . a post-feminist novel so sharp it cuts itself . . . The romance captures the heat and scents of summer in Southern France . . . and it has a great heroine.'
The Times

'An entertaining satire . . . spiced up with sparkling writing and pin-sharp wit . . . a thoroughly enjoyable read and an assured debut from a fine new writer.'
Yorkshire Post

Windfall

HELEN STEVENSON

SCEPTRE

First published in 1996 by Hodder and Stoughton
Published in paperback in 1996 by Hodder and Stoughton
A division of Hodder Headline PLC
A Sceptre Paperback

10 9 8 7 6 5 4 3 2 1

British Library Cataloguing in Publication Data

Stevenson, Helen
Windfall
I. Title
823.914 [F]

ISBN 0 340 61824 8

Typeset by Palimpsest Book Production Limited,
Polmont, Stirlingshire
Printed and bound in Great Britain by
Cox and Wyman Ltd, Reading, Berkshire

Hodder and Stoughton
A division of Hodder Headline PLC
338 Euston Road
London NW1 3BH

Part One

1

There can be nothing more disembodied than a human voice singing words you do not understand. I often used to listen to Elizabeth, with a wall, or maybe two, between us. Her voice was so young, younger than she; it had a quality of shocked freshness, like a footprint crushed into the dew. I could, had I chosen, have imagined the words, the scene: that count who was leaving for war again, or the portrait turned to the wall. I could have pictured her face with the odd look it wore when she sang, the refusal to tense the eye muscles or to lift the brows bringing a strange wistfulness to it, which made me imagine she was singing the sorrow of someone she had never met. Her hands were so familiar they could have been my own, palms upwards, fingers curled but never, never clenched, as though she were measuring two tiny ounce weights, but for something other than their weight, some quality that might be conveyed to the nerves in her palms, run shivering up her spinal cord and be transmitted in a kind of chimeric ecstasy in her voice. I could understand, in her voice, why people talk of the shadow of an emotion. A shadow is an absence, where no light falls; but the negative picture is thrown by the very thing which is illuminated. Where others had happiness, Elizabeth bore the strange subtle imprint of its absence. And so you could take her voice into your own head and sing with it yourself, and sometimes, when I had been doing this for only a minute, waving about, mentally, in my chair by the window, I would feel doubled up with emotion and my muscles would have gripped themselves rigid; but for her, always for her. I was the animator of her soul, that did not sing.

* * *

She came to me by chance. It was a kind of convalescence. It seemed that I was convalescing from life and she from death. We would sit in the garden in the early evening – at that time she used to go to bed almost with the light – when the sun was lower than the walls and there was a lit-up feeling to what was left of the day – and I would wonder how I could give her back her soul, or the sense of it. For I had not taken it, nor was it mine in any way to restore. I had no wish to mother her either. I had never really mothered anyone at all, except perhaps the odd kitten. There was nothing kitten-like about Elizabeth. She was strong, almost middle-aged; between two ages, you might say. I was strong too, but between two different ages. I have always felt most comfortable with old people, even as child, and now I am almost come to that myself, which should suit me. To look at, you would think Elizabeth had walked in out of another age, but in fact she is thoroughly modern. It is strange that we talk of the Middle Ages – if anything, the Victorians would have been much happier with the title: it conjures up such a picture of pouchy comfortableness, which goes not at all well with pestilence and disease and religious persecution.

Although I am an Englishwoman, I was married to a Frenchman for forty-four years and I have lived in this house for close on twenty-seven. Widowed for three. So that means his mother died after we had been married for twenty-one years. Fortunately he had no brothers and sisters. (Even in terms of property I think like a Frenchwoman). Before I die I will sell the house, to a young family perhaps, foreigners too. They will rush from window to window, hurling back the shutters against the walls and exclaim at the acres of leafy vines – all leased now, I no longer work them myself. And one morning in autumn they will draw back aghast at the view of those knobbled black stumps, nature's *danse macabre*, rippling away like so many fields of First World War crosses. Still, spring comes early in the south.

Every morning I bow my head at the bedroom window before these vines, in or out of leaf, and part my hair with the spike of my comb, a long clean pencil line down to my brow. Pierre used to say I would draw blood one day. It is not beautiful hair, not like Elizabeth's, but it is long and I am adept with the knot at the back of my neck. I fasten it quickly with a sort of pin which they don't make any more, and which I would have to have specially made were it to break. Shortly after Pierre died I had it all cut off into a neat grey helmet. It caused quite a stir at the hairdresser's. The girl who did it had an assistant standing by to sweep up the long grey locks as they fell, to prevent them from forming a pile. I think she felt that to have them lying there on the floor, as though they had somehow been wept there, would shock any incoming customers, giving the salon something of the feel of a pre-guillotine chamber. In fact, everyone was quite surprised at the end result. I looked so much younger with the short cut, a Joan of Arc combination of swagger and innocence, that the gesture was seen as one of liberation rather than of mourning. So I let it grow again, and people were able to say I was letting myself go and felt comforted that I was properly widowed and grieving. Soon I was back with the Spanish comb, cleaving a neat furrow along my scalp each morning. Let's hope I never see anything terrible out of my bedroom window. I did once, in Elizabeth's day, and the man at the wrought iron works mended my pin in his spare time, with his spare skills, which were no longer needed as everything now came out of a mould, where he worked. Pierre was right, I did, that once, draw blood. I'm more careful these days. But I still look out.

I was going to call this Elizabeth's story, *tout simple*, but then it occurred to me that it really wasn't hers at all. Like any other artifact, a Spanish comb, an aria even, the story belongs in the end to its creator. And while theological doctrine, which isn't really my strong point, reminds us that creation takes place *ex nihilo*, fabrication (which is actually quite a strong point) *prejacenti materia*, I'm going to think of this as my creation. The heretics had an expression which covers the points nicely: *Deus est creator sive factor*. Well if He can be so can I, (although the expression does remind me rather of a very cheerful 'rainy day' book we had as children called *Things to Make and Do*. It always strikes me as significant that God started off making the world when it was dark and raining. But did He manage to pull off whatever it was He had in mind? Was it all laid down, pre-conceived in lovely perfection? Did it all go wrong in the execution, so that a week later he awoke and shook His head sadly and said "that is not what I meant . . . That is not what I meant at all"? Or did He intend it to be like this, two steps forward, three steps back, with the constant anxiety that the light at the end of the tunnel might be a possible apocalypse?) God's world, not man's world. The tenant in the vineyard. Do not damage or consume; leave as you found it. It's an idea that's coming back into vogue. So, a little bit *ex nihilo*, a little bit of what's lying around, finest thread and shoddy scraps, *creator sive factor*, we'll skip the fastidious distinctions.

I spend a long time looking at these vines. The window is open this afternoon and there is a light wind, which will bring rain in a few hours. For now the sun is shining on the vine leaves, vivid lime-coloured shoots sprung from the twisted members of last year's woody growth. Each plant stands exactly one metre distant from its eight neighbours. A simple distribution of this kind makes calculations about yield per hectare very simple. It also creates strange optical effects, although the effect of custom is such that I have to blink before I see them now. Wherever you stand in the field, you become the centre of a radial clock, and wherever your eye focuses, a row of vines opens before you like a ten pin bowling alley. In late spring and summer I can almost see the shoots growing, the leaves shaking themselves loose in the light. There is something about a vine – unlike any other plant, it seems to unpack itself after winter, as though the shoots and leaves, even the flowers and fruit, have been in storage, minutely packaged away like a travelling medicine chest, with unbelievable yards and yards of lint and bandage rolled into the space of a thumbnail. When the leaves first open, in early April, they are freshly crinkled, like the skin of a newborn baby or a silk dress taken from your luggage.

I seem almost to live in this room now. At night I simply put myself away upstairs. Night time is not my time at all. I no longer even dream. Over the past months I have gradually brought everything together in this one room – the books I will still read, a favourite photograph, the grey Irish jug for flowers, pen holder, Christian's lucky horseshoe, my nest of marbled eggs. Tomorrow I will fetch the bedside table down, the spindly one on Pierre's side of the bed. I'll take the old Persian runner off it and put it over the back of that chair. It's too long for the table. There is a strange current in my blood at the moment. Sometimes I have imagined I could enchant an object, draw it into this room by the force of my desire. Then I go and fetch it and place it on the table in front of me. That little pan pipe leaning on the bookend now. Pierre made it for me on a picnic once, out of a splint of ash. It never worked, not a peep, not so much as a toot out of it for forty years. I brought it in before breakfast, out of the glass cabinet in the drawing room. There's a china doll left in there, and a little wooden model of a boat, with elaborate rigging made of black cotton. I don't think I'll move those. They can sit it out. I came in after lunch (I wait till the sun moves round to this side of the house) and was pleased to find the pan pipe here, next to the old pruning knife we used to cut willow. I am acquiring a talent for the happy disposal of objects, for the pleasing little ironies and references that arise through chance contiguity, like a chaotically hung exhibition from which a striking, unintended meaning can emerge. There's one stranger in the room. Something jars. What is it? The lamp? My plaster parrot? The leather-bound Shelley? Yes, perhaps Shelley was a false move. And the African book ends. They belong in a different exhibition. I'll put them back. But it's not that. It's that sampler, isn't it? Sampler: 1. A piece of canvas embroidered by a beginner as a specimen of her skill, usually containing the alphabet and some mottoes, with various decorative devices. 2. A young tree left standing when all the rest are cut down. (I like that, don't you? Elizabeth? Can you hear me? Elizabeth!)

The house is very silent, I've noticed that today. A footstep on the gravel would alarm me now. My hands are trembling. I'm not so very old, but my hands are trembling. Sixty-five, six; twenty years to go, at the least (the tenancies are tied up for that long. I can't afford to expire before they do). Let's go out and walk along the vines. Pascal, who manages the vines, came this morning to tell me that the roses are sickening. We planted them, Albertines, when we first came. The first sign of sickness in the rose comes a week before it attacks the vine, so you can take action before it's too late. It's rather a pity for the roses, like being the king's taster, privileged to exist, but essentially doomed. Our vines grow on their own stocks, which makes them particularly vulnerable to phylloxera, an aphid-like pest – generally results in severe discolouration of the leaves, followed by what the experts call "rapid collapse and death". So the roses are there to protect them. Pierre loved those roses. He wept whenever they succumbed. His heart was in the right place. Unfortunately its being well sited didn't actually stop it giving out before it should have done.

I'll put a scarf on over my hat, like a beekeeper, and go outside, when I've fastened this window back. It tends to catch the wind. The glass is so thin, like a sheet of ice barely formed over a puddle in the early morning, with a violet tint which comes from years of sunlight. Then I'll walk along the edge of the field by the roses, take my secateurs. If you're tired you needn't come. I can manage. I have a feeling they may sicken soon. I'll save a few blooms before the blight.

I was going to tell you before I got on to the roses. It's only a little thing, about the sampler. It hangs on a nail I found in Pierre's old tool box. The plaster jumped off the wall where I tapped it in with the heel of my shoe (which took quite a precise aim, I can tell you), but of course you don't see that as long as the picture hangs there. "Do justly, love mercy, walk humbly," it says, and what a little model of harmony of intention and action it is, with its pious injunction pricked out neatly in blue cross stitch. How the demure little needlewoman has toiled, her smooth brow bent calmly over her task, her modestly covered arm, in grey silk perhaps, quaker grey, capped by a white cuff. One day I came into the house and left the front door swinging in the wind, which swept up the hallway like a station master passing down the platform, slamming shut doors as the train prepares to leave. It ducked its head into my room with a brief, high cry, then whipped the door shut with an abusive clap, and the little sampler slid to the floor like a delicate lady in a swoon. The wooden backing fractured, and the glass glanced off the side of my table here and broke. I picked the frame up off the floor. The unhemmed square of embroidered cloth had been stretched and folded over it, like the lid of a shoebox, so that when I turned it over to look at the back it was like looking at an image which lay at the bottom of a shallow printing tray. The inverted image, vivid in unaged threads which had never seen the sun, was planted like an overgrown border in chaotic loops and bunches of ragged ends, and for a moment I glimpsed a second, impious message, like the name that flares on the grail and dies without trace, in the tell-tale wilderness of the needlewoman's angry stitching.

2

In the beginning, my beginning, though it seemed like the middle, nearer the end really for them, there was Elizabeth and Mark. Mark and Pierre had a vague academic connection, through the University of Toulouse. Word came, through Pierre, that Mark would be spending a few days with us at the farmhouse before the start of his autumn term, and that he would be arriving with an Elizabeth. When a couple is announced like that they come to you fresh, on equal footing, like names on a public letter head. It is easy to forget that they too have their separate pasts, their trailing shoots and tendrils, their new, old, and almost dead bits. But they did have their past, both as a couple, and as people who, for the greater part of their lives, had not known one another at all. They were not married, though Mark was married to another woman, so they had not consumed one another's pasts, as usually happens through official union – that economical clearing away of the afterbirth, the spillage which has allowed this new thing, the couple, to come into being, but must not itself be allowed to linger and reek. Nor were they new to love, a love, it is true, which lay slack between them, twitching only every now and again whenever the prospect of loss or change made them flinch. When love is new and you still have to run to keep up with it, your head tilted back, chasing the changing, billowing shapes of the clouds, you forget the past too, and the intensity of the charge sends the clocks whizzing, or stops them dead and consumes the calender, and the past; before you met was the old world, and you stand at the water's edge laughing at those who have thought to bring luggage for the journey. Later, of course, you have to go back for your own luggage, and then once more, for the things you had forgotten to pack. Elizabeth had met Mark during her final year at university, where he was a junior fellow in the French department. By then she was twenty-four and he was – already – ten years older. She had gone late to university, having spent a year in Bordeaux as an au pair, and another nursing her mother, who enjoyed a psychosomatic depression following on the death of her husband.

During this second year of forbearance she took up singing lessons. Her voice had been discovered quite late, at the back of a drawer towards the front of which she kept more obvious attributes, like beauty and sense. Her sense was not common, nor was it quite intelligence, it was like the secret knowledge of a child, which most people lose, the odd, angular perspective, the view before the veil of experience falls, and it came from her father, who had never seen the world quite straight; for him, life had been cast in a slightly quizzical mode; in Elizabeth the same perspective resulted in an impression of aloofness. When Elizabeth was fourteen, she and her father had gone to a concert in a cathedral, where they heard a performance of Fauré's Requiem, which is generally considered tuneful enough for children. It was one of the rare such occasions they shared. Elizabeth had held her father's hand with both her own, one below, one above, throughout the performance, because she felt it must be possible for two people who loved each other to feel an emotion together, to hear the music as though they shared a sense line, and that joining hands would be not just a symbol of, but actually a means of achieving this. Driving home through wet streets, with the windows misted and the darkness deepened a shade by the rain and lying in a film across the sharp differentiations of the world outside, Elizabeth had produced what had been meant to be an imitation of the soprano, not mocking, but she was, she thought later, definitely simulating, not emulating. In the way that certain animals seem to produce, on giving birth, not a helpless, scarcely formed infant, but simply a modified version of the fully blown adult form, maturity in detail having already been fully attained in another existence, so it was with Elizabeth's voice. It came out as the real thing, full and round and colourful. Father and daughter stared at each other in shock, under the choleric light of a neon lamp. It was as though, without meaning to peep at all, they had glimpsed a red, mature fruit nestling in a tray with all the others still far from ripened. When years later, she began her singing lessons, clandestinely at first, it was in memory of that moment, a secret which could no longer be kept between the two of them; because her father was dead, silence could no longer serve to keep their faith. Eventually her mother overheard her. She arrived back at the house from a meeting of the neighbourhood watch to find her own home full of song. The intrusion of feeling might have set the alarm bell ringing, had it not been a fake, the plastic box on the pebbledash wall but a frail deterrent, an empty threat. Mrs Faulkener at first adopted a Mrs Worthington position towards what she considered to be a preparation for a career on the stage, and expressed her alarm by pointing to the impropriety of Elizabeth's choice of "hobby" in the light of her father's recent demise. When she realised that Elizabeth was not set for a career belting out "Hey Big Spender" in the Blackpool ballroom and had more of a drawing-room bent, she changed her tune and to prove her acquiescence would invite Elizabeth to delight her with the odd rendition of "Poor Wandering One", which had always been a favourite of her husband's.

Elizabeth had been a quiet student; studious, aloof, quite aside from the shriek and paddle of undergraduate life. An affair with Mark had suited her perfectly. He had a cottage five miles from the university town, and Elizabeth would spend the weekends with him. They would walk, and she would cook meals for him. He helped her with her proses. He meant she didn't have to go to parties. He was very tall, and quite athletic in build. He made the undergraduates, among the more selective of whom she had a certain vogue, look provisional, identical in the way that saplings in a nursery often seem identical, unless you actually get up close and examine their defects. His hair was already grey in parts, and his eyelashes were long and abundant, so that she was reminded of those little children whose eyelashes, when their eyes are closed, trim their lids like an extravagant flounce, something to be grown into. He was young for a don, and far too old to be a student. She appreciated this double exile, the fact that professionally he swam between two waters. He was married to a woman who lived in Yorkshire, who never counted for her, as she believed she could not count for the woman in Yorkshire. When he returned to Anna for holidays and family gatherings, and it was rare, Elizabeth spared him. She never for a moment suggested he should end his marriage. It was a spotless relationship – owing partly to the necessity for discretion, partly to its having a present and no future. They were both able to be on their best behaviour all the time. If either of them felt at one time or another a little more passion than was strictly permissible within the terms of their agreement, that passion was never directed towards change, as passion will normally come round of its own accord into the wind and have a naturally accelerating effect, but in being contained, glimmered then died, like a short autumn day. He taught her a great deal about the more far-flung corners of the syllabus, which meant that her specialisations isolated her increasingly from the general flock of the faculty. He made love to her in a variety of manners, some less comfortable than others, and never offended her by asking solicitously whether she had had any pleasure herself. It was a courtly intimacy. After making love they drank herbal tea or the kind of wine which was expensive enough for you to be sure some of the money must have gone on ridding it of any headache-inducing impurities, and he would read troubadour poetry and, on request, her essays. She found the formality of their relationship rather exciting. There was a rigorously professional streak in her which made her want to do things well, and this necessarily involved a certain amount of artifice. The theatricality which this in turn entailed appealed to the exhibitionist in her, even though their affair was secret and without witnesses. She had often thought that she must really shake herself and find a proper lover, one who would not feel quite so much like a book borrowed from the library that may not be scribbled in, or even neatly annotated, since scribbling was not her style and marks are marks, but Mark suited her and did not want her children. She never thought much about the need to meet a man who would "give her children". The way she looked at it, perhaps the way most women look at it, the children she might one day have were all there, ready to produce, like a special bottle from the cellar, to the right man, at the right time.

After university she spent a year in Bath studying for a diploma in translation and arrived in London a year later. She bought a small house, refused her mother's offer of a chocolate brown sofa with matching armchairs, painted everything white and furnished it with wicker chairs which creaked for the first few months and then settled down in silence. She set up a small business translating documents, brochures, and occasionally, once her reputation grew, short stories and articles for university presses. During the first couple of years she drifted apart from Mark, who was spending a sabbatical in Toulouse. On his return he submitted his thesis on Jean de Peyrouth, a little known troubadour poet, to the Oxford University Press, who kindly completed the circle by asking Elizabeth to translate it. They took up together once again, and it lasted four more years, until the day he took her to a concert, the second decisive concert of her life, where Will discovered her and carried her off like a wolf child into his own curious, damp-warm, infinitely sensual underworld.

But it was the late summer of the year before this happened, a month before Pierre's death, and two summers before she came to me to recover from Will's death, that she and Mark came to stay. Pierre kept his distance from Elizabeth – she was a little bit on the stately side for his taste, so while he and Mark poured over footnotes, I took her to myself, and we spent three or four days driving around Occitanie.

This is old troubadour country, where the bright light (such a different thing from its plural equivalent) and the shimmer and colour of pageantry have hung in the air since long before the crusades; heat and sharp stone buildings, gentle glinting rivers, scraggy pasture of rocks and cork oaks rising with the mountain skyline beyond, to where the stern, paternalistic peaks soar above the gaiety of the towns. It is a world of contrasts, of light and dark, mountain and valley, passion and purity; of merchant and shepherd, red wine and springs, ragged and smooth, lush and spartan, echoing with the cries of "drink for tomorrow we die" and with oh such a brooding weight of silent history. In Occitanie the Dark Ages were conducted in piercing sunlight;

it must have been a bit like having Christmas in Australia. And here, before Occitanie was even annexed to France, while from the lips of the troubadours sprang their listless, joyous songs of desire and renunciation, and from the mouths of cloistered priests their thin and plaintive psalmodies, both on their knees, but their necks, as Pierre used to say, at quite a different angle (I used to think he meant the troubadours were looking up the ladies' skirts, but now I think he was probably being less Rabelaisian than I thought, and they were just kissing hands), a strange virus arrived from the east. While the lords and their vassals were away dying fly-sozzling deaths on foreign soil, steeped in the blood of the Lord, sleek men of the east were calmly shipping in their sugar and spices, sacks of deep ochre saffron spilling riotously over on the quay at Narbonne, cumin and coriander musking the sea salt air, the virus crept ashore, like a plague-ridden rat who has stowed away in the bowels of a ship. It came at a time and to a place which were so propitious that, had it not been for the papal and Carolingian war machine that moved west from Rome and south from Paris, it might still be alive today. Some say it still is.

The virus was a thought, an infection of the intellect, and it attacked a body social made weak and drunkenly tolerant by the celebration of light and love. It was a dualist heresy – what else in a country of such light and shade as I have described? It was an ascetic heresy – its councils of perfection so austere that only a select few, the "parfaits", could be expected to adhere to them. This was also, in a sense, true of the Catholic church at the time – the shaded and cloistered virtues of Cluny and Clairveaux, the world as Babylon well lost, with "many are called but few are chosen" exercising a nicely tuned system of exclusion from divine grace. But in the newly egalitarian society of Occitanie, the kind which always seems to emerge when the men depart to squabble over some great cause, the further away the better, grace was available to all – women and children and languid swains, at a pace of their own choosing. Oh God make me perfect, but not yet. In my next life maybe, or the one after that. There was always another chance. It might, I suppose, have seemed a laconic religion; maybe that's what made it seem so dangerous. You took it all more or less seriously, and even in purgatory you knew that at least the light of the world would shine, the familiar Mediterranean sun. At the top of the hierarchy you had the parfaits and parfaites, who had taken their final vows of purity, and whose lives were therefore dedicated to God and the world of the spirit. At the bottom, the stragglers, the rural poor, for whom life expectancy was probably so short that it was hardly surprising you needed a number of reincarnations to get it right. The ultimate objective of existence was that the soul be freed from its material prison, the world, the body, so that on death it might be reunited with its spirit and its celestial body, from which it had been painfully parted during its sojourn on earth. The world of matter, creation of Lucifer, the most beautiful and best loved of the angels, fallen so far that we know him by the name of Satan, will destruct or dissolve away when the last soul has been reunited with its celestial double, its spirit, which floats between heaven and earth; when the soul and the spirit meet, illumination occurs. The individual becomes pure, or Cathar, and experiences no further longing or desires. And the last soul to turn will be Lucifer's – conversion being the only possible means of truly vanquishing an enemy, bringing him round to your own point of view.

The world as dirty matter. It's an odd idea to have flourished in a country of such spectacular beauty. Maybe it was a reaction – the evangelism of the converted, Pauline passion. And nothing gives you back the sense of your soul like the experience of beauty. It's a paradox you have to live with, the way your soul aches and you hear all the music of the world when you see a lovely face. Desire and renunciation as two sides of the same redemptive coin. Something about the heresy worked a magic on the populace, and in the end, under threat of massacre, scornful of the offer of papal grace, confident of grace in the courts of heaven, a band of two hundred and fifty lords and vassals, women, children, merchants and shepherds, fought to defend the last fortress of Montségur, perched high on a rocky outcrop, besieged by the papal army of Simon de Montfort from below, but with the clouds parting in glory, so it is said, above their heads. The two hundred and fifty were a strange ragbag of sacred and profane adherents to the cause. Through twenty months of hardship, in cramped, insanitary conditions, with the army baying for blood and recantation at the foot of the hill, suffering the extremes of cold and heat in the winter and summer months, despite hunger and sickness and squalor, the parfaits managed to cling to their faith as to the rock face, to keep the peace and a belief in the purity of their cause. In so doing, they converted all their imperfect companions to the faith, the swashbuckling vassals who had seized the occasion to revolt against the Catholic king of France, their households and families. Of these, some were already *croyants* – that is, they believed, but had not taken the vow of dedication, the consolamentum, and were therefore still destined for further reincarnations; others, at first, had no belief at all. When the day of surrender came, the defendants were allowed a mysterious fortnight's grace by the defeating army. During this time, it is said, they smuggled out unspecified treasure – and it has been much argued that far from being gold and silver, possibly acquired by the Templars, with whom they were allegedly in league, it was an intellectual treasure, a piece of precious knowledge, which was to protect them from persecution over centuries to come. Then, as the memorial at the foot of the hill states, they delivered themselves into the arms of the papal army, and, on refusing to recant, were burned, singing.

Ever since, the tinge of heresy has lived on. Early protestants hid out in this region, spiritualists too, then esoteric groups of all kinds, attracted by the strange geology of the valleys and hills, which they say creates a powerful field of magnetic force out of the combination of telluric pull and cosmic rays. Rose and Cross, Templar, Masons, post '68ers, ecologists, you name it, and the book shop in the village, boasting a thousand esoteric titles, will be able to fill you in. Thank goodness for the intransigence of the Catholic church – to which we owe the continuing possibility of transgression and the bloom of heresy.

I took Elizabeth to Montségur on her last day. As we approached, coiling through pasture and pines, the play of darkness and light became dramatic and unreal, and though it was summer, as we passed through the last village before beginning to climb, a chill came over the car. We had to stop to let a shepherd cross the road, and I wound down the window and stretched out my hand to touch a glistening rock, running with clear water, with a mucus feel to it, mossy and prehistoric. And because the car was limping, it felt as though we were arriving by some primitive form of transport, more appropriate to the place than the Renault 5, however ancient. It was a Sunday, a day when heretics stay in bed. As you turn a final bend in the road, past the angora farm, and the bed and breakfast, it is revealed – the blunt mass of stone on its mile high cake stand, the shape of a Walnut Whip. It is like a natural folly – something of artifice in nature. The castle is held aloft in the sky, and you feel that the mass which supports it, up which we would shortly toil by a neatly kept path, had been meant to be invisible, a piece of stage apparatus. The gesture with which the stone held the structure balanced way up there in the sky, peaking above all the other mountains, reminded me of something. It was only on the way home that I said to Elizabeth, "Hold your hand up as though you were examining a skull," and she thought for a moment, then held up her arm at shoulder height and, with her palm facing upwards, crooked her fingers round an imaginary bowl.

Elizabeth and I stood at the top of the hill, inside the fortress, and we felt so little attached to earth, we might have been in a cage being towed across the heavens by some magical bird. The air was thin. On the summer solstice you get groupies of all kinds, particularly neo druids, who are strong on sunshine, toiling up to the summit to watch the first rays of the sun play intricate games with the geometry of the place. The complicated diagrams available in the book shop, drawn up by some Nazi freak in the 1930s, do seem to suggest that the fortress was constructed as a kind of solar temple, a prism of celestial light, a crucible for the purification of the soul. There was a cold inhumanity about the place, which I imagine was not in fact there at the period when it was inhabited, but which we have invested in it, the better to fit our metaphors of purity and unworldliness. Hitler planned to stage a huge production of *Parsifal* there when he had finished conquering the world, indicating that Montségur was the spiritual location of the Holy Grail of racial purity. The Nazi belief was that the secret treasure smuggled out to a place of greater safety on the night of the 12 March 1245 was the knowledge of a secret dynasty, traceable back to King David, the original shepherd king, whose genes were brought to these shores by Christ's children themselves, who sailed the Mediterranean and settled here after His crucifixion. (In those times, in Palestine, to be a rabbi, you had to be married with children, so it was not an unreasonable elaboration of the legend to endow Him with a few.) Transmitted to the Visigoth dynasty by some obscure union of a dragon and a woman, the magic genes were unseated by the impostor Carolingians, and sent out into the wilderness, to multiply in secret, virus-like in the dark, erupting and subsiding at key moments through the centuries. Keepers of the faith, and there are many of them, though we will not be overly concerned with them here, for they are really no more esoteric than cricket lovers or VW owners in the end, believe the area to be closely watched by the present French government for signs of insurrection. With the year 2000 approaching, they believe, the next shepherd king must be growing up in a town near here. Eyes peeled. Outside the schoolroom in the village we discovered a sign: *silence, on chante*. How I love this country of contradictions. Let us be black and white and all the colours in between while we still live, for tomorrow we die indeed, and who knows as what we may return?

Elizabeth and I went back down into the world of matter, of litter bins and tarmacked roads, and the fluffy angora sheep and the hard-bitten little fruits on the hazelnut trees. We drank a cup of tea out of the thermos flask to flush out the feeling of light headedness. She was looking particularly virgin motherlike that day. The heretics believed that Mary was impregnated through her ear, by the whispering of a word in her ear; I like that, it goes way beyond the seductive power of language. (The word made flesh, as John says.) Sometimes I wonder if the Word itself, the naming of parts, wasn't preceded by a kind of wordless song, an essence of expression devoid of all representation, primeval or ideal, depending on whether you are an Aristotelian or a Platonist and believe that the world is in progression or in decline, that sunrise is intimation or apotheosis, the glass half empty or half full. Elizabeth looked out at the landscape as we passed. We drove through a dappled river valley, with rippling fertile fields, and I remembered Pierre saying they reminded him of Venus, which was a gallant way of saying they reminded him of me, when young, and it is true that the fields looked as though they were clothed in some kind of new flesh. I looked across at her from time to time. She had an unused look. I did not know her well, had not known her long. Once I saw a sarcophagus in a museum, which was considered so splendid at the time of its creation, in the ninth century, that they put it up for preservation the moment it was finished, so that even all these centuries later it still looks new.

When we got back to the house, Mark was standing at the window of the drawing-room looking out at the vines. It was surprisingly hot inside, and I realised Pierre had lit the fire, though it was only early September. It had come on to rain towards the end of the day, and although it had now stopped, there was a noise of running water, like a leaking ship, as the gutters guided the new rain down into the earth. His face was sad – those dark eyebrows and eyelashes gave him an introspective look, shielding his eyes and thoughts from the light of the world. He stood with his hands in his pockets, his head against the pane of glass. Perhaps he was cooling his brow. He was leaning forward against the window sill. When I came into the room and dropped my bag onto the sofa he didn't move. I pretended not to notice something was wrong.

"Has Pierre looked after you?" I asked, and when he didn't answer, Elizabeth, who had followed me into the room, said sharply, "Mark!"

He looked up quickly, and smiled, and recalling the question said, "Oh, yes" and came over towards us.

Elizabeth gave him an exasperated look, and I caught the look he gave her, and it hung a long while after in my heart. It was a look full of longing and disappointment, anticipation and regret. You could call it an exchange of glances, but no fair exchange, for he gave everything in that one look, bared everything of himself, and she not only gave nothing back, but did not even register his look, so it was wasted, one of those feelings forever condemned to its relative, unfinished state, never to find relief in recognition. I worry about all those satellites, and crisp packets and various bits of twentieth-century debris shooting off into infinity as I have read they do nowadays, unleashed beyond the atmosphere, disposed of out of sight, but never undone. I like to think things might decay and disappear, or be regenerated in new form, or find at last that thing which cancels them out and lays them to rest, a kind of grace. That love should, lest it rage and roam like the lost soul in the story, searching hapless for its sundered spirit, be, at the very least, acknowledged. I knew Mark was married. I knew he wanted to leave Anna for Elizabeth, and that he had not told her this, but was waiting for a sign. He had told Pierre this on a walk they had taken through the vines. I wondered what Anna felt. I hoped she never met Elizabeth. It's no easier to swallow when your husband leaves you for someone you cannot despise. Pierre said that she was a history teacher at a school in the Border country and that Mark and she rarely met. They had no children, but Mark was a Catholic.

"So what?"

"He can't divorce."

"But he can seduce?"

"At least he hasn't got any children."

I always like to have the details pinned down.

"He must use contraceptives, otherwise Elizabeth— "

"Goodness, I don't suppose so. Not being Catholic. He doesn't look like a short cutter to me. Sexual sins are only sins in so far as they exclude the bringing of life into being or the nurturing of that life. Perhaps with Elizabeth he takes the risk. When people take risks they always seem to read the getting away with them as a sign. Anyway, she looks chaste to me."

I didn't agree. Physically she was ripe as a fruit; it was her soul that was unfertilised, barren as yet, but not shriven. She too was waiting, unconsciously, for a sign, and it would not come from Mark.

Dinner was strained that last evening. Pierre was in a world of his own making, invisible and apart. He and Mark had had a successful few days with their texts, and Mark had brought him over an as yet unpublished poem which had recently turned up, copied out in a seventeenth-century manuscript, attributed, and they had agreed between them, with accuracy, to their particular troubadour friend. Pierre could not have been more delighted if the troubadour friend had phoned and said he was bringing them over the original in person. Mark was in one of those moods where the courtesy required to disguise it only makes you feel the more intrusive upon it. Elizabeth was looking regal, in a long dark blue dress, a pale pink lipstick, which looked as though it had been dusted, not painted on her lips, and her hair loose on her shoulders. It was the first time I had seen it loose, and I was surprised how long it was. At her neck she wore a pale blue stone on a gold chain. It lay in the dip where her breasts rose from that part of a woman's chest which lies not quite like a man's, nor like a child's, sculpted but with no shape to it unless in the line which flows outwards to her shoulders. I admired the pendant. It was a stone the colour of a good strong six-o-clock gin, slightly blue with cold.

"Mark gave it to me. It matches his eyes." I looked across at him. He was listening to Pierre, turning the stem of his glass between his fingers so that a hair lip of inky red wine tipped gently up the side and retreated again. There was never a time when he was not aware of what she was saying. Maybe he thought that if he was attentive he would, in a chance moment one day, catch the word which would tell him all he needed to know. He looked across at her now. It was true, his eyes were a pale grey-blue. He looked slightly ill at ease, and I wondered whether she had ever pointed out to him before that she had recognised the scarcely uttered plea that lay behind the gift, which was lovely, but which I felt she wore whilst still refusing openly to acknowledge its significance for him. He smiled, not at her, at himself perhaps, and turned back to Pierre, who was still happily musing about some comparative reading that had taken place at the faculty in Toulouse the previous summer. He wanted Mark to come back the next year and give a paper.

"Not next summer," Mark said, although Elizabeth remarked to me a long time afterwards, that she didn't know why, or on the basis of what previous commitment, he had declined. "Perhaps the summer after."

Mark picked up the wine bottle and turned it between his hands. "What's this?" He pointed at the label.

Pierre took it from him, and pulled up closer, to show the picture in detail. He drew the candle over towards him, and their two heads came closer together, like an illustration in a children's Bible, the old, white-haired man, and the dark young one, bowed in discussion with the wine bottle and the broken bread strewn about them on the table. They might have been discussing a dowry, or a plot to kill a rival chieftain. Pierre held the bottle out towards the candle.

"It's the wine they make from our grapes. We bottle it ourselves. It's the new wine. We actually use the same bottles, washed out from the previous year, which, proverbially, we shouldn't." He looked up and smiled at me. He was always pleased when he was able to display familiarity with an English idiom. Elizabeth saw the look, without intercepting it, and I felt her soften slightly.

"We make these labels, for our own pleasure." He made it sound like a rather lascivious pleasure. He passed it over to Elizabeth, and she took the bottle and examined the picture closely.

"It's Poussin, isn't it?"

"Yes. The Shepherds of Arcadia."

"I think we saw it in the Louvre. Didn't we?"

Mark nodded vaguely. I wondered whether he was remembering some other, intensely personal moment, the kind a pair of lovers might well experience as they wandered round the Louvre one holiday weekend, which would have led to the particular painting being somehow registered in his memory according to a classification which for her had never even existed, making retrieval by the same reference almost impossible.

"I remember it," she said. She was talking to Pierre, but she never forgot to glance at me, randomly, so as not to appear artificial, regularly, so as not to appear remiss. "I'd always thought it was big, like his others, but it's only— " She boxed the air vaguely with her hands, horizontal, vertical, sketching the size. "I remember thinking how strange it was, us looking at them, them looking at the empty tomb – like the Louvre itself, really, all these penetrating gazes, focussing in an emptiness, in the end. It was as though there was no object there, the grave stood for emptiness."

"For death," said Pierre, quietly.

"It always seemed like a picture about looking at pictures. Although it is quite a big tomb, isn't it?" she said, peering at the picture. "Why did you choose it?"

Pierre took the bottle back. He had taken out his glasses, little half moons slung low on their backs, and he worked them onto his nose with one hand, then carefully looked over the top of them as he examined the picture again. Mark had pushed his chair back from the table, and crossed his legs. He sat watching Pierre, and the way he was cast, idly in his chair, a position of true repose, suggested he would make no further contribution to the conversation, almost as though he were invisible, in the dark, from the stage where the players continued to chatter and act.

"Fouquet, the chancellor to Louis XIV, wrote to his brother, who was a priest in Rome and asked him to get hold of Poussin, who was living in Rome at the time, to do a picture for the king. His brother wrote back and said that Poussin had agreed, and would paint a picture whose secrets, if ever revealed fully, would make the king of France tremble in his boots. This is the picture."

"Why? Why would it make him tremble in his boots?" Elizabeth leaned forward with her elbows on the table, and the little pendant swung forwards to hang in a perfect vertical. Mark watched its swing subside and Pierre said, "No one really knows. There's been a lot of nonsense talked about it. That the tomb represented the secret knowledge of the shepherd kings, who would come to unseat the French throne, assume power one day."

"Well that's not very likely is it? It's already been done."

"Fouquet fell inexplicably out of favour in 1661, five years after the commission – he was arrested, and replaced by Colbert. It was discovered that the tomb in the picture appeared to be based on one in existence not all that far from here, in the Ariège. Colbert had the whole area searched – even the archives of the local churches, where people thought the secret might be kept. That provoked a lot of snooping and speculation. Free masons, Rose and Cross – all the esoterics were involved. Then the farmer whose land it was on bulldozed it away the other year. Since then people have said it was only a replica of the one in the Poussin picture anyway. Nothing's ever come of it. But it's become a sort of local picture, on a local theme. And we like it. That's why I chose it. It goes well with wine. *Et in Arcadia Ego*. Even in Arcadia we die."

After dinner Pierre asked Elizabeth to sing. She made no fuss, didn't flutter a protestation as people often do, particularly when they really aren't all that good, but got up from the table and went to look at the music on the piano. Mark helped me clear up. He looked tired. He had caught the sun during their stay, and I wondered whether he might not have fallen asleep in it, for the creases round his eyes were a web of white.

"Do you often hear her sing?"

"Hardly ever."

She chose a song by Henry Lawes, out of my book of English love songs. It's a restoration number, from the court of Charles I, with words by Sir John Suckling:

No, no, fair heretic, it cannot be,
But an ill love in me, and worse for thee.
For were it in my power,
To love thee now this hour,
More than I did the last,
T'would then so fall, I might not love at all.

Love that can grow and can admit increase,
Admits a well, an ebb, and may grow less.
True love is still the same,
The torrid zones and those more frigid ones,
It must not know, for love grown cold or hot
Is lust or friendship, not the thing we have.

For that's a flame would die,
Held down or up too high,
Then think I love more than I can express,
And would love more could I but love thee less.

A sweet, rather vain conceit, I thought, as I dealt the notes out carefully on the keyboard, pausing for her here and there as she led us through the plaintive drama of its little ironies. Pierre had opened the window. It was almost dark outside. Mark was standing in an unlit part of the room, a deferential withdrawal, but also, I thought, a way of refusing to be an audience, so that he could reserve the right not to be consciously touched by the song. When she had finished, I turned the pages of the book slowly, looking for something else she might know, and the turning of the pages was the only sound, no applause or comment; a church silence, which admits no end or beginning, pretending to a continuum despite the pause, which may be anxious or blissful, depending where your thoughts are.

Nymphs and Shepherds? She gave a little shrug and nodded with a slight smile, but when I looked at her to start, at the moment when she was about to take breath, she stopped and looked round quickly. I dropped my hands lightly into my lap and chipped a note with my ring finger, and it sounded awkwardly and alone, like something dropped through carelessness.

"Sorry," she said, and looked across at Mark. "I thought I heard footsteps in the garden."

"Just the rain," murmured Pierre. He was sitting with his feet up on the sofa, curled up slightly, dreaming. Mark moved out of the half light and came and leaned over the back of where he was sitting, watching Elizabeth now. She frowned at him slightly, then smiled the frown away, uncreasing the moment of irritation. One more song, the evening was over. When we waved goodbye to them the next morning I remember feeling that two separate people were leaving, almost by coincidence at the same moment, by the same transport, and I went off to see the roses, feeling unaccountably sad.

I had been lining the shelves in my kitchen cupboard with wallpaper on the morning Elizabeth returned. The old sheets were gummy with rings left by jars of previous years' pickle, sealed in the English manner with little circles of greaseproof paper, clamped down with a thin elastic band. There was some rhubarb and ginger, and I noticed from the date on the label that I'd made it the day before Pierre died. I remember, now, waking up in the armchair at dawn with an aching back and smelling the ginger on my hands, and thinking that the straw-coloured horsehair that was bursting through the seams of the upholstery was actually shredded ginger and imagining the pale shiny roots piled up inside like bones in a pauper's grave. I noticed that Pierre was gone – dead and gone – some time in the night, and fell back to sleep again. When the doctor came to sign the certificate and I told him that, he set his teacup back on the little table at his side and looked at me very hard, as though he had just recognised in my grief-free features the approximate lines of the artist's impression on some wanted poster.

The sky had started cloudy, which was why I was indoors doing the shelves, but by eleven o'clock it was hot, and there was a dry, prickly feeling to the day. Before then there had been no guests that year. We never did any kind of publicity. Christian sent us a steady trickle of folk he met on his travels. A friend of Pierre's wrote us up once for some English bed and breakfast guide which went out of print in the seventies, and that's kept us going pretty well. Now, I naturally tend to get the kind of person who enjoys browsing in second-hand book shops. There's a photograph of the house in the book, somewhat fudged, so that it looks as though it's shivering slightly in the heat. The white stone runs in a streak across the picture, between sky and parched grass, and Pierre is walking across the front of the house. He's trying so hard to look as though he's unaware of the camera that you might think he's pacing the building to check the square metrage, which would have been difficult for him, as he never had much of a stride. I was telling you about setting the vines each a metre apart. We planted a new field fifteen years ago, around the time when Pierre, who must have been getting on for sixty even then, was taking modern dance lessons from a young girl we'd met on a course in Quimper. Her name was Carmen. In the mornings, the two of them did a lot of meditating about space and movement in the mind, then they threw themselves about a bit in the afternoon. Pierre always reminded me of a fish when he danced, there was a bit too much sinuous expression and not enough technique for my taste, but he did enjoy it. I was outside in the new field in front of the house, going along with my metre rule, sticking in little bamboo twigs to mark the spot where we would plant, doggedly following my lines of string from one end of the field to the other. Pierre came out of the house holding Carmen by the hand and led her to the top of my next lane. Then he bent down rather ceremonially and removed her dance slippers. She had long, prehensile toes which left a substantial drill in the dry, lumpy soil. Slowly she lifted her right leg and took a high, vaulting step into the air. As her foot bore her weight down into the soil, her left leg came up and over in an arc, and she moved slowly through an 180-degree turn. And so she moved down the line of my string, revolving slowly, marking with her feet my metre points, like a pair of compasses being walked across a map. Pierre's greatest pleasure was in movement, in the float and glide and drum and tap of his various dances. After he retired from the law and we came to live down here, we would spend at least a month every year in pursuit of a new dance for his collection. He wanted to become a kind of repository of traditional knowledge, which he would not allow himself to record except in the memory of the steps themselves, as though his body itself were a kind of instrument of transcription. I've always felt uncomfortable with the idea of the deliberate acquisition of tradition. It reminds me of those people who resort to the *Dictionary of Quotations* when they need something apposite on robins, say, or death. I expect myself only to employ cultural quotations – whether in dancing or writing – if they are part of my genuine repository of knowledge, acquired through the natural course of things, each in a context once known, if now forgotten.

My least favourite was the sardane. We went down to a little place on the Spanish border, only a couple of hours from here, on the Mediterranean side and wound up the last road in France to a little walled town of perhaps two thousand inhabitants. It wasn't that difficult to get to, only an hour's drive from the coast. There was one road in, and another one out, and the one that led out turned sharp away south over the mountains to Spain. In fact the road didn't pass through the town at all, nor even did the river. The fortress for which it was famous was placed nicely out of reach up a hill, as was its hideous Gothic church, and away at the back was a spa hotel where white-coated staff trod the gravel paths moving patients about the gardens in their wheelchairs, following the shade through the day and discussing with them the pH of their morning urine (the mineral water was particularly efficacious in the treatment of renal diseases).

Pierre and I stayed in the Hotel Renée (people often wrongly assumed from its name that it was connected with the cure), which was run by Alistair Ambrose, an elderly gentleman from Weymouth. Mr Ambrose had that peculiarly pained manner of speech which distinguishes a certain kind of fastidious British homosexual. He was assisted by a cherished little Italian, and a disillusioned British school dinner lady they had met on the ferry over. The Italian had had the misfortune to learn every word of English he knew either from his friend from Weymouth or from the school dinner lady, who had served nine years in a canteen in a school in Trowbridge. This, along with his skittish way of bustling to and from the kitchen, added to the rich atmosphere of end-of-pier farce which prevailed in the dining room. Pierre and I walked during the day, then presented ourselves at the Maison de Culture at seven o'clock every evening for our lesson. The classes were conducted by a married couple, he very thin and anxious, with thick steel-framed spectacles and a different pastel shade of short sleeved, beautifully ironed shirt every evening. Madame wore a white trouser suit and little red espadrilles with those laces that cross over and wind up and over your ankle, finishing in a little bow at the front. We'd all stand in a circle and mime out the steps, which were fantastically complicated, up on our tippy toes, tripping along like little dainty fairies first clockwise, then anti-clockwise, all holding hands and whispering in step with Madame *des petits pas, des petits pas, des petits pas, des petits pas* . . . till it came to the point when, in response to a change in the music (which we weren't allowed to have for the first four days of the course), you suddenly had to start leaping into the air. Oh it was horrible. On the last day, which was Bastille day, we danced in our own special idiot circle in the village square, while all the locals and those smug revenants who'd done the course the year before swirled and hopped about us. I wore my special *Heat and Dust* dress, which is a sort of cream linen shift with broderie anglaise at the hem, and a floppy hat. I thought it would be a good costume for sitting things out in, but instead I just got extremely overheated and dusty and threw out the rhythm of the whole circle. Afterwards they presented proficiency certificates to everyone except me. The only good thing about the holiday was the black Madonna in the church, who had the crossest face you ever saw and extremely large flat feet, just like mine. For a pantheist and a Catholic icon we really had quite a rapport.

I used to amuse myself on these trips by collecting material for my pamphlets. Prompted by the little success I had had with my book on the Cathars, I took to writing guides to the regions we visited, always with a good dose of historical background. A friend of Pierre's in Paris, who had often produced legal documents for him, ran up a couple of thousand of each for me and I used to come to an arrangement with the local *syndicat* of each region, whereby they took a thirty per cent cut of the cover price for straightening up the pile on the table every evening before closing. Shortly after Will's death, Elizabeth came across one I'd done in Brittany when I was on the run from some ghastly morris-related jig. She wrote to me on the headed notepaper of her company, and asked whether I would mind if she produced English versions to each of my guides. It was an oddly impersonal letter, I thought. I wrote back to her suggesting she should come and stay with me for a few days, so that we could consider the idea. I was basically in favour, but I wanted to be sure. I have a suspicion of translators – you have to get the right one for your own style, otherwise it's like having your clothes washed along with someone else's non colourfast cottons.

She didn't reply for a couple of weeks, then I got a letter from her business partner saying that Ms Faulkener had been unwell and was resting her voice. I couldn't see why I should need to know about her voice, or why a strain on her vocal cords should stop her doing written translation, but it turned out later that Frances, the partner, had produced two sorts of letters on Elizabeth's behalf, one to be sent to the various churches and charitable organisations for whom she was booked to sing that spring and summer, and the other to people in the translation pending tray. There was a mix up and I got the wrong one. Eventually, I received a letter saying she would like to come around the beginning of June.

When I heard Pascal's car coming up the hill with her from the station I quickly put the pots of pickle back in the cupboard and went to wash my hands. When you come out of the front door of the house it is like coming out on to a badly lit stage. The wall of light is so hard you could almost crack your head on it. Pascal was opening the passenger door for Elizabeth, who was looking slightly indignant and walked straight round to the back of the car to fetch her own bags out of the boot. Pascal shrugged at me and felt in his pocket for his crumpled pack of Gauloises. The cigarettes were always crumpled too, but he maintained it gave a better smoke. He offered me one, but I refused. If I do, and I don't much now, I roll my own. Pascal had cut the grass in front of the house a couple of weeks before and it was now dry and stalky and crawling with insects, which Eliot, my cat, was pursuing in hectic little leaps and darts. It made a slight cracking noise under my espadrilles as I went forward to greet Elizabeth. She, on the other hand, was wearing heels, which left hot little dents in the earth. There was a smell of petrol about the car, and heat waves rose from the bonnet so that above it the air shimmered weakly. I touched the door handle and it was scorching under my fingers. There is always a moment in a story like this, when you have to say – it was then, that was the crucial second, here, in this place I have brought you to, and I have brought you here for a purpose. Here, everything stops. Elizabeth dragged her case out from the boot and rested it against her knee as she brought the hatch down with a bang. I took her right hand in mine and laid my left gently on her shoulder. All I said was, "I'm very pleased you could come," but for some reason she looked at me in a way that suggested I had spoken words with an extra, coded meaning, and that from now on she thought help might be at hand.

Sometimes you can carry an experience, a piece of knowledge, even an emotional condition around with you like a parcel for weeks, months without unpacking it. You feel its weight, you are bowed down by it, sometimes you leave it somewhere and are compelled to return to collect it. Your fingers hover over the knot – it is too tight, too difficult – but as time passes it may fray and snap. And so you fold back the paper and the contents of your parcel appear. It may be difficult to identify, although, if not what you asked for, far from it, you have known for a while what it was. I have always found it difficult to receive gifts. I am not, perhaps, a particularly gracious person, but I have learned, as you do with age, to thank people calmly and convincingly. When I went through my rather theatrical thirties I had a phase of shrieking thanks, of feigning genuine pleasure

– no, but really, it is exactly, etc. – until Pierre had a word with me one day and suggested I tone it down a bit, which was a relief really. But it's not just saying thank you. It's the way the transfer of ownership occurs. One moment the parcel, whatever it is, is in the possession of your friend, the next wheeeeee, over it comes like a cricket ball, and it's yours. It's already yours, and you don't know what it is, which is not normal at all. In normal circumstances, surely, a thing becomes ours because we in some sense know it. Knowledge is concomitant with possession. He knew her. Ah, yes. And how can we know but through the experiences of our senses? It can take me years to come to know a possession of my own, a piece of clothing, a pottery bowl, a perfume bottle. A book? Yes even a book. The smell, the touch, not just of the pages, but of the story itself, everything I know, even facts of a certain kind, have a fragrance, a shape, a colour, a texture which can only be experienced slowly, with time. And so with loss, and with love. There is a shock of love, and there is a shock of loss, and the one is not so dissimilar from the other. But after the initial shock, just as love grows as you acquire knowledge, not only of the beloved, but of the condition itself, so can grief. Knowledge of a new kind must be acquired about the person we mourn; we grow to know them in a new way, a way that was not possible in their lifetime; and at the same time we acquire new knowledge of the condition of grief itself.

She arrived wearing this pair of court shoes I've already mentioned. I imagined they must be for travelling in – likewise the oatmeal-coloured linen suit. People do like to be smart when they travel. I suppose changing places makes them feel naked, like vulnerable molluscs who've bolted from their shells. It's quite an art, getting it right; like style in anything, it is at its best when it's both comfortable and expressive. You need something you can wriggle about in your seat in (especially on trains, I find I tend to stick to the upholstery), walk in (no hobble skirts or silly heels), run in if you're late; something to be not too hot or not too cold in; no hats or scarves (remember Isadora Duncan); and always bear in mind that the whole ensemble has to compensate for the absence of the bolstering home environment, the one you made earlier, conveying a spare but significant range of information about class, wealth and possibly education. I have observed, lately, a growing trend in travellers to adopt a kind of attire known as the shell suit, which goes to show that my mollusc theory was entirely in line with current sociological thinking. With the literal mindedness of the age, some clothes manufacturer has come up with the obvious solution – get that shell on your back!

I took her in and showed her round. Although she was such a smart, confident girl – woman – it did feel a bit like taking her in, as one might a waif from the streets. There was a sense that she was seeking sanctuary. I took care to give her a different bedroom. Neither of us wanted this second visit to employ any of the old threads. Too much of life is knitted up with the unravelled yarn of a previous garment, which once sat well, but having fallen out of use with fashion and the day has singularly failed to readapt to the new design. I had told her on the telephone that I was widowed, and her particular kind of tactful formality, which put just the right amount of invention into the stock phrases, the most delicate hint of interpretation and ornament, had dealt with the situation in a way that allowed us to avoid any further mention of it until we were much more closely acquainted. Her bedroom this time was in the main bit of the house, which is strictly renovated (not lovingly restored, I'm afraid, neither Pierre nor I was the type). There are a lot of very straight, rather thin walls (the magic of plaster board) and the predominant colour is white. The floors are laid in terracotta tiles, bought by the palette at the local DIY. A single vase here, a picture there, a spray of dried corn on the wall. It's too hot for much detail, although you could say it was a little bit starched, I suppose, if you wanted to criticise. In a sense my house is my travelling kit. My journeys take place at home.

Elizabeth didn't speak much at first, and I remembered the friend's letter about her losing her voice. When she did, her voice was as I remembered it – that of the perfect public speaker, no trace of elocution, but a clear carrying tone, at once impersonal and intimate. She adopted pitch and expression precisely to her words. Perhaps that came from the musical training. (But I told you: in the beginning there was no singing at all.) Her soul was frozen over, like that of the little boy in the *Snow*

Queen. I'm giving you my impressions, the inferences I drew from her appearance and demeanour, rather than the details themselves, which I suppose makes me a bit of a literary tyrant, but does save time and lets you imagine for yourself what she looked like. She made little reference to her previous visit. I asked after Mark early on, to get it over with, and she said she hadn't seen him for a year and half, so that was that. One of my early impressions had been that she possessed – and this is rare – what *Schiller* called a *Schöne Seele*. A character in possession of such a thing does good naturally. And so, as a dramatist, he preferred the naturally bad character, whose malevolent, creative energies could be readily converted, at the flick of a coin, into a positive force. I wondered about that too, whether the creative force per se is naturally good. (He's so creative! say mothers of their little boys; stop creating! my grandmother would say to me, although I suppose that must have been short for creating-a-mess.) Now here is the nub of the heresy: for the creation of material is attributed to Satan, and all that is material is satanic. All souls were originally *schön*, and corruption is only a degree of forgetfulness and imprisonment in matter, the world, the body. And though I never went along with the philosophy myself, it was clear that this was Elizabeth's particular drama. Her perfect physique and features, so carefully cultivated and maintained, gave the illusion of a soulless topography. All her grief for the loss of Will had been assumed by her body, and in the sculpture of her face, like a well kept tomb, inscribed by the mason's chisel. She allowed herself no feelings. When you rolled away the stone, the tomb was empty.

Her room was spartan, almost like a nun's cell. It was immediately above the kitchen, and as I stood at the window washing the salad I could hear her walking about; her suitcase must have been on the bed and she returned to it after each little sortie across the room; here a sliding drawer, there the placing of a pair of shoes; laying her clothes in the drawers, an uncreased paperback by the bedside table. A bottle of scent? There was something she left until last, something she could not place – there was hesitation in her tread. It was as though she held in her hands an article whose placing in the room required a decision which went beyond convenience or appropriateness. Not a bible, surely, although people do have their ceremonies about bibles in a room. I don't put the car keys or my spare change down on it either, but that's more a tic than an observance. In the end I think she put it on a shelf in the wardrobe. When she came downstairs her tread was regular and precise. She had taken off her jacket – gently does it, layer by layer, Elizabeth – and the short sleeved shirt underneath was gravel coloured and smooth as a well worn pebble. No sweat. I was relieved. I have known visitors change into something which bespeaks "holiday" within minutes of their arrival, and the precipitation is just too much. You show a nice gentleman in a suit to his room and, before you can say *bienvenue*, he's rubbing sun lotion into his bald patch and displaying his bunions through the canvas of his espadrilles. Even the second-hand book world isn't what it was. But Elizabeth's process of acclimatisation was at once drawn out and imperceptible. She was fragile, handling herself with care.

She worked on the translation. Occasionally, at meals, we discussed points of language – the delicate inflections of meaning and style which, properly perceived, reflect the most sensitive contours of the brain without giving anything away about the actual nature of the terrain. How you say it does create what you say. The utterance precedes the statement. The style precedes the sense. Do we believe in the possible existence of an unfashioned, clear born thought, product of an immaculate conception, involving no coupling of words and fact? We do not. (As the old lady said, "How do I know what I mean before I see what I say?") The words of the text were my own, and in so far as they were already there on the page I suppose that, yes, essence preceded existence; but she took them, as though dancing with a rag doll, and made such a living, light and mobile thing of my bare-boned text as made me feel that my own version had been the secondary, hers the true one.

There were aspects of her behaviour that implied the whole of her was temporarily bound in some kind of sling, suggesting that during the healing period only the very slightest movement would be advisable. Gossip wasn't really in her line – I don't think she knew how to, it wasn't just a period of austerity when she hadn't any, a barren year. Nor confession either, that related addiction; but if you took the time to read her it was apparent enough that her soul was bruised, and that where the greatest damage had occurred she was, like mishandled fruit, or a windfall, ready to weep.

It was the end of the first phase – although, having said that, there had been very little exposition. Perhaps it had been a prologue. We'd had the statement of a few themes, but the character was not really apparent. She also wore dark glasses a lot of the time. You know when the dramatic moments in life are occurring, the big bangs, the irreversible reversals of fortune; but the structure – the ends of acts, beginnings of scenes – is harder to see until you look back in – nostalgia, usually (that's when we make the best shapes). Sometimes, though, even in *media res*, you feel the lights dim for a second, and you know that something is shifting irrevocably, and that when you look back at the whole picture, perhaps walking back, tracing it along the wall, like the Bayeux tapestry (1957, sword dancing in Normandy, dreadful heat) you will pause and say to yourself, there was a seam there, something happened.

We had a basket with two plastic boxes and lids in. Elizabeth was carrying. I was walking a little bit behind, so as not to spoil her view. I wanted her on ahead, although she didn't separate from me – occasionally she would throw her voice, and sometimes a smile. I thought I noticed that day, for the first time, a certain lasciviousness in her enjoyment of her senses; the tiniest of thaws setting in. I had always considered her care and attention to the very simple features of her own appearance rather in the light of the busy career woman who keeps all detail in the home to a minimum, with mechanisation wherever possible. Clean surfaces, efficient storage space, hygiene and simple elegance. There was something machine-like about her body – it was well oiled and polished and certainly gave no trouble. It was well cared for in a way that meant that she had not had to develop, or had been able to suppress as superfluous, any personal gestures, the brushing back of her hair, the licking of the lips. I suppose it was the air hostess look. People don't want eccentric tics when they're whistling through the air at two hundred miles an hour. They find it unsettling.

But it was a hot day – a Tuesday, I think. Her shorts were quite modest – and by that I mean they were long, not skimpy, the epithet being transferred (modest woman/modest meal, ah! it's all coming back). I had brought my book with me, even though I knew it was unlikely I would read that day. Some women won't leave home without a handbag. I always take a book. It's almost pure accessory, but you don't have to worry about it clashing with your clothes. She had a tendency, like one of those American lady attorneys in television serials, to look air conditioned into ice maidenhood, so I was pleased to see the heat was tinging her with just the slightest hint of blowsiness. I thought she began to notice the colours of the hard beaten earth and the wild, gorgeous *fougère*. She was taking in the rich, fruity smell of decay and life which hangs in a forest, particularly when it is warm. (Have you noticed that the sense of smell seems to work best at somewhat over moderate temperatures but not in great heat?) I had noticed before that what might almost come across as austerity – in her dress, her modes of speech, her appetite – was actually a strange, and very clever kind of sensuality. It was dampened down by something, and yet it seemed an unused thing still, as though young green shoots had been stifled by clods of earth. Perhaps I say that because I know. She used her sense organs with what seemed like tentativeness, but was actually the peak of indulgence. I used to find myself quite incapable of watching a wine tasting – the combination of sense-gorging and delicacy made me want to dash the glass to the floor, or better still, simply slug it back like some grizzled Napoleonic campaigner who's stumbled on a keg of Rioja. I imagine I would have felt much the same if I'd lived in an age of snuff takers. But although Elizabeth had something of the wine taster in the relationship between her senses and the material world, it was done in such an unconscious way that it could only delight me to watch her. Maybe all I'm saying is that she had learned that, in times of convalescence, a little is enough to give you more than an ordinary sense of pleasure. I can't quite say she scrambled, but she took a higher path, that ran along the bank, beside the regular one. She caught her leg on a briar, and after a little gasp watched with an odd kind of satisfaction as the long white scratch on the well-waxed calf slowly seeped a little snail's trail of blood. We didn't talk: I haven't any words for you yet, and the sounds of the forest were not something you could translate. But I'm taking you there too, nothing is missing.

We reached the end of the track, where it suddenly drops onto a plateau. When we used to bring the horses up they would break into a gallop the moment it came into sight. You can see the real mountains from there and there is a small, stone hut, the *bergerie*; I planted 200 saplings on the plateau last year, a mixture of ash, mulberry and apple. Each sapling is still clad in a little plastic tube, like the things you pick up golf balls with. They stop the deer from eating the foliage; out of the top of each poke a few bright green leaves, looking ridiculously like some naïve attempt at camouflage. To Elizabeth I said: "Take the basket and make your own way down." I'd pointed out the wild strawberries along the path as we came up, small scarlet blisters on the undergrowth, almost like insect bites on the foliage. She thought she would be bored to pick them, people always imagine they will, but I knew that once I left her to it she would start idly and then her interest would grow, and the humble business of eye to finger would consume her; the hunter's instinct is as evident in fruit gathering as it is in the pursuit of a beast, just a bit less bloody.

"I'll go by this path through the woods. I have to get back for Pascal. Take the track back down again. If you meet a wild boar, stand your ground," and I set off through the trees like a satyr (feeling, not looking, I know, but it's the spirit of the thing).

I'd been making my way for only a couple of minutes when I found a clump of amber chanterelles among the oak leaves. I thought we'd have them for supper with shallots and a little sorrel in an omelette. I made a sack out of my handkerchief and started to pick, working my way across the patch, enjoying the way the stalk breaks softly from the humid earth, the damp, male smell of the flesh, mingled with soil. The leaves on the surface were dry and a pale brittle brown, but underneath there was a clammy world of activity and disintegration, decay and growth. Twigs snapped and cracked underfoot and the odd brave bird cruised between the trees on a fiendish flight path from light to dark, ducking and skimming among the branches. When I had gathered enough I laid my bundle down on the ground and sat for a moment on the edge of a bank, where the ground dropped quite steeply away into shrub before the next belt of trees. I thought Elizabeth would be pleased with the chanterelles; she was good at taking pleasure in details. I remembered a theory about the short story which had impressed me in the days when I used to think I could write – that it should be like watching a pan of milk boiling over. Sitting there thinking about it I couldn't for the life of me imagine why.

I heard a car pass far below on the road to Montillon. In the old days that would have been like hearing the telephone ring from afar and wondering who it might have been, but the traffic is heavier now, and it's never for me. Pierre and I used to come up to the plateau together, and sleep over in the *bergerie*, and he would bring his paints and set up all his things with great care and I would sit and read a book. I read the whole of *Heart of Darkness* once, and he'd only finished the outline of the mountains. What would he have made of Elizabeth now? One of yours, my dear, perhaps, he would have said and gone back to stretching and bending with Carmen. His hair was long and white, soft not dry and bushy, and sometimes, particularly for dancing, he tied it back with a shoelace or a piece of twine – never something specifically designed for the purpose, it had to have the air of a makeshift solution, and he wasn't a macho man at all, but there were limits. When I laid him out (the language of the post mortem, not the boxing ring, we never rowed, except about religion), I tied it back off his face and as I drew it off his forehead and temples the skin tautened – suddenly the texture of youth was there, and his features, sharp as the bone underneath.

It will sound irritatingly like a narrative device in a fairy story when I say "I fell asleep", but I'm really quite old, for me, which is how it always feels, and I did, lying back among the leaves. Ophelia at seventy. I don't recall any dreams. Meanwhile, Elizabeth, who had already half filled her box with strawberries – and no, her lips weren't stained, this isn't Mills and Boon, but her fingers weren't quite up to the usual standard, came across me lying there in my bower of leaves, and, quite naturally, I suppose, presumed me dead. It's the kind of thing people begin to assume about you after a certain age. You only have to miss your regular bus stop through a lapse into reverie and people reach for your pulse. That happened to me once when my eyes were open, you know the way when you're in a bus and your eyes are actually focused on a particle of dust on the window pane next to you and you're thinking of something entirely different. Usually I'm trying to remember who played the husband in *Brief Encounter* or the name of one of the lesser Shakespeare claimants (I've noticed I always forget the same things – for years I couldn't remember what the art of sculptural hedge cutting was called, and when the memory lapse came round again I would chase it down the familiar lanes like the hound of heaven itself, until one day it stuck, as though I had cornered it in a blind alley of my memory and it would no longer ever escape me. I no longer have the same enthusiasm for the word at all – *on n'aime que ce qu'on ne possède pas* – but that's wrong, it's not possession, it's knowledge.) Anyway, to return to the bus, a carnival float or a man on a penny farthing passes by and you don't so much as blink, because you don't see it. I forget actually what it was I was supposed to have registered, my indifference to which was suggestive of a stage only one step short of rigor mortis, but I was given a good shaking and dropped the tray of eggs I was holding on my lap.

You might imagine I was awoken by Elizabeth's scream, which rang like the whistle of a stone pitched into a deep, distant gully, but in fact I awoke a second or so before that, feeling the vibrations of her footsteps by my head and she screamed not for finding me dead but because, having believed me dead, she saw me move. I sat up and said, "It's quite all right Elizabeth, I was just picking these mushrooms for our supper", (although at first I couldn't see them because they'd rolled out of sight down the bank, so it seemed for a moment as though I was fabricating, which almost detracted from the veracity of my assertion, which quickly followed, that I was not dead at all but only snoozing). She wore such a stricken look, I was quite touched at first, but then I realised that the expression was the outward sign of a pain remembered, suddenly livid in the light of her shock. It was a look I once saw on a mother's face who had lost her child in a supermarket, not in the moment of panic itself but in the seconds when, after much searching, it became apparent that the child had almost certainly been abducted. It was the intellectual registering of shock that created the most horror. I found that interesting at the time, although of course I was doing everything possible to help the mother, but you know how as you get older you can't help becoming a little bit detached from these things. Of course shock can be caused just by sheer incongruity, the grotesque. I paid a visit to a farm where I occasionally buy milk the other day and the old lady who always ladles it out so neatly in her clean pinafore, with her glad-to-be-old-and-gracious face was stripped to her vest like a navvy and ducking her soapy head into a barrel of rain water. She looked like some hideous parody of those advertisements you sometimes see on the television where some ethereal twenty-year-old blonde trips through a field of corn and you're supposed to think of her as Ceres herself, and make the connection that you too could be a mythological beauty if only you bought the right bottle, and I must say I got quite a shock. Perhaps that's what Elizabeth felt coming across me like Isolde in the forest in a posture of abandon, stirring sensually at the sound of Tristan's tread. My mind runs away, and I am unfairly using hindsight to light the scene in a particular way. She was shaken though, and dropped the strawberries, which was a waste, because picking them from the plant and picking them up off the ground are two very different things, and the latter tends to do them no good at all. Half of them rolled under leaves and into little gullies and in the end we left them. It's all part of the propagation process, but Elizabeth seemed to feel almost guilty for the waste, even though I told her nature didn't work like that and we could always get some more on the way down. When we got back to the road we put the chanterelles in one box and passed the other between us while we picked more berries for supper. It was soon done and, as she was still a bit shaky, I took the basket from her, not wanting any more accidents, and led the way this time down back towards the house. I want to get us down the track fairly quickly now, as in my mind I'm already there in the kitchen before supper, peeling the shallots, and hearing her go to the cupboard in her room, open the door and take out the object which had, on that very first day, aroused my curiosity.

There are three things now – no four, counting you, and

wherever you are when you read this. As for the first – which is me, telling you this, well, I'm here, in this room which you know, with my things about me and the green fields beyond the vines and the sound of Pascal clipping away on the old growth. We have made cider from the windfalls – it's cloudy, like pastis with the water added, but we are going to strain it through muslin, and it will come out translucent and honey-coloured as a young Chablis.

Then there's me and Elizabeth herself sitting at the kitchen table with the terracotta vase between our plates for all the world as though it were just the pepper pot, and her quiet voice, and then there's her *récit*. Until then I had known nothing of her story, having only asked briefly, as I said, after Mark. I had gathered he was not part of the picture, and also that her condition when she came to me was not connected with him in any way. It seemed to me that whatever had happened to her, she needed Mark, and that I might well end up by suggesting this to her, but it obviously wasn't the time for that sort of intervention, so I kept him back, like the war husband you place in the summer house – stay there, I'll go and see how my mistress is today. And perhaps he would have to return day after day – no, she is too weak, I can't tell her yet that you have come, no, today she must receive Lady Butterworth, come again tomorrow, maybe. I feared that Mark would be growing sad and old, but I knew she would not have him yet, that her own drama was too fresh. She was in that peculiar situation of the woman who grapples with her own terrible personal loss, which is all the more hideous for her knowing that it is tiny, scant in the face of the wretchedness of the world. She suffers for the absence of wounds – which is why women tear their hair, I suppose, except Elizabeth would never do that; she kept quite still, with her hands in her lap. And she kept her nails short.

The *récit* was well told – I could not recreate it in her words, because even as she was telling me I was hearing it in my own words; her blank delivery left room for the intervention of my imagination – that thing which makes images out of the simple material of fact and statement. So when she told me about Will, for instance, I had to match him to something – someone – I knew, and when she talked of places in London, they were to me as I had last seen them, in the fifties. Sometimes – with the South Bank, for instance, I had to stop and mix a fresh colour, because that particular one didn't exist in my day, there was no provision for it in my paint box. But for the most part, even though it distorted, my method of transposition held good.

Things are multiplying rapidly – how many did I say? Three, not counting you? Elizabeth's experience, Elizabeth's *récit*, my rendering of it to you, you listening (that's counting you). We'll stop at that for now. Pascal says I'm allowing myself a little too much free rein these days. The other day I was mopping down the kitchen floor – with all the chairs up on the table, like at night in a café – and the table was pushed up against the wall. I started in one corner, and, humming to myself (my rhythm is better than my pitch, though I tend to lose time – I would be good dancing to a wind up musical box, we could slow down in perfect tandem, with the pitch dropping and feet dragging as though it were all part of the performance), I stepped out onto the floor with the mop and moved across it with a series of complicated steps which might quite well have appeared to the uninitiated to have no justification whatsoever. I tried to teach him that evening, but he could see no sense in it at all, no sequence or logic. Pascal tried to make up a rhyme to jog his understanding. All the lines began with g or d, for *gauche* or *droit* (of feet, two left, in his case, which didn't help), and at that point we gave up, because I said that this smacked of the worst kind of last resorting. You may well say acronyms can be very useful, but in my opinion anything you have to remember with an acronym isn't worth remembering. Anyway, what he hadn't grasped – and this may have had a lot to do with his own faulty execution – was that properly performed, the dance led one to cover every square inch of the floor without stepping on the wet bits. You have to be pretty agile – there's a fair amount of leaping and striding, but it does make the time pass quickly, and if that's not what dancing's for then I don't know why we bother. I know it's not everyone's answer – it certainly wouldn't have been Pierre's, but I'm speaking for myself while I've still got breath to do so, because you're a very long time silent, as Pierre himself can testify. So what follows is really my way of covering the floor, which may seem a little erratic at times, but

I think we will end up with everything having received the right amount of attention, with nothing gone over more than once, before moving on to a time after the *récit* over the pepper pot, which will be a lot easier for me, as I was there.

Part Two

5

The letter about Will's ashes weighed five ounces. It took three days to get from Reading to Elizabeth's door in London. The postman, who objected to Elizabeth's letter box because it was the heavily hinged brass type that snapped shut on his fingers, left the letter tucked under a pint of milk. A schoolboy pinched the milk and the letter trailed a little sideways, fanned by the breeze, and became caught in the coils of a winsome clematis, where it looked like a card of condolence stuck into a wreath.

It was her thirty-third birthday, and there were the usual cards from the natural card senders. She placed them in a brass letter rack by the coat hooks in the hall and went back to work. She wore high heeled shoes already, although it was still early morning and her own flat, and she moved back into the drawing-room with the slightly fettered grace of a Jamesian heroine. Her dark wiry hair was fastened at the nape of her neck with a black ribbon, and through a loop of this, pinning it to the hair which was drawn tightest against the skull, she had slid a clay modelling tool, a tiny personal device of the kind a painter, having taken his mistress as model, might add to the image of her, as a discreet reference to their intimacy. The modelling tool had been Will's, and he had made a present of it to her by simply declaring a change of use. As she was shortly to read in the formal language of the letter entwined in the clematis, all that had been his was now hers, so that the few gifts he had given her, to which, not being a sentimentalist, she had been unaware of attaching any particular value, were about to acquire, with hindsight, a certain charm for having had so short a life.

She sat down again by the window to finish the piece she

was translating. She was well ahead in her work. She would enclose the invoice with the finished copy. With Elizabeth, clients tended to be prompt in payment. They were always pleased to participate in so pristine a transaction. Outside, the white-painted walls of her garden showed faintly grey in the city sunlight. A withered ornamental cherry was splayed with a clutching gesture against the south wall, like some phantom hand clawing at a window in the night. In the terracotta pots she had brought back with her from Portugal the soil, mixed sixty/forty with compost from the garden centre (no fetid potato peelings here) had set rock solid and was shrinking away from the sides and cracking. It was a fair sized garden for London, but since Will's disappearance she had not set foot in it, except to put the rubbish out. To the interior of her house, on the other hand, she had paid scrupulous attention, dusting pictures, cleaning cupboards, rearranging furniture and reordering all her books by spine colour and height, so that the bookcase in her living room looked like a decorator's pantone chart. Gym sessions and swimming sessions and appointments with hairdresser, manicurist and sunbed had left her looking similarly polished. Only her voice was unexercised.

She was typing up a fair copy of a document she had translated from the German for a classical record company. She typed on a compact word processing machine. The handwritten translation was held in a pincer device which screwed on to the edge of her desk. There were few crossings out even on the handwritten sheets. There was a flawlessness about Elizabeth's presentation to the world, a kind of matt, non-reflective, but still non-absorbent surface to everything associated with her. Even her speaking voice was cool, and her skin had the hue and texture of the finest pencil shaving. Over the years, from earliest childhood, her implacability had made her a certain number of petty enemies. She seemed not to care what you thought of her, a trait more forgivable in the ugly and selfish than in the beautiful and good. She rejected both good and bad opinion. Even her virtues, her kindness, her foresight, her generosity, showed a measure of competence which made them seem more like skills than character traits. In other words, she was as a sounding brass or a tinkling cymbal, for she appeared to have no love.

There were no photographs of Will in the house. They had known each other for only eight months – not even time for new life. He had been more difficult to photograph than an insect or a bird. Only when he worked was he still, and she would no more have photographed him then than she would have a priest blessing the sacraments. In her presence he had been so vivid and mobile that the thought would never have occurred to her, and when he was not with her, not immediately with her, but down at some water's edge, say, or taking someone else's hand, it would have been a trespass. Where Elizabeth took life always at the same unchanging pace, so that others treated her almost like a human metronome against which to measure their own variations, Will had as many possible speeds as the natural world itself; the slow stealth of an unfurling leaf, the crack and flare of fire on brittle kindling or the dangerous swoop of a falcon. No fit subject for a photograph. And he had said there was no point photographing her, trying to capture her, for she always gave the impression that she was already in repose. A few weeks after the clay modelling tool, he gave her a candle encased in a glass sheath, so that the motions of the air would cause it not the slightest flicker. She still has the candle, but the glass blew over and smashed in the wind.

Frances, Elizabeth's partner, was a chaotic parker. Hearing the car crunch and scrape, and then reverse and idle, Elizabeth wondered whether she had decided to go back to Pimlico and take it from a different angle.

"You'll have to come and open up for me!" she shouted at Elizabeth through the front window, "I haven't any hands."

As Elizabeth opened the door to her, Frances shoved a white cardboard cake box, the kind that are made up by deft fingers and tied with ribbon, into her hands. "Take that, I'm going back for the baby. Happy Birthday."

She returned with the baby to find Elizabeth back at work. "Elizabeth, it's your birthday," said Frances patiently, all scarf and mittens and baby, falling back against the front door to close it with her arms full. "You can't work on your birthday. I'm taking you out."

Elizabeth carried on typing and smiled. Frances noticed a faint henna tint on her hair, which was new since the weekend. "Out? Or out of myself? How's the baby?"

Frances looked for somewhere to put it down. "Cat napping. Out stealing cats. Look at him. I read them all *Orlando* last night, you know, the marmalade cat, not Virginia Woolf." She looked over Elizabeth's shoulder. "Save me or I will be abandon-ned!" she read off the screen, making it sound like the response to a psalm. "What is that anyway?"

"Programme notes," said Elizabeth, ordering the machine to print. "It's a new recording of some Schumann songs. I didn't think it was your line."

"Certainly not. Here's the stuff for the pot people. How to use your Rumtopf. It's a bit free, perhaps. What do you think of hedgerows for fields? I thought it sounded better for the Rumtopf crowd, whoever they are. I don't imagine they fancy themselves out in the fields all that much. I thought hedgerow was classier. I was dying to use garner, but I couldn't work it in. Do you think we'll get a free one? I could keep the bills in it."

"Is that the final copy? It looks a little bit blobby, Frances. I think I'd better type it up again before we send it. It won't take very long."

Frances was about to argue, but stopped herself. It was slightly blobby, it was true. "But not now," she said, "we're going out now aren't we?"

"It depends what you have in mind. Are you taking me to the circus? On a trip up the river? Will I have to change? I'm waiting for this to print out. Would you like some of your cake?"

"OK, but it's yours. I bought it for you . . . I meant to make one, you know how it is, then I thought you'd probably rather I didn't bother, so I bought one. Yes, it's definitely coffee time. *Kaffee und Kuchen*. Watch Billy for me and I'll go and put the kettle on."

Making a cup of coffee in Elizabeth's kitchen was a strangely mimetic experience, like flying a simulated aeroplane – it seemed quite removed from the reality of water and steam and grains and possibly the washing up of an earlier mug. Frances clattered about a bit, just because she felt some noise would do Elizabeth good. She almost wished Billy would wake up and make a row and possibly a bit of a mess. When they had shared rooms at college there was never any squabbling about who cleared up the mess, because it had always been Frances's. Somehow it had never seemed to worry Elizabeth. She had simply stepped around it, had had a knack for finding her own library books amongst the collapsing piles that Frances had heaped up in an attempt to fake order and tidiness, and had somehow kept her life separate whilst continuing to live in the midst of Frances's chaotic whirlpool, in which strange life forms and inert matter seemed to appear out of nowhere like replicators in the original primeval soup. Years later, when Frances first met Will, their eyes met involuntarily as Elizabeth carried in a cardboard box of shopping, packed with the tailor-made precision of a Fortnum's Christmas hamper, with Will following her through the door, his arm still in a sling from his driving accident, eating a chocolate biscuit from the torn open packet he had salvaged and was holding tucked between his plaster and his white shirt. It was a hot day and Elizabeth had taken the packet from him and emptied it into a tin, which she then put into the fridge. Will, carrying on a conversation with Frances about her most recent baby – he was telling her about Shelley stopping a mother with a baby in her arms on Magdalen bridge – went over to the fridge and took the tin out again, and munched his way through the entire packet, considering Elizabeth's intervention as nothing more than a comma, a pleasing little stylistic gesture in the general, uninterruptible flow of things. Elizabeth leaned back against the gleaming white fridge and smiled and watched, and Frances noticed that she who was never tired or creased was looking both and was happy. When he had finished the biscuits, Will put his arm around Elizabeth's shoulder and placed a chocolatey index finger on a small, single mole below her left ear.

"This is where Elizabeth keeps her secrets," he said, smiling. "This is her dark broom cupboard under the stairs. All her evil thoughts and dirty washing, condensed in a single spot."

The coffee was almost ready, she was just waiting for the moment when she could send the plunger down to the bottom, with that peculiar hand over hand gesture – she was trying to think when else you used it – there was one other thing, in an amusement arcade perhaps . . . or detonating a bomb. The mugs were out on the tray, Elizabeth liked a milk jug to be used, which was quite right, if you had the time . . . There was no noise from the other room, although she half believed she could hear the swish of Elizabeth's skirt, except it would have to be skirts, for some reason you always heard the swish of ladies' skirts . . . was it a sign of ultimate respectability? Did they wear two, just to be on the safe side?

Elizabeth appeared in the doorway. "He's woken up," she said. "You'd better come." She had never yet shown any affection towards Billy, who had been born just at the time Will disappeared. She would stare at him for long periods, and trace a line down his cheek as he slept, one long, beautifully kept fingernail running along the line of his jaw. But she never held him, never spoke to him as she had with Frances's other children.

The night Will and Elizabeth met, the very same night, Elizabeth believed she had conceived, but it proved to be a child of her imagination – almost like Will himself, who now, nearly a year later, could almost have been no more than that. He had told her from the start that he must leave her after nine months. He had said it as though it was all the time he was going to be allowed, at the end of which he would be recalled to the place from which he had come. Afterwards, when she had asked him fearfully, in the pale, mean hours of morning, what he had meant, he had laughed, and she had chosen to believe it was because he had been joking. The symptoms of her growing phantom child persisted in her mind as their love – not grew so much as swelled up to reach its natural, ample size. She had known when, after the eighth month, he had disappeared, that he would never come back. She had chosen to take his disappearance as a further proof of his love for her. Perhaps each relationship we have has a natural length, like a gestation. They had been allotted their nine months. But as those months clocked by, it became clear that there was some kind of error, for they were set for an epic – there was no end in view. It did seem as though they could continue so for ever. They had eaten of the tree of knowledge, and what wonderful fruit it was. And as anyone who has ever eaten of it knows, banishment comes not as a punishment, but to prevent the lovers from approaching the tree of life, upon which they become like gods. Banishment was there, waiting, and, pre-empting its sting, Will had chosen to disappear a month before the end, to drop early from the tree, so that the drama was never brought to term. They subverted whatever destiny it had been, but by choosing an end more abrupt and tragic still.

She had never had word from him, nor expected any. They had never cheated on the jealous God. On the last day of what would have been the ninth month she followed a funeral car to the church, any car, any church. It was, by chance, the funeral of a young man, who had been trampled by a horse on holiday in France. She sat near the back, and wept for Will, and for the young man who had fallen from his horse, and for the child she called Tristan, who would never be born. As the service proceeded, with mechanical kindness, she took stock of her own presence. Ethereal Elizabeth, who, through Will, had been made into flesh and blood, had, like the little mermaid, exchanged her soul and her voice, and gladly, for human love. For nine months, she had not sung. Her singing voice, which until then had served very nicely as an image of her soul, had left her, and she had not cared. Frances had been shocked by her not caring. She felt somehow that Elizabeth might need it later on. Until the day she met Will she had probably sung every day of her life, sometimes out loud, sometimes in her head, like the rest of us. When, a week after Will's disappearance, Frances virtually forced her entry into Elizabeth's house, she had been reassured at first, to find her friend more beautiful than ever. That at least, was intact. She had recaptured that characteristic calm and cool she had had before Will. She hadn't visibly fallen apart. She was as physically astonishing as ever. But still she did not sing. Somehow Frances had thought it would return straight away. But for a further month, she was like a clock which did not strike – this time for grief. When she got back from the funeral she rang Frances and told her that during the service she had found herself singing above all the rest, like some diva joining in the chorus of "Land of Hope and Glory". She heard herself looping the notes together way above them, opening her throat while around her the untrained squeaked and the grief stricken stood silent. She felt her body take over her voice and every part of her and she realised, she said, that the soul was not a thing apart, that her voice was just one more part of her body, and her body was all she had, all that she was, and that when that was gone to ashes there would be nothing else, and certainly no more singing. She would sing with her body from now on, and it would do very well, but she knew now that there were no choirs of angels.

Frances brought the coffee with her into the living room. "I've poured out already, can you bring the cake? Ah . . . did you have a lovely sleep darling? Did you catch lots of pussy cats? Did you really?" She goggled at the child and lent her ear to his gurgling. "I suppose you're a hungry boy now?" She began to unbutton her blouse, settling the baby in the crook of her arm. "Lots of milk Elizabeth please, then if I spill my coffee all over him it won't be too hot. Do you think he's grown?"

"No, he's about the same."

She was remembering a day when Will had cooked her breakfast, a violently yellow kedgeree, while drinking pernod because, he said, the colours matched. She had come down into the kitchen and watched him as he sang to himself through last night's hangover, something rich and nineteenth century. It was as though he could smell the music – it made him shake with pleasure and toss his head in imitation of an opera singer, rather as an adolescent boy will bite his lip and scowl wretchedly over an invisible guitar. The previous night's washing up was piled in the sink and his cigarette was poised on the edge of the table, about to burn down into the wood. The tip of ash was already wilting dangerously towards the floor. There was the reckless extremism of youth in his every gesture; his fingers too were yellow where the nicotine had aged them.

She took her coffee, and looked out at the street, although she knew that he would not come. Be on your guard then, since ye know not the day nor the hour. But of course, even if he had been going to come, and she knew he could not, it would not have been now, not today, even though it was her birthday, since he would have been privileged to know her every movement, and would not have chosen a moment when Frances was there. She rationalised his nonappearances, whilst knowing he would never ever come, like a Seventh-Day Adventist, who bravely pleads his own incompetence, or the dislocation of the cosmic calender, prepared to swallow a thousand local disappointments rather than accept the hopeless infinity of his expectation.

Billy was feeding. Elizabeth watched her friend, breathing gently, her eyes half closed, just fluttering over the tiny head through her eyelashes. She had pushed off her shoes, and was stretching her toes. She looked a little used. Elizabeth considered inviting her for a day to her gym, but what would she do there? Frances would much rather play a good comradely game of doubles, even though Elizabeth had pointed out that it was only pretend exercise, it did nothing really for your figure, particularly not the vodka and coke in the club house afterwards (all right diet coke, but it was a pretty helpless gesture). If our own body is the only thing we can ever experience through any means other than the senses, if we can somehow experience it as, what was it, a will to live, as Will had seemed to do . . . which had translated almost into a vigorous will to die sooner rather than later . . . how was it that people like Frances, who certainly appeared to have no sensual relationship with hers, could get along by doing neither, by simply floundering about in it, like a comfortable old sweater? . . .

Elizabeth closed her eyes – without smell, without touch, without sound, without taste, without sight, how could she be aware of herself, how could she know she was there, in life? And yet, if she could not know it, could not be sure, if she must at a stretch even assume, when her senses were in abeyance, that she wasn't there, did not exist, what was this thing that was asking the questions – not her brain, her brain was just one more material thing that could not be perceived except by the senses – unless, unless . . . she panicked and opened her eyes. Her hands were weak, there were tears in her eyes. The machine was functioning normally. Frances was watching her and holding the baby as she would have liked to have held Elizabeth, to have wiped away the tears, just to have helped. Frances had cried over Will too, and out of her own sadness she had tried to fashion an image, for reference, of Elizabeth's, as though she could hope thereby to simulate the conditions of Elizabeth's world, and learn how to tread within it. It was not easy to estimate the contours of Elizabeth's interior world – it never had been, and since Will had almost landscaped it, bringing out the natural features, enhancing the existing qualities of the terrain, she found it had become a place which was lovelier but more foreign than the one she had previously guessed at.

She put the baby in its carry cot, a snug little hold-all with a row of ducks, threaded like beads along a string, suspended across the middle. Her bag was by the door, waiting for someone to fall over it, Elizabeth would have said. She picked it up and fished out a large envelope.

"I forgot, Lizzie, this was outside the front door. It looks like a wedding invitation. It's not David and Annie, I've had theirs . . . it was huge, like a Sunday newspaper, all in sections about travel and dress and faxing confirmation to the hotel."

She turned the letter over and looked at the post mark. "Perhaps it's a personal telegram from the Queen. A computer error. I'll get Alistair to come and see to that clematis for you. It needs something doing to it."

"It needs watering. I'll do it." Elizabeth took Frances's mug and the envelope and went through to the kitchen. She stood at the sink, with clear, seven times recycled water splashing away the coffee grains from the sides of the jug, and opened the letter. The solicitors had written to inform her that Will's worldly goods were hers to keep, and his ashes, his earthly remnants hers to dispose of. He was deceased. She looked hard at the word, trying to find a double negative in there somewhere – de-ceased, could that not mean "living", still-with-us . . .? Looking out into the garden she noticed with the indifference that can evoke an ache, a sort of lament for lost feeling, that the cherry tree, untended, unpruned, unwatered, was just coming into flower. In the next room the baby spun his little plastic ducks and chuckled happily to himself.

"What was the story about Shelley and the bridge?"

"Shelley was crossing Magdalen bridge with a friend. They were discussing anamnesis, the theory that we come from some sort of eternal home, and that life is a process of forgetting. Like Wordsworth, you know 'our birth is but a sleep and a forgetting, the soul that rises in us, our life's star Hath had elsewhere its setting and cometh from afar And not in utter nakedness But trailing clouds of glory do we come . . .'"

"Dear me," I said, rather briskly, "What do we go out in then?" but she ignored that.

"A woman was crossing the bridge, coming towards them, with a baby in her arms. Shelley took the baby from her and said, 'Truly, if only this child could disclose to us all that he knows, then we would be wise, my friend.'"

"What did the mother say?"

"'He cannot speak, sir', she said."

And Shelley said, 'Why of course not, otherwise he would tell us all he knows of heaven and earth.'

"Something like that, yes."

"That's a bit like drowning witches. If they die they were innocent."

"By the time the child can speak he's forgotten."

"And Will. Had he forgotten?"

"That's a funny question. What do you mean?"

"You describe him like a fairy childe. All-knowing."

"Maybe. Maybe I do. But I don't think he'd forgotten. Not quite."

She travelled up to Reading the next day for a meeting with the solicitors. Mr Heythrop, of Heythrop, Marsh and Wainscott, spilled his cup of tea all over the papers on his desk, which added at least ten minutes to the interview. She wondered who was paying his bill. She saw his hand reach vaguely for the telephone, which the secretary had carefully moved a few inches to the left in order to make room for the tray, while he was still clutching about with his other hand after the letter with the instructions in it. She had bobbed involuntarily and made a little movement inside her head which had had no time to be translated into action, reminding herself of her younger brother, David, who was incapable of watching sport on the television without anticipating the muscular reflexes of the participants, so that when he was watching the show jumping you had to be careful not to come too close to him for fear of receiving a sharp kick on the knee cap. David had left home for Australia just a year after "we buried your father" as Mrs Faulkener put it, as though trying to urge collective responsibility for an act of unjustifiable interment. It was as though David refused to believe he was dead and had gone to look for him, even though they all knew perfectly well that he had died of a heart attack on the local village green whilst batting for Little Harkness after three pints of Guinness and a whisky chaser. Elizabeth hadn't seen David for ten years. He worked for a pizza delivery firm in Sydney, painted houses, combed beaches, sold double glazing . . . these reports had trickled back over the years in postcards which were always written in the style of one who has only gone away for a short break and will be back next week. Elizabeth never expected him back. She had been told fourth hand by an acquaintance of Frances's husband that he had last been spotted in New York waiting for a girl outside the Rockefeller Centre, sporting a copy of the *Wall Street Journal* and quite a bit of extra weight.

Mr Heythrop's mopping up operation had been fraught with the same kind of hazards as those which frequently attend a clean up after an oil tanker springs a leak. The more he mopped, the greater surface area seemed to become affected by the spillage, and the fundamental cause of damage, the large puddle of quickly chilling tea, had not been at all adequately dealt with before subsidiary considerations began to claim more urgent attention – the steady drip over the edge of the desk onto a cream-coloured rug below, the salvaging of a draft petition for divorce which was sustaining extensive damage on Mr Heythrop's eastern seaboard, between the telephone and his touchingly kindergarten-ish pencil case. He began to look like some eccentric naval general who has embarked upon an improvised simulation of a historic sea battle with the equipment to hand on his desk.

Why was it that death was so beset with humourous possibilities? Elizabeth knew it was partly just that a guffaw echoes louder in a morgue than it does in a circus tent, but even so . . . it wasn't merely that old chestnut of mocking what we most fear, it really was the case that everything to do with death had the potential to flip over into absurdity. Maybe grief makes us clear eyed in the face of absurdity, she thought, but that would only explain why people found the paraphernalia of death so funny, not how that paraphernalia accrued in the first place. She remembered sitting in the car behind her father's coffin between David and her mother, sizzling with suppressed giggles, their faces wet with tears, as the undertaker strode down the road in front of the funeral cars, bearing a staff like an Old Testament prophet. This might perhaps have been very moving, and have entrenched their grief in a way solemn ceremonies are supposed to do, for your own good, had they not known that his name was Sid Sissons and that he normally drove around on an ancient motorbike with a sidecar for his wife. The humourous possibilities of the conjunction of this idea with that of the transport of dead bodies was just too much for them. Even as Elizabeth wept her way through ''The Lord's My Shepherd'', during which there floated across her mind an indistinct vision of early Sunday evening on the village green, with her father watching over grazing sheep with his pint of Guinness overflowing, the image of Mr Sissons tootling past at three miles an hour en route for death's dark vale with a couple of stiffs in the side car sent her into a sort of snorting splutter like a car backfiring.

"How extraordinary," said Mr Heythrop, but he did not go on immediately to explain. Elizabeth sat quietly as he flapped papers up and down and pulled out drawers with the quick, urgent tug of someone reloading a gun. Frances had wanted to come with her, but she had asked to come alone. She did not comfort herself with the idea that Will was there somewhere, watching, reaching for her hand. There was no comfort in the idea of a dematerialised Will. Her grief felt still as an urn, with the potential violence inherent in the most fragile objects. The only time she had wept was when Frances, reading the solicitor's letter, had said, in a scandalised voice, that it was like something appearing on your Access bill months after you thought it had already been paid for.

"Oh God, Lizzie, I'm sorry – it's just – I don't understand, who's done this?"

"I don't know."

Elizabeth stood by the window squeezing her hands together. The baby began to wail and Frances pushed the carrycot out into the hall and came back, shutting the door. The noise persisted, and, so as not to duplicate, Elizabeth stopped crying herself. Even the little and meek can do something useful.

Frances wanted to ring Heythrop immediately and find out who had sent them the ashes.

"We have been instructed," the letter said, "to purvey the ashes of William Makepeace to you. They will be available for your collection during office hours . . ."

"I don't think I want to know," Elizabeth said. "They don't say. Perhaps it's one of those things they don't tell you."

"But it means he must have a family." Will had always said he was quite alone in the world. If he spoke of his family at all it was as of a house that had burned down, a single item, non-extant.

"I don't want to know," Elizabeth repeated. Frances saw that it comforted her to see her own role as entirely predetermined, with no room for freedom of action. She would go immediately to collect the ashes. She would not ask any questions, because in delay, and in questioning, she would have altered, in however small a way, the outcome of the story, and thus introduced a note of deviation from the version Will had selected. Already she had chosen to encapsulate the whole of the past year in a mould, like a hard, precious stone set in a rigorous clasp. It was unmodifiable, and to that extent unassailable. It was also unapproachable. She could not relive the joys, the extremes of feeling she had experienced with him, for the sense had gone out of them, they were set in stone, and she could no longer even perceive how it had been – her senses held no memory – she guarded vigilantly against any renewal, eschewing the madelaine like a hot kettle. So she went through the motions adequately and unquestioningly. Frances favoured demystification – if only Elizabeth had been prepared to ask a few questions – what had happened, where he had died, whether it was his family, or some anonymous hospital visitor who had acted on Will's last wishes and made these arrangements. Looking at Elizabeth, Frances felt it really was a question of ashes to ashes, for there was in her face the cold, mineral immobility of something sculpted from stone. Will's sculptures would outlive her. When the life had gone from her, they would still be there in representation of her. When what had gone from her? The paradox of her relationship with Will was that he had brought her to life whilst convincing her that life was a delusion. At least, she said, she realised that her body was a machine for something. For what? Frances had asked, in some exasperation. For creating the illusion of a soul, Elizabeth said. All those oscillating neurones and genes, to cite but the most elemental pieces of material, drove the machine and drew up its specifications, and the body responded and collaborated and the Great Mystery, the unfathomable energy was created, which was no more than the huff and puff of the machine but gave us the sweet impression of being in life.

"That's consciousness, though," Frances suggested, batting around for something to connect with.

"A cat is conscious too," said Elizabeth, "it's hardly miraculous. When it perceives something, a mouse, say, its neurones reach an oscillation level of forty megahertz per second. That's all consciousness is. I imagine it's when we perceive the illusion of a soul that our megahertz are at their most frantic. It's only a question of degree. To perceive an illusion which we can be conscious of we just have to up the megahertz level."

"You don't believe in anything anymore," said Frances, "not in beauty or love . . ."

"Exactly," said Elizabeth, "anything you have to 'believe in' like that has to be an illusion, otherwise it wouldn't require faith, would it?"

"Faith is a supernatural gift from God which enables us to believe without questioning whatever God has revealed", said Frances rather wistfully, as though she were quoting an old love letter or a line of poetry.

"You were lucky to come out of that convent with a brain at all," Elizabeth replied.

Frances felt rather lost in these conversations. "She doesn't cry," she told Alistair. "If she could cry she'd be able to dispense with all this rationalist nonsense."

"I expect she's frightened of rusting up the machine," observed Alistair from behind the sports pages.

"Or getting wrinkles."

"She'll come out of it," he said.

But Frances felt that Elizabeth had been vouchsafed a vision of hopelessness, a sort of negative revelation. "I bet they keep records of that kind of vision in some locked chamber in the

Vatican. The ones they don't want people to know about. Like the MOD and sightings of flying saucers."

Elizabeth found she was feeling rather irritated with Mr Heythrop. She looked over his shoulder to the photograph on his wall, a large portrait of his wife and children. It looked like a detail from a larger photograph that had been blown up, without being of sufficiently good quality to support the magnification. You could see they were just made up of little dots, blobs of pigment, and she wondered that the photograph didn't make him feel less secure about his family, rather than more so. Maybe he put it there out of spite, to show all those people who came to him seeking divorces that even though he did not look up to much, he did actually have a happy home life, that his dealings with misery were entirely professional.

"Most extraordinary," he repeated. "I don't seem to be able to lay my hands on it." He pressed a button on his telephone and bent forward to speak into a little microphone, so that Elizabeth could see the pink pate which was forming in the centre of his skull, as though someone had picked a flower from it and left a void. The flower of his youth, perhaps.

"Miss Elton, do you have the letter we received last week concerning the receptacle of ashes to be forwarded to Miss Faulkener?"

Miss Elton's voice came back through the outgoing microphone, and for all Elizabeth could understand she might have been announcing the next departure from Reading to Paddington. Mr Heythrop sighed and sat back in his chair.

"There *was* a covering letter," he said, as though it had not only been lost but had actually ceased to exist. Perhaps that was his excuse. "I had it here only yesterday. Or was it the day before?"

Elizabeth said nothing. She hoped fervently that there was some etiquette debarring him from inquiring into her relation to the deceased, or expressing condolences. She could not imagine that there had been anything in the letter which could have enlightened him on the subject of her eligibility as custodian of Will's final remains. And above all she wanted no explanations, because any explanation would have been more incomprehensible than the absence of one. Mr Heythrop was most put out by his own incompetence, in fact he seemed to feel it represented a misfortune of equal dimensions to her own. The atmosphere warmed between them slightly. She felt it would not have been inappropriate for him to turn the family portrait to the wall.

"I . . . er . . . concerning the possessions— "

"There aren't any," said Elizabeth. "He didn't live anywhere. I mean, he didn't have things – or at least, I don't know where they would be. I really don't want anything. Would it be all right if we didn't go into that?"

Mr Heythrop looked surprised. "Well, I expect, yes, something could be arranged. As I can't put my hands on . . ." he looked vaguely askance at his desk and dabbed a drop of tea with his jacket elbow. ". . . I seem to think there was some reference— "

"I expect you're thinking of someone else."

"Often," suggested Mr Heythrop, ignoring her intervention, "people like to choose . . ."

"No."

"I see," said Mr Heythrop. "Well, I'll just ah— " and he got up from his desk and left the room. Elizabeth noticed that the sole of one of his shoes, having come into contact with a tributary of tea, left unrecognisable prints on the wooden floor, a partial picture only. She felt like someone who has been granted a child for adoption, and that the moment had come when the child, beribboned and best-frocked, was to be brought into the room, and she was to come face to face with what she was to live with from now on. But they were only ashes, they represented, at this juncture, no more than the information, which in a way was a relief, that he was dead. His handing them over to her would be a ritual gesture, like a knight handing a glove to his vassal, a gesture in confirmation of her bereavement. But pictures, ornaments "to remember him by", as people said, why, she could not for the life of her see how anything of Will could be transposed into her own consciousness, how anything, even a memory, could be salvaged by the possession of a material object which had once been his. The very idea was somehow primitive and tribal, as though she could be expected to believe that wearing a lock of his hair in a pendant next to her skin could exert any pull against the huge, indifferent current which ran to the oblivion which succeeds death.

Back he came, empty handed. He cocked a finger in the air – he had it now, one more second please – and pulled out the bottom drawer of his desk. "They were here all the time," he said, as though it had been some kind of coincidence, or irony. Elizabeth even smiled politely. But of the letter there was no further mention.

He clearly felt under the obligation – and she wished he wouldn't – to make an appropriate speech. She was reminded of a prize-giving at her old school, at which she had been asked to sing (an idea of her mother's, which had embarrassed everybody, but which the headmaster had had to accede to as Mrs Faulkener was a governor). A boy had been summoned up to the stage to receive a prize for long distance running which had been awarded by the county, and he had arrived up there with a kind of little leap of triumph, making for the trophy with the justified tread of one who has a righteous claim on it. The headmaster had held him back slightly with his hand and gone on to address the audience on the subject of the character forming aspects of the sport in question – patience, discipline, solitary determination – while the poor boy had stood there in front of the whole school, having become transformed through the headmaster's cunning address into one who, whatever trophies might line his path, had patently yet to attain the greater moral prize, shifting from foot to foot, with his eyes on the gleaming cup. As the speech had dragged on, he shifted his gaze from the trophy to the headmaster, then quickly looked away in annoyance and boredom, at his own feet, then out of the window. Elizabeth had the feeling by the end of it that the boy was somehow being punished for his glory. When the headmaster finally handed over the cup, the boy took it and handled it in a way that suggested it had been sullied for him by the intervention. She felt it would have been only right for him to ceremoniously take out his handkerchief and remove the man's fingerprints before the whole assembly.

"People often feel," Mr Heythrop was saying, "that the back garden is a little close to home."

She was slightly confounded by this statement, and waited for him to expand on it.

"The importance of the moment does tend to incline one in favour of a somewhat ceremonial emphasis. Obviously certain precautions should be taken regarding the weather. I should not advise you to attempt dispersal in wind or rain. Things can, if you will excuse me, come back in one's face. Bridges, ships, that sort of thing, are of course very popular. It really is a question of personal choice, and of course of the dignity of those we have lost."

She wondered what image, through her, Mr Heythrop had formed of the deceased, of Will. She felt that he was looking for clues, the better to be able to advise her, as though she had ordered a cake for Will's birthday and was required to supply ideas for an appropriate theme in the design.

"I'm sure I'll think of something suitable," she said, moving things along rather, wondering whether the ashes were even now damp with tea. She didn't fancy having to scatter anything coagulated. He passed over a small carton box, sealed with masking tape, with Will's name on it in black felt tip (no delicacy spared), as though he were the addressee and not the very contents themselves. The ashes were inside, in a little urn which was apparently a sort of house speciality of the crematorium. You got to keep the urn.

"Some people actually keep the vessel and contents intact on their mantelpiece for years," Mr Heythrop told her, "so it is as well to make provision by providing an urn which will not . . . ah . . . create any aesthetic disturbance, clash with the other ornaments, you know."

Elizabeth gave nothing away about her intentions. She found the idea of Mr Heythrop picturing her disposing of Will somehow voyeuristic and wondered how he would have reacted if she had smashed the pot and tapped the contents into the waste paper bin. She uncrossed her legs and picked her bag up off the floor. Elizabeth had thought to bring her most capacious handbag, and the box fitted comfortably inside it. She tried to imagine that Will was some kind of pet whom she was smuggling through a border to avoid quarantine laws, but since she knew it was no more than a pile of ashes, ground to the finest dust as though in a pestle and mortar, there was no call to be fanciful, and anyway, by nature, she wasn't. Mr Heythrop had patted her arm after handing over the box and seeing her to the door, as though he were groping for words, but not those words, to say "I hope you'll be very happy together . . ."

Everything is an instrument of everything else – to this extent I suppose one can believe in Providence – there seems to be no effect that is not also a cause. There are days of which you say, with hindsight, there was something in the air, it had to be that day of all days; and others of which you say, it was so strange, uncanny, almost, that it should have happened on that day because I had not the slightest inkling. Whichever way you put it you can make something extraordinary of it.

Elizabeth and Will met on a summer day in London. She and Mark, following the habit of a number of years, had been attending a series of concerts at a church close to Westminster. Mark spent the day at the British Museum – he allotted himself one day a week there, which meant he could get to see Elizabeth once a week for certain. It was barely enough to survive on, but it was there, and guaranteed, like the minimum wage. In his mind he was forever working on strategies for leaving his wife, though he never spoke to Elizabeth about this. Anna lived in relatively happy ignorance of the affair. Whenever it occurred to her that Mark seemed to survive remarkably well on the small amount of affection they spun out between them and wondered whether he might not be topping up elsewhere, she dismissed the possibility as fanciful; he could not afford to leave, his work on troubadour poetry was his highest priority – a love affair would have been damaging to his concentration, and his work, he always said, was going well. Elizabeth never asked questions about her. It was a rule of protocol, rather as some married couples have a rule about not talking shop.

Mark had rung during the afternoon to say he would be early, as was his way, so that, removing an element from her day (a visit to the library to consult a specialist dictionary) she took time to walk through the streets towards their meeting place by the river. It was a warm evening – the news vendor's boards told of a heat wave, as if the moment required a caption. Already she had plotted her route. She was never late. She calculated her arrival at the church for a little before seven. If you had stopped her in the street and asked her for her own directions she must have paused a moment, bringing the information up on a little mental screen, before reading off the landmarks with their estimated times of arrival – the palace, Scotland Yard, Conservative Party office, then the huge baroque building itself, more like an observatory than a place of worship. Perhaps that was what had been intended – a vast, sceptical camera obscura turned on the heavens, sweeping the empty skies for signs of divine activity.

Waiting for the lights to change as she crossed Piccadilly, she felt the shudder of an underground train beneath her feet, and for a fraction of a second something dragged inside her in sympathy. Four hundred feet beneath the paving stones, which were warm as an evening sea, Mark's train coiled without wake through the tunnel system and the electric lights of the underground picked out a precisely etched network of early lines around his eyes. He had passed the day in the sunless world of the library, and if he closed his eyes and laid the pads of his middle fingers over the lids he could feel blood pumping through the web of fine capillaries. The light of the world, meanwhile, shed long shadows on the emptying streets where Elizabeth walked towards their last lovers' meeting, before the sun disappeared and individual shadows spread and merged like water on a flat surface.

She turned the corner into the square, where the church sat round and comfortable as a draughtsman in its box. Churches, unlike chapels, always seemed to occupy their own space – never squeezed uncomfortably into a terrace like a dessicated flower between the leaves of a book, but with a generous skirt of ease – known as property – spread wide about, girding the consecrated quarters like a crinoline. She saw the crinoline as a gadget wildly in advance of its time, describing to an inch the necessary measure of personal space long before psychologists began to speak of it. She stopped at the pub on the corner and went into the ladies, passing through the warm beery smell of the bar into the disinfected world beyond. Drying her hands at the hot air stream, she tilted her face to one side, not wishing to achieve the effect of having just spent a day on the ocean wave. She deepened her lips a shade and ran a pencil across her eyebrows. Her fine fuse wire hair was held back with a leather thong, to expose earrings small as grandmother's beads. Ivory silk billowed slightly above the high waist band of her skirt, sharply tailored to show the fish bone arch of her hips. Whilst being thin she somehow conveyed an impression of breadth – her wide brow and horizontal cheekbones gave her face a full frontal look – nothing was receding. It was almost a flat Botticelli face. Confronted with the mirror image you might have imagined her profile could only be a shadow, a distortion against the light.

She made her way out onto the crowded pavement. People were drinking Pimms and other cocktails – the heat had brought a weekend feel to an ordinary Wednesday evening, and habits of home and holidays were seeping out from under shirt cuffs and collar. She wondered whether they might not all shortly troop off to the garden centre together, cracking the habit of a career in estrangement to muse companionably over parasol bases and thermal-lined picnic hampers. Then, when the rains came later in the month, they would retreat again, the impermeable membrane of propriety tightening like a chapped upper lip in the wet and the cold. Bells all over London were ringing seven o'clock, each to its own parish, but overheard in distant dioceses, a Dickensian anachronism, so that even had they been ringing for the death of the monarchy itself they would have sounded glad as ever, celebrants first and foremost of their own survival. Meanwhile, in the same city, in theatres, taverns and down in the night-lit tube stations, the timely squeak of watches was also sounding – eek! The idea of the personal timepiece was one more indication of the fragmentation of society, each to his own. She pondered for a moment the idea of whole counties, countries even, being infected by the sluggish contagion of one solitary clock, from which all the others took their tune, like a choir humming the initial notes of a part work to the "la!" of one whose once perfect pitch has dropped an imperceptible semitone over the years. Now everyone had their own way of checking, errors became personal, not communal, and if the dance slowed for one, he must fall out, while the others stepped on in perfect time.

As she approached the entrance to the church, Mark stepped out to meet her and they kissed gently but formally, like a couple who have once been intimate, meeting at a funeral service of one they have both loved.

But it was, after all, an ordinary Wednesday evening. Mark had brought the score. Elizabeth had imagined herself enjoying the concert in the comfortable shade of a pillar, with the possibility for lapses of concentration available but not on a plate. Instead, Mark had decided they would go up to "the gods", as he put it, which in view of the church setting, was an uncharacteristic gaffe. They climbed upstairs and he held back to let her pass before him into the row. She sat herself down and smoothed her skirt. Mark lent over the rail to look down into the belly of the church, scouring for a familiar face. She wondered if it was someone in particular he was looking for. He came and sat at her side. Reaching for a gesture that would affirm, without actually being a feature of their intimacy, she laid her hand over his fingers and they rested there together, with a sort of mutual quiescence.

Across the gulf, on the opposite side of the gallery, sat a woman with long pink crinkly hair and a wildly painted face. Her dress was a theatre reconstruction of 1930s' elegance, and even at a distance of thirty metres Elizabeth could see that a shaking hand had drawn in the eyebrows. She pondered the strangeness of the fashion for removing the real thing to replace it with an inaccurate facsimile of the same, thinking of an article she had read about some caves in France which had been closed to the public to preserve their prehistoric wall paintings. Next door an exact replica of the paintings had been created, and the public went with undiminished enthusiasm to peer at the fakes. She was about to mention this to Mark, but, anticipating his response – roughly, that it was quite right, since the originals were sustaining damage through even the little light that was provided to inspect them by – she said nothing. But her mind dwelt on the paintings, in the same spirit as she had often reflected on the pine tree that falls in the middle of the Antarctic when there is no one there to hear – does it make a noise? It did not seem incongruous to be thinking along these lines. She would not have been surprised the next day to scour the papers and find no mention of the concert, or even to read of its cancellation.

She had scarcely spoken since they had met at the door. Mark slid his hand out from under hers. He was so painfully in love with Elizabeth, and so committed, by precedent, to a demeanour which belied the messy, urgent and irrational character of his feeling for her, that in order for him to express what he really felt, underneath his aura of gentlemanly nonchalance, it would have been necessary for him to be incarnated afresh, like an ex-mafia man, and to re-embark on his courtship of her (preferably with a memory of the mistakes made the first time round) from an entirely different angle. They had known one another for seven years. When he had first seen her he had been attracted by her ability not to impersonate – that was the wrong word – but to incorporate, perhaps, essentially to be, all women in all ages. She had a Mona Lisa quality, but Mona Lisa repainted on a different day, with her eyes fixed not on her own knowing smile, but on some brighter light, in anticipation of spiritual, not sensual pleasures. There was the small child, the leggy girl, the assured young woman, the lover, the mother, sybil and sphinx, each glimmering into or out of life in her face and the inflections of her voice. All the instructions for life were there in foetal form, and would unravel in their various guises and aspects through the years, so that the man who had known her had, in knowing her, known all women, at all times and in all places. He knew that in harbouring these notions about her he was making an idiot of himself, even if the notions themselves found no translation into a language by which they could be rightly judged as ridiculous. Friends told him he was making an ideal out of an enigma, and an enigma out of a sealed, but empty tomb. The book he was writing on religious imagery in erotic poetry and erotic imagery in religious poetry (1220–40), had been conceived shortly after he first met Elizabeth. For the first time he had been able to see what the troubadours had really been getting at. "She is your *dame blanche*," his friends told him.

This was not quite true, but Mark recognised that he had made the error, early on, of allowing their intimacy to bear the same character as their exterior aspect as a couple. It was as though, on walking into a house he had found himself wandering through endless inner courtyards whose walls were all replicas of the outer façade. The doors which promised access to a warm, personalised, and possibly, on occasions, disordered interior, proved to be no more than alluring trompe l'oeils, by which he was each time freshly deceived. He wondered whether like the knight in search of the grail, he had only to ask the simplest question – perhaps Parsifal's question, "What ails thee?" and the door would open – except Elizabeth would always have just appeared fleetingly at a window, answered "nothing!" and withdrawn. In praising her beauty, the clarity of her thought, in failing to find fault with her, he had somehow prevented their relationship from taking on human form – so that it could neither wither nor flourish, nor change in any way, nor follow the seasons, nor grow old; they were locked in a kind of inhuman, pre-fall condition which was neither corrupt nor innocent, but as static and immutable and cold as a snowflake, conserved artificially at constant temperature. His hand, disengaged from hers, but still retaining the shape of the clasp in which he had held it, was damp.

"I'll go and order drinks for the interval." He passed her the score. Pergolesi – "the Stabat Mater". She was surprised. She had been convinced they were there to hear Carissimi's "Jephta", and the switch, not so much from Carissimi to Pergolesi, but from Old Testament to New was strangely unsettling. She felt as though she had slept through something.

Mark went down into the crypt and into the men's lavatories. He felt sick and his heart was clapping oddly. He leaned against the wall and laid his hand on his forehead. His fingertips were slightly numb. When he clenched his fist so that his nails pressed into his palm, the joints cracked. His head swam. He reached into his breast pocket and took out his diary. He wanted to make some mark, to plant some evidence to show he had not been a dupe, to be able to say, I knew, I knew it was the end. But all he could think of to write was, "Pergolesi, St John's 7.30", and was immediately aware that it read like an inscription in memoriam. Then he unbolted the door and went out to the bar, which was almost empty. He gave his name, the money and the order. The girl behind the bar was talking to a man in a white shirt. She wrote out "Mr Chester – 1 white wine, half lager" on a piece of paper and placed two glasses on top of it. Mark dropped his change back into his pocket and turned away from the bar. His feet nudged against something soft and there was a squeal and a shuffle as a large black dog got to its feet and looked up at him, stretching its front legs in a movement that looked suspiciously like a limbering up exercise.

"Sorry," he said automatically to the man in the white shirt, who turned round quickly at the sound of Mark's voice. Mark was shocked – he had imagined an older face – he was young, with a sweetness in his features which was not disguised by the premature lines that ran from the corner of each nostril to the sides of his mouth, nor by the black smudges under his eyes. He looked down at the dog with an expression that mingled affection and an inability to remember how the animal had come to be there. Then he looked up at Mark with a glance that had clearly been prepared in the moment of hesitation during which he had been looking at the dog, as though he had been swiftly topping up his expression from a secret inner source. His eyes, meeting Mark's, seemed to have taken aim a split second before. It was a naked look of insolence, the look given by the beggar who has unseated the rich man at his table. When the last came to be first and the first last, when the Day of Judgement finally revealed, as though there had not been sufficient warning in advance, that there was, after all, no justice in this world or the next, the truculent latecomers would look like this at the righteous. Mark had been singled out for dispossession. At the same time the dog was dribbling on his shoes. It had already started.

"Shylock!" said the girl behind the bar, and the dog looked up at the boy and crept away under his stool.

"Sorry Mr Chester," said the girl, reading off the ticket, which Mark felt was an impudence, since one's name was after all something to be given voluntarily and solemnly, like a handshake. He hoped they did not think he was sweating because of them. He heard someone snigger and saw that the girl was laughing behind her hand in a pantomime of restrained mirth, designed, with arch hypocrisy, to convey her senses of both propriety and humour. The boy continued to look at him. Those who have power to harm and do none are undoubtedly, he thought, the most vicious. Their quiver is full, and tipped with venom.

Elizabeth was sitting cool as stone, the score unopened on her lap. As he sat down, she turned to him and said, "I saw something strange today."

He took the score from her, and smoothed out the page. "What was that?"

She wondered why he didn't just say "What?" as though he were really interested. The addition of the extra two words was a sign of a lapse, compensating in the length of the phrase for the lack of attack in the single interrogative. I am beginning to criticise him, she thought. See through him? No, not that, although she wondered why the discovery of transparency, the quality which allows one to focus, without distortion, on what lies beyond, should also signal the beginning of the end, a breakthrough into disillusion.

"What?" he asked again.

The little painted lady opposite was craning round to look up at the window behind her, miming interest in the simple pane itself, as though it were in fact set with rich stained glass which she alone could see. Elizabeth had the sudden feeling that in fact the woman could hear their conversation, and was feigning interest in something which did not exist in order to hide her curiosity.

She explained that she had been walking through Paternoster Square, on her way to an appointment. A small gallery near St Paul's had commissioned her to translate a text relating to a French minimalist whose empty spaces seemed to generate an awful lot of sound and fury signifying, as far as she was concerned, nothing. Mark was about to interrupt, but she looked down into the pit of the church as she spoke, and the lack of eye contact made it impossible for him to override her. A flock of girls sat on the grass, she said, their pale legs exposed to the sun, chattering among the remains of their lunch. Mark stopped waiting for a comma and listened. It was not at all the kind of detail she would normally have included. Elizabeth felt she could have walked through them unobserved, that they would have been aware perhaps only of the slightest chill, the lift of a frail cotton skirt, a wisp of hair displaced, something passing like an echo of a former presence.

All day she had been in this dream-like state, uncertain of her own footsteps, afraid of falling, conscious of heights and depths, of the empty spaces between material objects. It was most unlike her. She had dreamed that night, with a force unfamiliar to her, that she had given birth to a child, but a child who was not of her own flesh. In the space of a few minutes, no more than a few seconds in the dream, it grew into a man, and lay down, not beside her, but over her, covering her body like the saint in the story who lends his body to the unknown leper and shields him from the night wind. Now the sensations of the dream clung to her like a cobweb, and she could not shake off the chill she had felt on awakening.

As she came into Paternoster Square, instead of turning into the little street towards the gallery, she was drawn away from the shadow of the buildings, and had the sudden feeling she was being moved, not physically, but by the strength of a thought not her own. Her movements had that perverse random quality which belies the presence of a deep hidden strategy, like mutations which turn out later to have been uncannily advantageous. In the middle of the square she found a drawing, executed by a pavement artist, roughly etched in coloured chalks. It was a windfall moment, something wonderful and unexpected laid at her feet.

"You remember?" she said. "When we went to see those people last year, about your book."

"The Occident expert. Pierre." Pierre had had some interesting things to say about Occident philology, but for Mark's money had been a little too much concerned with broadening the Englishman's understanding of the social and historical context of twelfth-century France, heaving with both elbows at the walls of his narrow focus, a veritable Samson in Mark's temple whose motto was an emphatic "*An den Sachen selbst*!"

The singers had started to file onto the platform. The soprano and alto, a classic combination of thin one and fat one, came out last, to a burst of applause, which followed directly on Elizabeth saying: "It was the picture on the wine bottle. It was supposed to have some mystical significance."

Les Bergers d'Arcadie. Mark flattened out the score. His bowels were feeling loose and noisome, his head rather light. The applause subsided, and Elizabeth leaned back in her seat. When the singing began she was surprised to discover that it was in fact the fat one who was the soprano and the thin one the alto; it was one of those inversions that, had it not been superseded by more significant events, could have made an otherwise run-of-the-mill performance rather memorable.

The concert began and for once she closed her eyes. Normally she was an attentive concert goer. The price of the ticket was usually higher than that of a recording, so it was as well to ensure that you had a satisfactory visual experience too. As a singer herself, she watched for technical detail – breathing, stance, the infinitesimal movements of a singer's body, a fractional representation of the whole available range of physical gesture, like a singly dropped wink in a potentially expressive face. She had not sung in public for well over a year – the last time had been at a garden party held in Mark's college, where, in a linen print dress and garden hat – as though she were fresh in from deadheading the roses – she sang through the Noel Coward song book with a certain forced gaiety. It had been slightly windy – her voice had been lifted away like ashes from a bonfire, and she had had to peg her photocopies of the pianist's music to a stand. The stand itself had proved rather unstable and she had laid her hand on it as she sang, with an anxious retaining gesture which she tried to make look as though it were related to the nineteenth-century gesture of laying one's hand expansively on the piano lid – a proprietorial gesture, similar to that of country landowners in portraits by Gainsborough – a hand on the mane of the horse, the top rung of a gate, the trunk of an ancient tree.

She opened her eyes abruptly – she had been close to dreaming – and placed her hand on Mark's knee. He started at her sudden movement, and the score slipped between his legs. He had been treating the concert as an opportunity to take time out of contact with the world – the cultural equivalent of a long bath. She could not, after all, end it while the music was playing. When the soprano and alto took up their long, sinuous duet it sounded to Mark as though they were discussing something terribly female and intimate rather than lamenting the death of the son of God. There was an all too enjoyable complicity between them which belittled the subject of their exchange. They sang in perfect amiable harmony, the one fresh and virginal, the other resonant with a kind of ample calm. The irresistible blend of maiden and matron was expressed in a single song. He too closed his eyes for a second, and was visited briefly by the bizarre image of Elizabeth and Anna, either side of a garden wall, deep in a conversation whose words – like church Latin – he recognised but did not bother to translate, knowing as he did, their full weight and impact, if not their intrinsic meaning. The image laid itself down in his head and with resignation he shifted his ideas to make room for it.

After the applause had died away and the singers had left the stage, the audience below began to move purposefully towards the crypt. For a few moments, perched high above the throng, Elizabeth and Mark sat in their own silence, unable to move from the passive to the active register, where movements, decisions and mistakes were waiting to be made. Images of the building and people passed unrecorded, the slackness of perception that accompanies the slow emergence from sleep creating a moment of lapsed time between what they saw and its recognition by the brain, so that they both separately experienced the curious feeling of having been there before, in this moment, which had passed a fraction of a second ago and could therefore be recollected. Elizabeth twitched and felt a chill on her upper arms. Someone walked over my grave, she said, and smiled at Mark, taking his arm. As they moved towards the staircase the rays of the setting sun hit the glass of the window opposite, and a million tiny particles of dust danced in its beam, as though the whole world of matter were beginning to revert to its original state, each atom alone and formless in the atmosphere.

Down in the crypt there was a crush of concert goers in random motion. The audience which only minutes previously had been settled into a single obedient mass had, with the lifting of restrictions and the rise of temperature down below ground level, become volatile and wayward. They collected their glasses and sat at a corner table under a low arch. It was cramped and noisy. Mark, in particular, felt overcome by the heat. They had nothing, he thought, to say to one another. It was not that they had run out of steam, but that somewhere a whistle had been blown. They had run out of time. There was no reason why it should have happened on this evening rather than on any other, but the end was no less final for being arbitrary. Having so long experienced Elizabeth's silences as a positive sign of strength he realised that their quality had changed, that her serenity had sagged, to expose a void of interest within. The people at the next table were laughing at something. They were young – in their mid twenties. He had not noticed them earlier, when he had been ordering the drinks. It appeared that the music from inside the church was relayed over speakers and could be heard in the crypt during the concert. The people at the table had been there throughout the first half and obviously regarded the taking of seats in the bar by the rest of the audience as a sort of inverted attendance on their own alternative entertainment. They were like servants at ease while their masters attended to the serious business of a formal dinner; feet up, ribald and collarless. Elizabeth wondered what they did when they were not at play.

"Will!" A boy with his back to her, and to Mark's back, pushed back his chair and stood up, holding on to the table with both hands, so that she thought he might be about to heave it over, glasses, bottles and all. But in fact the dramatic moment had passed unperceived while they had been upstairs listening to the music and Will watched the girl pour out wine from a bottle into Elizabeth's glass. As his acquaintance – stooge, even – called his name the other people at the table all stopped talking and looked over to the young man in the white shirt sitting at the bar. Two of the girls looked at one another with a quick, furtive glance. Then one of them got up from the table and left.

"Will!" the boy shouted again. Elizabeth saw a head turn. Mark, feeling tired and ill, stood up.

"I'll just go to the loo. Don't wait. I'll see you up there." And he left, missing nothing, least of all the fact that she did not answer.

Will, the boy at the bar, seemed to grow older as he drew nearer – as though he were making a passage through time, instead of through a crowd. He was looking directly at her. She thought she knew him, then realised it was the *déjà vu* effect again, because the profoundest impact had been made in the first split second so that at all moments thereafter he was strangely familiar to her.

He was not tall – perhaps about five foot ten. His build was scraggy – jeans loose around the waist. He was fingering one of the buttons of his shirt as he moved across the room, with the other hand holding high his dark pint, with its fraction of a creamy head. His hair, Mediterranean black, long and slightly straggly, had long since grown out of a short style of which it retained the form. Elizabeth later thought there was something touching about this, that she had been able to read a different, anterior Will into the one she first saw. The sleeves of his white cotton shirt were rolled up beyond the elbows, D.H. Lawrence-style. His forearms were quite pale, but his face – unshaven, high-browed and long nosed – had been in the sun, and was drawn from the same palette as his hair. He had the look of a young Galilean on the threshold between two eras. When he smiled at her she saw his teeth were tobacco coloured. His top right incisor was missing. Frances later claimed this was a sign of madness. For now Elizabeth simply registered that he smiled with one side of his mouth only, a sideways grin which held the promise of a rarely materialised laugh. The boy at the next table got up and pushed a chair towards him. "We thought you'd disappeared!"

Will spoke as though his throat were grazed, or he had not used it for a very long time. His fingers were a shocking yellow brown, and his nails bitten to stubs.

"I did. I came back to get someone."

As a bell rang – for the end of play – the room started to empty. His eyes held on to Elizabeth's – they were a primitive blue – the kind of blue that must have existed at the beginning of time when first there was light. He sat down in Mark's empty chair and after a while the dog came and settled at his feet. He looked at her half empty glass and she placed her hand on the stem and was about to drink the rest when he reached and took it from her. In the single gesture she read that he was both taking the cup from her and commuting her sentence.

She never told me what he said to her, which words he used, but she spoke of the seduction in terms used by those who believe they have been vouchsafed an experience of speaking in tongues. Revelations always seem to come in an undecipherable language. It was like Pentecost – you had to be there. The effect was of a vestige of a forgotten language, spoken by those who communicate not by the flesh but by the spirit. Others might have said, not with words, but with the body. In her narrative the sacred and profane were equal, if opposite, forces and the vocabulary was often interchangeable. They stayed down in the alcove of the crypt, where the sound of the concert up above had been cut off, due to an electrical interference – Will had this effect on certain days. She explained that normally he would have changed tables, but on that occasion it was impossible, because it was a meeting whose co-ordinates had been drawn up long before, though the instructions had taken light years to arrive. Mark came to the doorway twenty minutes after the start of the second half. He checked himself on the threshold and withdrew. He understood with the kind of clarity which accompanies only awful, never joyful truths, that she was lost to him. He too, strangely, as the outsider, was included in the experience by being subject to its power, which told him to leave, and which he unquestioningly obeyed. He missed the end of the concert – there was no longer any point in it; the evening had turned out to have been created not by the willing co-operation of singers and concert goers, but by the young stranger in the crypt, so that it was natural that it should remain incomplete, like the devil's bridge, where the creator's imprint is a single missing stone.

2

They spent the night in a place he took her to, which she could not situate; it was not a house, or a hotel; it was a room in a vast disused building in the centre of London somewhere. There was a bed, and it was warm, and not until day was beginning to stretch across the sky did they feel tired and sleep. When she woke up he was still there. Whatever the enchantment was, potion or passion, it prepared her to be indulgent of the utter strangeness not only of him, but of the whole physical world in which he moved.

They were in an attic room, with a white painted roof. Set into the ceiling, just above the bed, was a cracked window, the size of a paving slab. Lying there on her back, she saw a cloud race from one side to the other of the glass with the speed of a passing car.

The bedclothes were cleanish white cotton, as though they had been issued by an institution which made it a priority, even at the expense of any other grain of luxury. She checked above and below, leaving alongside for last, and arched herself up slightly to look ahead. The room was quite small. There was a window opposite. The curtains had not been drawn. Outside she could see, at some distance, the Post Office tower. It was another hot day. She had no idea of the time. Perhaps it was mid-morning. She had the impression the room faced north. She could hear the low diesel rattle of black taxis down in the street, and the sound of slowing, idling and roaring-off-again traffic, characteristic of the city centre. The wallpaper had been painted over white, and there were lots of holes on the wall on her left, as though someone had gone over it with a fork to allow it to breathe.

She realised it had once supported rows and rows of shelves, the removal of which left it with this rather toothless look. The bed was imposing wrought iron. It even had what she supposed must be bed knobs. It was far too big for the room. In the corner was a table covered in streaks and drips of spilled paint. Will had dropped his clothes over a back of a chair. Then she realised that those were her own clothes, and that his were on the floor by the window.

She looked down at him. He was lying on his side, twisted towards her, with his hands under his cheek, like a child. His shoulders were bony and slight as an adolescent's. He breathed huskily, and there was a watchfulness about him even in sleep. The room smelled of sweat. Only a single sheet, nothing more, because of the heat. In gathering her thoughts, she gathered only those which had to do with Will, and though the few hours for which she had known him represented only the minutest fraction of her life, they excluded all recollection of that other life. On ordinary days – every other day of her life, it seemed – she woke up with a sense of her own history, often randomly selected, as though for a temporary exhibition in a museum, taking what turned up and seemed to make the point, in the form of images of herself and her past and present life, which had stuck to her like tiny clinging seed pods, in the night. Elizabeth Faulkener. This, this and this – and this; perhaps something from childhood, something from yesterday, a thought of Mark, an idea about her work and what she might wear that day, the words of an aria half memorised, not yet learned. And the familiarity of her surroundings, each element of which reaffirmed her co-ordinates in the world, morally, historically, geographically. She was that sort of person, who wore those sorts of clothes to go to those sorts of places, and lived in this sort of house. This morning, there seemed to be only the knowledge of the last twelve or so hours, and there was enough to fill up more than that length of time in reflection.

He smiled slightly in his sleep. He had a fragile adolescent beauty and the implacable authority of a cat, its insolence and stealth and seduction and faultless intelligence which betrays no calculation but whose thought is ripe in the instant of its conception and is executed while it is still fresh as an instinct.

She wondered if he was one of those the gods loved. Whatever he had said to her, and his silences and his quick movements and long caresses had worked on her like music, her response, the inversion of all values, her trust in him, a stranger, had unlocked a world of feeling and joy she had not believed existed – perhaps here and there a glimpse, a suggestion of beauty here, a shadow of a grand emotion lingering there, in a churchyard, or in the performance of a piece of music which might once, in the composer's ear, have contained something of the original glory of the world's dawn. He opened his eyes. She had to remember not to look away. Last night she had looked away as he held her face between his hands under a lamp on the embankment, and he had pulled it back and stared at her again, and for longer this time, to show her it was not possible, that she had to stay there for as long as it took. She told herself he was mad – she wondered about hypnosis – but it was the kind of madness that makes the rest of the world look foolish and lost.

"I'll have to give you a new name." He had moved towards her, laid her head back on the bed and spoke into her ear. His breath was smoky and stale. Then he turned her onto her side, so that her back was to him, and moved up against her. "That's what happens if an angel wrestles with you till daybreak. You get a new name."

He was a few years younger than her, in the flesh, even though his flesh seemed as though it had been worn longer. There was something maternal about the milkiness of her. It seemed to revive him. When he stroked her, passing his hands over the contours of her body as though memorising them for a time when he might be blind and unable to see her, the touch which she had always received passively in the past seemed to bring her into life, to draw her into him – it was a creator's touch. There was an illumination where his fingers and lips passed. At once she felt her body alive, as though her mind was not just in her head for once, but in every part of her. His fingers were calloused at the tips. His lips were at moments full and childlike, at others tense and aggrieved. His fingers and lips worked together, his whole body seemed to be employed in making love to her, every digit and organ and surface and sense was there, like an opera, in which every art is called into play. In the last moment, as he flung himself against her and she clung to him, with a cry that was not a completed noise, but was the sign of a cry, no more, she felt de-materialised, as though she had been thrown by a wave and twisted around and flipped on her back and stood on her head and could not locate, for a second, the solid surface and the sky above, adrift in space for a moment lost. They lay, collapsed into one another, for some minutes. Elizabeth believed that this was love and was happy that she had not known until now how pale a simulacrum everything which had gone before – Mark, there was, really, only Mark – had been. The world – centuries of writing and singing and sighing about love – seemed a different place. No wonder. No wonder people behaved as they did – passion existed and had the energy of madness and madness's own furious drive. He leaned over the edge of the bed for his tobacco and papers.

"What do you do in the day?"

She checked herself. He sounded as though he believed she worked by night – at this. "I translate things. I have a singing lesson every lunchtime at the Academy. I live in my house. I see my friends. In the evening I sometimes see Mark. Where are we?"

"Just south of Piccadilly." It was a shock to find herself in such well known territory. Her friend Monica worked in the Economist building, only a couple of streets from here. She had been past here a thousand times, a public place – a location known to the world; overnight it had become, for the rest of her life, secret and private.

"I told you last night." He ran his tongue along the edge of the paper, bit off a bit of tobacco that stuck out of the end, and spat it across the room, with a sound like a wood fire popping. He lit the cigarette and pushed his left arm under her shoulders. "Budge up." He seemed to move from the sexual to the fraternal with total naturalness. "It's a gentlemen's club. They're going to pull it down. Not for a bit though— " as though it was somehow up to him.

She would miss her singing lesson. He gave her a pair of his jeans, which were stained with paint but clean on. He had a pair of espadrilles which were worn down at the back and which she borrowed. "It's all right – if we meet anyone you know they won't recognise you," he assured her. There was no mirror, but she was quite prepared to believe even her features had changed. Her handbag was there on the floor. She only remembered it as she saw it, so the thought that after all he might be a crook, a thief, a con man occurred to her in the same split second as she realised it couldn't be true. She looked at him quickly – he was standing by the window, scratching his ribs and smiling. When he saw her look up at him and realised that she had for a second distrusted him he flicked the tab of his cigarette out of the window and came and laid his head on her shoulder.

He looked up – they were of the same height. Elizabeth, down from her high heels, with her hair unclasped, felt childlike – she could have held his hand and darted among rock pools and collected small creatures for racing against the tide, with Will shouting, "Run, run!" as the waves splashed against their legs and they heard the sea roaring at their backs. Their eyes met, and although she had known since the moment she saw him that for her, this was the encounter that tells you everything you really need to know about the world, the light by which everything else can be read, but only read and not lived, because after all the rest is a stale business, only knowledge, the fact of existence and not its breath, it was the first time she realised that it was the same for him, even though he was himself the light, he had needed her, felt the want of her until now, and from now on, with life starting again this summer morning, they would be together.

"Come and see my father's house," he said, and she started and dropped his hand. "It was his club," he corrected. "He used to come here when he was young – my age. Then," – he kicked her hand bag under the bed – "we'll leave that there – he dropped out – went sort of native, abroad. I think he killed somebody or something. I'll tell you one day." She was looking alarmed. "It's OK," he said, "it's only a story. Everything that happened once is only a story. Once upon a time."

They went hand in hand down the corridor, past doors with faked panels created out of rectangular cuts of wallpaper, beaded for depth. Will explained that when the gentlemen's club had gone bust it had been licensed for a short while as a brothel, in the sixties. "They didn't need to change the decor." The various materials which had been used for covering floor and wall and window were rich and warm, like the lining of some internal organ. It was so dark and dusty, so sepulchral, that Elizabeth had the feeling that the entire building had only just been unearthed, or had erupted from beneath the earth's surface and that outside the police would be waving people back, cordoning them off with fluorescent tape and bollards, and phoning to the papers to say it was all a hoax, a publicity stunt for some film or other, and reporting secretly down un-networked lines to MI6, or whoever it was who suppressed all evidence of other worldliness for the good and security of the population.

They came to the head of staircase, a long ripple of burgundy-coloured carpet, held in place with chrome-coated rods at the join of each rise and tread. The banister rail was shiny as the seat of some minister's pants. Will kicked off his shoes and threw them down to the landing below. He let go of Elizabeth's hand and hoisted himself up astride the rail, then slid, face first, with his front polishing the woodwork, right down to the bottom, and she was reminded of Peer Gynt, the wild fantasy boy, rollicking through his dream world in search of sensation and truth. He was at the bottom, wobbling one of his teeth uncertainly. "Are you hurt?" she called down, and he looked up and laughed. "Now you!" but she shook her head and came down the staircase in a way she felt, afterwards, a ghost might walk, a gliding movement, sliding her hand, sensible to the way a generous staircase can supply details of form which belong to another age, so you could feel the swaying crinoline and the grip of tight laced corset and convention, the grace of the female body beneath the fetters of the day. When she came down to the bottom step he was standing there as still as ice. She put out her hand and he smiled and placed his palms either side of her face, as though he could cool her, or warm himself.

They found a library – volumes and volumes of parliamentary speeches, genealogical tables, prints of houses and people who were no doubt extinct, laid up on record here for nobody's future reference. There was a large fireplace, muzzled by a hideous Victorian surround. Above it, a portrait of the last queen. The room was cold, and Elizabeth remembered that outside the pavements would be warm and butterflies would be dotting among the rhododendrons and azaleas in the park, and the cold blooded reptiles would be baked into inactivity in the glass house at the zoo. Will had taken some playing cards from a drawer and had constructed the first two flights of a house of cards. He was breathing cautiously, and for a second she did not recognise the sound and believed there was a third person in the room, snoozing lightly in a chair by the empty grate, and she started and turned quickly to where he would have sat and Will's house fell down in the current of air and there was, anyway, no one there.

"Can we go now?" she said.

"One more room." But to get to the one more room he took her through many more besides, dining rooms, and antechambers, and smoking corners and a snooker room where the score was still chalked on the board and the last player had left his cue propped up against the table as though he had just gone to ask for another glass of port. But despite these human details, the place was dead as dust. There was no spirit of past players lurking in the corners, you did not feel that hearts had been sad there, or that young men had rejoiced over a lucky horse, or hidden a trembling hand with a stamping of feet, whistling falsely over a pair of pistols and a brandy in the early morning while the house boy was stoking last night's embers towards a possible flame. She wondered whether it was because she could only have felt the presence of a woman, and there would have been no women there, apart from upstairs where they had come from, where they had been women only anatomically speaking and were otherwise as little capable of leaving an imprint of their soul's particularity on the stale air of time as if they had been pieces of furniture or portraits of themselves, statues with no voice or movement.

By the time they arrived at the door to the last room, she had lost a sense of whether they were below or above ground level. They had passed through kitchen quarters – no maggoty carcasses, she was relieved to find, no rancid churns of butter, but rows and rows of pans with burnished bottoms and hooks suspended on pulley systems and hierarchies of knives. There was the same smell of untouched books, damp paper – perhaps that was just because it was a smell you rarely came across except in second-hand book shops, so that you imagined it was the smell of old books, whereas in fact it was the smell of age itself. For the first time, as he stood aside to let her into the last room, she felt afraid. She passed in front of him, and he laid his hand on her neck and ran his fingers under the collar of her blouse and along the line of her throat and down beneath the silk and bent slightly to kiss the groove from her hair line to the top of her back bone as she gave a little gasp, at his touch, or at what she saw. The room was bright as the day outside. It was a kind of work shop. Around the walls, at waist height, ran a work surface, veneered with slate, so that she could not imagine how the walls bore the weight. Everything was covered with a fine layer of white dust, as though someone had sifted flour into the room from above. Every movement they made would be recorded in the dust, so that it was not for fear of making a sound, but for fear of leaving traces, that she stayed quite still as he caressed her, her eyes cast directly ahead, hooked like a cloak over what he had brought her here to see. On a pedestal in the middle of the floor was a plaster cast of a human head, a woman's head, Elizabeth's. For a moment she could only imagine that he had taken the cast while she was sleeping, in the same way as that morning, when he had run his hands over her on waking, before, even, he had seemed to be fully awake, she had had the feeling that he was registering her, taking her imprint on his fingertips, so that when she was gone from here he would still have the sensual image of her body and her slightest feature, lodged with him safe.

Outside she could see a garden – a tangle of honeysuckle at the window and grass and for a moment it was like one of those fairy stories where you chance upon the hole in the wall that leads to another kingdom. Somewhere a bell was ringing for midday, and she thought of Oscar, her singing teacher, who would be dusting the keyboard with his handkerchief, and looking at his watch – Elizabeth, he would say to himself, was never late, and would happily take advantage of her absence to chat up her accompanist, on whom the attention would not be entirely wasted. It seemed that midday was a kind of witching hour, that whatever questions she was going to ask would have to be postponed until later when she was out in the world again – and perhaps Will would emerge into the world by daylight as a man much like all the others, and she would be able to show him to

Frances and say this is Will, he's a sculptor and she would see that it was quite right that the two of them should be together, and would invite them for dinner and allow Will to tuck up her children as Elizabeth sometimes did.

He moved behind her, as he held her there in his arms; they looked together at the image he had made of her, before knowing her, as though he had called her into life and she leaned her head back against him and told herself it would be all right. The risk run would turn out to have been an inspired one, the key you have to try in the lock, knowing the door will open, and fighting your fear. It would turn out that Will had a cousin she knew by sight, and often drank in the Three Bells on the corner by the Opera House and whatever had been happening for the last sixteen hours had been, not quite a stunt, but one of those times in life when you stepped out of the ordinary for a while, and saw the splendour of the world, and something of its meaning, and afterwards felt you have been vouchsafed a rare vision which would dim with the years but never entirely fade and always linger with something of the glory of a dream. Which is what it is to fall in love, she was right, and it never does leave you, even if you only keep it like a fragment of cloth you found caught on a nail and carried for years in your wallet, in case you should ever come across it again, and could match it up and buy it in yards or by the luxurious, never ending roll.

He stayed in the workshop while she went back upstairs to the room they had spent the night in. She changed back into her own clothes and let herself out into the street. He had not wanted to come out with her. He was going to stay and sculpt his white clay. She hadn't said, "but the sun's shining." Walking alone up towards Oxford Street, she felt him with her, because together they had changed the course of things, and that would never alter now. Everyone out in the street seemed familiar, as though each of them could have embodied something of him, there was something of him in everyone – in so much as ye do it to the least of these my children, ye do it as to me. She understood how you could walk with a stranger on the road, and talk, and only in the gesture of his breaking bread, or lifting his glass at night would you say, "Oh, it's You." She was full of him, like a fine wine the details of whose provenance and history can be gleaned from a single sip – anyone who even tipped her elbow in the street, or caught the glance of her smile across a counter would know from that tiny brush all that there was to know. Love, in the first hours, brings an extraordinary equilibrium, a shifting of values, and all the pettiness of the world can fall away, so that if you had to make the world, you would do it in seven days yourself, less, even, because the pattern is there, you can distinguish what counts from what doesn't, and how to select, and what order to do everything in, because when you are on that level, there are only a very few things left worth doing.

Oscar met her as she was going up the steps into the music college. He was perfectly forgiving.

"It happens to the best of us, my dear." He held the door open for her. They went into the windowless practice room and Oscar switched on the light.

"I am sorry. I knew I was going to be late."

He looked her up and down. Her clothes weren't crumpled, but there was something about them that said they were not today's choice. They didn't go with her face.

"Sorry nothing. I'm free all afternoon. Let's have a sing song then I'll take you for something to eat. I'm not going to ask you if anything's wrong. If you've been burgled you are obviously well insured. You look like a peach."

"I haven't been burgled."

"Good. That huffy boy's gone home. You'll have to sing without him."

Somewhere down the corridor a girl was singing in an empty room, with that crying in the wilderness effect that comes with unaccompanied song, the heroic quest for order and sense in a deserted world.

Oscar handed her a page of music. "Let's try a little bit of this."

She placed the sheet on the stand by the piano. *"Frauen, Liebe und Leben?"*

"You know it?"

"Yes, but I've never sung it."

"Let's try. *Seit ich dich mit diesen Augen gesehen, glaub ich blind zu sein."*

He rumbled the opening bars and Elizabeth pulled herself up to sing, filling her lungs a second before the entry of the voice, framing the vowel sound, her tongue lifted back in her mouth for the sibilant, pitching the note in head ready to strike.

Silence. Where her voice should have fallen was an abyss of black night, an emptiness.

"Sorry Oscar, I missed— "

"We'll take it again," he said sweetly and went back to the beginning.

The same thing happened.

"I don't know what's wrong— "

"In your head," said Oscar. "Sing it through in your head. It happens."

He played the song through once, and she followed the music, singing, as he said, in her head, and she heard it all perfectly, her own voice, silent, singing inside her. But when they tried a third time, nothing came out.

"How very peculiar," said Oscar, smiling. "Has this ever happened to you before?"

"No." Elizabeth laughed. "It's blocked off."

"I've never seen you so relaxed," he said, getting up and coming over to her. "You've gained a dimension. Where's ethereal Elizabeth?" He squeezed her shoulders together. "Come on, let's go and have something to eat." He shut the piano and they went out of the building into the hot streets.

They ate in an Italian restaurant, with deep earth-coloured walls. "Let us have rich food and wine," said Oscar to the waiter in Italian. "We celebrate the lady's hunger satisfied."

"Is that what you meant to say?" asked Elizabeth as the waiter bore the news off to the kitchen.

"No, it just came out like that." Oscar looked a little surprised himself.

Over lunch she entertained him, lavishing attention on him in a way which contradicted his previous experience of her. But the attention came with a dose of largesse, breadth not depth. He realised that her mind was elsewhere, that this charm was all for someone else, someone she could fancy was there in his place, under his skin. It wasn't that she was practising on him, that would have been too crude. There was a weight off her mind. Something had been assured somewhere. She had stepped forwards, from a place where she had always kept herself quite remote, a defensive position, now abandoned.

"What about this singing business, then? One might almost say that the cat had got your tongue. Were you out on the tiles? Shall we go and steal across the roofs of London, like Mary Poppins? Perhaps it will turn up? Or are you being a little mermaid? Do your feet feel all right?"

She wiggled her toes. "It is odd. I expect it will come back. I suddenly – I suppose I didn't want to. It must be that. Perhaps it's just the weather."

"The Italians seem to manage."

"Well, yes . . . we'll see. Perhaps I'm just tired. I'll maybe give it a rest for a few weeks. You're going away soon anyway aren't you?"

"Capri."

"So, maybe I'll leave it for a bit. I'm awfully busy with other things."

He looked sceptical and said, "I've noticed."

"How's your young man?" he asked later, dipping down to the bottom of a ball-shaped glass to scoop up the last of his ice cream. Elizabeth said that last time she had seen him he had been as usual. She knew that unlike many people who might have asked the question Oscar enquired out of genuine interest in Mark's well being, which she felt was over-personal, as they had only met once. "Delicious," said Oscar, referring to Mark under cover of the ice cream. "Have you had enough to eat? You could do with a bit more wobble on that chest – here, taste this" – he passed the last bit of ice cream over to her on a spoon with a handle as long as the glass was deep. She opened her mouth.

"It takes a long spoon –" he said,

"To sup with the devil."

"You said it. Right. Shall we be off?"

He licked his spoon with his little lizard tongue and popped it back into the glass. He finished off the last of his wine, fixing his eyes on Elizabeth as he drank. She watched him happily.

"To *Frauen, Liebe and Leben,*" he said, and handed her a flower from the table.

She smiled beyond the measure of her immediate happiness, and leaned across the table and gave him a big kiss on the cheek.

"My oh my," he said dreamily, "Who's been putting what in your drink?"

"Elizabeth, Frances here, Thursday morning, could you give me a ring please?"

"Elizabeth, Frances again, er . . . two o'clock, I expect you're out singing now, perhaps you could ring me when you get in. Thanks."

"Hello, Frances here again – call me please."

"Elizabeth, where the hell are you? I've had Mark here all day, he's in a state, Alistair's given him some pills or other. Ring me."

"Frances."

"Elizabeth, thank God for that. What's happening?"

"I'm here."

"What's happening?"

"I'm home. I'm just running a bath."

"Oh . . . Listen Lizzie, is everything, you know . . . normal?"

"Everything's wonderful. I've been in the park with Oscar. We went to the zoo."

"Oh. Because you see, Mark's –"

"Hang on, I'll just turn the hot off. OK."

"Mark turned up in a state. He's says you've been kidnapped. He was a bit – well, drunk, I suppose. Very strange. He's asleep now. He spent the night at his club."

"What club?"

"Somewhere in St James. It's like 'pub', only you get drunk by the bottle and you can stay the night. Shall I keep him here? I suppose you've had a row at last. About time too. You couldn't carry on being so good and true all the time. Anyway he's flat on his back now. Do you want to come over and kiss him good night?"

"No."

"Oh. Oh dear Lizzie. You sound a bit – he's –"

"Frances, I don't want to see Mark."

"Oh heck. What's he done?"

"Nothing. It's me."

"Who is it?"

"Oh . . . I— "

"Has he got a name darling?"

"Will."

"I see. Mark says you met him at the concert. He was a little indistinct."

"No. I . . . I didn't meet him. It's not . . ."

"Not what?"

"I can't explain. I don't know . . . I don't know what it's like."

"You mean it's not like anything else?"

"Yes."

"Oh. I think you'd better show me him, Lizzie."

"He's not like Mark. It's not . . ."

"I know. It's not like anything. You said."

"Frances?"

"Yes?"

"I know it's awful about Mark. I can't explain. Do you see?"

"Do I see?"

"Understand? A bit?"

"Yes. I think I know exactly what you mean."

"When did you? Alistair? No . . ."

"Ages ago. Something in Sydney."

"Upside down?"

"Oh yes, the whole lot!"

They both burst out laughing.

"This has to be seen. You are seeing him again?"

"I suppose so, yes."

"Well, haven't you arranged?"

"No. It wasn't like that. But yes. Of course."

"Tonight?"

"He knows where I live."

"Goodness. You'd better hop in that bath."

"What will you say to Mark?"

"I shall tell him you want to be on your own for a bit, and suggest that perhaps his wife wants to be on her own a little bit less for a bit. He has to sort out what he wants. That's always a good one. They get so self absorbed it takes them at least twice as long as it would if you told him to bugger off and leave you alone."

"He doesn't need to sort out – for me, Frances. I knew that before, when I got to the concert, I'd known all day. It was as clear as if someone had sent me a letter or something."

"An edict."

"Yes."

"Perhaps."

"It's not perhaps. It's really over."

"You're in love."

"Perhaps."

"It's not perhaps."

"No."

"Is he married?"

"No."

"Does he drink?"

"A bit."

"A lot."

"Yes."

"Got a job?"

"I don't know. He sculpts."

The doorbell rang.

"Frances, I have to— "

"All right. But quick. What's he look like?"

She saw the handle move, and the door opened. Will walked in carrying a large white plastic bag and a pack of beer. "Chinese," he said, and kissed her ear. Then he went through to the kitchen. He seemed just to know where everything was. He whistled as he put the beers in the fridge and the food in the oven.

"Lizzie— "

"What?"

"Where are you? Where've you gone?"

"I told you. I'm home. I'm just running a bath."

"I asked you a question. Is that him?

"Yes."

"Is he there?"

"No. He's in the kitchen."

"I'm in the kitchen," shouted Will.

"Goodness. I hear him."

"I'll ring you tomorrow."
"Lizzie?"
"What?"
"I asked you a question."
"Did you?"
"I said, what does he look like?"
"What, or who?"
"Who?"
"No one?"
"What, then?"

Will came into the hall and sat on the stair, two steps below Elizabeth. He rested his head back on her knees and smiled up at her, munching a spare rib. She placed her hand on his head and leaned forward, so she was speaking into his hair.

"He looks— "
"Yes?"
"He looks just like an angel."
"Goodness. Of light or darkness?"
"I haven't really looked. I'll tell you another time."
"You'd better. Be careful."
"Good night."
"Good night Lizzie."

When Mark picked up the telephone a few minutes later to call Elizabeth himself, he found it was wet, with an imprint of the last user's hand telling him more of the conversation than Frances had reported to him. He dropped it back into its place and without saying goodbye took his jacket and left, closing the door quietly behind him, so as not to wake the sleeping children.

"Will used to say a child's mind was full of poetry because he knew so little and an old man's so devoid of it because his experience is so wide. But I don't think Will knew any more than he needed. What he didn't need to know, he forgot. Sometimes I got the feeling he was *trying* to forget that he had known something so much better, and it had gone, and he needed to obliterate all the memory of it, by constructing other things. Like his sculptures. It was as though he was trying to fill the world up. And he was always busy, you didn't have time to think. We were always tearing around doing things –

not museums and things, just in the way you do when you're a child. Busy all day."

"Did Frances really like him?"

"Of course. But she said he was bad."

"Bad?" It sounded like a baby word from her. Or something you'd say of a fruit.

"She said he was sick. Mephistophelean. But that sometimes you had to do it anyway."

"And do you agree with her?"

"That he was like that? Or that you had to do it?"

"That he was like that. If he was, I don't imagine you had a lot of choice."

"About selling your soul? No. You don't set the price. You'd do it for nothing."

"I fancy you would," I said a little wryly. "And the singing?"

"Oscar said the voice was the seat of the soul."

"I'm not sure that was really very helpful of Oscar."

"Oh it didn't matter about his saying it. I mean, it would have if he had been wrong, because then I would have thought there was a connection where there wasn't. But he was right."

"It's strange," I said, "when you saw me asleep in the woods yesterday, you screamed because you thought I was dead, and then I wasn't."

"I'm sorry, it gave me a fright."

"And I had assumed you lost your voice because of grief."

"Ah," she said, and smiled over at me.

"You lost it for happiness. It was the other thing."

"It was full of opposites," she said. "'All for love and the world well lost.' Isn't that it?"

"Yes. Some bore or other."

"It wasn't that. It was all for love– "

"'And the world well gained.'"

"That's it."

"And now?"

She sighed. "And now."

"It's still here, Elizabeth. The world's still here."

"Don't tell me. All that stuff about – with all its lies, treachery and broken dreams, it is still a beautiful world. I saw that in a dentist's waiting room the other day. I know it's still there."

"Here," I corrected, as though it had been a typing error.
"It's here, yes. But I don't want it any more."

She missed her train back to London, and had to wait for another one. Despite the presence of his ashes in the terracotta urn in her handbag, she did not feel that she was getting away with space for two for the price of one, because she had no sense that Will was any more with her now than he had been before. This relic, the bare stubble of his life, was not a keepsake, but neither was it a formal acquittal. She travelled forwards, and watched the countryside filing backwards past her, until she got the feeling it was she who was immobile, along with the train and all its other occupants, and that the scenery was being flashed past on some kind of screen, like the one of those fifties films about a couple on honeymoon. Perhaps winter weddings were more fashionable then, since the man is usually wearing a rather hunky overcoat and the woman is wrapped up in a glamorous head scarf (a now obsolete fashion item – no head scarf is glamorous – Elizabeth mentally congratulated the Queen for being quite possibly the first woman in history to have made an item of clothing go out of fashion by her association with it). There they are, driving down a mountain or along the corniches beside the Mediterranean, or at least through some landscape that is particularly sculpted so as to require a more than usually dexterous handling of the car by the man in the overcoat, and you suddenly realise with one of those eye-bulging readjustments to the optical nerve that in fact, although the man is throwing the wheel about with the kind of imperious rigour normally reserved for women with two left feet on a dance floor, the car is in fact completely static, parked in some studio in north west London, and that it is the simulated landscape which is tearing along at a rate of knots. They probably got the idea for this by watching the sun, she thought. *Eppur si muove . . .*

At Paddington, the human traffic all seemed to be going the other way; everyone was wearing that slightly closed off anxious look that is the insignia of those with private concerns in very public places, and a platform is far more public than a train. That twilight world between work and home had always seemed to her to generate a certain sexiness; there was something of the office party about it. When you were "going for" your train, you couldn't be sure who was friend or foe, you just assumed no one else was headed for the same platform and pushed deliberately through regardless. It was only when you achieved a seat and an assured passage that you opened up your face a little and acknowledged the human bondage of a common destination, so much so that she imagined that if the 5.40 to Oxford ever got stuck in a snow drift there would only be a token time lapse before somebody successfully organised a community chorus of "We All Live in a Yellow Submarine!"

Automatically she looked around for Mark. Towards the end of their affair, although they had not known it for that at the time, since Will and not natural wastage saw Mark off, he had often come down on Tuesdays for a meeting at the British Museum, where he held some advisory position on French mediaeval manuscripts. She would take the day off work and meet his train. Her flat was close enough to the station for them to be able to go back there for a couple of hours before his meeting. Sometimes he would phone her before leaving: "Look, I'm sorry Lizzie, it's just not possible," and she would go down to the Serpentine and walk all afternoon, tight-lipped and mute as a swan, and be sad, not for not seeing him, but because she did not believe there was anything in the world that was not possible.

She thought at first that she was looking round for him in order to avoid him. Already, in looking for someone in order to avoid them, you're looking for them, and somehow they count. She sat on a bench with Will's ashes in her handbag, which she nursed protectively on her lap. His disappearance had become a death, an absence had become an inert presence, and she found suddenly that she was unable to remember anything of him as he had been during the eight months before he disappeared – she could only remember the last day, and the time when he had not been there, which now seemed like a period of grace, because although she had known he would never return there was something still living about it. Until today it had been a story which still continued. His absence had been an image of death, as strong as, even interchangeable with the real thing, but somehow less desiccated, less hopeless than this. Her raincoat trailed slightly on the floor, and she twitched it clear, and crossed her legs – a position for waiting in, not one in which she could exactly claim to be poised for flight. She was tempting fate, an expression whose exact meaning had always rather escaped her, like begging the question. Neither expression had she ever really understood. It was something to do with saying, "Mark may be here, I do not want to see Mark. If I look for him, wait for him, the law of averages, the disappointing end of the law of chance, will mean I don't. Otherwise it would be too much as though I had summoned him up. If I see him I must be careful not to let him see me, but if he sees me first that will be fate and I won't be able to do anything about it." It was true that she had no wish to see him, that she was simply pursuing a little obsessional thread, because she found herself in this place at this time. She had thought so little about Mark in the past few months. Frances had told her that he was suffering, that she had never understood properly how he loved her, but she had only logged the information, not understood, or absorbed it. It was there in note form, for possible amplification at a later date, a freeze-dried sort of knowledge, of the head but not the heart. Will had brought about an inverted eclipse of the world, the kind of dazzling light that leaves you blind, groping in the blackness, illuminating nothing but itself, and that self illumination brings about, in the end, a more total kind of darkness, a black hole at the very centre of things.

There had been no real warning. She could not really look back and identify, picking it out like a subtle pattern in a mosaic, a carefully structured lead up to departure. There had been no orchestrated moment of solemn leave taking in a garden, with a meal beforehand, a doom laden ringing of bells.

She had woken on the last morning to find herself face to face with him. Usually he slept with his back to her, and she with her hand placed on his side, in the vulnerable dip between the end of the ribs and the hip bone, the soft, unprotected bit, you could so easily pierce with a knife. That morning his eyes had been open, looking past her, accustomed already to the light. She could see he had been awake for a long time, staring like that out at the tree in the garden. His face looked slightly sunken, perhaps just because of the lie of the mattress. You could have pressed your knuckle into the hollow underneath his cheekbone. The shade of his two day beard emphasised its leanness; his lips were dry, and because his cheek was pressed downwards, his mouth was slightly compressed at one side, so that the lips hung forward, fuller than usual. The lines on his brow too were more obvious, he looked more than ever like something new which had been crumpled, not by age but by misuse. He was lower than her in the bed, having discarded the pillow, and slipped during the night.

Then she remembered he had touched her neck with his lips in the night and she had taken his hand and held it loosely in her own. As she had flickered awake at rare moments, she had been aware of him, not sleeping, watching, a kind of vigil. Sometimes a vigil has a reason – it can be penitential, ritual, or just watchful. Could ye not watch with me one brief hour? Was this petulance, or a lesson – that to watch in the small hours is the greatest sign of love. It is a sign of love – so often we do it only for the dead, when it no longer counts for them, only for us. To watch with our friends – it's something we hardly ever do, through the long winter evenings, on silent walks, suffering their remoteness, feeling their pain. It doesn't really protect, although that is another of the uses of vigilance. He had not been watching her sleep. It had been a night with scarcely any moon, and although there was the soft chemical light of London outside, it was not direct, only reflected in the sky, and not enough to see by. She thought afterwards that through his wakefulness he had changed the quality of the time, so that it had not been lost, unmeasured, wasted, to be regretted as time unused, but lived for her by him, in his knowledge of what was to happen, sparing her, letting her sleep. It was a kind of sacrifice. A clock can mark the moments passing, but they can only really be said to have done more than pass if someone lives through them for us, making sure the clock hasn't cheated, thinking thoughts for us, holding the world in the conscious palm of their hand while we sleep. Watch over me this night, people pray. They hope the saints will pray for them, clapping their hands in faith so the soul won't shrivel and perish. That's what He's there for. To count our hours, to keep the world in consciousness while we sleep. Don't let me slip away. So that of course the natural cry in the garden is that of the tired watchman himself – could ye not watch with me? Here's a heresy: God too needs someone there, He needs the evidence of His opposite to be sure that He exists. And if His opposite cannot face Him, at least he marks the time, or requires Him to be vigilant Himself. Everybody needs somebody.

He looked at her now and touched her mouth with his finger, tracing it along her lower lip, as though pencilling her in. He always made love to her in the morning, and she became so accustomed to his caress, so sure of it, that it was, in a very simple way, as though his touch brought her to life each day, from essence to existence. During the time he spent with her, he had made her, as she told Frances later, come to see her body as a beautiful machine, but a machine for life, for love, at least, so that it was not pure materialism. There was a kindling in his touch, in her response to it. He might, as Frances said, have imprisoned her soul, but in doing so he also identified it, made her familiar with it, in the form of her love for him. Maybe the soul takes many forms. Maybe it's just a portmanteau in which you keep the gifts you can't account for. Maybe it's like the magic stone in the fairy story. You have three wishes, and with each wish it will become transformed into whatever you choose – a song, the child of your imagination, or a physical love which was not simply sexual but physical in the sense that it was vividly present and tangible, existing of itself, like an atom. It was a far cry from Mark's aching troubadours – for whom speech alone, word after word, image after image, phrase upon phrase had been the only tool capable of bringing the inert into life – consummation was already death; the lover's cry, cajolement, lament, his articulated desire – there was life, plucked from indifference into longing for a state which would never be achieved. For him the words changed things, utterance altered the world. Maybe it was no more than a literary streak. Not that Mark had deferred the act of love, but because he had always had this sense of beseeching, of persuasion, of which, moreover, he could not speak. With him she had always had the sense that the act of making love was hopelessly relative and time bound, and thereby became less a consummation than a poor reflection of the glory it should have possessed, or invested them with, if it had truly represented his love for her. Later she realised that it had been guilt which had tainted their love-making at the source – his guilt, of which he had never spoken, for fear of infecting her with it, for fear of bringing it veritably into life.

"Where are you going?" He was dressing quickly, pulling his shirt and jumper over his head in one piece, as he had removed them in one piece the night before, hopping into his jeans. She lay on her side with her hand propping up her head and her hair tied back with a ribbon, a nude of perfect proportions, full and slender at once, but her expression caught amiss, not sensuous or knowing, just caught in anxiety, at the end of a question. He was dressed now, apart from his feet, which were bare and, she noticed, needed a wash. He was standing by the window in the same position she remembered – the first night he had come here, with his head against the frame, looking out quietly, with his arms not quite folded, but laid across his chest, as though he had felt a sudden chill.

"It's almost the last day of winter," he said. He had a surprisingly deep voice, for someone whose frame was so slight you sometimes imagined it must be made of something like wicker. He began to roll a cigarette, very slowly, thinking, concentrating apparently on the little action, using the time, the concentration, to pace the room inwardly, in his mind. He came back to sit by the bed, without lighting the cigarette, smoothing the join where he had stuck it down, with a teasing movement of finger and thumb of his left hand. "You been to see a doctor?" Elizabeth turned onto her back and pulled the sheet up to cover her.

"No."

"You should."

She didn't answer.

"It's not normal."

"What?"

"To miss eight months. There's something not right."

She sat up. He had lit his cigarette, and the smell suddenly made her feel sick. She turned away slightly, leaning against the pillows.

"I'm not ill."

"Maybe not. But you're not pregnant either. It's psychological. A mythical baby."

Elizabeth had only mentioned it once, when she first noticed what was happening to her body. The test was negative. But her body was producing evidence of something, by closing itself off from any possibility of fecundation. It was not at home to callers. She had known it wasn't a real conception. A friend had once told her that you knew, the second you conceived, that it had happened. She had felt something like that, but it had been something else that had been conceived, something less material than a child.

"It's not that. It's not a fantasy, or a delusion. It's just my body. It's stopped for a bit."

He got up off the bed. She watched him go over to the window. He had a graceful, dancer's walk, but quite unconsciously, so that if you had told him he would have stopped dead in his tracks and stared at his feet, as though he did not know where they could have picked that up. His cigarette ash toppled and fell onto the floorboards before he got there. He gave up on the idea of opening the window and took the lid off a pottery dish she kept jewellery in and came back to sit on the bed with the lid in the palm of his hand as he smoked. "Promise me you'll go and see a doctor."

"No."

She reached out and touched him, turning him towards her slightly, by the elbow. He seemed reluctant to look at her, but eventually turned his face to hers. She had never seen him look so solemn, so expressionless. Almost all his usual expressions were of mirth, energy or desire. There was a rare stillness there. His eyes were slightly red.

"You never ask me to promise anything. You know 'promise' doesn't mean anything".

He sighed and rubbed his forehead above his right eyebrow with the fleshy pad, just below his thumb, crooking his fingers away, so as not to singe his hair.

"If it doesn't start again after next month I'll go to a doctor."

She wanted to test something, her notion. She had not forgotten what he had told her that first night in her house. Nine months, no more. She might disbelieve it, but she still remembered. It had set up a pattern, an idea of a structure in her mind.

From a drawer of the desk by the window he took a cassette,

and slid it into the player. He lay down next to Elizabeth and switched it on by remote control. His left hand was tucked under the back of his neck, his bare feet crossed at the ankles. Elizabeth lay with her eyes closed, breathing peacefully. He rolled over to look at her, watching her eyes open at the sound of her own voice. It was an aria from the *Magic Flute*, recorded a couple of years previously at a concert in a church in Suffolk. The interpretation was inseparable from the song itself, or from the voice singing it. She lay in silence on the bed, apart, uninvolved, unresentful. It was a symbolic act, theatrical in its way. It had no practical use – it wasn't for entertainment, it was unrelated to any other element of the day. He brought things into life – an idea, a sculpture, an event – then dropped them. They might continue to exist, like the cassette, which, once the song was finished, he switched off, forgetting ever to put it back in the drawer, so it stayed there for months, but without his attention they were sapped of their meaning. He leaned down and kissed her, his lips dry against hers, she thought it would be just for a second, but he persisted, waiting for something to ignite. She pulled him towards her, and he lay like that, covering her body, with his mouth pressed against hers, supporting himself on his forearms, with his fists clenched against the pillow, so he would not cry, but when she moved and took him in her arms she found his face was wet with his own tears, not hers.

They rarely arranged to meet. He was just there, or she was, not in a habitual way, almost as though each time they met it was by chance, which it was in a way, or it seemed like that. They had thrown out so much of the unnecessary world that the space they occupied was small, a tiny village, of which they knew every detail, every fallen stone, every path through the backwoods. When he left that day he looked back up to her window to see if she was there, smiling, knowing he would be back soon. For once, she wasn't, because the phone had been ringing and she had gone to answer it, which he never knew. She came back to the window and looked down the empty street for the traces of his absence and sensed there was something amiss. And because it was the first time, she might have made the connection and realised that it would also be the last time, that with him there were no degrees, he was either there or he wasn't.

"He must have had an accident. Something's happened to him," Frances said, when she eventually tracked Elizabeth down.

"How long is it?"

"I don't know."

"Oh come off it Lizzie, of course you must know. How long? How many days?"

"Five."

She was standing in her kitchen, in a grey shirt, and black trousers, a sort of designer version of the kind of clothes Will himself would have worn, cupping one hand in the other, as though they hurt. Frances was impatient.

"For God's sake Lizzie, I'm going to phone the police."

"No."

"What do you mean? You're crazy."

She saw the look on Elizabeth's face and came away from the phone.

"You can't phone the police because your lover leaves."

"You had a row?"

"No."

"Did he seem different?"

"Not quite."

"Not quite?"

"Sad, maybe."

"He was ill. Really ill. It was true."

"Yes."

"It wasn't—?"

"No."

Frances took her hand, the one she had been cradling in the other. She made her sit down.

"Why didn't you ask him more? Why didn't you worry about it, for God's sake? You just ignored it? Didn't you believe him?"

Elizabeth put her hands up to her brow, splayed, with her thumbs stretched, a web of protection. Then she looked up, pinched her lips, sealing them for a second, then shrugged not carelessly, but hopelessly, and said, "I don't know. In a way, yes. But I'd stopped counting."

"Counting what?"

"The months. Till the day he left. He reminded me. Even then I didn't worry. There was still one left. It could have changed."

Frances was at a loss. "You're not going to try and find him? Have you been to his place? The workshop? Shall I go for you?"

"No." To enquire would have been a breach of the promise, the one, fundamental promise which meant that there was never any need to promise individual things.

"You think he's dead, don't you?"

"If you like."

"What do you mean? You think he's dying?"

"No. Yes."

"Not just disappeared?"

"It's the same thing. I can't—" she stretched out her fingers, and pulled them back, then placed her fist where her heart was – "I can't change anything. I never could. I can't bring him back. It really is finished."

But Frances had done all the checking up in the end, and because it turned out that Elizabeth was quite right she never mentioned it to her. There were no traces – no police or hospital records – she watched the place he had once lived in on and off, randomly, which seemed to her as sure as a twenty-four-hour watch, seven days a week, and he never came or went, and she understood that Elizabeth was right. He had gone, voluntarily, which was the most final, incontestable way of disappearing of all. She did wonder why there was no body.

Elizabeth had never seemed to be perplexed by this. She seemed to feel it was quite normal that if Will was not with her, his body next to hers, he was nowhere. Now, with his ashes in her lap, she could not help but think of them as ingredients rather than remnants, a little dusty pile of something that could be mixed with something else to bring about a chemical, or maybe alchemical change. The gesture of bequeathing his ashes to her had seemed at first quite out of character both with Will and the manner of his leaving her, in which she had chosen to see a very sophisticated kind of tact. He had been quite capable of deliberate bad taste in life, but in something like this, it surprised her. It lacked his lightness of touch, it was heavy upon her, explicit, an image which was scarcely an image, it was so literal. If the voice was the image of the soul, these ashes then, were they really an image of the body, of mortality? She could not work out what psychology was supposed to lie behind the gesture of dispersing them, of irretrievably separating herself from his last remains. Love is a kind of magic, and magic dies when there is no more illusion, when there is only one person left. Something remains, longing, desire, desperation even, frustration and heartbreak, but not the same magic. The magic gets blown away on the wind, carried away like the voice in the wilderness, lost on absent ears. All this she felt on one level, not the cutting edge, a deep, underlying seam, where poisonous deadly gases no doubt lay, and no canary sings. Nearer the surface, she worried about her raincoat and the slight tarry fleck near the hem, and about Mark's timetable, and the pigeons and a meeting with Frances in the morning.

With stealthy curiosity she watched to see if Mark would arrive. It wasn't that she had any great yearning to talk to him, she thought, or resurrect their friendship in any way. She was just curious to be reminded what he looked like, to see whether his clothes were different, or if he had transferred his allegiance to the *Independent*. He was so absorbed in his study of mediaeval French documents that any modification of his clothes or method seemed exaggeratedly frivolous and to have more than usual curiosity value, rather like the prime minister shopping in Safeways to assure people that ordinary concerns were, after all, perfectly natural and nothing to worry about.

After a while she grew tired of scanning the crowds and the pigeons were beginning to get a bit close to her ankles. She decided to walk home through the park, but to ring Frances first and remind her of the meeting in the morning. She didn't like to ring too late in case Billy was asleep. Short of change, she went into the bar, which, for some reason, was so designed as to look like someone's idea of a bar in a train, although Elizabeth wasn't sure that such things existed. This seemed a rather over-zealous approach, since the whole point about being here was precisely that one wasn't on the train, that was the one place you definitely weren't. It was Mark, with his sharp eye for error who had taught her to think critically like this and, despite her preparations, which she had allowed herself to indulge in, in the knowledge, if not the belief that they were only pretend, it was another reason for being surprised to see him sitting there in a corner bay underneath a simulated communication cord, chatting up a girl.

"Mark?" Her voice managed to be cool in its mode of address and warm in itself. He looked up and she knew that he must have seen her before, when she was sitting outside, or when she was getting her change. He was not unprepared, but his not quite mastered confusion was no improvement on anything he might have improvised if he had not been forewarned.

"Elizabeth." He moved along his bench to give her room to sit down. "Polly, this is Elizabeth. Elizabeth, Polly."

Polly was a happy looking student with the manners of a forty-year-old, only the experience to catch up on.

"I was just going to get another drink," she said, "Would you like one?"

Elizabeth asked for a coffee, which was her way of saying that she wasn't staying, that she had something she needed to keep awake for, that this was refuelling, not relaxation. Having pushed it this far she was now horrified to find herself confronted with Mark. Being the last person she wanted to see this day, she had unconsciously sought him out, an odd inversion of her real intent. Mark asked for a pint of bitter. Elizabeth felt awkward sitting next to him, as though they had been strangers on a bus. For so long she had been living in a country of the heart which she believed he had never visited, never would visit, that she had acquired a quite different set of mannerisms, unlike those which had previously been characteristic of her, mannerisms of thought if not of speech, although it sometimes spilled over into that. She knew there was no point trying to explain how things were, because he didn't even know what things were, or had been.

"How's Oxford?"

Mark looked at her, moved slightly away. For that kind of conversation, he seemed to imply, he needed to take up a different sort of position, one in which to conduct a superficial exchange of banalities. His face was closed up and he was fiddling with his cuff button. He was, she thought, deliberately acting distaste for her in a way that he could be sure she would know he didn't feel, so that she would realise quite how much her presence disturbed him, that he was obliged thus to disguise his emotions. He took a breath and said in a sour, chatty sort of voice, "Oh, more and more teaching. I've got rooms in college now. Thomsett retired."

Elizabeth, with the kind of elision of ideas that seems quite normal once you have become used to discoursing only with yourself said "And Polly? Are you with Polly?"

It was like bad improvisation, where someone was urging you, "Think! What would they really say?" and you did say the first thing that came into your head, forgetting that they wouldn't have, and mistaking spontaneity of invention for a precise use of the imagination.

"On and off. As a matter of fact, we've just been to mass. Her father's something to do with the Cathedral School. There was an awfully good Magnificat. She's much in demand though."

He looked up. Polly was standing at the bar talking to some friends who were waiting for the next train up to Oxford. She hastily picked up their drinks and brought them over.

"Do you mind if I . . .?" she gestured over to her friends. Elizabeth felt rather old all of a sudden, as though Polly were bringing them breakfast in bed. For the first time, Elizabeth felt that she and Mark were the same age. Had Will, the master of child's play, done that to her? Mark asked her if she were doing any singing.

"I had some concerts but I had to cancel them. We've got a lot of translation work."

"It's going well."

"Yes."

Mark took a gulp at his beer, the first gulp of the glass that always looks, thought Elizabeth, like a precaution, to stop things spilling over. There were some things that all men did the same. Her bag was on the table between them. Mark suddenly turned sideways and pushed it away from them. She clutched at it in panic, drawing it on to her lap. There was a silence, the kind that occurs after someone has made a silly mistake driving, causing all the other passengers to gasp, after which no one comments for a few seconds, because it's hard to follow the naked gasp with words. Mark looked at her without saying anything. Then he picked up his drink and stared at it for a few moments. For a moment, when he had seen her walking towards the bar, he had thought she had come to find him, that she had come for him. It was sickening how quickly he had been able to read in her eyes that she had not been thinking of him, that there was no real shock of meeting him, because she was quite indifferent to him now.

"I'm sorry Mark," she said, "I'm a bit jumpy. Running into you like this. It's almost as though you're irritated with me for being late."

"I don't remember punctuality being one of your problems."

This is awful, she thought, I only wanted to know if his appearance had changed. Was that all I cared about? Did I just want to rest my eyes on him and be reassured? Black sweater, blue jeans, classic lecturer's jacket. She looked down at the file in front of him. Perhaps it contained Polly's latest effort on structure in *La Chanson de Roland*. He had written his name in the top left hand corner, like a little boy, but with the same young lady's handwriting, with the black italic nib. Polly came over.

"I'm going to run," she said. "James is having a party down the road. We'll come back up tomorrow. I'll see you Mark. Goodbye Elizabeth, sorry to be rushing off."

They watched her leave, pulling her coat on after her as she elbowed the door open. Elizabeth, sitting there in her dark blue raincoat, felt that as usual she was present, correct, but in the wrong place. She never seemed to be able to settle anywhere. Her coffee cup was empty.

"I'm going to get you a proper drink." Mark got up from the table. "Cold white wine, perhaps?"

"OK." She had forgotten about the last order she had made, in the crypt. She sat there toying with an old receipt that had gone damp round the edges from the ring left by Mark's beer on the table, and remembered Mr Heythrop's disaster with the tea. She dropped the receipt in the ash tray, and wondered where and when she would scatter the ashes. She saw herself tipping them out like an empty ashtray. Why not? Mark sat down beside her.

"What are you thinking about?"

Elizabeth reflected that people only ever asked that when they assumed you were thinking about them, really.

"I was wondering. What does the Catholic church say," she asked, "about the resurrection of the body?"

Mark sat back with a sigh as if to say, "I guess that's as much as I could have expected."

"'By the resurrection of the body'," he recited, "'I mean that we shall all rise again with the same bodies at the Day of Judgement.' Question 129. Are you thinking of coming over?" he asked, rather sardonically.

For a moment she thought he was inviting her to snuggle up next to him, then realised what he meant. Thresholds, darkness into light, temptation into sin, faith into belief, knowledge into certainty. Will you won't you will you won't you will you join the dance? He had converted to Catholicism when he was twenty, and his faith had always just sat on him like a beautiful cufflink, tucked away up his sleeve, glinting occasionally, buffed effortlessly to a sheen by just the right amount of outside friction.

"What do they mean, with the same bodies?"

"It doesn't really matter what they mean, does it."

He smiled and spread out his hands on the table. They were beautiful hands, not at all like Will's – less often put to use. "We're talking about a revealed truth. It's impossible to believe it without faith. A truth above reason, revealed by God."

"You make it sound like an edict from the politburo."

"It's a bit like that, yes."

He'd never really seen Elizabeth look puzzled, but it was the kind of puzzlement he was accustomed to seeing on the face of examination candidates who believed there must surely have been some misprint on the paper. He decided to plough on in this coarse, pedagogic vein, if it was the only idiom in which he was to be allowed to address the woman who for unbelievable long years had been his lover, and of whom he dreamed day after day, if not night after night, because he rarely dreamed sleeping. As long as he answered, slowly, she could not run from him – he would hold her by a straw, if not that of intimacy, the short one he would have chosen himself.

"The idea is, I think, that the violent separation that takes place between the body and the soul – well, violent to some, it depends what you believe in that area to start with – is something that God never intended, something that came about as a consequence of the Fall."

". . . You mean that if it hadn't been for the Fall, man would have been immortal in his physical form . . ."

"That's the idea."

Elizabeth shook her head. "Honestly," she said, "you really have to have a desperate need to believe, almost a total disregard for the evidence . . ."

". . . So that the redemption, you know, Christ's dying . . ."

". . . I *know* what the redemption is."

"Remedied the sin of the Fall, so that eventually when it's all sorted out, we'll all be able to be reunited with our bodies. It's not so mad, look at you. It's seven years since I first met you on that bridge. Remember? In seven years every cell of the body has been replaced by a replica of itself. You are no longer the woman I met. Your body has been entirely reconstituted. And your hair's gone red."

"It's a rinse."

"Not at all the same woman."

"But I understand that. I mean I understand about cells replicating and DNA. It's not a mystery."

"What do you mean, you understand it? Of course you don't, you've just read a few magazine articles, you've taken it on trust from some academic. You ought to know better than that. You've got too much faith in the wrong things. Why is everybody's scepticism directed at the church, for God's sake? What is it, a persecution? Flush out the unscientific method?" He paused and sat back. "I see the glimmer of a conversion coming on. What's up Elizabeth, have you developed a hairline crack? Quick, patch it up. Another drink."

"No thanks."

Mark went to the bar and came back with a drink for her anyway.

"Mark, you know I don't . . ."

He sat down, opposite her this time. "I don't know what the hell you think you are doing here," he said, "but you might at least have the courtesy to let me buy you a drink. If you didn't want that you shouldn't have come. I have spent a year forgetting you. You're not going to breeze in and out of this bar and leave me shocked at having seen you, ripping out my stitches with your nails. At least allow me to give this unfortunate meeting some shape."

"Not here."

"Then go." He picked up her bag off the table and she gave a gasp and took it from him. "Go on Lizzie, go away. Let's keep it brief. Get out, leave me, and never come back. Go on, just go."

The sudden change in his behaviour reminded her of someone, an old person, of the type who fights against illness, pity, frailty, age itself until one unknowable moment when everything cracks and they just sit down and stop coping for themselves. Her grandmother, fit, wiry, with a wasp of a tongue – no use for anything but give you a sting to remember, her mother used to say – who had turned meekly to her one day and asked her to help her to the lavatory. Mark had the same air of not caring that his life didn't work any more. She resented his not knowing what had happened to her, for being grief-stricken on his own behalf, but then, if he had known, he would have had to pretend to like her more. It was his assumption that she was happy that was making him bitter towards her. Elizabeth was completely astonished, but with a dull kind of astonishment that made her feel hard and resentful. She had to remind herself he knew nothing. Frances had simply told him Elizabeth had fallen in love with someone overnight and was no longer the same person. That was what had hurt him most. To give her love and her identity away to a stranger. He was sitting with his head in his hands, like, she thought, some old drunk. She thought that now he really hated her – for all those hours and days and weeks when she had forgotten him, for each neglectful second, he had notched up a score against her. When he had been ill, he would have resented that she had not rung; when he had been lonely, her absence would have irked more than all the unsolicited attention of the others who comforted him; when a natural disaster occurred within a hundred mile radius of his home he would have hated her most, of all those who did not ring and ask whether he had survived. All this time she had felt nothing against him. She had been careless with his love. She had even assumed he would be relieved, like her, that a *deus ex machina* had arrived. She had never asked Frances about him. But it is one thing to be swept out of the path by the god, and another to be entertained by him – there is an ending for every character according to his needs.

"Please go Lizzie," he said, looking up. "I don't want to walk out on you. But I don't want to see you either."

In fact he could not bear that she would leave, it was a way of praying that she would turn to him, and in refusing to leave him, reassure him that there was a chance he might be loved. She got up, uncertainly, moving very slowly. Each action, picking up her bag, standing up from the table, was conceived in thought before she performed it. Everything seemed to take twice as long.

"Bye then."

"Bye." He caught her hand as she was leaving, and she looked down at her hand, not at him, as he spoke. "Does he treat you properly? Does he love you?" Later he would tell Alistair he had said unbelievable things to her. "I wanted to be barbaric, but I was just stupid," he said. "And drunk."

"He's dead," she said. "It's finished."

As she turned away, Mark felt he was about to cry, and Elizabeth mistakenly thought she saw a slight smile break on the corner of his mouth and wished she had not drunk her wine. There was always the urn with the ashes in, but though atoms were atoms, cinders cinders and not transformable into anything higher, whatever the fairy story said, she drew the line at chucking them at Mark. In that one false perception she found evidence for her need to hate him, to blame everything on him. She wished she had never known him. He was the one detail she might have altered, to make history different.

"I tried to be civilised," she told Frances the next day. "He was so different."

"I felt like telling her she's a selfish bitch," Frances said to Alistair.

"But she's not."

"I know, but she can act like one. How can she not realise what she meant to him? She behaves like a complete half wit."

"That's not the same. She's just been in shock for a year. Mark can look after himself."

"I'm sure he wasn't laughing at her. Let's have him for dinner."

"Leave it a bit. Honestly, I saw him a month ago. He was fine." Alistair rather envied Mark's availability to the kind of women he was easily able to attract. "He's got a string of undergraduates dying to mother him."

"But she said he was all – bitter and horrible, and drunk."

"Course he is when she's around. I assure you. He's fine. Just tell her to keep out of the way."

Meanwhile, Elizabeth, deceived by Mark's unhappiness, felt like a wife who has discovered an infidelity with a woman so totally opposite to herself in every way that it is the personal slight that hurts more than the actual betrayal.

She had a friend who, when her husband left her, told no one for the first couple of months. She travelled a bit, as though geographical distance from the scene of the break-up would delay the impact, postponing its arrival like a forwarded letter. It wasn't so much a case of needing time on her own to come to terms with it, more that she wanted the option of not having to face it quite yet. Elizabeth had similarly avoided telling people about Will's death – in the end, of course, it had backfired on her, because people were able to date her loss back to a time which also predated occasions when she had been seen bright and artificially smiling, so they thought she was heartless, as well as less deserving of sympathy than she would have been nearer to the time. By the time she got round to telling casual acquaintances she found they already knew – "it's common knowledge" – so that she felt she had not tended the release of the news as she should and that Will and her loss of him had been cheapened by her reticence. In telling Mark she felt she had almost been guilty of reporting losses to the enemy and of thereby strengthening their hand. He had had his own unhappiness to stand against it, and she wondered whether it was actually only people who had never suffered in any way who could be genuinely understanding of another's grief. "I know, I've been there too," wasn't a comfort at all, it was a kind of veiled boast, usually, and even when it wasn't, it at least involved an erosion of the personal character of one's grief, a sucking into the abstract, as though one's widow's mite – an unremarkable grief, but mine own – were being chucked into an overflowing wishing well for the general assuaging of pain.

Instead of walking straight home she took a bus down Park Lane and got off at Victoria. She was angry with Mark, with herself too. It was a meeting which should either have been avoided, or more carefully prepared, not the haphazard outcome of a flirtation with chance. She found she was dwelling on the incident with a furious kind of concentration, as though the sharpening of her recollection of it, and of her anger, could in some way punish the two of them and expunge the memory of the meeting. She walked down Vauxhall Bridge Road towards Frances's house in Pimlico, where, since it would be the children's bedtime, she would just put a note through the door to remind Frances about tomorrow's meeting. Brightly lit buses swung past her with a bronchial wheezing of doors and air brakes. A black cab, its reading lights illuminated within, drew slowly away from the kerbside, like a smart item of luggage under the X-ray at an airport, its occupant, open newspaper, legible headlines and all, unwittingly exposed under a bright naked bulb. She walked quickly and her heels rang out a cheerful clatter and tap on the pavement, the relentless, despairing accompaniment of the dance-till-you-drop-on-the-pier-end-and-don't-forget-to-smile routine. Her father used to teach her steps when she was little. "Come on Lizzie, kick those legs up, shoes off, skirts up ra-ra-ra!" She had been a determined little dancer, with a strong chin which Mr Faulkener had said they must tie up in a bonnet like Elizabeth Bennet's. Mr Faulkener had been the gay, melancholy joker in her life – he had a brilliant sheen like a new playing card, but a knave's sadness, always the baggy-trousered prankster caught out in the rain. He had a dull job in customs and excise, and scooted home like a teenager after work to get ready to go out in the evening. As president of the cricket club, male lead in the drama society and shareholder in the local wine bar he was never in danger of outstaying his welcome, because he had an air of being himself the perpetual host. He had married Mrs Faulkener because in those days you had to, and looking back, their cool and proper daughter would not have made a very good illegitimate child.

As life and prejudice chipped away at Mrs Faulkener's charm to sculpt something really rather bitter and tired, the couple became increasingly estranged, but neither seemed much to mind that. Jack took her out to dances and dinners from time to time, where they would mix with his younger friends, often the ones Mrs Faulkener did not see fit to invite round to dinner at home. She would sit and toy in embarrassment with her *isle flottante*, her new hairdo tight as a dried hydrangea on her head while Jack, who never betrayed his antipathy for her by so much as a breath of the irony he was famous for, offered votes of thanks, and charmed everybody with his theatrical wit, and in particular his famous woe-is-me-turn which first time round Mrs Faulkener thought was for real – the hilarity of the party only convinced her the more that the company Jack was keeping was not in his best interest. When he died you could see "I told you it would end in tears" written all over her face.

Elizabeth had inherited his dark colouring and high forehead, his un-Englishness. It had been out of her very sympathy with his high, somehow Mediterranean spirits, that she had developed a complementary kind of earnestness – "Daddy, don't drink it please, please daddy," as though it had been hemlock and not just the end of the bottle that Mrs Faulkener claimed made you into an alcoholic. She wondered what other home truths Mrs Faulkener had had up her sleeve and whether they had been sprinkled like unwanted baptismal water over David in late adolescence and been the cause of his leaving home. By the time she realised he wasn't coming back, she had already gone herself, and had met Mark, and was cleansing herself through method, order and good health of the tatty, sometimes-with-ribbons unhappiness of her childhood. Now Mrs Faulkener lived in a comfortable little modern house on the genteel side of Manchester, where she had been brought up. She watched a lot of television – nothing with sex or violence – indeed, the set was housed in a cupboard in the wall and if you pressed a switch on your remote control, a machine-woven representation of a scene out of the *The Book of Hours* descended to screen it off from view.

A couple of weekends previously, Elizabeth had arrived unannounced from London, and Mrs Faulkener, caught short watching something less than suitable, had pressed the "descent" button instead of "off" so that the love scene had the curtain drawn down on it while it still carried on underneath, like a scene in the theatre that has gone horribly wrong and from which only the severest recriminations can ensue. Elizabeth could still hear them shuffling and grunting behind the screen as Mrs Faulkener, in her confusion, went to put the kettle on. She looked round for the remote control and picked it up from the table, where it sat next to an open box of chocolates, and clicked the power button, so that the action stopped. A few minutes later her mother came back into the room.

"You don't know what it is you're watching these days," she said.

Elizabeth glanced at the television guide which lay open on the same table. "It says there's the bowls on the other side," she said, unkindly.

Her mother set out two cups, rattling them in their saucers, a spoon laid to the side of each.

"In my day," she said, not looking at Elizabeth, "there was still some romance. I'll let that stand a minute." The teapot was clad in something that looked as though it might be distantly related to the anorak family – quilted and ungainly. It even had a zip.

"Was there?" Elizabeth's only image of anything that might have resembled any one of Mrs Faulkener's days, which could surely not have been very numerous, was derived from films of the period, when, quite obviously, they had not shown the sex not because no one was doing it, but because you weren't allowed to show it in the cinema. It seemed quite possible that such films had spawned a whole generation of young people who took it from the films that you didn't do it, so they didn't. As Jack had leaned over to kiss his bride-to-be at the bus stop in the rain, it could only be supposed that time stopped, that when she opened her eyes it was the next day and her friend at work was already saying, "Did you have a lovely time with Jack last night?" How did they spend all that time that was cut in the films, if it was not in doing what they had cut from the films? Days must have flashed by in minutes, nights were non-existent (unless it was a French film, of course, in which case it was altogether different – she had noticed that in films and in novels, if you wanted people to do something out of character, particularly in that line, you bundled them off to France).

"We bided our time," said Mrs Faulkener, grimly, falsely, and the set of her mouth seemed to be trying to suggest that the wait had been difficult and testing, and that they had probably had to have their legs tightly crossed and read magazines on earthworms in order not to explode with the pressure of unconsummated passion. "It was very nice. Nowadays –" how Elizabeth hated that expression, tagged as it always seemed to be with the implication that this was a disgusting generation, cuckoos in the nest of the preceding one, who had done nothing to deserve it, and certainly not fornicated – "nowadays, it's not so much a question of boy meets girl as boy grabs girl. There's no romance in it now."

And how romantic had it been, Elizabeth wondered, all that distaste and shame, denial and frustration? Had they needed to hold sex at bay in order to enhance their love lives? Couldn't there be a giving, and a generosity, which would create more of the same? It wasn't even give and you shall be given unto, it was give, and not having to count the cost, because you loved and you lost nothing, nothing was taken from you, you reaped, without planning, without even caring, a thousand fold in joy and yes, in friendship. Blessed intimacy. I am blaspheming, she thought, and reached out to remove the tea cosy. Mrs Faulkener reached out her hand.

"No, no, she said, that's the beauty of it."

What, thought Elizabeth, are we to talk of beauty after all? Are the scales about to fall from the flocked wallpaper, will the unspeakable be mentioned within these walls? Beauty? Love? But I don't believe in them any more than she does now, she thought. How can I defend them? I can only speak as an historian, or as someone who has seen the glory, and from whom it has gone. She had never told Mrs Faulkener about Mark. She had dealt with her own guilt over his being married, had noted that she did that marriage no harm, that he was kinder with his wife. She had not wanted to put her position to her mother, to hear the conventional arguments against her actions. She had enriched his life, she had been his friend. Perhaps he should have stayed the poorer, but faithful.

Perhaps even he thought so now. But she could not admit that it had been dirty, or greedy, or an example of low living. She could not believe that her mother thought her still a virgin. Indeed, she was probably a lot more of one than her mother thought, because what with all that intimacy and friendship and adult communication, they hadn't had quite as much time left over for sex as those who exercised denial imagined. And as for speaking of Will, no, a thousand times no.

"That's the beauty of what?"

"This cosy! You don't have to take it off to pour. I found it in Lewis's."

Elizabeth might have laughed at the poor teapot, condemned to do the one thing it did well clad in a Y-front sort of arrangement, but she was angry. She picked up her cup, then found she could not hold it without its rattling, so she put it down and said, "There is nothing more romantic than sex with the person you love. It does not matter whether you have said in a church in front of a god you do not believe in and do not have the honesty to confess you do not believe in, that you will love them for ever and ever until you are – old and living huddled over a teapot and watching television because he never speaks to you any more and goes to his separate bed each night aching for someone he maybe never even met. It doesn't matter. If you love someone, and are fearless about the future – even if you are wrong about it – that is faithfulness, it is already there, you have your faith in that person at that time, and you have his faith too. That is love, and sex is the most delicate representation of that love, like – a song." She had exhausted herself, she wished she had not spoken, but it was out now.

"You seem," said her mother, licking her lips and reaching for a plain biscuit, "to know a lot about it." Elizabeth sat back in the armchair. Her body was weak with the effort of her heart to speak of those things she had never found words for before. Her stomach relaxed, and swelled slightly under the stretched fabric of her skirt. Mrs Faulkener looked over at her daughter, waiting for an answer.

"I'm thirty-three," said Elizabeth, but thinking that she could be eighteen, that if she had been able to find those words at eighteen it would have been true just the same.

"Hmm," said her mother. "Well, I can't say I'm surprised."

"I haven't been making a confession. I'm just telling you where I stand."

"And what about the little ones in all this?" said her mother.

"Little ones?"

"I suppose you take something – so as not to get caught out?"

"If I had conceived a child with the man I loved," said Elizabeth curtly, "I would have borne that child. If I had not felt able, for some reason, to assume the responsibility of giving that child a proper home and family, I would, as you say, have taken something. It didn't happen."

Mrs Faulkener had finished her tea. First things first. "They say there are more people alive than dead now," she said.

"Nowadays," corrected Elizabeth, but her mother took no notice.

"The world population is a scandal. There'll be no air left for us to breathe. No food to eat. No green grass anywhere."

"I don't believe," said Elizabeth, "that your argument against sex has all of a sudden become an ecological one. 'Procreation equals extinction.' You were saying only a moment ago that it was a moral objection."

"Oh," said her mother with a sigh, waving her hand, which meant, these great concerns are mine own, you just go off and hump the night away with some man no better than the ape he's descended from, I'll bear the worry of the world on this one. "Oh, it's just all so very sad."

"No," said Elizabeth, "it is you who are sad. And we who must lie and deceive you in order that you will not be sad. David and I."

Her mother looked up with tears in her eyes, and Elizabeth felt guilty for having gone too far. "David is my son," she said.

"Yes. And he is my brother, and I would very much like to know where he is. But not in order to bring him back here, for – his loins to wither and his collection of dirty magazines to start making the bed stand up off the floor."

"Elizabeth!"

"Oh I'm sorry," she said, and she was crying too. "Oh, don't cry, I am sorry. I don't know, I don't know. But I let you be,

I don't shout at you, or tell you this or that is wrong, and your generation was hateful and corrupt. I let you live without censoring you all the time. Don't say these hurtful things."

Her mother came over and crouched by her chair. "There," she said, "don't you cry. There's nothing to cry for. I can't help my age. Maybe you're right. Let's not talk about it again," and Elizabeth had not had the strength to say, "Yes, yes, we *must* talk about it, and talk about it again, until there is no fear or misunderstanding left, and one day I can tell you, my own mother, how I loved him, how I bared body and soul to him and it still wasn't enough, not for him, nor for me, and not because we were wrong, but because separation erupted like an earthquake among innocents, and there is no healing after that."

She wrote her note to Frances on a piece of paper specially cut to size, a sheaf of which she kept strapped with a gold band to a little leather-bound board, for leaning on, in her handbag. Once Will had drawn silly faces and pin men illustrations of the *Kamasutra* on the wrong side of all her pieces of paper and slipped them back into place, but she noticed his finger marks and left him a neat little note: "Will, before you can sully my reputation you will have to wash your hands. Elizabeth." She slid it through the letter box and controlled the bright snap-to of the brass flap. so that she could steal away back into the night without being caught on the doorstop.

Walking past Westminster Cathedral on her way to the tube station, she remembered Mark and Polly and how he had made a secret of his assignation with her at the church by mentioning it with an evasive smile. He had the weirdest taste – not Polly, but Polly and mass. Did they meet for coffee before confession and check their stories, she wondered. "My soul shall magnify the Lord." It made your soul sound like something made of glass, for artificial magnification, over and above real size, a deforming vessel for closer inspection, like the singing voice she had lost, which had again falsified the world, shapen a bewitching, but mendacious image of it – I shall sing your praises, let me sing you love songs – a beautiful means of inducing comfortable falsehoods. Not that Will, whose life had been dedicated to such manufacture, was guilty of bad faith, but he had somehow died of his belief in joy, of his delight in the sensual accessibility of the world. It was as though he had been flying high on the buttresses of some dizzying cathedral, his exaltation blinding him to the clash of the bells and the spin and crack to earth. Her fallen angel.

She was standing under a street lamp, so that everything was in shadow, and the façade of the cathedral, variegated as a sweetmeat with pinches of white amongst the rosy pink, all under a mackerel sky, might have seemed sinister and somehow tricked out for something not quite nice. The paving slabs laid end to end were like marks on a ruler, "one step two step, tickle you under there". Elizabeth's anti-ecclesiasticism went a long way back. Her father had always jokingly taken their hands and scuttled them past churches, "Come along children, no dawdling now," as though it had been, which it was for him, a place of ill repute. Now, as she stepped forward into the shadow of Mark's trysting place, she felt a strange sympathy for the gloomy edifice, as though it were not a living place but a relic, somehow pale and pathetic in the moonlight. Her foot knocked against something and she bent to pick up a coin which had been left on the pavement. She turned it over in her hands, thinking that since she did not know for what this coin had last been given in exchange, it was impossible to know what it was, as though if the world stopped tomorrow and the currencies were all frozen, each coin would somehow be trapped in the condition of the thing for which it was last swapped, like people able to override the content of their entire lives by a death bed repentance. It was too small a coin for propitiation, and yet she did not want to keep it. She dropped it again on the ground and it wheeled off and lodged in a crack.

From inside the building, seeping like vapour through – what? – the stones themselves, since there were no open windows, or doors, came the sound of a choral song – the choir, running through their paces in preparation for Sunday, day of rest, when songs fly up to heaven. This was Tuesday evening, between work and play, and already they were in there, rehearsing the notes, repeating difficult phrases, eliminating the errors, but holding back still, because this was not the real thing, not yet. My words fly up, my thoughts remain below . . . Come Sunday, up they would go, launched on a sense of occasion, sincerity converting mere meaning into sense, and giving them wings.

She would go home and have a bath, remove the silt of the day and replace it with oils and lotions from bottles, tidy her house, prepare it maybe, to receive this odd new object, which would be unlike any other, in taste, certainly, but in status too, since she had not selected it, but accepted it. She had been standing, listening, absently minding the crack in the pavement. She noticed that her handbag was open, and that out of the top peeked the terracotta urn. There was something so awful, macabre and kitsch about it, that she almost couldn't take it very seriously. It was like carrying a kidney from the scene of an accident in a Sainsbury's bag. It had an animated air, you could easily imagine it developing facial features, a mischievous little imp who would soon turn on a speaking voice, and start directing her life. It would get rather cute, putting spokes in her love life, expressing disapproval of her opinions at dinner; each time he would pipe up embarrassingly loud and she would have to take him to the bathroom for a talking to, like some American sit com, threatening sharply to chuck him clean away if he didn't . . . what on earth was she thinking? Crazy day. There was a touch of Sid Sissons about it all. But I am broken up, she told herself. Just because her fancy hadn't entirely left her didn't mean she was a hard hearted bitch.

She remembered being taken to see Lincoln Cathedral as a child. Her mother had relatives up that way. Her father had been overruled. It had been winter, and she had been wearing a little red muff with white down at either end. She and David had scampered round the Cathedral looking for the Lincoln Imp, a tiny device left by the mason. *Et in Cathedra Ego.* Me too. For this one little aberration of the sculptor, the Cathedral had gained more fame than for all its architectural splendours, and yet it was a mere thimble's worth of stone when placed against the Gothic immensities of the Cathedral. Afterwards, they had all had tea in a hotel, and everyone had been happy, they had felt like a family. Elizabeth had kept on looking round at the other three, thinking, this is a family, this is my family, and feeling grateful to the imp. Then, no, she said to herself, I am not going to let it take me like that. Will is not going to become my lucky charm.

Immediately she had rejected it, the idea became quite repellent, and she almost had an urge to run clatter clatter on her heels down to the Thames's edge and fling him down into the petrol filmed waters, that unpleasant churn of effluent that would say no to nothing. But instead, because she was one of those people who are able to desire something passionately and yet at the same time be equally capable of anticipating, experimentally, for size, the regret she would feel if she allowed this passion to dictate real actions, she turned instead to make her way back to the tube station and home. There was a sound of tearing paper at her feet. She looked down. Her shoe had caught on the edge of a large sheet of what looked like brown wrapping paper, which had been stuck to the pavement with a broad brown border of scotch tape. Only now did she see the chalked drawing on the ground, framed, within the border of sticky tape, in its careful outline of white, like a picture postcard. *Et in Arcadia Ego*. A light wind was blowing, lifting the tiny chalk particles into the air, as though the artist were blowing on his paper to clear the dust. Here too is death. She felt a sudden dragging in her insides, the memory of her phantom pregnancy when she had allowed herself to believe that there was new life within her. It was something she must walk round. Forgive us our trespasses. She had stepped on the picture and torn it slightly with her shoe. She must not step on it again – for luck, for reverence.

She looked up from the pavement, not at a sound, but alerted by a kind of silence, filtering like a singly held note through the other random noises of the London night. A little boy was quietly playing by the wall of the cathedral. He came over, but did not seem to see her. She was quite sure, beyond any doubt, that if she had taken a photograph of him now, his image would not have appeared on the film. Now he was walking tight-rope style along the edge of the picture, heel to toe, with his arms held out at his sides. She thought perhaps he was a truant from the choir, a little lost penny, but he was too young for that. He was singing quietly to himself, she thought she could hear him, a little mewing sound, lost in himself, no phrase complete, as though the rest were sounding elsewhere, in her own head, perhaps, or someone else's. The child was known to her, once familiar, now forgotten, through long absence, seen now through a second sight, which sees more, and differently. Tristan, she would have called him, and perhaps it was his resentment of the name that made him haunt her like this. He would have been only newly born, and yet would appear, from time to time, no guise altogether different to the one before it, nor altogether the same, like a dream character with endless changes of costume and walks and lists of the voice, though Tristan never spoke. She turned and walked quickly towards the tube station.

The next morning she said to Frances, "I need to get away."

"Yes," said Frances, "I can see that. To be alone or to be with people?"

"Different people, maybe." Elizabeth had hardly been sociable over the last two months, but she had not been a recluse either. There were always dinners, or chance encounters that led to invitations, or somebody who was in a play, or singers you couldn't not go and listen to, because one day they would do the same for you. People had become used to her not being very available over the past year, however, and certainly she no longer saw any of Mark's friends. Only his closest friends had known Elizabeth anyway – the others moved to a distance, to show their support for his wife, and now even the ones who had known Elizabeth had moved to a distance to show their support for Mark. She never lacked for company when she felt the need for it, but it was precisely on the occasions when she felt the need of it that courtesy, an unwillingness to use her acquaintances as a side show, kept her to herself. The cast was down to very few. Herself, Frances, Mark, the little boy. The terracotta urn and its contents, which could almost have been a hallucinatory drug, some imported powder that could enslave or release her.

"I thought of Marguerite. The woman who writes the guides. I told you about her. There was an idea I might translate them. I'm sure she'd have me to stay if I asked. I need a holiday." She didn't really think she needed a holiday, but it was a formula for something else she needed, which she couldn't find the words for.

The kitchen slowly started to seep from black to grey, not imperceptibly, but unremarked. It was a light I rarely see, and it was a little like coming round from an operation, where waking takes place within a discernible and protracted moment; it's a privileged moment, because for the short time it lasts you can be aware of consciousness as a condition, of which you are still a stone's throw short, like throwing a lamplight on a star. Then I blew the candle out and we slipped back a little into night, and hurriedly, because of the danger of the blue dawn when you are feeling low, in the last moments of what could still be called night, I sent her off to bed. She appeared wide awake, but it was a brittle, startled state, like that of one who has only momentarily been awakened from sleep. I watched her walk in the pale grey light across the courtyard and up the wooden steps. When the cock crowed she did not pause on the stairway to listen, but hurried on, with her cardigan draped around her shoulders in that fifties heroine way that was a little her style, as if she were afraid to hear it twice more before dawn. It is hard to know the difference between laying to rest and summoning up. They seem often to have the same characteristics in the first stages. She moved in a mist, always muted – not by the sense of loss, because the loss itself had rendered her insensible, but dimmed, as though the curtains had been drawn.

I came into my study here and laid my head against the glass pane. The sun had now risen and there was a cold, reflected light moving over the vines. It seemed to spread across the soil which was hard with night still, lapping around the roots of the vines like silvery water, and it struck me that at dawn the sun's light is most like that of the moon.

This is not quite a love story, not as I've written it, nor was it a love story as she told it. But when, from a glimpse in the street, you extrapolate a whole marriage – from one harsh word, or a hand held out in heavy traffic – what you imagine is more often than not quite close to the truth. Elizabeth gave me this much, which was incomplete without being enigmatic. Its curt synopsis was there in front of us in the little terracotta vase, a little to the left of the salad bowl, next to the carafe of water. By the time she had finished telling me the beginning, I realised that in fact from one point of view, mine perhaps, it was no more than the end of the story of Elizabeth and Mark. The twenty-four hours which she related in detail, the first meeting with Will, and the realisation that it wouldn't be the one and only, which makes the second meeting, his arriving at her house that night, more important, in the end, than the first, were only the flotsam of their sunken affair. Because I had met Mark, I felt indignant on his behalf. I could not understand – she could not express, though that is no real excuse – what it had been in Will that so possessed her. All she could do was describe the phenomenon, like the results of an experiment for which one has no hypothesis. It had in her telling the uninflected indifference of a revelation – "I saw a new heaven and a new earth." I took her word, though I have not perhaps always given it faithfully back to you. It might be possible to discern a hypothesis of my own somewhere in there, though it will not have any scientific status, being hunch-like if apparent at all. If, in those few days she had been with me, I hadn't been witness to the difference between the young woman I had met only two years previously, and the version I had before me now – veiled, not quite by misery, but by having lived too intensely – like those people who after taking LSD, find themselves unable to settle for the world as our ordinary perceptions render it to us, I might have believed that her experience with Will had been, from the outside, thoroughly banal. Perhaps he was like an item of clothing which, worn by someone extraordinary, becomes a raiment of light. She used no colour to describe him. She never said, oh! it was so this, or that. She never once said she couldn't find the words, because for her the very simplest words sufficed; she called him by his name, that being enough, for her, to summon him by.

That day she slept. From where I lay resting in the early afternoon, with my head facing east and my feet tilted west, I could hear a light, beseeching wind, which had stolen up on the house and hushed the trees. Poplar, lime, white willow and plane, these are the best trees for music – an ensemble of mixed woodland. Not oak or beech, they are too stiff. You could plant for future music. It would be a long time in the composition, but you could be sure that when the saplings grew to full height, their leaves frothing one unimaginable summer from now, it would sound to you then as it did at the time you first imagined it, for the music is all in the ear. There was no clapping of doors, though, it was too light a wind for that, but there were still currents moving through the house. There was little to lift, nothing really for a wind to animate. A curtain here or there, a woven cloth hanging from the back of a chair. A silk print suspended between two fragile pieces of bamboo. Pierre's own work, with little more to recommend it, actually, than that it was created by one hand, the master's. Perhaps this is the premise on which monotheists base their assumption of superiority. Made by the master's hand alone. I see no particular virtue in it myself. I'm a religious relativist if ever there was one. My symbolic drink would be one of those orange juices, "made from oranges from different countries throughout the world". How can people settle for a slogan which uses the same preposition twice over? Who let that one through? Or the co-operative wine, from grapes of many vineyards.

The house is tiled throughout with rectangles of terracotta, their surface puckered with air holes, like a cake just risen. There is no glaze – they come straight out of the kiln like that. It is a soft stone, and even when you walk in your heaviest shoes, there is little noise, no tip or clog of heels. But someone was moving around the house. I think, but can't be quite sure, it was my sense of hearing picked it up. Or maybe one of the other senses, one of the ones we haven't codified yet, identified it on the horizon and brought it to my ears' attention, passing up responsibility to a higher authority. My bedroom is above the drawing-room. The architecture of this, the main part of the house, is as simple as a double-decker bus. I sleep in the corner room, by the top of the stairs, in a room which faces west, towards the vines, and north, into the courtyard, Every room in the house has a window looking out into the courtyard, of which the main farm building forms the one straight side, the whole being like a D or penalty area. You could have a choir practice with only one person per room, if you opened all the windows. The curve of the D is made up of a barn, a brick wall, and a once provisional, now never to be touched wooden building, with storage space on the ground level and a flight of steps leading you to a first floor outer landing or gallery. Two doors here, one for Christian's room, the other Elizabeth's makeshift office, where I had provided her with a couch, an old *lit bateau* – the type with scrolled boards at head and foot, Madame de Pompadour gone heavily rustic. It was dressed with a white lace cloth, dowry style, and underneath, showing through, a red cotton throw, which peeked through the holes like berries in snow. Christian brought the red cotton back from India.

She had slept there that night, this morning. Maybe she preferred it to her bedroom in the house. I had also added an old table – Pascal and I brought it up from the *caves* before she arrived. It's about ten feet long, of oak, with a drawer for each person down its length. I was told it was a nun's table, that it came from the convent when they had a clear out, and that each nun kept her pewter plate and cup in the private drawer. There were no signs of locks. Perhaps a locksmith never sets foot in a convent. Perhaps there are no secrets. It would be one of those lateral thinking problems. Why did the locksmith go to the convent? Is it something to do with valuable treasure? No. Was he there in a professional capacity? Yes. Was he going to put a lock on a door? Not necessarily. You can't have not necessarily. All right then, no. I had put it underneath the window, so she could look out. The vines are round the other side. Here you looked out at the pale hay fields and the dark woodland that meets them like the water-shadowed lip of a sandy beach. The hay was long and feathery, reminding me of those eyelashes which are so pale, the colour of untreated wood, that they can be no help against the light at all. It is a long room, it sticks out into the hayfield like a preacher's pulpit, propped up on posts, banded with lint and glue to defy the field mice. The floorboards are rotten in places, and you can see not daylight, but down into the gloom of the storage room below as you walk. The room is warm with the half lush, half dusty smell of late ripening fruits, because I store the apples down below in winter. She worked by the window at the far end, north-facing, so she must have had her back to the sun all day. Usually she left the door open so the sun came in from the south and brought her plenty of light to work by. She had a little portable computer, but she didn't seem to use it much, and often worked by hand, only typing things up in the evening, printing the smooth, perfect sheets, which emerged as from a mangle, out of a little laser machine that I sometimes heard sighing and giving little moans as I worked on the border at the end of the day. She had a couple of dictionaries, but otherwise just paper and pens. She had nearly finished the translation of the second book, and the finished work lay in a clinical plastic folder, pristine and apparently untouched by human hand, with a careful hierarchy of headings to correspond to my own.

I had taken a short siesta after lunch – that makes it sound like some sort of drug, but it didn't work anyway. It was a day when you feel you have undone too much, are too keen and alert, in your fatigue, to the impressions the world can leave, as though your wings were wet still – because you have cheated the sun, the clock, your own body. The curtain of habit and routine, whereby the similarity of each day to the next creates a sense of reliable probability that all will be well, as it has been more or less on similar days, is rent. I felt still slightly sick with tiredness.

After my siesta, I combed my hair through quickly with the Spanish comb. Pascal was walking among the vines with one of the men from the co-operative, discussing the crop. Every now and then they would stop and part the leaves and touch the grapes thoughtfully with finger and thumb, pressing them lightly, then looking up at one another to discuss, still holding the fruit delicately between their fingers. From the other, smaller window, I could look down into the courtyard, though it's a space more decorative than that word suggests – because the buildings are all so low it gets plenty of sun, and is more of a secret garden really. I don't know why I say secret. To the outsider, perhaps, though you can pass quite easily into it, through an arch which in early summer is thick with dusty wisteria, like a ribboned and powdered wig. The door to her office was open. She must be about or working. I heard a door open below and looked down from my window. She had come out into the courtyard and was holding the terracotta pot with the ashes. She was holding it as if it was a church candle, with two hands clutched around it. For once she was only half dressed – I don't mean she was wandering around naked in the garden (naturism, they call that, I believe, practised by those who think we can remedy the Fall just by taking our clothes off. Again, the literal mindedness of the age), but though she wore a long cotton dress, pink flowers on a white background, heavy, dusky pink flowers, more like the kind you find on curtains or upholstery material than on fabric for a frock, as Pierre used to call them, her hair was loose. She wore no jewellery, no detail in the hair to show she had prepared herself, with however slight a gesture – a slide, a comb, the sculptor's tool – for presentation. Her feet were bare. There aren't that many people who look scarcely dressed just because their feet are bare. That should tell you something about her. She stood in the hot sun, holding the urn, and looking down at the garden hose, which I had left running earlier that morning, to dampen a patch of earth to which I was going to transplant some seedlings in the evening. It had a tiny leak, which was sending up a fine vortex of mist, and for a full minute I saw two rainbows, one cutting across the other's bows. I don't know whether that means luck.

I came downstairs into the kitchen. She had forgotten the kettle, which had boiled bone dry and was hopping up and down on the stove, like someone dancing on scorched earth. I turned off the flame and set it in cold water, to take the heat from the stinging metal. I had hung huge bouquets of sage and lavender and verveine from the beams, to dry. They were already crisp, with all the moisture gone from them, but the steaming kettle had dampened them again, and they had wilted and fallen soft. The window was misted over, creating two kinds of weather, one inside and one out. I passed my sleeve over the glass, and looked out. She was still there in the garden, holding the urn, unchanged from the image I had seen a few minutes earlier from my room. Seen like that, through the mist, from one season into another, she appeared to me to have come from a different time, as though it was the blurring of something in my mind that had allowed me to step across an invisible barrier and glimpse her there. I've seen it happen too often not to have been alert to the possibility that Elizabeth might resent my having heard her story. We had a friend who began writing poetry after the death of his child. He met an editor at a party and in a moment of weakness told her about the poems. She flattered him into showing them to her and asked to be allowed to publish them. He agreed, thinking perhaps, and I remember that he was never quite rational again, if any of us ever are, that if his poems reached a wider audience there was a greater chance that his dead little child would hear his voice. But the day the poems were published, one of them appeared in the review section of a newspaper. He rushed out to buy a copy. There was a terrible scene – he wanted to suppress the edition of the paper, and went round ripping out the poem from as many copies as he could lay his hands on. He soon found himself having to explain to the chief of police who was, fortunately, a sympathetic man. But you see it isn't only Muslims and photographs, you can give a piece of your soul away before you can say "lend me your ears", if you're not careful. The poet's wife had to take him to Guadaloupe for a year, till the collection was out of print. The indelibility of our words and actions – the impossibility not just of turning the page, but of tearing it out and still having as many left as you started with – governs so much of human behaviour, action in time, that I often ask myself why people don't accept that heaven is simply non-existence, the end of time and action, both of which entail relativity, eternal into temporal, spiritual into material, perfect into imperfect (and every schoolboy knows the imperfect is much easier to form than the perfect).

So she had recovered the ashes. She had left them behind her when she went to sleep, in her workroom, at dawn. I hadn't known what to do with them. I knew I didn't want them in my room. Should I have drawn the urn together in a huddle on the kitchen table with the salt and pepper grinders? Or found a handy plinth to set it on? In the drawing-room is a dresser for the best glasses, with glass-fronted doors, so you can peer through glass at glass. Sometimes, when the sun is low in the west, a shaft of golden to copper light will slice across the room and strike off the crystal and out again, and the room is filled with piercing yellow rays, spotting the opposite wall with a bright shadow like a torchlight. I had placed it there, in front of the glasses, and there she had found it and carried it out to the garden. When I went out myself she didn't turn round, not at the sound of my moving, but only when I switched off the hose, alerted by the new silence. She was sensitive only to absences. She smiled at me and stepped onto the first plank of the wooden staircase, to return to the room where she had been resting. When she walked, wherever she walked, it was as a sleepwalker, whose rising from the bed is a transgression upon the state of repose, which is suspended, to be resumed. You had the feeling that the greater part of her had been left behind somewhere, that this was only the waking image of her, almost like a photograph. It was broad daylight, but in her long cotton dress and bare feet she looked, for a moment, like a child carrying her candle back to bed.

I didn't see her again until the late afternoon. I was sitting at the table in the courtyard, where so many things get done, mending the hose pipe with an old bicycle repair kit. I fed the hose pipe through my fingers, looking for the little point I had marked with a black cross. I had not spoken to her since we parted at dawn. The knowledge shared, her story told, you need to keep a silence, in the way you keep a secret, letting a skin of trust grow. Nature moved with a kind of unostentatious lack of concern, over the scene, butterflies whispering their wings among the great sage bush, though it was July and its flowers dried to brittle brushes. The slight trickle from the hose pipe, once I had reduced the pressure and put an end to the rainbows, had cut a minute, imitation river in the dry soil, which the sun had now caked to a river bed, in tiny proportions, with banks and tributaries and minute pebbles blocking its whole width. A slight wind moved in the leaves of the creeper. On the road, which passes close by on its way to the village, a hundred yards from the house, you could still hear it rippling a hushed glissando through the shady plane trees. A tractor moved slowly towards the village beneath their shadow. Silence and stillness and against them the flutter of faint noises, an old branch shifting, perhaps as it might only once in a decade, set now, in its ways, dead matter and sapless; the distant hum of a tractor, a sign of the world beyond, came to me as to a child who lies in attentive silence in the night.

I didn't hear her take a breath or smooth a page, or see her shoulders rise and the muscles tighten, so that the song was there one moment where it had not been the second before and I thought at first that it had been going on for a while and for some reason I had not been able to hear, as though a door had suddenly been opened into a world where she had been alone, singing, unheard until now. Her voice – was it her voice or the song? – came to me through the window of her bedroom. It was only slightly open. To open it fully you would have had to have taken a pair of shears and hacked at the virgin vine. She must have crossed over during the afternoon. It was an English song, though at first I couldn't make out the words, which were deformed by the walls of her room, by the scarce open window. Later she showed me the printed page: "A Blacksmith courted me. I fear the scorching suns will shine and spoil his beauty. And if I was with my love— "

The song broke off, a clean cut of new silence in the air. I sat quite still and my eyes were closed, in concentration, perhaps, that fine needle point of precise attention to a particular soul, or to its absence. Then the kitchen door opened and she came out into the yard. I looked up – I was holding the hose pipe with an oddly inappropriate gesture, finely between the fingers of both hands, as though it had after all been a piece of thread, and I had been about to stitch, with all the fluid grace that a good seamstress can bring to her work. I plunged the pipe into the tub of water on the table in front of me and edged it along, until the bubbles started to rise from the spot I had marked with my pen, guessing where the puncture lay. She came and sat at the table, watching me for a while. I wiped down the pipe with a cloth and laid it in the sun to dry off before I applied the rubber glue.

"Are you hungry?"

She was looking at her nails. She had applied a very pale pink varnish to them, though varnish wasn't quite the word, since it looked more water colour than oil. She still wore the heavy cotton dress – it was almost a tea gown. At least those were the words that came to mind. Tea gown. It's not something of which you could say, "I wouldn't know one if I saw one," even if you had never seen one before, and had no idea what one looked like, because it's one of those rare articles whose whole expression is found in the word itself. It's not onomatopoeia. I suppose it's that the age in which they were worn, the spirit of that age, finds such perfect expression in the two slightly odd words used to define it – tea, and gown. Nothing like day dress. Nothing like evening wear. There's something about the word, that slightly aromatic, faded feel, like old tea, perhaps. It dipped low at the front. She had added those few extra details which had been so glaringly absent earlier in the day. A comb in her hair, a smudge of grey under her lower eyelashes, pearl earrings, and a pair of slip-on canvas shoes, pointed at the toe, and with a slight heel.

"No."

"A drink?"

"No thanks."

"Why don't you have a lie in the sun? It's perfect now. Not too hot."

"I think," she said slowly, "I might go and sit by the pool." There was a a sort of plunge pool behind the house, fed by a spring. The water was freezing cold.

"Make sure there aren't any snakes. And watch your hem. It would be a shame to spoil that dress."

"It's ancient," she said, "it wouldn't matter." It was true – I hadn't noticed, but it was truly faded, not just muted for the fashion of the day which said it must look faded to simulate age. It was old, and my care that she shouldn't damage it arose from the feeling it was old and fragile, which is not something you normally associate with clothes. Her old clothes were older than her, but still preserved, not put out for gardening, for spoiling. More often than not she wore clothes which had a ring of newness to them, a crisp, scarcely worn look. The range of old to new spanned at least eighty years. She must have had a grandmother with a dress sense. But it added to the feeling that she could have come from any age. Her linen tea gown wasn't off the peg from Liberty's, it was out of some ancient chest, it had a real past. Still she didn't move. Then she reached over and picked up the pipe, and held it out so that I could rub the glue onto it. She was careful to leave a silence before she said, "I was singing."

"I heard." I kept my eyes on the pipe, squeezing a tiny amount of adhesive onto the spot where it was punctured. "I wouldn't have said you'd lost – you know, to me it sounds like a song. Would you mind if it wasn't recognisable? If other people couldn't tell? Anyway, I thought you'd renounced it."

"I thought maybe, yes. And then I was thinking this afternoon, it's such a mechanical process, really. If I could only overcome – you know, this awful association, as though it were almost unprofessional, of feelings, expression, the theatrical sincerity, the method, coming to feel what you ape . . . becoming what you pretend."

"You could do it cynically, you mean."

"I think that's what I must have done before. Always, I mean, before – this last year."

"Before Will." I thought we'd better knock the idea of not saying his name on the head early on. Not daring to speak his name is the related opposite, the mirror image, of it never being off your lips. "No, you're muddled. We do things the way we do, because we don't know any better. It's a state of ignorance, and the ignorance makes us innocent. Not knowing. I don't know if it eliminates the wrong, the failing. It's the experience of acquiring knowledge, whether it comes from loss, or just from living, or from love – I don't think, personally, it counts if it comes to you on a piece of paper—

"—that's just the 'learn by your own mistakes school'. If you think that you have to throw out the whole idea of instruction—"

"I'm talking about a moment of illumination. Instruction comes before. Preparing the soil and so on. Knowing, comes in a single action."

"You really believe that?"

"It's a bit like losing one's virginity. When it works."

"Which isn't necessarily the first time."

"Rarely. In the history of woman kind, at least."

"The blinding flash?"

"The discovery of something that changes everything. *La jouissance.*"

"Say it in English."

"It's ugly in English."

"Yes," she said, "You're right. I wonder why."

"Cynicism comes after. It's the improper use of a revelation. You've been told, you've been given the chance in a million, and you still think you know better, or different. So you just reinterpret the knowledge so that it means what you wanted it to mean, so the revelation is denied."

"The 'he would say that' school?"

"Sometimes the alternative is paralysis. Not scepticism but not faith either."

"Or like me – ventriloquism."

"Don't do it then. Wait."

"For what?"

"Wait until you can— "

"Recapture that first fine careless rapture?"

"Not at all. There's never a second coming. Or a going back. You could sing your heart out, like the chaffinch, and your throat would bleed before you found it. Never."

"Then what?"

"Becoming as a child again. Through experience, hard work, patience with time, assimilation of pain. Aforethought and deliberation. Become a cynic who loves. There's an achievement for you. Give me one Alceste for a thousand Romeos."

"A living sacrifice?"

"A saint without God. A realist."

"Who can still sing?"

"'The crow doth sing as sweetly as the lark when neither is attended . . .' Yes, of course."

"Aren't you talking about an illusion? A self delusion?"

"No, I'm talking about faith."

I set the hose pipe to one side, and began to gather the bits of equipment back together in that little box they come in – unmistakable for any other kind of box, long and slim, and rounded at each end, a bit like a mouth harmonica. I got up from the table, pushing myself up slightly with one hand pressing down on the wood, the other on the top of my thigh. I was, I remember, wearing a pair of seersucker trousers, an old blue sweater and a pair of old rubber gardening clogs. I picked up the garden trowel, thinking that if I didn't do it now, while I could see it, I might lose sight of it for the rest of the summer. I tapped it against the wall of the house to free the soil which had dried to it. It made a ringing noise. Elizabeth looked up at me. I leaned it against the wall and came back to sit with her. I wanted to show her she had lost nothing in the telling, that I would never make use of what she had betrayed about herself. In certain languages, the word for translation is the same as that for betrayal. I wouldn't even allow it to colour my view of her in any way. I was going to let it pass as something that had never been, if she liked. But at the same time I sensed that she sought from me some confirmation that she had actually told me, that it had not been as in a dream, when you wake and find you have it all to do again.

"Are you feeling any better?" It could have been the tiredness I was asking about. She was silent for a while. Her face was as still as if it had been painted. Her mouth was caught though, in a position of strain, one of those intermediate stages between two expressions, the kind that can catch you out on camera, the painful moment of transition between two states of grace – a smile, say, and composure. I realised my question had been refused. Unhappiness, awareness of loss, a sense of banishment from the world of ordinary pleasures, all this had become a habit of mind with her, so that when she sang, even, she was incapable of enacting any other mood. We all act, all the time, miming our emotions, so that eventually they come and flood the form, like a moat round a castle on the beach, and we could almost say the water was made for the shape we have fashioned for it. From the moment it inhabits our actions, emotion spreads with ease, even into the deepest recesses of life. But when something goes wrong, when there is a terrible breach, so that none of the emotions proper to the little events of life are present any more, there is a great wave of anguish and pain, washing the whole, destroying the feeble fortifications in the sand, and while you survey the destruction, the little hills flattened and laid low, you are still railing against the event, still fighting back the wave, digging trenches, in vain. I sat looking at her, with my hands joined in front of me, resting on the table. I spent ages doing that. Just looking at her, like a picture you knew wouldn't jump from the wall. This was where I had come home to. This was the scene of my latter years. It was, in a sense, a waiting room. Many people feel most at ease in waiting rooms. It's not as though you don't know what's going to happen to you. I could sit here, in my garden, in my oldest clothes, mending the hose pipe, talking quietly to myself or whoever was there. My memories were there too. Others would come, and go, refuel, depart, leave other memories, take away their own. There were, for me, no straws to clutch at. I had, in a sense, all my time before me. There was nothing to dart about after, seek out, or go back for. It was all here, in this house. Still is.

"If you go into my study", I said, "you'll find a photograph on my desk, in a walnut frame." No, I wouldn't have said in a walnut frame. There's only one. I took the picture from her when she brought it out. It was odd to see it out of doors. A photograph belongs inside, like a piano or an inkwell. I held it out of the sun – not just because the early evening light was still too bright for the frail photographic image, but for the subject too, a memory, my weakest spot of all. Elizabeth hadn't sat down again. She looked suspicious, mistrustful even. She had her hands clasped in front of her again, like a humbled but bullish servant, you know, the gardener who's been summoned to see the lady, holding his hat timidly, with both hands, just below his belt. Except she had no hat.

"I showed it to you last time?"

"No. No, I'm sure you didn't."

"I thought – when I showed you – no, maybe not." Perhaps it was somebody else.

"Who is it?"

I was surprised. There was – I can't have mistaken it – there was fear in her voice. She picked up the skirt of her dress, and came to sit sidesaddle on the bench beside me, laying the dress out to her side so it hung down towards the ground. I looked down and checked it wasn't trailing in the pool from the leaking hose. Always the same images recurring – her dress, the water, the leaves in the evening air.

"Who is it? Marguerite?"

"Sorry." I had been looking at the photograph. I put it face down on the table. She picked it up and turned it over. I could tell she had seen it before, the face, if not the photograph. Then she laid it back on the table.

"It's Christian." Like you, she knew the name. That's Christian's room. Christian brought that back. When Christian comes. I often wondered if that was the name he was first given. I don't know why, but I felt it couldn't have been given him by his parents, that he must have found it elsewhere, discovered it for himself.

"That must be just after he came to us. He must have been – twelve, maybe."

"I sort of thought – he must be your son."

"I have no children."

"No. You said."

"Who are his parents?" It seemed a strange question. Christian's parentage had always seemed to me one of the least important things about him. Like everyone, he had some, but to me they were just eggshells, the thing that had fallen away at birth to reveal my marvellous boy, who had come, after twelve years of childhood, to his true home, where we took him in, and treated him as our own.

Christian's real mother, who spent most of her life in the café at Simpson's in Piccadilly, and had once been photographed for *Tatler* – though not, I hasten to add, when about to become one with Christian's father, which was an event more likely to be recorded on a police file than in a society magazine – died a couple of years ago in some kind of prematurely old person's home in California. But in her London heyday, when she was still able to reap a decent yearly crop from her early seed-sowing as a model in the sixties – the odd rich American lover, a contract with a skin care company to show off her hands washing a younger woman's body and face in the shower – she still had nominal care of Christian, who spent most of the year at school, depending for affection on the gruff comforts of a kindly matron. Every summer she sent him to stay with his father, who lived near here. He had a forge in the forest where he sculpted hideous objects out of smelted iron and lured beautiful women to cook for him and rub sweet smelling unctions into his back which was coarse as oilskin.

Vincent was a wild, clever man – it was rumoured that he had an impressive career as a political activist on the wrong side of the law, and had escaped conviction only by escaping detection, but I always thought if that was true he would have got his teeth fixed, for they, and consequently he, stuck out a mile. In the winter he lived in Toulouse, in some *atelier* down a back street near the railway station. Though he aged more quickly than time, partly because of his drinking, his girlfriends seemed to get younger and younger, which generally meant each one seemed to him less competent than her predecessor of the previous summer at the things Vincent expected a woman to excel at – rounding up and feeding his horses, cooking his meals and washing the caravan every morning. He would pick Christian up from the airport every summer, where he would entrance the girls behind the desks with his smell and his rotten smile, and bring the child out in his battered old lorry to a newly reconnoitred patch of forest. He would drop him in the forest half an hour before sunset, park the lorry, and slip off under the trees down paths known only to himself, while Christian stumbled after him, twisting through imaginary alleyways, following lines which led nowhere, desperate to keep track – and yet more frightened still of what lay behind than in front, for the worst part of the game was Vincent's Return, when he would suddenly double back and creep up on his son from behind, dragging him silently to the floor like the Erlkönig, except he was both demon and father at once. Christian was not so much frightened of the forest at night, as of the brute initiation rite which must be enacted not once, but over and over again. Presumably Vincent was waiting for the day when Christian would wrestle him to the ground and smash his face with his foot (it might have been the moment for a teeth job), but he never did. He was still only a child.

Once they arrived at the appointed spot they would bed down on dirty mattresses to sleep till dawn. Then Christian's dreams of the red-bricked school and the Wiltshire downs would ease warily aside, wallflowers to the rampant ogres that now whirled and span across his night time consciousness, which was more treacherous than a thin-iced lake. In the morning he would be put to work alongside his father who sweated and swore his way through the undergrowth with a scythe from his own forge, clearing a patch of land for the caravan, slashing at the bracken and brambles with a sort of whipping action that did not seem to belong in the gentle forest. Christian would fall in alongside, chopping wood, steering the horses into a new clearing, dragging his little mattress out under the trees away from the caravan, singing his own magical songs to himself to ward off his evil father. He had learned one of these songs from the daughter of one of the beautiful women, who had been brought along to play with Christian, and in whose company, that last summer, he had built a house of sticks and stones, which far from breaking his bones, provided the first real home he could remember. He said he knew it could have been home because it hurt to leave it when it was only a few days old.

At first, his father accepted the gesture of independence, but emerging from the caravan one morning to find Christian sitting on a log chiselling at a piece of cork oak bark with his knife and singing to himself, he took it into his head that his child had magical powers and was fashioning an image to torture him by. For Vincent, initiation was a process by which the protective, magical cloak of childhood was stripped like skin, so that as pain became a more real and constant threat, the gritted iron of manhood might assert itself to the tune of an ever increasing sense of personal triumph. He sprang at the child and tried to wrench the little piece of wood from his hand. Christian obeyed his truest instinct, leaped to his feet and ran. He fled toward the edge of the forest, and across the fields until he came to the track which leads to our house. Fortunately Vincent's pursuit was cut short when he ran slap into a tree and cracked his head, splintering his skull like a boiled egg. According to local legend, for which Pierre was largely responsible at that time, he lay cold-stunned on his back in last year's leaves until a she-fox came along and swapped his head for a cleverly disguised cabbage, stuffed with leaves and maggoty dung, using Vincent's own noddle as a foul-reeking bait to deter the huntsmen who were on her tail. From that day on, at least, he became a milder man, and the only cries that filled the summer forest were those of his and his mistress's pleasure as he romped his way into early senility.

Meanwhile, Christian had found us, and we him. The first time, he stayed with us three days, chattering earnestly with each of us in turn – why had we no children, they said his father had many many more in Toulouse, that they lived in a den by the railway (had we read *Oliver Twist*?), that Vincent could probably spare him to us if we wanted. Pierre walked back with him to the caravan after the three days were up, and found Vincent convalescing on the step, picking his teeth with a razor blade. He accepted the money Pierre gave him to compensate for the loss of his under-age hireling and in return stuffed a horse shoe in Christian's little backpack, for luck. I think he thought Christian was leaving for ever, as in a fairy story, quite possibly to walk round the world, though he was only twelve, and our farm only an hour's walk from there.

So Christian always thought of us as a refuge, and when he became a fisher of men, having left his school at sixteen and taken off, somewhat belatedly, no doubt, in his father's eyes, to travel the world with his skill of chalking pavements, he would pick up strays and guide them, sometimes directly, sometimes by use of subtle bait, to the farm. I enjoyed these encounters, for Christian had good taste and knew how to choose only those who would benefit from my special brand of careful neglect.

"So you see you are not alone in this story."

She looked at me as though I had forgotten to finish my sentence.

"Christian drew those pictures. The *Et in Arcadia Ego*. After the Poussin. After the wine bottle."

She smiled and passed her hands over her eyes. "I thought of you – I said – when I saw them. It wasn't a coincidence."

"Of course it was a coincidence. But not so great a one. Christian gets everywhere. He must have been to every European city by now."

"But I saw it twice."

"A double coincidence? Sometimes, yes, it takes two coincidences to convince one."

"Or," she said, slightly oddly, "they cancel each other out, and it just seems like the normal course of things. And where is Christian now?"

Always that question. Where is Christian now?

"I don't know. He's been away for two years. He was here just after you and Mark for quite a while. Then he went off to Italy. Pierre died in the September. He turned up the morning after Pierre died. He has the sixth sense."

"You believe that?"

"Of course. Except there are more than six, probably dozens more, but they all seem to do the work of the sixth sense. But he would have come for the *vendange* – you could see it like that. Pierre died in September. That was when he had his accident"

"Who? Pierre?"

"No. Christian."

"What happened?"

"Someone threw a chair at him. During the party after the *vendange*."

"Was he badly hurt? Was it serious?"

"No. No, I don't think so. Not damaging. But he's never been the same again. At least, I don't think he has. I haven't seen him."

I looked up at the sound of a footstep on the gravel. The west door to the courtyard garden opened. Because the house is on a hill, I just saw him outlined against the evening sky, no landscape, no friendly surround, as the painter might fill in the gentle hills, a corner of brick, a river even, threading by in the distance, somewhere behind his shoulder. He was tall, and slightly gaunt, like a fearsome preacher. His face was a pale olive colour, stippled with grey. He had come a long way. Mid-forties to fifty. I recognised him at once for a schoolmaster. English. He seemed to know I wouldn't refuse him entry. Elizabeth had her back to him. She turned and shaded her eyes. Even the setting sun seemed to hurt her. I stood up and went over to the gate. He took a card from his jacket pocket – jacket, I thought, this is July, but it was one of those items of clothing that has nothing to do with protection, bodily at least, and said, "Madame d'Astige? *Je suis bien au Mas Colombe*?"

"Yes," I said in plain English, forgetting to smile in welcome. He held out the card. He seemed to think it was a kind of invitation.

I took it from him. It was Christian's card, a reproduction of the painting. He had bought them by the dozen from the shop in the Louvre. Even though it wasn't the only painting he did, he kept the cards on him for luck and if he met someone he particularly fell for, he gave him the card with my address, sending them to me, maintaining contact – it was also a way of telling me where he was. I met him in Prague, they would say, or Lisbon. I don't know why he never wrote or phoned. He was exercising some kind of discipline on us both. Ever since his crack on the head, or perhaps it was Pierre's death, though I don't think that would have made a difference. I had no idea how long it might last. But I knew straightaway that this was not one of Christian's choices. He brought with him the air of an impostor, one who has tricked an innocent, overheard the magic word so that it exercises an influence for evil where it was meant to do good. Although he was a handsome man, it had not been put to the good. His flesh and lips had that pale, protected look, a kind of sensuous austerity. It is true that very often we can read in a person's physiognomy the secrets of his soul, not just the good being beautiful, not as simple as that at all, but nevertheless, there is a cartography of the face, and probably to the voice and the touch of the skin, if you are blind.

But something told me to take him in despite this, a look in his eye, maybe no more than that, one of appeal mixed with the threat of a curse. I must have been very tired. I made no comment on the card. He had a couple of bags. He had taken a taxi from the village. The taxi had driven on now. There seemed to be no choice about it, no more than if he had been delivered to an island by the last boat.

I decided he must stay. I led the way upstairs. The house was suddenly growing dark, and I flicked on the light switches as I passed. No quicker way to bring on the evening than to go indoors, it's like leaping a season in the calendar.

"How long were you thinking off –?" Importuning us, I was going to say. He ran his finger underneath his shirt collar, the way you run a knife round a cake when it comes out of the oven.

"I . . . em . . ." He gestured about him rather loosely, looking for something to tie up maybe. I stood in what was to become his bedroom door and waited for him to look me in the eye. He stopped. "I hadn't really thought."

I led the way into the room, and forgot to tell him to duck, so he cracked his head on the top of the door frame. He insisted that it didn't hurt.

Elizabeth raised her eyebrows at me as I came back out again.

"He had Christian's card," I said doubtfully.

"He's met him?"

"I don't think so. I wouldn't think so."

"So strange, that he should come like that, just at that moment."

"You say that" I said, turning on the hose to test the puncture, "but perhaps I told you then, because I knew he was coming. Perhaps it was me making the shapes."

"Really?"

"No," I said, "not at all. But you always have to consider the possibility someone has information you don't have. 'I'll do that first because . . . I'll make the rain fall before I make the plants grow. I'll make the plants grow before I make the fish and the fowl.' Like that. Beware, storyteller."

I looked up at his room. There was no noise coming from it at all. I wondered if he was just sitting there on the bed with his head in his hands, not moving. I sighed. It would have been nice to have someone rather cheery. Elizabeth sensed that I was feeling a bit down with it all. "Come on," she said, "no more watercress salad and a bottle of white. Proper cooking. We'll do it together."

"We didn't really need anyone else."

"It'll be different. It'll make me behave," she said. We were walking towards the vegetable garden, where we were going to sacrifice a courgette and some beans. Cutting along the edge of the vineyard as by the sea's edge, we saw a small team of men working their way down the rows, spraying a mist of something onto the leaves. Pascal came up and stood with us, watching them move on into the distance. He bent down and picked a rose. He held it out to Elizabeth and she reached out for it. "No," he said, and pointed instead to the leaf, where a grey dust lay in the little veins. "Mildew."

"Not too late?" I asked.

"Should be all right. Hope not. We lost thirty per cent in the frost," he explained to Elizabeth. "We can't afford to lose much more."

Pascal is one of my favourites. He's been with me since he was twenty or so, when he'd finished the army. He wears Pierre's old clothes to work in, and when we have to go to church for a wedding or a death, when he represents Pierre, rather like someone representing the Queen. He needs a good wife. Elizabeth was a world away from his type, but just on that one evening I suddenly wished I could join their hands there on the edge of the vineyard and send them both off to a village hop, where he would lead her through the dances and kiss her as they walked back by the light of the moon. There's age for you.

Over dinner that evening, our new arrival, Mr Goodman –

and it clung to him more like an ironic title than a name – said very little. Elizabeth talked mechanically, politely, about the region, which she was by now quite well boned up on, thanks to translating the guide. I did not ask him about Christian. I knew he must have seen him, it couldn't just have been that he found the card in the street, or had it handed to him by a stranger, because his manner was slightly reverent and knowing, as though we all shared the same secret of Christian's extraordinariness, the sense you have in his presence of there being more to life than you had previously suspected. In my own case it was exacerbated by my love for him. Take any boy you love – remembered, gone from you, or still there, precious in the last years before manhood, your Christian. You cannot have forgotten the way he ran, the way his skin was still miraculous as a baby's, the way he smelt, the uncreased skin around his eyes in the early mornings, the way you marvelled when he went away and came back unharmed, and you imagined it must be because he had the secret of goodness, so that the world could not harm him, and the evil spirits of the woods seized up and shielded their eyes because that marvellous boy had passed, and they felt their powers shrivel before his innocent gaze.

I recognised that in the way Elizabeth had spoken of Will. The greatest power you can have over someone is exercised by disappearance. It's not just the questions it leaves unanswered, though that is a torture in itself. It's not just being robbed of a present that could have been full of them, and changed your every minute and with each altered minute the course of history. For Elizabeth, since she had received confirmation of Will's death, which you might have imagined would be the beginning of the period of healing, the world had lost all possibility of happiness – though, as I reminded her, she was not poor, or homeless, or hungry. If she had been, if she had had that to worry about, it might even have helped.

At least I knew Christian was, as they say, out there, alive. I wasn't unhappy in the raw way. I knew he was choosing not to come home. And I am old. That helps. The desire to rectify the pattern, balance the design changes as you grow older, it does not have that sharp, selfish, possessive nature that it has when you are young and still believe everything is possible. Elizabeth herself seemed to believe that once she scattered the ashes she would have done with it. There is a debate about whether when you see flames about to consume you, you feel fear and the fear tells you to run, or whether your instinct shouts run, and on running you feel fear. I had told her that she must not believe that scattering the ashes would bring about her recovery. She must wait and watch and when the moment was right she would do it, like setting free the birds at a moment when you know they will fly. The moment when she no longer needed to have them with her, when she could say "I accept", and recognise that there is more to life than dust and disappointment and loss, then she could let them fly, and it would not be a question of where, or how, or with what solemn words or thoughts, it would just be an action in the moment that indicated that she was whole again. A simple matter of letting go. It is a common cliché that letting go implies a kind of repossession, that ceasing to mourn in quite the same way enables you to recover life and the one you have lost, and hold them close in a different sort of embrace, instead of thrashing and flailing and trying to stop them slipping away.

It was a still evening again. The clock seemed to be making a ridiculous amount of noise, the way people sometimes hum in an exaggerated fashion to brush over the cracks in communication, or simply indicate time passing. We were sitting in the dining room. As always when you are three, there was an empty space, and for each of us it was a different person who was missing.

Elizabeth touched my hand. "Marguerite?" I had probably been doing my semi-comatose trick again. At least she touched my hand and said my name, and didn't do that awful thing of waving a hand ironically up and down in front of someone's eyes, which always means reproach, not real concern.

"I'm sorry," I said, reaching over for her plate, "I'm very tired." I took Mr Goodman upstairs again. It was one of those evenings when you're really glad of the banister. "I must just show you a few things."

He was in the room next to mine. He looked tired, and I brought him a bottle of water to have at his bedside, because it was so hot, and he seemed to have come so far. I noticed he didn't unpack, not so much as empty his pockets while I was in the room. He just stood there by the bed, taking in my information about what to do if he wanted to keep the shutter half open to get a bit of air, and what time we had breakfast, like a soldier who is being briefed, recording the information as though it had no personal relevance. It was not a leisurely use of formal conversation to ease into acquaintance – nothing on those lines at all. He was wrapped up tight in a kind of worry, which I was afraid might have had something to do with Christian. The only question he put to me, as I passed in front of him – "excuse me" – to replace the box of tissues and pin up the mosquito net, which he said he wouldn't be needing (I think he thought it was for honeymooners) – was whether I had any family. No, I said, straining with all my force upwards to drive a drawing pin into the ceiling with my thumb, to catch up the mosquito net and stop it trailing where he didn't want it. I clambered down off the chair and put it back against the wall and asked if there would be anything else he would be needing. For some reason I found myself behaving like a kind of Dorcas figure, a Victorian maid. When I wished him good night I was about to draw the door very quietly behind me, humbly withdrawing to my quarters, then I thought how ridiculous, and gave it a good affirmative bump.

"Go on now," said Elizabeth, when I got downstairs again, "up to bed. I'll see to all this." She came in a few minutes later to say good night.

"Do you want the shutters open or shut?"

"Shut please. I might try and sleep in in the morning. Oh no, I can't, he'll want his breakfast. What are you doing tomorrow?"

"I thought I'd go to Albi."

"Take my car. There's plenty of petrol in it. Is Mr Goodman driving you away?"

"Not at all. He's a cold fish, though, isn't he. Do you get many like him?"

"Never. What are you going to do in Albi?"

"I want to show the editor the first translation. I need to clear up the contract. It's very simple, but I'd like to get it out of the way. I thought I might have a look round. Do you need anything? Can I bring anything back?"

"No thanks." I spoke from the bed, feeling strangely hospitalised, with her hovering like that, being good to me, putting me to rest. I knew she liked to look after me. It was the instinct

– convents and hospitals are full of broken hearts, and not in the patients. You give your love to God, or to humanity, when one frail human has spurned it. You give it to those who can't answer back, who can't say no thank you. God and the feeble get people on the rebound. This was not quite my case, but perhaps she was trying her hand. On the other hand I didn't want her to get too attached to the role, spend the rest of her life singing hymns to the aged, with the life gone out of her. For it was the lifelessness in her song that had made me think of Christian, the absence of something joyful, and that was what had prompted me to speak.

"It's two years since he came," I said, allowing myself to be just a little pathetic, lying there in my bed, with her standing at the window.

"You were going to tell me—" She was looking across at what had quickly become Mr Goodman's room. Another of those too rapid handovers. He had done nothing to deserve the naming of a room, scarcely enough for the attribution – and certainly no deposit.

"He'll come back one day," I said, not wanting to talk about it, and realised as she was closing the door behind her that it was the worst thing I could have said.

I sat there looking blankly at the opposite wall. I felt I was straining to hear something, waiting for a sign. The cicadas were – not singing – peeping, perhaps. The frogs gave out their irregular chuckles, as though reading Wodehouse tucked up in the flower beds. Not far away an owl fluttered his night noise across a field or two, that strange billowing cry, which has the quality of the human voice at the loudest undercry it dares. (hist, Romeo, hist! – bondage is hoarse and may not speak aloud.) I could hear the pipe of the water supply groaning as an animal drank from the trough. It was like being in the percussion section, without being able to hear the main body of the orchestra, its song. When I was a child I would spend hours in my bed at night, sending telepathic messages to my loved ones, over and over, do you hear me, do you hear me? Do you, will you receive me? Receive my prayer. They never mentioned that they had done. It *was* a kind of prayer, a beseeching of the airwaves. I had made myself believe that if I ever fell asleep during the sending of one of these messages the gift would be taken away for good. I expect I must have fallen asleep and not remembered, for there was never any evidence that it worked. But it's important to keep trying. When they do eventually discover how to do it I'll be well in training, first in line to receive the magic word that makes the message pass, the code word you have to prefix your communication with, before it can hope to get through. Perhaps it's just pure flattery, like "O Almighty God". Or to one you love, "my darling".

"My darling", I said superstitiously, because at least the thought counts, "may He keep you safe, and protect you against the dangers and darkness of this night." The words comforted me, though I did not know whether I was talking to Elizabeth, who would be, not curled up, laid out under her single sheet, dreamless, I hoped, or to Christian, wherever he was, in whatever foreign place, though nowhere was foreign to him. I felt still, in the eye of me, and full of a sort of summer bounty which was cradled, as in a basket, by the night.

Part Three

12

Aiden Goodman changed his life for ever on May Day, but it was not until a month later that he gave his first sign of distress. (Or plea for help, as his brother, Robert would have called it, although Aiden would correctly have pointed out that the two are not always the same thing.) Aiden was fifty years old and was developing a slight stoop. They were travelling along the ring road outside Caen and Aiden noticed a very large modern bridge coming up. He didn't like bridges, It seemed a good time to go. Very quietly, he asked his brother to stop the car. Robert pointed out that they would be at the hoverport in twenty minutes' time. Aiden, having checked there was nothing behind them (he had never passed a driving test but was the very model of cycling proficiency), leaned forward from the back seat and placed his rather cool, long fingers over his brother's eyes. Robert screamed – a real scream – and banged on the brake and clutch with his feet, a movement not dissimilar to that with which he bounced up and down on his compost heap every Saturday afternoon. His wife Janet gave a sort of bark and clutched at the dashboard. The car stopped as though it had been an order she had barked.

"Thank you," said Aiden, and climbed out. He walked very calmly round to the back of the car to remove his case, brushing imaginary chalk dust off his left lapel as he went. He took his case from the back of the car and closed the boot. Robert was sitting staring rigidly at the steering wheel. Janet had wriggled round on the seat of her shiny trousers to stare at him like some graceless child, he thought, through the back window of the car. The image of her face was artificially lined by the de-misting stripes, through which the scene inside the car looked like some photograph which has been cut up and reassembled.

He walked back to stand beside the driver's door. Robert fumbled for the switch to operate the electric window, and lowered it with precaution, as though he were about to accept an entry ticket to a safari park.

"Good bye," said Aiden coolly. "Please drive on," and Robert, as though he we were being operated by his brother, took off the brake and slid away.

Aiden's heart seemed to have taken up a syncopated rhythm. Bum! Ba-dum! Bum! Ba-dum! He was very white in the face and was invisibly biting his lower inner lip with his incisors. It seemed to him later, when he reconstructed the incident, tasting the salty, ferrous flavour of his still bleeding lip, that in his anger he must have been making use of his teeth in a rather rodent-like way which had become otherwise obsolete in humans. (Except, he added in a footnote, when biting off a strip of sellotape).

Robert was Aiden's twin – non-identical, that is, to all intents and purposes, completely unalike. Their mother had enjoyed an easy pregnancy. She was a great fell walker (her husband called her the Striding Edge, which Aiden had always, as a child, assumed to have a slightly odd sexual connotation and to be not altogether affectionate) and had still been marching parties of reluctant day trippers, dreaming, for the most part, of cocoa and the box, up and down and roundabout the dales until well into her seventh month. If there is one advantage to having twins, she used to say, it was you got over in nine months what would normally take eighteen. And in one night what could normally be expected to take two, Mr Goodman usually added, grimly, in his mind's voice.

But in the same way that she was quite likely to double the size of a walking party to include, indiscriminately, a group of writers from a retreat in Ingleton researching topography and its literary function in the Great English Classics and an annual outing of the Furnace Liners' Brotherhood, she had, with Aiden and Robert, if not killed, then at least inflicted a period of prolonged unpleasantness on two birds with one stone. She of the Great Outdoors had had no truck with confinement – that had been the lot of the twins alone, each with their bristling embryonic backs to the wall of the womb; a grimly born co-habitation, and one in which, owing to Mrs Goodman's trenchant Fresh-airism (this in the days when an -ism indicated a disposition in favour of the preceding substantive rather than the reverse) involved a good deal of being thrown together which might have been avoided in a more conventional pregnancy.

In the end, Robert was first out, this side of midnight, and Aiden always thought of him as the brash cuckoo in the womb. The birth was attended by an immigrant Italian midwife who, on arrival at the scene, had gone round opening the doors of all the chests and cupboards in the house to weigh odds in favour of an easy birth. No one had suspected twins, but it was obvious, once he got moving, that Aiden was more than the mere afterbirth of his brother, so Mrs Goodman braced herself once more. If she had more of an A.J. Wainwright than a Dr Spock approach to childbirth, it could at least be said that she was exercising her right, which in later generations became an inexorable one, to do it her own way.

They were born on the cusp of two star signs. Robert was a midsummer baby, Gemini just; Aiden who, as it seemed appropriate to reflect at this moment, would always much rather miss a boat than take it with Robert, was Cancer, a crab. It was as though he deliberately dawdled to avoid the taint of twin-ness on his highly personal escutcheon. Neither of them had any interest in astrology, but it was a useful tool of differentiation. In the same way, they had conveniently been born in a town which maintained two distinct and rival football clubs, so that as children they had been able to go quite separate ways in pursuit of a common, if short lived passion.

At school, where alphabet and calendar had conspired to bring them together, nature turned out to have made helpful provision by setting Robert up with some asthmatic genes. Aiden always felt a sense of personal satisfaction about this, as though he had in a sleight of hand, slipped Robert the Queen of Spades.

University offered escape from the tightly woven nest of the family home, which was neither poor nor happy, nor rich, nor tragic, but very boring. Childhood was another long confinement, a prudish affair: the boys, had they been sensible of, rather than emotionally inured to their condition, would have seen that they were treated rather like pieces of Victorian furniture at the height of the vogue for puritanism. (Who created that? surely not Mrs Goodman, who was always out and about, and surely not Mr Goodman, who regarded the family home as a place for keeping things, like an all purpose tool shed – furniture, food, children, not much else, and whose job involved a lot of travel; Mrs Goodman's mother, no doubt, who herself had been reared within a community of closed brethren. It was she who looked after the boys and sat them down to do their homework after beans on toast, and watched the clock, as though it were an entertainment, through the evening). Aiden went off to St Andrew's to study languages, and arctic terns at the weekend (although it should not be thought he was a man of spun Arran sweaters and a tweed cap – he dressed for his ornithological expeditions rather as though he were going to spend the night in an unheated library). Robert went off to Sussex and studied social sciences, where he met Janet sitting next to him on a floor. She aroused a sense in him of the meaning of compassion on a truly inter-personal level, so often submerged in the collective political consciousness, by stirring his powdered milk into his coffee with the long end of the wooden crucifix round her neck. She explained that it was a secularised symbol, that the ancient religions were rich repositories of imagery, which could only be enriched by subsequent borrowings on the part of later movements. Aiden had suggested that this was like saying authors should be delighted by their three pence in the pound from the Public Lending Right, but on the whole the geographical distance between the twins afforded few opportunities for skirmishes of this kind, and Aiden, briefly, flourished. He had time and energy enough for two.

He wondered in his fastidious way, as he watched the Vauxhall estate take rather falteringly to the highroad of the bridge, whether it might not have been Robert's confident happy-holiday use of the word "hoverport" which had finally unleashed him. Aiden had spent a week in a house in Brittany with Robert and Janet, talking things over, as they had so wanted him to do, and listening in a taut, brittle fashion to their counsels.

"No self blame, no self pity. That's the bottom line!" Robert had insisted. "You have to go back in there and face the kids with who you are. They can take it. Can you?"

Aiden remembered the moment when a feeling of disgust had abruptly leaked out over his resolve to make the best of the holiday.

"I cannot understand," he said, with a sort of pale venom in his voice, usually reserved for those of his pupils who manifested problems of conjugation with the verb *avoir*, "why you find it necessary to adopt the vernacular of an American probation officer."

Robert and Janet discussed him in bed again that night, as they had almost every night since it had happened. They were in clover, heavy-scented lucky clover. Aiden had a problem. Aiden was, after all, in disgrace. They were here to help. They had seen it coming, of course. If it hadn't been this, it would have been something else sooner or later.

"Somewhere down the line he was always going to have this happen – it's like— " Janet pushed herself up onto her shoulder, getting really interested in her own analysis – "like he subconsciously willed it, you know?"

Janet was a great believer in people subconsciously willing things she felt they ought to feel more responsible for than they did. Even when she had told that couple with the baby that they wouldn't be able to go through with the house sale and they would have to find somewhere else to live, she maintained that they had somehow willed their own misfortune. "She looked so, oh, I don't know, defeated," she said, "with that long greasy hair, and that awful skirt she was wearing."

Robert, who was proud of his wife's intuition, had rubbed his luxuriant grey beard and mewed sympathetically. Aiden's problem was he didn't know who he was. Aiden's problem was, he had this bitterness against the world.

"It's more like – a cosmic bitterness," Janet thought, but Robert was convinced it was a fundamentally social thing. "He's never fitted in. Always out on a limb, arrogant— "

"stuffy, prim . . ."

"– always right about everything . . ."

"– always sneering at things he doesn't understand . . ."

". . . I shouldn't say this, he's my brother, when all's said and . . ."

"What?" urged Janet rapturously, as Robert approached his climax—

He had leaned over and whispered in her ear, which was pink with excitement, and she drew breath with a pleasure tinged with wonder, as though she had just seen her first rainbow.

Aiden managed to flag down a car fairly quickly. It was still early morning, and there was a regular stream of cars on their way into the nearest large town. Dressed in his beige suit, holding his canvas bag and Panama hat in his left hand and indicating his need for a lift with his right, he was not the usual cut of hitcher. In fact the only reason why the driver of the very first car of all didn't slow down for him was that the lady behind the wheel had thought that he was in some way rather kindly registering his approval of her or her vehicle, with his arm stretched out at a perfect right angle to the perpendicular and an embarrassed little smile seeping over his face as she approached. Indeed this might have been the case. Perhaps Aiden thought the gesture meant, "Yes, that's a well-maintained vehicle, I'll travel with you a little way, madam." As a second suitable looking candidate came round the corner, Aiden ornamented his gesture slightly, with a suggestive little flick of the wrist, which sent his thumb into a sort of windscreen wiper-like movement backwards and forwards, implying the possibility of some kind of negotiation. He met the driver's eye, and the car pulled over, its tyres crunching in the dry gravel at the edge of the road. Aiden stepped back a little, to save his shoes, which he had polished only the night before, then leaned forwards to open the door. A success! He felt like one who has survived a night in the wild, improvising a bed of leaves and bracken under a starry sky. He asked to be dropped at the railway station, where he bought a ticket for Paris.

The train arrived at the Gare St Lazare in the mid-afternoon. He had never seen the station before, and had always found the name slightly exotic. He half expected to find stalls spread out along the quay, selling flimsy sandals and fake ivory goods.

Instead there was just a trickle of people leaving the train, banging the doors emphatically behind them, as if to say, "That's quite enough of that!" Aiden had never understood why people did not realise that in fact it was quite unnecessary to slam a train door. He had tried to demonstrate this by vivid example over the years, every morning (twice – on and off) and evening (likewise) on his way between the suburb where he lived and the town centre station, close to the school where he taught. All you had to do was step cautiously from the train (once it had reached a standstill, as the notices advised), with your briefcase in your left hand, using your right to twist the door handle very gently through a quarter of a turn. This drew in the snib so that the door could be closed as softly as if you had just crept out of the room of a sleeping child. Four times a day he had performed this stealthy trick, while all about him the clash of metal on metal shook the carriages in their gauges. To him the gentleness of the movement represented a tiny triumph of order and reason, like the sharpening of a pencil, the neatening of a pile of books on his desk. He felt it was quite possible that someone rather like himself had written the Creation story, with God methodically creating a little bit each day and then having a rest. Just calmly and quietly going about His business, gently does it. Definitely not a big bang. Oh, please, no, not a big bang.

Paris was warm and his burden was light. He set off in the direction of the river, passing the deep burgundy-painted cafés with their brassy pavement tables and waiters moving crisply about with their note pads, rather, he thought as though they were booking their customers for parking offences. The idea put him off stopping for a cup of tea, and instead he turned in the direction of the area between Les Halles and La Bastille, where he reckoned he would still be able to recognise the hotel where he had stayed in 1963, when he had spent a night on his way to a job interview in Switzerland. He had not been offered the post, that of junior French master in a small international school, but it was the most glamorous thing he had ever nearly done, and he remembered the whole trip with wondering nostalgia, laced with the smell of the metro and croissant. In fact he had spent almost the entire time on one train or another, and Switzerland had been so heavy with cloud that he might as well have been in Norfolk going to visit Audrey and her mother, but the few hours in Paris had coloured it all, as though the whole episode had been written on scented paper.

He crossed the wide boulevard at the lights, waiting with a group of young people for the little green man. As soon as the sign appeared, they swarmed in front of the waiting cars, and for a moment Aiden was tempted by habit to stand in the middle of the road and shepherd them all across, with a mixture of protectiveness and irritation, which was the manner he had developed on school trips, a sort of irascible Saint Christopher. "Come on, come on, out of the way, quickly now, Dankworth, stop playing the fool. Hopwell, I won't tell you again!" A nasty face that boy had, always chewing something, though if he'd told him once he'd told him a thousand times, despite having so often threatened not to tell him again. What exactly had he meant when he said that? What a silly expression! As if the next time the boy could expect to get away with it unadmonished. It was not a phrase of his own making, he must have picked it up from the other teachers. And yet it was half familiar from another context . . . Audrey, the waiting taxi, the dark figure out on the street holding open the car door, his last words to her as he stood in the doorway of his own home, not seeing her out, just watching her leave, and calling into the night, "I won't ask you again!" Once was enough for any man. You couldn't plead with a woman and still have her respect you. Or so he had believed.

He made his way down the street, walking quickly, overtaking couples who stood hesitantly outside cinemas and bars, past tourists, planted like trees in his path, rooted deep in the network of lines printed on the map before them, past red-coated fishmongers flipping open oysters at their stalls as they chatted to their customers, not even checking, he noticed, to see whether there was a pearl inside. The chances were fairly slim, but not to look seemed to show a reprehensible indifference to the possibility of good fortune. He had attended a rather unpleasant staff meeting once, about the "viability" (though what it had to do with money he couldn't imagine; did they mean advisability?) of continuing to insist on one year of Latin before the adoption of the second foreign language. As head of French, which every child had a chance to gnaw at, with however ghastly an outcome, Aiden was rather regretful that the issue did not immediately affect him. The German teacher, who, he suspected, was none too sure of the difference between a conjugation and a declension herself (he had had to correct her once, in front of several other members of staff), had quoted some line from Bertolt Brecht about preferring a healthy oyster to one who has produced a pearl in response to the irritation of a grain of sand. Aiden wasn't actually all that keen on oysters himself, but he was all in favour of the production of pearls. The German teacher had even taken to the use of the term in a derisory way: Mr Goodman's little pearls. The precious few, who had loved his subject and had made it all worthwhile, who had entered with him into Arcadia and had understood. Mr Goodman's little pearls. It put him in the mind of a novel he had read at college about a man who was so rich that he was able to indulge a natural tendency to decadence by encrusting the shell of his pet tortoise with rubies and emeralds and having it roam all day through a deep pile carpet. The character would just occasionally catch a sparkle of emerald as its reptilian porter waddled slowly across the room. Aiden thought it was one of the most hideous ideas he had ever come across.

He found he was standing in front of a shop which sold very expensive shoes for women, staring hard at a pair which seemed to be made out of crocodile skin, with a little gold chain across the toe cap. While he had been thinking of other things, the strange image of the pair of shoes had left a print on his mind, and as he turned down the Boulevard Haussman, he began to examine it with a feeling of repulsion. It was not that the shoes were of crocodile – he didn't give two hoots about that, though he could have named at least three colleagues who would probably have marched straight in and started ranting at the shop assistant. Perhaps it was just that there is almost nothing quite so smug looking as a pair of expensive shoes just sitting in an empty window, neatly side by side. They represented the poise of a certain type of woman. He ran over the women he knew who might have worn them – there were none. For a moment he felt a bit like the prince in Cinderella, desperately trying to force the foot of this and that woman to the shoe which told him everything he knew of its owner.

And then it came back to him, and he knew who would have worn them, when she grew up, and why he had stood looking at the shoes for several minutes while he was thinking of Mr Goodman's little pearls. And he allowed himself for a second to remember why he was here, why he hadn't been able to return to England with his brother and why when term started in two days' time he would be untraceable, and would have to send a letter or a telegram or whatever was possible these days to explain that he was not coming back, to apologise for not giving three months' notice (and to express the hope that his pension would not be in any way prejudiced by this unavoidable course of action).

It would have to be a letter. There was too much to say for a telegram. In fact for once, he believed he could have filled exactly the amount of space available on a picture postcard; for once he had something to say that would come out at exactly five sentences. It was rather a shame that it would be so unsuitable a way of bringing his career to a close. He could try for something apposite. A picture of Père Lachaise Cemetery perhaps? Les Invalides? But of course that would reveal his whereabouts. He didn't want that at the moment. He wanted to have his crisis, or whatever it was, where he was invisible even to anyone's mind's eye. It seemed to him that the only reliable way to convey a brief, unrevealing message to the headmaster would be to send it via Interflora, no flowers. This seemed to him at once such a good and yet such a thoroughly unconventional idea that he wondered whether he might not be on the brink of one of those rather radical personality changes that seemed to afflict austere northern European men when they travel abroad in novels – think of Aschenbach, or those people in Gide, all falling to pieces and or catching syphilis or eating over-ripe strawberries. Those people had never seemed very convincing to him. The idea that austerity of thought and manner might be in him devices of self-restraint, rather than the perfectly adapted channel of his natural tendencies, had only ever occurred to him when he had read the interpretation in another's eyes. They would not let him rest the way he was;

they would have it that he had been traumatised into austerity by some searing playground incident, shriven to chastity (he was unmarried) by a wanton mother, tied, stake-like, to his dignity by the negative example of a brawling father. He saw Freudianism as another manifestation of decadence – for like decadence, it blamed everything on the past, or, at least, decadence always had a Freudian explanation.

It took him over an hour to find the hotel. It was in a little cobbled street just west of the Marais. He crossed the Rue Sebastopol just north of the Place Beaubourg, narrowly missing a confrontation with the Pompidou Centre, and stopped well short of the Place de la Bastille, where the new opera house gleamed like a huge ingot amid the whirling traffic. He threaded through the streets like a man looking up a word in a dictionary, for whom each element is nothing more than an indication of the whereabouts of what he seeks.

The name had changed – it had been, oh, what had it been? *Hôtel Dauphine*? *La Régence*? Something surprisingly royalist. There had been a very nice lady in charge, who had clucked at his rather good French, and mentioned a visit she had once made to Lyme Regis. This was it, definitely, but it now had a neon sign in pink, edged with green: *La Jacarande*.

He opened the door and noticed that the handle was greasy and slipped in his palm. As he stepped into the vestibule his nostrils picked up a whiff of spiced meats. Inside, he recognised nothing. To his right stood a collection of large potted plants, real or artificial, he could not tell – he tended to regard all indoor plants as artificial, in the same way as he considered domestic birds in cages as not really live. Set into the wall, which was panelled with thin strips of palely varnished pine, or even balsa, was a large fish tank, where a hideous pink and black flat fish, dressed to the nines as for some gruesome Christmas dinner dance, was wafting motionless, under the arch of a miniature subaqueous cathedral. The desire came to Aiden, not in a flash, but growing with a kind of contemplative relish, to punch his elbow through the glass. He could almost feel that there would be no sudden gush of water, no flailing fish to be trodden underneath the sole of his shoe, that the broken glass would simply reveal the apparatus of trick photography, a row of tiny coloured bulbs and some spinning silhouettes.

To his left was a reception desk, which was unattended. Behind was a row of pigeon holes, each numbered, with hooks for the key of each room. Although it was only mid-afternoon, many of the keys were missing. To the right of the pigeon holes was a large print of a Swiss chalet in spring time, with snow-capped mountains and cows. An amber-coloured curtain of synthetic velvet was drawn across a concealed door. Aiden had the distinct impression that someone was waiting behind it, like an actor during the playing of the national anthem, making lewd gestures at the audience and whispering "*merde*" under his fetid breath for luck.

The curtain flicked aside, and out came a round little man in a vest and trousers. He spoke with the intonation, but not the volume, of someone trying to convey a message to another person standing on the opposite bank of a very wide river, which created a very odd effect. He supposed Aiden wanted to see the *patronne,* and winked. Aiden was very much mistaken if that wasn't a Marks and Spencer vest he had on.

The little man twitched the curtain to one side and shouted through, "*Eh! Lou Lou! Il y a un client!*"

Lou Lou made an imperious entry from behind the curtain. She was small and beady, a little cock robin of a woman, sixty-five if she was a day, and her black hair was cut short in a tufty sort of style that Aiden associated with the late seventies. She wore a pair of glasses on a chain around her neck, and held them up on the bridge of her nose as though they had been a pair of binoculars. She looked at Aiden and then at the ledger which was open on the desk. She appeared to be making him some sort of appointment.

Back out on the street again, he burned up the pavement with shame and embarrassment. The woman had taken him up a wrought iron staircase which led onto a gallery around a courtyard, which was open to the sky. Outside each of the rooms off the gallery, was a large cane chair. In one, a large Marocain-looking girl in a red woollen dress sat carefully knitting. Potted plants again, everywhere, and a greenhouse atmosphere. Somewhere a sparrow flew with frantic swoops, as though an invisible skein barred its way back to the world of free flight. She had left him in a room furnished with an iron bed and said that someone would be with him in a moment. He was reminded of a room he had had in a private hospital, where he had been given a pre-operation injection and had struggled as the world closed in and distorted itself around him, as though the very walls were leering. When she was gone, he seized his things and fled down the fire escape. Two large aluminium bins gave off a rancid stench of uneaten lunches and as he lurched into the street a dog began to bark. He began to walk towards the river, checking over his shoulder that he was not followed. Soon he reached the Place des Vosges, where sixteenth-century apartments had once lodged the royal household, and now the very rich lived in very small portions of the former lodgings. He crossed the river by the Pont d'Austerlitz and walked up alongside the cool, quiet flow of water, in sight of the spires of Notre Dame.

Outside the cathedral there was barely room to move. Groups of tourists bunched round their leaders, who were checking numbers and waving rolled up newspapers to attract attention. Aiden sat on a bench in the paved area before the west door, and fanned himself with slow trance-like movements of his hat. He was suffering the malaise of the familiar, yet unknown, that contempt bred by the prostitution of an image in books, magazines, picture postcards and on film, which renders the lovely unlovely and the majestic mean. He thought of Pascal, who had asserted that even the greatest philosopher of reason would refuse to walk a plank connecting the two twin towers of Notre Dame. He wondered if the thought were connected in any way with the idea of the leap of faith and his head began to swim.

On the whole he could not be pleased with the building. His guide book told him to consider it the definitive masterpiece of French Gothic art, possessing perfect unity combined with total clarity of exposition. Well all right, he thought, but what do they mean? Was it like the perfect essay, presenting one overwhelmingly persuasive argument whilst fluently citing minor illustrations which demonstrated *in parvis* what the whole seemed to convince of like a punch to the mind? The house of

God – as though He could be found At Home there on Sunday mornings for discussion of the advisability of double glazing the rosary window. My body is my temple, no no, that was worse than ever, surely He couldn't live there! Should he try and see the building as a representation of the innate idea of God, which Descartes had suggested was implanted in our minds by God Himself, to be, as it were, an artist's mark impressed on His work? If so then what were all these bits and pieces doing, stuccoed across the great design like so many little nit-picking clerics having vicious little colloquies in the shadows? The trouble was that when people talked of harmony, Aiden often couldn't see it at all. He couldn't hear it either. He could only understand it as simplicity. The heaviness of the world bore down upon him as he sat alone on the slatted bench, the pullulating clutter of creation heaving about him like the sea, a manic whirligig around the minute fulcrum of his own pinprick consciousness. He put on his hat, as though to protect the fragile seat of his little sanity.

The vast cap of blue sky was beginning to cloud over. He sat in the shadow of the cathedral and watched a boy on the other side of the square who was crouched down on the ground drawing in chalk on the flagstones. Aiden judged he was around twenty years old, though it was hard to tell, very thin and brown with brown-blond hair, which he wore quite long. He was kneeling on a little mat – it might have been his coat, Aiden thought, but his experience of young people was that they no longer wore coats. At his side was a little hessian bag, where he kept his chalks. From where he sat, Aiden could see nothing of the drawing, and his curiosity was aroused by the reactions of passers-by who stopped to admire, never speaking to the boy, even behaving, surely, as though he were deaf, or inhabiting an unreachable dimension, cocking their heads as they assessed the quality of his work. The boy continued to draw, absorbed and alone, and as a crowd gathered round him and he became partially blocked from sight, Aiden had the strong impression that the boy exuded some electrical force which held his critics back, providing him with a magical circle of protection. From time to time people dug into their pockets and sprinkled a little small change onto the flagstones, where the boy let it lie, and continued to draw and to colour and to move about on his knees, so that it was as though the passing tourists were not rewarding him for his work, but rather sought some magical cure at a shrine, or hoped for a wish to be granted.

Aiden sat on, watching, through the afternoon, and the strange notion came to him that there was some link between himself and the boy and that the clue to what he must call a mystery lay in the painting. He would not rise from the seat, though, and go and mingle with the crowd. He would wait for a moment when he could go unobserved. He felt he already had some hidden knowledge which must eventually be made plain to himself, and which made him say in his head to those who drifted by, "but there standeth one among you whom ye know not." And as he repeated the words over and over again until he was enchanted by them, a pigeon flew down from the high buttress of the cathedral and came to land within a few feet of the boy, who sat back on his haunches and held out his hand. The bird fluttered towards him, hopped onto his palm, then flew in a circle about his head, alighting on it for a few moments before flying off back up to the tower. The boy stopped work and looked up smiling after the bird. Aiden resisted the desire to go over and see what he had drawn.

The boy looked down at his picture, softened a line or two with the toe of his shoe, then bent down to pick up a piece of paper, or card, from the floor. This he tucked into a pocket in the side of his hessian bag. He drew the coins together, again with his feet, while he looked back up at the tower, where the bells were ringing for six o'clock. When he had made a little pile, he scooped up his earnings and put them in another part of his bag. He turned his back on the picture, and Aiden wondered whether it was finished, and he would simply leave it there as a piece of public art, or whether he would return to it in the morning, as though his square of pavement were no more than a place of work, and the availability to the public of what he produced there no more than an unintended side effect. He was walking in this direction. Aiden bent over quickly and fiddled with his shoe lace. When he looked up the boy had passed. Aiden waited for a minute or so, then left the bench and went over to the drawing on the ground.

2

Christian stopped outside a doorway in a narrow cobbled street on the Isle de la Cité. It was Friday evening and a soft light glowed in the third-storey room of number eighty-four. The woman he had seen come and go from the building was home for the weekend, and was moving around in her drawing-room, laying a table perhaps, touching a glass with a delicate finger to test for traces. Until the end of the previous week Christian had worked there in her apartment, which was rented out by the month to foreign employees by a bank who had taken a short lease on it. He had cleaned the kitchen and changed the sheets and picked up the magazines from the floor, wiping clean the slate of the temporary residents' existence, for them to return to each lonely evening in the foreign city. Now the owner was back and was gathering the house around her once again, and the agency had asked him for the keys back. Normally he had picked up the keys every morning before he set off on his round of apartments with his little holdall of cleaning equipment. He had only held the job for a month, but quickly these habits had come to feel long established, as though he had brought them with him to Paris from some other existence, like an itinerant guildsman. Now the weather had cleared he had gone back to drawing on pavements. Number eighty-four was some way from the others on his circuit, and he had been trusted to keep the keys until the end of the week. He took them from his back pocket and twirled them on their little metal ring around his forefinger. He was curious to see the apartment with her in it, with her shoes kicked off on the floor and her books open on the desk. She was a writer, he knew. The lady at the agency had told him that when he had commented on the collection of books. He had thought that must be more of a hindrance than a help, like trying to paint in an art gallery. "I expect it's so she knows what's already been said," the woman replied smoothly.

The lights dimmed in the room, as though she had suddenly decreed evening, and at that moment the bells of Notre Dame rang for half past six. He knew that switch, it was to the right of the door, above the table where the telephone sat. He shifted his hessian bag with the afternoon's takings to his other shoulder and crossed the street.

She was obviously expecting someone. The door buzzed several seconds after he pressed the bell. He arrived at the third floor to find the door of the apartment open, but he knocked anyway, since it would not be him she was expecting. He heard her footsteps crossing the wooden floor of her bedroom and she appeared in the hall. He held out the keys, not speaking, since she was still some distance from him, and remembered the gesture from the afternoon, when he had held out his hand for the pigeon to alight on.

"Excuse me," he said. "These are your keys. I've been tidying your house for the agency, but you're back now. I thought I'd let you have them so you wouldn't have to go over."

She came forward into the doorway. She was at least ten years older than him, in her early thirties, pretty, but with tired eyes. Whoever it was she was expecting, she hadn't dressed up for, not in the way women did in that part of the capital. Her feet were bare and she was wearing a dark green dress and one earring. As she looked rather blankly at him, she slid the second earring through her lobe and then twisted it slightly as she held out her hand for the keys.

"I think I may have something of yours too. Do you want to come in for a moment?"

He waited by the window while she went to fetch something from her desk. He looked down into the street to where he had been standing. For a moment he imagined he could see his own pale image in the doorway of the house opposite and his mind flicked forward to the moment, minutes later, when he would be out there again, glancing up, and it seemed as though his whole life were held here in a pair of endlessly receding mirrors and he had no material substance, only eyes to see his own reflection where he had passed.

She came back into the room and held out a card.

"You've been visiting the Louvre," she said. It was a reproduction of Poussin's *Les Bergers d'Arcadie*. "Are you an art student?"

"No. I'm just wandering about at the moment. You can keep it." He touched his hessian bag. "I've got lots of them. It's like my calling card. In fact that means I owe you another one." He took out a second card and wrote on the back with a finely pointed stick of charcoal. "You're supposed to spray it to fix it, but I haven't got any. There doesn't seem much point at the moment, it's raining such a lot."

She looked puzzled.

"I draw on pavements," he explained. "So it would get washed away anyway. I've been doing that Poussin lately. People seem to like it. I don't know why."

"Is this your address?"

"Sort of. It's where I stay sometimes in the summer. It's a good place. For writers," he added. "In case you ever feel like going south. The lady who lives there's quite old, she'll leave you in peace. She's a sort of aunt. I'm going there soon, I got some money for the train today."

She showed him out. She looked so sad and puzzled, he wanted to kiss her hand, or give her some kind of benediction. As he came out into the street the first few drops of rain were starting to fall. He looked back up at the window and held his hands out in a wry shrug, indicating the darkening pavement and she copied his gesture faintly and rather helplessly and smiled.

3

We all know someone a bit like Aiden. He stands unblinking and immobile at bus stops in the rain, tight muscled as a soldier on duty, his stomach a snake pit of terror, coiling and recoiling lest someone should offer to share their umbrella. He walks smartly through the park, averting his eyes from kissing couples, willing them to drift out of his path before he draws too close – and the intensity of his fear is so great that the magic works. He is not superstitious, but his passion for order is related to ancient placatory rituals. An ornament askew leaves a crack in the door where chaos may softly lodge its foot, biding the next slip, the dropped guard, the invitation to the dance. His lodgings are small, and run like an institution, but we will never know for sure how he occupies them, nor be able to observe the exact steps of the slow courtly, solitary dance of routine that gives meaning to his life. We might try to catch him as he browses in the library on Saturday afternoons. He will start in an exaggerated way as we lean over to ask him the time; it is the same response that makes him cough rather sharply and possibly put a handkerchief to his nose, when he has only wanted to make a tiny clearance of his throat – but the small noise would have been too personal, too related to his own malaise, have given too much away. He occasionally attends concerts and plays, but it does not seem quite polite to peer along the row to see whether he has smiled at the slightly risqué joke. It would be an offence against a kind of Hippocratic oath, taking unfair advantage of his appearance in public – an unavoidable consequence of his necessary attendance. It is a Shakespearean comedy, but the divine poet has a Mozartian tinge, and Aiden, his sour Salieri, would that he only walked with kings. The common touch – sharing mugs in the staff room, joking about "the kids", singing on the bus on school trips – does not so much elude as repel him.

He teaches French. As head of the department he is able to assume most of the sixth form hours. Unlike other teachers he discourages the less able from pursuing his subject. He thinks it hardly likely, he says, that any benefit will accrue to them from a study of the seventeenth-century dramatists, which will be occupying a good portion of the hours this term. The choice of texts is at his discretion. Racine figures prominently. Racine, unlike the wanton Shakespeare, has a vocabulary of only four thousand words. Aiden is safe in his acquaintance with each of these. There is little likelihood that any one of them will have alarming secondary meanings.

It was a hot September day, a couple of days after the return from the summer holidays, which Aiden had spent walking in the Dolomites. He was looking tanned and well, and several of the women staff had given him a second glance as he had walked into the staff room on the first morning back. There was something mysterious and alluring about this change in his appearance which made one speculate how it might have come about. A couple of them considered, not quite jokingly, the possibility of a double life, a sultry Greek mistress, an acquaintance in French-speaking Algiers. The young English teacher, watching him stir his coffee at the window as he talked coldly with a junior member of his department, had a fleeting and disturbing vision of him stroking the head of a wraith-like north African child on the cusp of adolescence, who picked his pocket, but made him glad.

"You'll have to show me her reports," Aiden was saying. "I must say I'm rather surprised to see her joining the sixth lowers". (This was one of his exasperating adoptions of public school idiom, a remnant from his few terms teaching at a crammer as a new graduate). "I had understood she was not university material."

Miss Chambers blew her cigarette smoke pointedly out of the open window and ground the stub out on the window ledge. Aiden had a way of drawing in his features in alarm or disapproval which seemed to reduce the surface area of his face by almost half, as though someone had run a thread round it and pulled. He did this now, and the young English mistress dropped her gaze and went rather wearily back to her marking.

"She's extremely gifted. She's never worked because she's bored. Her home background is extremely unsupportive— "

Aiden interrupted with a facial question mark.

"—orphaned, lives with her grandmother, housing problems, you name it. Alicia's GCSE results are a triumph for the pastoral system of this school. The headmaster is very keen for her to continue."

Aiden thought that the headmaster probably would be. He suggested that Miss Chambers arrange for Alicia to visit him in his room at four o' clock.

Miss Chambers found Alicia leaning on the wall by the tuck shop, surrounded by a group of boys. She was chewing reflectively and listening to their talk of the new ice rink, where one of the upper sixth would be holding his eighteenth birthday party that weekend.

Miss Chambers interrupted their circle.

"Give me that, please Alicia," she said flatly and held out her hand. Alicia took the gum from her mouth and pressed it into Miss Chambers's palm with her thumb, leaving a discernible print, like a footstep in cement. The boys jeered appreciatively, and Alicia smiled. The bell rang and Miss Chambers sent them off to their classes.

"A quick word, please, Alicia."

Alicia picked up her bag. Miss Chambers closed her fist around the gum and had to raise her voice against the racket of voices and feet.

"I've had a word with Mr Goodman. He'd like to see you at four o' clock. In the French room."

Alicia had a languid way of talking, as though she were deep in some reverie of white palaces and golden sands. Her white blouse, with its distinctly non-regulation collar, deepened the colour of her skin, a delicate mulatto, and she touched the thin gold chain around her neck. Her fingers were fine as a thief's.

"OK."

"OK what?"

"Miss."

She disappeared into the crowd and Miss Chambers stood looking after her, clutching the little grey blob, moistened with Alicia's spittle, which later proved remarkably resistant to the carbolic cleaning agent dispensed from a plastic container on the wall of the ladies' loos.

Aiden kept a red plastic bucket in his cupboard, on top of the twelve copies of *Phèdre* which, later that week, he would deal out like precious food rations to his new pupils. When a lesson reached its natural conclusion a few minutes short of the bell he would walk to the cupboard and take out the bucket, which he would fill with water from the tap in the boys' cloakrooms next door. As he came back into the room the chatter would die and his pupils would stare furiously at their books, holding back great tidal waves of laughter, which, unheard of within the cloistered walls of Aiden's teaching room, must surely have caused the windows to shatter and crumble in shards and splinters onto the floor. Aiden would carefully wash the blackboard in long regular strokes, very gently, as though it were sick and tender. It was a curious rite, and one which exasperated the teachers who used the room after him and whose chalks slid hopelessly on the glassy surface left behind after Aiden's ministrations. It was like entering a secret code into a computer so that the screen would show blank to any subsequent user. But after all, he could have wiped it with the dusty blackboard rubber if it was simply a fear of disclosing information which prompted his discretion.

He had completed this ceremony and was standing at the window watching the drift of children move across the playing fields towards the bus stops. He noticed with tenderness a small brother and sister who had just joined the school, twins of eleven or twelve, walking a little apart from the crowd, talking solemnly. They were in his first form, had come from a prep school in Berkshire, and already had two years of French behind them. Their father was something high up in the coal board. He earmarked them, like something that had been brought in that was too good for jumble and would have to be priced separately.

He smoothed his hair back from his brow and straightened his tie in the glass of the cupboard door. A small noise of shifting feet made him start and he saw Alicia's face superimposed on the red bucket, staring out at him calmly, though she was standing a few feet behind him. He felt a rush of blood to the head at being caught out in this little vanity and gave the glass a petulant wipe with the cuff of his suit jacket. The chalk dust clung to his sleeve and he dashed at it in vexation, with his hand. Alicia just looked at him and swung her bag from her forefinger thoughtfully, as if she were watching someone else's child at play and would move only if it threatened to jump out of the window.

Aiden sat at his desk and straightened some papers.

"Alicia Fellows?"

She didn't reply.

"Are you Alicia Fellows?"

"Course I am. Miss Chambers sent me."

"I assume that you are here of your own free will, since you have expressed a desire to pursue your French studies to 'A' level. I consider it entirely pointless . . ."

"Yes."

"Yes what?"

"Yes, sir."

"No, no," said Aiden crossly, "Yes, *to* what?"

Alicia looked at him as though he were mad. She dropped her bag on the floor and came towards his desk, which was raised on a little wooden platform, a couple of inches off the ground. She walked, even in her school uniform, as though she trod barefoot in soft, newly washed sand. Her black, glossy hair fell in natural ringlets onto her shoulders, her skin a perfect matt manila.

"I want to do bloody French," she said. "Don't you understand English?", but it was said with a smile, as though she had made a joke for his benefit. Aiden just sat there looking at her for a few moments, then opened a drawer in his desk and took out a file. He handed her a photocopied sheet.

"Bring that back to me in the morning. I'm afraid you'll find it rather beyond you, it's already a big advance on GCSE. But you see the others have been reading up in the holidays. This is the standard I expect from my group."

Alicia took the paper and put it on his desk.

"You can't make me."

"What do you mean, I can't make you?"

"You have to have me in your class. It's a right. I got good marks in the exams."

"Unfortunately," began Aiden, "a certain level of accomplishment at GCSE does not necessarily indicate that the child – "

Alicia picked up the sheet of paper and went over to perch on the radiator. Aiden stopped talking, aware that she was simply not listening to him, so that it would not be an admission of defeat to trail off in mid-sentence, simply an economy. She waved to someone down below, and Aiden thought that in her smile whoever it was would be able to read the whole story of her present encounter. He wondered if there was someone waiting for her at the gate. Alicia read the first sentence and translated quickly.

Aiden was surprised. She had put down the paper in front of him and was picking up her things.

"Very well. I'll expect you tomorrow. You'll find details of the timetable on the board outside."

"I did that already. It's OK."

She paused with her hand on the doorknob and her bag hooked over her shoulder. She smiled brilliantly at him and Aiden had almost begun to smile back.

She nodded with her head at some point below his eye level. "You got chalk on your chin," she said, and pushed open the door.

"What?" Aiden stood up in alarm and knocked his file to the floor. Alicia held the door open with her foot before it swung closed behind her, looking back into the room at him with a lazy smile.

"On your chin," she said. "Sir."

4

To begin with Alicia was unremarkable. She sat near the back of the classroom and spent a lot of time looking out of the window, where the sycamore trees on the playing field were shedding their leaves, provoking the groundsman with his stabbing stick and broom to ever more frenzied sallies out on to the hockey pitch. The trees took their time about it, fluttering here and there, then seeming to freeze for a while; the groundsman sometimes stood out in the middle of the pitch, poised with his stick in his right hand, balancing it in the palm of his left, waiting for the wind to send the leaves scuttling up into the air like a beater on a shoot. Occasionally Aiden would stop in the middle of his recitation of Racine and stare at Alicia in annoyance. The silence did not seem to rouse her. She seemed to be capable of blocking out sound and silence alike, like a child at play; Aiden wondered if she heard inner voices which drowned the noise of the lesson, as though she were watching a television programme in her head.

"Could you carry on from the end of Phèdre's speech please, Alicia?"

In the silence, the other children lifted their heads from the tightly printed text and grinned at one another.

"Alicia!"

She would turn her head slowly, as though marking well the last position of the object of her attention like a lookout on a ship, before bringing her blank gaze back into the narrow compass of the classroom.

"Yeah?"

"We are reading Racine, Alicia, I wonder if you would care to join us?"

She smiled and snuggled down in her seat, stretching her legs like a wakened cat under the table, propping the book up in front of her.

"Where from?"

Aiden paused and enacted that little pantomime of patience that is part of the stock repertoire of the school teacher, clasping his hands with his thumbs beneath his chin, his two forefingers probing the inner corners of his eyes. Then he sighed, and smoothed the page, to indicate his oh-so-admirable mastery of his own irritation.

"Line 49. Théréméne is talking to Hippolyte. *Pourriez-vous . . .*"

Alicia, who was a little short sighted, lifted the book and angled it towards the light from the window. Her eye flicked down the page, as though gauging the whole speech before beginning to read. She read slowly, in a dull, but clear voice, and the words seemed to pass through her like a stream of light through glass.

"Pourriez-vous n'être plus ce superbe Hippolyte,
Implacable ennemi aux amoureuses lois
Et d'un joug que Thesée a subi tant de fois?"

She continued to read, and Aiden knew she would not stop until he intervened. Her mechanical delivery, combining with the strange musicality of her voice, produced an incantatory effect, like plain chant. Her range was limited and expressionless, but her sense of rhythm was flawless, and she seemed to pay out the speech like a silken rope through her fingers. Suddenly the high cool palace walls seemed to swim before him as the voices of princes, queens and half-god creatures aloof from the ordinary trials of the world trembled in the early evening shiver of a warm, rising wind, their reasoned utterances, taut as desert tents, straining with the onset of emotion.

Her accent was good – she had a gift for mimicry. He had arrived a little late for a lesson one day, and the children were sitting around on desks laughing as Alicia, perched on the edge of his own desk, sang, in a low, evening sort of voice, a tuneless rendition of "Zank 'eaven for leetle girls", with unmistakable borrowings from his own repertoire of mannerisms. He had watched for a moment through the porthole in the classroom door, and the scene struck him as something normally only accessed by the placing of a penny in a slot. Sure enough, as he pushed back the door, which was propped half open with a little rubber wedge, the tableau dissolved, and the pupils scrambled back to their seats. Alicia looked up at him as he came into the room and placed her hands on the side of his desk to push herself off.

"If you could mange to adopt the same accent when speaking French you would find the effect remarkably similar to that created by a native speaker," he said as she moved back to her own chair. One of the boys in the class had a reputation as an actor, and Aiden asked him to take his copy of *Brighton Rock* and read the opening lines with his heaviest French accent. Each of them took a turn, and then Aiden got them to do the same while reading from a French novel from the store cupboard. The effect was remarkable. The success of the lesson created a glimmer of rapport which excited the whole class. They had not supposed Mr Goodman capable of such caprice, he had been charmed by their sudden enthusiasm. Somehow he had hoped to find approval in Alicia's eyes, but although she took to the game as well as the others, he read in her manner a secretive condemnation of his method, as though she suspected him of attempting to curry favour. He quickly resumed his role of tetchy grammarian, even dropping the *"Bonjour mes enfants,"* with which he normally greeted the class.

The bell pealed shrilly and Alicia stopped reading in mid-line and looked up at him. He found he was staring at her finger nails, where the cheap lacquer had chipped away to expose fine little caps of mother of pearl and he was reminded of those closed down shops in the high street where the windows are daubed with a cheap wash of streaky white in a half-hearted attempt to conceal the empty premises from view. He breathed in sharply and closed the book in front of him.

"Thank you," he said quietly, and there was a tiny pause before the first chairs began to scrape back on the floor and children were cramming their books back into bags and making for the door. He watched them leave. Alicia was showing a magazine to a friend, flicking through the pages to find a particular article. Her eyes were running up and down the pages, and she checked back to the list of contents to find the page number. When she found what she was looking for, she shared the magazine with her friend and they read the first few sentences together, and their heads bent over the article as though they were following a hymn sheet in church. Alicia finished first, and looked up at Carol with a smirk on her face. Aiden picked up the two books on his desk and bounced them lightly on the surface in front of him to make a neat edge. The girls both looked up with a start and burst into laughter. Still laughing, Alicia grabbed her friend by the arm and dragged her out into the corridor. When Aiden went next door to fill up his bucket they were leaning against the wall, still laughing like demonic mechanical dolls that must laugh and laugh until the clock winds down, and Aiden lifted his head into the air and pretended, in the manner of his noble seventeenth-century heroes, to be insensible to the peck and worry of this little tainted world.

5

After a comfortable night in a hotel near the Quai d'Orsay, Aiden decided to go to the Jardins du Luxembourg. He had never been there before, and was pleased with what he found. They were very neat and tidy, but the flower beds, for all that they they were rigorously formal, had a gaiety normally associated with freer, more English types of planting. He noted the almost profligate use of annuals, some of which would certainly have to be replaced before the end of the summer. That at least fitted in with his preconceptions. He had always had a picture of the gardens and palace being much more florid and baroque, because of associating Luxembourg with luxury items like tax-free watches, which is why he had always thought Luxembourg itself appropriately named – that first syllable couldn't just be coincidence. It seemed a suitable place to sit and consider the life to come, which was so surely going to be different in almost every way to that which had preceded it that it would have to be very carefully planned, being unfamiliar and possibly dangerous. He was not at all sure how one went about it. Obviously the geographical leap was something quite considerable to start with. Distance could be extraordinarily useful, creating sweeping effects with a very simple kind of effort. Done that bit, he thought. He was as much of a *tabula rasa* as any man of his age could hope to be. Financially, he was reasonably secure, for the time being at least. English lessons were the usual recourse of men in his position. He didn't feel much like Christopher Isherwood at that moment, but it was an option.

What he wanted was to be unblemished. That was his main driving force. He felt that life had always been against him, showing up his weaker sides, leering back his own unflattering image when it really would have cost nothing to be a little kinder to him. Now this incident which had sent him into exile – exile, he liked the word (other famous exiles . . . er . . . James Joyce, Ovid, Robert Graves? . . . expatriate didn't have quite the same heroic ring) – was going to have to be dealt with. In seeking to erase it through the experience with Robert and Janet in Brittany he had merely smeared it all over the page and got himself somehow messier than when he started. I was not wrong, he said to himself, I was not wrong. And yet. He could still see Alicia's face, even, particularly, when he closed his eyes. He had dreamed about it last night in the little hotel room with the orange and violet wallpaper, and had got up to wash his hands and clean his teeth, having dreamed the taste of the blood on his hands in his mouth. What upset him most was the thought of his reputation. He felt that if only he could be cleared of any suspicion, if only his former good name could be restored, he would be able to get on with the job of examining his conscience properly, but with all this false report and maliciousness to cope with he couldn't possibly think about feeling guilty as well, about repentance or self examination. He had to be on his own side for the moment.

He was smartly turned out again, in the austere garb of the ultimate dandy. His mode of dress was almost clerical. It was a way of wearing clothes that said, I despise clothes, but I will not draw attention to the whole vain, narcissistic concept of dressing by doing it badly myself. No free publicity. It was like the practice of washing his hands, which he did at least ten times a day, and of combing his hair whenever he came in out of the open air. Some might have thought it was because he was overly concerned with his appearance, but the "not a hair out of place" concept can actually be the sign of the least narcissistic person in the world. A man may fear drawing attention to his appearance, and therefore make sure that it differs not one jot from the prescribed norm for men of discreet taste, because he is secretly disgusted by appearances. It's very simple, really, Aiden thought, why must people always complicate matters by dragging up the subconscious. If I have a subconscious, he mused, I am certainly not aware of it.

The morning was coldish for June. A crowd had gathered before a flight of steps. A man with a megaphone was waving them back. (Aiden had his own theory about men who wielded unnecessary megaphones. He had developed it while sitting on a solitary classroom chair keeping scores on the touch line of the running track last sports day, and honed it to a keen point as his loathing for the priapic Mr Foxton, master of physical fitness, had assumed increasing importance in his life). They shuffled in retreat towards the flower bed in front of Aiden, determined to hold their positions, to reserve their right to observe whatever happened in a public garden. At the top of a flight of steps was a girl of about nineteen or so. She was wearing a long Miss Havishamish sort of wedding dress, romantic and cobwebby, and over her shoulders was draped a huge army greatcoat. Her head, and this Aiden noted with alarm and felt that if the girl had been a little bird, which she certainly looked like, he would have reported her minders to the RSPCA, was shaved down to within half a centimetre of her skull, but a looping tracery had been artfully left in relief, as though her head were a patina-ed fabric, luxuriant to the touch. He imagined running his hand over her head, and felt suddenly disturbed. He was not used to being aroused by abstract images, by his imagination. She had a tiny pale face with heavy eyebrows and looked as though she hadn't eaten anything but gum, which she now chewed in a vaguely derisory way, for a month. She also looked, Aiden thought, extremely cold.

At a signal from the man with the megaphone, she stood up and let the coat swing open, her hands now deep in some pockets which must have been sewn into the dress. When she stood up Aiden noticed that she was wearing heavy Doctor Marten shoes, as though she had forgotten to change. She began to walk slowly down the steps, with a hard rodent look in her eyes. The coat swung from side to side. Aiden was repulsed by this as an image of beauty, and at the same time fascinated by the spectacle. There was something grotesque about the whole scene, something which profoundly disturbed him. The girl looked like a criminal. She did not look at all like a prostitute. He could see she was a model, but her naked, startled, *cold* look made it seem as though they were somehow experimenting on her and she had not the will to protest. Every time she reached the bottom of the steps the director would wave her back up, and she would turn, in her heavy, too big clothes and clomp up the steps again with an entirely different walk.

Time and again she repeated the sequence of steps, and the crowd, whilst remaining constant in size, was entirely different in its constitution after about twenty minutes, as some people moved on and others attached themselves, so that Aiden was soon the only person who had been watching from the beginning and he began to feel that he alone knew the girl. It was as though she were in a laboratory and they were testing her learning capacity through repetition, trying to ascertain some statistical fact which could only be established through long and relentless reperformance of the same trick.

Down she came again, and again Aiden marvelled that she caught no one's eye. He had been sitting directly opposite her for half an hour and her gaze never once engaged with his. Suddenly the man with the megaphone gave a cry, as though of pain, but it turned out to be of anger. He dropped his instrument on the grass verge behind him and crouched down on the path, while the other members of the crew fell completely silent and stared at him, some of them already half in retreat. Then the man, a vicious looking sort of fellow in a leather jacket and a worker's cap, which Aiden had enough innate political acuity utterly to despise on sight, stood up slowly, walked halfway up the steps until he was just below the girl, and almost on a level with her. His shoulders seemed to jerk upwards, then very quickly, as though he feared someone might intervene, he lifted his hand and slapped her hard across the cheek.

For a couple of seconds perhaps, no one reacted, and for a moment Aiden wondered whether this was not the denouement of whatever it was they were filming, and hoped rather weakly that the man might produce some luxury item (hence the venue) which would win her forgiveness. But it was not so. The girl lifted her skirts like an eighteenth-century heroine in flight and suddenly ducked past him down the steps. Pulling off the coat and the dress in ripping movements, as though they stung her skin, she flinched from the various hands and arms that stretched towards her – as she passed, the members of the crew turned wordlessly towards her, as in some over-stylised dance routine. She kicked her way through the flower bed, beaded little head on a stick-like body, like some dessicated seed pod in late summer, as though you could shake her in the wind and get more of the same in the spring. Underneath she was wearing a pair of black cycling shorts and a beige-coloured tube on what Aiden thought of as her top half, so that for a moment she seemed like a butterfly whose wings, outrageous disguise, have been plucked in the interest of scientific enquiry, exposing the helpless little grub beneath. When she drew level with Aiden's bench, she turned and chucked the dress back into the churned up soil of the flower bed. "*Espèce de crapule! Fils de chienne*!" she screamed at the man, and her voice had the desperate screeching tone of a machine in pain. Because only she and Aiden were facing inwards towards the steps and all the other people involved in the drama were looking their way, Aiden had the feeling that he had somehow staged all this, that he was the director of directors, and that the girl was shouting from the wings, invisible now. She began to run towards the gates. "Ariadne!" shouted a woman who was standing with her hand on the megaphone man's shoulder, but she had already darted through the gates onto the Boulevard Saint Michel.

When Aiden left the park after a stroll along pleasant pathways under the trees, he came out on the Boulevard himself. He sat down at the café on the corner overlooking the hamburger restaurant. Ariadne was sitting at a table close by, sucking up frothy pink milk bubbles through a straw. He would have liked to offer her his jacket, as much to cover her nudity – which, though only apparent, was still somehow shocking – as to protect her from the bright morning cold. She seemed to be humming to herself in that preoccupied, slightly childish way he had known his mother to have when his father stormed out of the house after a row, leaving her to resume normality, to spit and polish the façade for the boys. He ordered a cup of coffee and the waiter clicked his heels in what even Aiden could see was a kind of contemptuous reference to his English gentleman bearing, which a Frenchman will often mistake for militariness. Traffic was grinding up and down the street. There seemed to be schoolchildren everywhere. Aiden felt suddenly, rapturously happy at all this activity which was not his, which he did not have to organise, or explain, or fit in with in any way, this unfamiliar, wonderful city which had evolved over hundreds, thousands of years, like some hitherto unknown and yet miraculously advanced life form, throwing open new windows onto the vast, remote possibilities of existence.

Ariadne was hunched over the table, rolling her straw paper into a ball, and scratching her knee under the table. She looked up as a shadow fell over her empty glass and the pavement artist was there grinning at her across the table. He pulled one of the white plastic chairs round so that he could prop his feet up on it. His back was slightly turned towards Aiden, so that he could only see glimpses of his face as he talked. Ariadne was smiling now. They looked so young, as though they dated from a very early civilisation. They looked Arcadian. At one point Aiden wondered whether they might not be aware of the middle-aged Englishman who observed them from a nearby table. The boy was telling her a story. She had drawn her legs up onto her chair and was hugging her knees. She said something to the boy and nodded at Aiden, but the boy did not turn.

Earlier that morning Aiden had bought a packet of envelopes and some writing paper. He now pushed his coffee cup away from him and wiped the table with his handkerchief. When he had finished using the handkerchief he folded it inside out to the way it had been ironed and then used, so that any contagion from the table top would not come into contact with the lining of his pocket. As he wrote, he occasionally glanced up at Ariadne and the boy, so that anyone watching him might have thought he was actually writing about them, a tender portrait of youth.

Dear Mr Capstan,

In the light of the regrettable incident which occurred on the evening of May Day, I feel unable to continue to fulfil the terms of my employment at St Catharine's. Although a whole half term has passed since that unfortunate evening, I find myself constrained in the performance of my duty, such that I now consider myself, pedagogically speaking, less than equal to the task of instruction. I realise that my absence will have placed you in a difficult position, and hope that you will have found an adequate substitute, who might be trusted to pursue the high level of achievement I have sought to maintain throughout my twenty-five years of service to your establishment. When I am next in England I shall contact you to discuss arrangements for the official termination of my contract. Until that time, I should be grateful if you would forward any correspondence to my brother, the Rev. Robert Goodman. (He gave his brother's address).

Then he began a second letter.

Dear Robert,
I have gone away for an indeterminate period. Do not attempt to contact me. I should be grateful, however, if you could contact my landlady, Mrs Coleman of 30 Brookland Drive, and explain that I have been directed to travel, for my health. I consider it expedient that you visit my house and switch off the electric current and water supply, and contact the telephone company and cancel the telephone.

In case of emergency you may contact me—

The bells of the Pantheon struck twelve. The boy stood up. He was now facing Aiden, who had been watching the couple covertly but closely, with that close attention that actually prevents one from seeing the whole, bent over his piece of writing paper, whilst thinking that he had no way of finishing the letter. He felt that to eavesdrop on people speaking a foreign language was an innocent act, not incompatible, in fact, with the pursuit of high levels of achievement in education – so he did it.

"I can't," Ariadne was saying. "I have to stay here."

"You don't. Come down with me."

"I haven't got any money – it's a guest house. Everybody has to pay— "

"You don't. Other people yes, or she wouldn't make any money. But she wouldn't mind you."

"I can't. Not after— "

"You don't want to come?"

"Oh yes. I love it."

"We could walk," he said. "You'd get better there. Everyone does."

"Yes I know. But I can't"

The boy stood up. He seemed to be looking directly at Aiden as he said, "Don't you miss Arcadia?"

Ariadne smiled. "Yes," she said, "Of course. But I can't go back. You go. I have to stay with him."

The boy's face was – what was that phrase again? – suffused with pity.

"Come on then," he said, "let's get you some clothes anyway."

She looked as though there was something she couldn't remember – where she was supposed to be that afternoon, perhaps, or where she had left her first set of clothes. The boy went round to her side of the table and stood behind her while she counted out some small coins on the table. She looked as though she were having difficulty adding up. He ran his hand over her head with a smile, slightly roughly, as though she were a dog, or he were massaging her skull, then bent down and kissed her on the ear. Later, towards the end of that day, Aiden lay on his bed thinking about that moment with a sense of shame, that something so primitive and innocent should have been appropriated by him with his adult mind, transformed and made ugly, a painful, erotic rhythm which drummed with an insistent, synthesised, never-diminishing beat, all from a tremor that should have been left to echo and die in the natural acoustic of an Arcadian landscape.

He paid and left. Passing the table where Ariadne and the boy had been sitting, he noticed that a card had been left face down, pinned by Ariadne's empty glass. He stopped and checked around him, then quickly removed it and slid it into his pocket, walking off hurriedly up the street, almost expecting the officious tap on the shoulder: *"s'il vous plaît, monsieur,"* and for a moment he found his muscles seizing and realised that he had imagined the scene to the point where he would swing round and hit anyone who tried to intervene. He felt as though the morning's images were all interrelated, as in a dream sequence, where symbols hopped promiscuously from one context to another, fickle metanyms with no particular rhyme or reason.

Ariadne and the boy had wandered off down the Boulevard on the opposite side of the street. He started walking south, with that odd, contrary feeling that walking south uphill creates, something biologically askew, like walking widdershins. He was making for Montparnasse, where he had it in mind to visit the cafés made famous by writers he had never cared for, nor ever would. After walking all day, like a hunter who cannot return home until the sun sets, even if his bag is empty, he arrived back at his hotel room at around six. He hung up his jacket on a coat hanger and went to wash. The neon light in the bathroom was viciously sharp and the mirror gave back an image of an older man, showing every crease.

He took out the first letter and put it in an envelope. Perhaps it was the fact that he had written it in the presence of these children – his mind only half on it – that had made him commit the lapse of calling the headmaster by the name the pupils gave him. His real name was Caplan, but being a *gauleiter* of the cricket pavilion and the bike sheds, he had earned himself the soubriquet of Capstan, the strongest cigarette known to man. This address did not predispose the headmaster to view Aiden's communication with anything short of righteous anger and contempt. He had been willing to overlook the incident. The girl concerned had left the school. The other master had agreed to swap one wrong for another and call it a right, ("a right cock up" he actually called it, and almost sent Aiden the bill for having his front tooth fixed, till he realised he got it on professional insurance). He took another job, in a progressive private school down south. He had never been happy in the north anyway.

Aiden took up the letter to his brother. He carefully copied the address on the back of the boy's card – that picture again – and sealed his resolution with a flick of the tongue, which left a tiny cut on its tip, which made it more real, somehow, more binding. Then he closed the shutters, thinking he would have a rest before going out to eat later on.

He closed the train door behind him, picked up his brief case and walked down the steps to pass under the tracks. Up the other side and out past the scrutineer. He *knew* Aiden had a season ticket, and yet every evening he peered suspiciously, then waved him past as though it were a concession he was prepared to make this once, just this once mind. There was a poster at the exit, a blown-up colour photograph of a man claiming to be Aiden's station manager, who was available for sympathetic consultations at the passenger's request. The word "impostor" came to mind. Someone had stuck chewing gum on the end of one nostril.

He had been back at work for four weeks. At five o'clock it was still light, but it was visibly a light which had had its day. It was his favourite time of year. After the plenitude of harvest time, the slowing of the sap pleased him, the leaves growing brittle, cracking almost to dust under his shoes. It pleased him (he always thought of pleasure as something received, not conceived, a *mihi placet*, not a *gaudeo*) to see a grimace of branches, stripped against an autumn sky, and all its summer glory, wasted at the feet of the tree. There was something particularly poignant about town trees, a greater sense of loss and waste, with the gutters mocking any thought of dust to dust, or regeneration. But here someone was burning off raked leaves. He was always astonished by the *rus in urbe* character of these suburbs, the cottagey Lutyenesque houses with their garden gates and roses. It wasn't as though the real thing had been swamped by the city – once there would have been what, fields, cottages, yes, but nothing like this, this was the town offering back to the country a glamorised version of itself, but not before it had ceased to be itself entirely. The fake rural look was, he thought, unmistakably suburban, and thoroughly reassuring, in the way that fakes are – you don't fear the loss or damage of them.

And yet he had never meant to live here. He had only ever seen it as a kind of pending tray, somewhere he could reside while he was deciding what to do with himself. In the meantime he had taught at St Catharine's, which was not particularly convenient – it was the very inconvenience of it which encouraged him to believe even fourteen years later that it was a provisional arrangement. He saw each day as a blank page still, which was encouraging, but at the end of the day he hoped to be able to look back at the blank page and see that it had been duly transformed into a neatly written exercise, with no spills or errors. It was a way of pedalling to stay on the spot. In the present climate, stability was of the essence. He felt he was keeping himself for something that was going to happen later on in his life, as though keeping still at constant emotional temperature (coolish) would keep him in condition for that moment when his noble destiny would become apparent. Other members of staff chatted in the staff room about their growing families, their moves from this house to that, with a pitiful hint of a belief in the idea of progress in their talk. From the outside it was so achingly plain – he almost wanted to shake them and say, "Look! This is your life," not in the congratulatory manner of the television programme, but aghast, as though holding up a mouse by its rancid little tail, "This, I'm afraid, is your life."

No, he had no delusions – he knew this was not it, but that one day, if he was vigilant, something would happen to him – he envisaged it as a kind of dramatic elevation of the type that occurs in Gilbert and Sullivan – we all know that foundlings don't exist, but the conceit that they do facilitates the interesting comparison of different states and conditions, so that although Aiden would not turn out to have been a prince all along, he would suddenly find his talents and strengths and sensibilities taking wing. As Aristotle said, "it is better that our heroes be noble, kings and princes, for in them we see in purest form the effect of the human heart on its reason." Perhaps he was preparing himself for a kind of republican kingship, as others become lay preachers. In the meantime, he was being as vigilant as ever old Mrs Goodman had been as she watched the clock through autumn evenings, as though bedtime were a cuckoo to be grabbed by its insolent beak before the moment was lost. *For ye know not the day nor the hour* . . . His briefcase swung well at his side, like a good walking companion, satisfactorily heavy with marking. They were into a rhythm now. This was their first piece of written work on Racine. He hoped he was in for some surprises.

He crossed the road at the roundabout and began to climb the hill past the playing fields. The retired gentleman at the bottom house was creosoting his fence. "Nice evening," he said to Aiden through the slats, which made Aiden start slightly, like a warder being addressed by a prisoner he has not noticed behind the grill and Aiden answered, "Indeed." A bit higher up he met Mrs Plowden coming out of her garden gate. Mrs Plowden suspected that if anyone on the road was the neighbour of whom everyone says, after the event, he was such a nice, quiet man, always kept himself to himself . . . it was Aiden. "I feel weird, every time I look at him," she would say to her husband, after they had passed Aiden in the street, "Poor soul, I don't know, I've nothing against him at all, but it's always the harmless looking ones isn't it?"

"Nobody ever says to the paper, oh yes, he had it written all over him, that one, do they?" said Ned Plowden reasonably. "They always make out it was something they couldn't possibly have foreseen." Mrs Plowden felt that Ned had hit on a profound insight there, but though she sensed its weight, she could not exactly put a value on it.

Aiden hung his jacket on a wooden coat hanger and placed it ready for the next morning, by the door, removing the two pens from the inside breast pocket, in case they leaked, and his wallet, which he put in the top left hand drawer of a chest next to the shoe rack. These arrangements came so naturally to him, he might have been setting out a chess board or a deck of cards.

It was an ugly house, with a pleasant garden, but its ugliness endeared it to him. The furniture was not his, but through long familiarity it had seemed to become so, so that if he had had to move into new quarters and refurnish from scratch, there is no doubt that he would have gone to some lengths to find replicas of the oddities he had come to consider the only possible, the truly conventional adornments of a house for living in. Gate-legged tables, bamboo umbrella stand, shabby armchairs, with white woven headrests, faded to cream by the sun. A dark red carpet, which did not quite reach the walls, giving the impression that somehow the level had sunk by four or five inches over the years. The walls were painted a pale coffee cream – Aiden organised for them to be repainted once every three years, during his annual summer holiday. Mr Holden, who was a painter and decorator of the old school, made a good job of it. They had laughed together, when Aiden returned from his jaunt in the Dolomites ("See the weather held up for you then, Mr Goodman, shocker it's been here") at the decision of the paint manufacturers to market standard cream under the lofty title of "magnolia". "Rose by any other name, I say, Mr Goodman." The woodwork was washable gloss – until this most recent redecoration it had always been strictly white, but Mr Holden had been emboldened, since his truck with magnolia, to experiment with hues and tints, and had persuaded Aiden to accept that woodland white would be more restful on the retina. What they ended up with was the not quite white, not quite ivory of a brand new pair of false teeth. The kitchen was rather like that of a rustic holiday home – nothing fitted or aligned or matching, but comfortable. The cleaning lady had been in and removed the used tea towel, replacing it with one a shy third former had bought for Aiden on a school trip, because everyone else had clubbed together to buy a present for the bouncing geography mistress, who was leaving to go and dig for soil samples in Morocco, and no one had thought of Aiden. The tea towel was of the instructive variety, illustrating a range of edible mushrooms and their poisonous false friends. Though it was by now quite faded with age, and the third former was married with two children and had a part time job as a cashier in a local garage, Aiden could not say that in all these years he had ever really looked at it. From a drawer by the bed he took out a jersey – burgundy v neck – and pulled it on over his shirt. He ate rice and eggs at the kitchen table and washed up the plate before the spare yolk congealed. He answered the telephone, which went dead as soon as he announced the number.

At seven o'clock he sat down at the table by the window with a pile of essays in front of him, a red pen and a blue pen and a copy of the play they were studying. There were eleven pupils in the class. He could not yet recognise their handwriting but it would become familiar over the next two years. Here was Dickson's paper – well, he'd made a stab at the question, the application of Aristotle's law of three unities in *Phèdre*, but what shoddiness in the presentation. It betrayed a total lack of organisation in the thought. The moment of attack – poor mind to poor subject matter – stab? – pen to paper – stab! was registered in each hapless word represented on the page. He was tempted to write, "Tracing your argument is like tracing the path of a wild animal –

piles of excrement loosely connected by a random trail of muddy prints," but instead he wrote "Presentation! Organise your ideas *before* you begin to write."

And here was Melanie Preston – a serious girl, good material, well presented. She had carefully outlined what was meant by the three unities and proceeded to discuss time, place and action as though they were the three little maids from school – not exactly filled to the brim with girlish glee, but at least neat and pleasing and to be relied on not to step out of line. At the end of the essay he wrote, "Good. But what implications does this have for the drama?" He regretted this immediately afterwards. "Sir?" "Yes, Melanie?" "It says what implication— " "Yes, Melanie, it says that because I wrote it at the end of your essay."

"Sir?"

"Never mind, Melanie, we'll talk about it later on in the term."

"Yes, sir." What a gloomy girl she was. He predicted a quiet career in librarianship and wondered whether, in thirty years' time, as she worked late one evening, meekly classifying and ordering at her computer, the entrance of a bibliographer of world renown – a knock on the door, a paper falls to the floor, the walls begin to shake – this is theatre, Melanie – would provoke a shiver of an echo of Mr Goodman and Racine's three unities.

And so it went on. By nine o'clock there were only two papers left to mark. Nicholas Carter. Ah, the Stud of the Sixth. His prose bore certain marks of influence – NME editorial, caustic and wordy at the same time. At the bottom of the essay he wrote flatly. "You have not answered the question", a statement Carter was to take as the starting point for an angry assault in words and music to the accompaniment of bass guitar and drum kit at the May Day rugby club ''event''. "Try asking me a question, That I can understand . . .," it went, but Aiden never responded to this invitation to continue the dialogue.

The bells of St Thomas's down the road were striking late – he checked his watch – ten minutes late. In twelve hours' time he would be back in front of the class again. "Well sixth lowers," he would say, "we certainly have our work cut out this term, some of us— " he would look over at Dickson – "more so than others. Has anyone seen Alicia this morning? Melanie?"

"Sir?"

"Have you seen Alicia this morning, Melanie?"

"*No,* sir!" – as though "seeing Alicia" were a euphemism for something unmentionable.

He poured himself a meagre glass of port from a decanter on his desk and set it by a table lamp. She would arrive late as usual, her hair still wet from her morning shower. She carried her books in a shoulder bag made of loosely woven rope, the kind you might use for fetching fresh produce from the market. "Sorry I'm late, sir," she would say, winding through the desks to take her seat. She never explained – there was no tale of woe, of missed buses or forgotten hockey sticks – "that's all right, Melanie, perhaps next time you could tell me at the *end* of the lesson, thank you" – and apart from her wet hair and, sometimes, an undisguised weariness in her movement, there was nothing to show that she had even been alive during the hours since the last lesson. Sometimes he felt that she only existed when she was there in room nine, listlessly following the lesson with half a presence. He was reminded of the fairy story in which the seven brothers are turned into swans and the princess weaves cloaks out of stinging nettles which will give them back their human form. But morning comes before the cloak of the youngest brother is finished and in the place of his arm he has a white swan's wing which, despite its beauty, he carries like a fatal injury.

Back at the table again, he took up Alicia's paper, which he had left until last, the longer to preserve the fictional image he had made of her, which had so little in common with the girl herself, but was pleasant to entertain. The white wing of his own fancy had, for once, the upper hand and it was rare for him to succumb to, or even be tempted by, anything that was not the real world. Or rather, his imaginative world was simply a kind of quotidian utopia, inhabited merely by ideal forms of the degenerate world he was obliged to live in. His fancy generally looked backwards, not forwards, it was a process of recuperation, not of invention. Before reading Alicia's essay he went back to Dickson's effort and wrote after his own comment "Fair copy to me by Friday morning."

He was a bit chilly, but it was too late to bother with the heater. He eased about on his chair and straightened Alicia's pages. She had written on alternate lines only. Her handwriting was the most childish of the batch – it had nothing of the affected adulthood you usually found in adolescent script.

Racine always wrote about princes and princesses because he didn't know any ordinary people. They never went outside their palaces because it's better inside – there isn't any mess. Everything happens in a short time because nobody ever goes to sleep, or even to bed. The King – Louis XIV – who was called the Sun King – preferred this because then he knew that no one would do anything embarrassing on the stage. When you get to the end you know no one's going to say "what happened next?" or "there's someone at the door", because there isn't any time or place to have any action in, it's all been used up, like when you die. At the end of French, Mr Goodman washes the blackboard so that no one can see what he's put, and when it's finished nothing has changed. But in fact there's been all that going on in our classroom – then it's like a play by Racine, because there's no mess, or none you can see, at least. This is what Aristotle meant by the three unities. He doesn't understand that if you're OK on the inside it doesn't matter if your life's a mess or there's crap on the floor. All these princes and things, like Phèdre, they're really unhappy and selfish. They think it's fine till it makes a mess in front of everyone, and then they say it wasn't them it was fate. I think that's dishonest and crap.

The end of French. She made it sound like the end of time. Aiden sat looking at Alicia's comment for a while, then got up and was about to pour himself a drink when, unable to find his usual glass, he realised he had already done this once. He drank, and then took his blue pen – there was nothing to mark with the red pen, nothing of which you could say – had you put it like *this* or spelled it like *this* or organised it like *this* it would have been correct – and wrote, "You have used the word mess four times." The direct address to her seemed to exhaust him. He got up and poured himself a second glass, which already felt like the third, because of having forgotten the first one. Then the doorbell rang. His landlady had installed the doorbell and chosen the chime, which was not what he would have chosen himself, and it rang so infrequently that it was scarcely familiar to him, with the result that whenever he did hear it, it was as though the visitor had brought it with them, part of their own apparatus, rather than their first point of contact with his own house. It rang again. He remembered it was Tuesday, scouts night at church. Were they collecting jumble? He had no jumble. He was not someone who ever had anything that could be described as jumble. Then there was a hard knock on the door, the more direct approach. Whenever callers came brandishing a Bible he adopted a technique his mother had always used and excused himself on the grounds that the cat had just died. It required a certain amount of sang-froid to carry this one off and last time he had brought it out he had had the uncanny feeling that every time he said it a cat did die somewhere, in the way that some people believe that every time you light a cigarette from a candle a sailor dies. If anyone had ever accused Mrs Goodman of deceit in bringing out this excuse for not entertaining on the doorstep, in short, of being a liar, she would have said that it took one to know one.

The knocking continued – three solemn knocks followed by a short pause, then three more. You might conceivably expect failure to respond to such a summons to be followed by the imposition of a penalty.

When he opened it, when he had, irrevocably, opened it, he found himself thinking that "too late" could come awfully quickly, like that other night, which of all the nights between it and now, was the only one like this night, this moment, when he had looked out into the street and the taxi had been there ready, and she had gone; too soon it had been too late, no, then he had acted too late, and now he had acted too soon, what he meant was that in both cases it was too late to have done otherwise by the time he had opened the door. "I have to come *in,*" Alicia said, as though it were part of a set of instructions.

His first thought then was that there would be someone watching them from the road, a car, with its lights off, parked between two lampposts, and he pictured it in black and white, which for him was the medium of fact, of information, while colour was for fiction, for things that were not true, so that instead of telling himself not to be stupid and scolding Alicia and sending her off into the night, into tomorrow morning, when this would be something which had not happened at all, he thought he would let her pass. He wondered afterwards whether more people let in strangers by night than by day, even though it seemed even less well advised to admit the unknown in the dark, because strangers who arrived in the dark seemed to have special rights, because they had walked in the night, alone, and either needed no protection or had indicated, by not being afraid, that they were of a kind apart, to whom special favours must be granted, the finding of a stable, the lighting of a lamp.

It did not occur to him to ask her how she had found his house. He did not feel as though she had bridged the two worlds of school and home – as he did every day – by deciding to look up Mr Goodman, who must have some private life, with an address and telephone – he did not think of the phone call and the line going dead – but more as if it were by some extraordinary coincidence that she was here; he could almost think that she had come to find the house, and that he, like some hapless traveller, who just happens to be staying in an inn the night the ghost of the soldier killed in battle returns to find his mother, just happened to be there in that house, so that the extraordinariness of her being there at all was only compounded by his being there too, and the two were in no way causally connected.

She was ill, that was it, she was cold and ill, and it was, of sorts, an emergency. She stood shivering by his desk. It was her, wasn't it, it wasn't just that he had – for some reason – been thinking of her – oh God, no it *was* her, and then it really was like waking up and finding that something you thought was a dream was real, that you'd dreamed it *and* it was real, a double dose, whichever way you looked. Then he remembered there was a way of dealing with the unknown, which consisted of assuming it was an element of the real world which was just like all the rest, except no one had explained it to you – yet – and he said quietly, "Alicia. What are you doing here?"

"Oh," she said, looking up at him, and then past him, "you're going to be nice. I *thought* you'd be different, but it was a bit risky." He suggested by a herding sort of gesture that she should go through, and swept the road with a covert glance before closing the door again.

He was standing about four feet away from her. He found he was rubbing his forearms, and it was quite cold in the room. It occurred to him that unlike a novel or life itself, in which each person has a hundred thousand little arrows pointing off them – he thought of those diagrams in the geography room, labelling parts, points of interest, past history, future direction, background, heredity, recorded knowledge, even rainfall, moments of high drama – yes, Melanie, this is theatre – moments like this one didn't need any amplification; all detail not contained in the moment itself was irrelevant, no greater knowledge could ever augment or intensify it.

"Are you ill?" he asked.

"You don't have to be rude," she said coldly. "Of course not. I just had to come. I'll tell you."

Aiden couldn't begin to explain to her that this was an entirely unprecedented, and quite possibly – he'd have to look it up – punishable action on her part. He couldn't say he was about to go to bed – that wouldn't do at all, but he needed to mention the lateness of the hour, perhaps she would recognise that that, if nothing else, placed her coming to see him very high in the batting order of contraventions of the law concerning behaviour of pupils towards masters in a liberal democracy.

"It is ten o'clock," he said, and she looked up suddenly, as though the speaking clock had just walked into the room.

"I don't go to bed till late," she said. "Listen, I'm freezing. I've been in your garden since six. I let you get your marking done. Was it our lot?"

"Yes."

"I spent ages doing mine. Did you like it?"

"It's not a question of whether I like it, Alicia, it's not a homemade birthday card, it's a practice run of an A level essay. It was deplorable."

"Oh."

"But very original."

"Oh good. Is that good?"

"To begin with."

"Later it's not so good?"

"Not on its own."

There was a silence. Aiden did not want to be the first one

to raise the question. She was no longer in school uniform. It looked as though it was going to be an ethical and not a legal matter. Oh dear. That was altogether more delicate.

"Can I have a jumper? I'm freezing. I mean, just for now."

He didn't want to let her out of his sight, but it was a choice between that and giving her the one he was wearing, which would entail taking it off, and ruffling himself. He chose the second option. He pulled his arms out first and then eased it over his head, very carefully. He held it out. She took it and reversed the process, placing her arms carefully in the sleeves, then putting her head through the hole as though it were a noose, and this the final, well considered action. He suddenly thought of something he had read about the mediaeval practice of reading prayers backwards, that it had been popularly supposed to have a maledictory effect.

"Have you got some tea?"

He sat there looking at her. She was squatting by the cold fireplace, and her faith in it as the warmest place in the room, even though no fire had burned in the grate for over forty years, showed a touching kind of superstition – and perhaps an effective one. Aiden himself always felt warmer in red than in blue. He said, "You'd better come through," like a doctor who has decided to appease an hysterical patient by agreeing to a blood test.

He was glad, ridiculously glad, that the place was tidy. There were no chinks. Armour, what armour? he asked himself crossly as he rinsed out the teapot. He still kept silent. Of course he was panicking. Of course there had never been anything like this before – except the night of nights, backwards again. He had, he was sure, just been rinsing out the pot when she came in fastening the belt on her raincoat and said breezily, "None for me. I'm off." "None for me?" Was that really what she'd said? "None for me?" Suddenly, after all these years, he almost laughed. He wondered sometimes if Audrey hadn't really been a little bit silly, a little bit stuck up, in her nice pale blues and floral blouses, and that knitting pattern cover girl face, the colour of a powder puff. No one would ever have called Audrey Striding Edge, she was more of a pin steps sort of girl, if anything – Mrs Goodman had put Audrey's physical timidity, her air of never wanting to get her frock dirty, down to the fact that she had swallowed an umbrella at puberty. Perhaps she'd got this notion from the credulous midwife, who had got it from someone who had seen it with their *own* eyes, the metaphor reverting to its factual, primitive roots – there's always *one* who remembers, who was there and who *saw*.

Alicia was now sitting at the kitchen table. She wasn't pretending to be demure. She slumped slightly, her head in her hand, and her fingers pushed back wearily through her hair. Her elbow rested on the table. He found himself wondering why no elbows on the table had been one of the prime prohibitions of his childhood. That and not singing at the table. Or reading. He hadn't thought of that for years. Not *singing*? Yes, he was sure, wearily sure, it had been that. Did he ever do any of them? No, to be quite honest, he didn't think he did. He put the teapot down in front of Alicia – he had made Lapsang Souchong, feeling that there was something more on the ceremonial than the chummy side of tea in this choice, and sat down opposite her, placing his right elbow on the table experimentally. Alicia looked at him queryingly, as though he had been testing the temperature of the water and was about to announce that it was OK to get in.

"I expect you want to know what I'm doing here? I mean, it doesn't feel that weird to me, but you know, I do funny things, I don't expect you do, do you? Do I have to call you sir and everything? I think I shouldn't, it sounds rude outside school. What d'you think?"

"I don't know."

She twisted her wrist, three times. (Was he developing a fixation for the past, or had that not been the "I'm turning left and my indicators have gone" signal he had failed on in his driving test back in 1957?) Her bangles slid down her wrist and over the cuff of her shirt. It was a washed out blue silk, crumpled, the shade of a round-the-world matelot's shirt, and emphasised the impression she gave of having tasted distant lands and their unexportable fruits, the kind that wither in a day. She wore baggy trousers that clung to her ankles, and sandals, sprayed gold.

She sat toying with her cup. "It's hot this tea isn't it?"

"You want some milk?"

"No, it's good like this. Is this what you drink? I mean,

my gran's neighbour, he drinks whisky. Like that? Is it your tipple?"

Aiden smiled.

She put her cup aside. "It's nice, but I'll wait till it's not so hot."

Aiden didn't know whether or not to be pleased by the implication that there was no hurry.

He had decided to keep his own participation down to a minimum. She was the one who must explain. She could have no idea that during these last few weeks he had begun to coil his fantasy around her, that she represented for him the possibility of redemption from boredom and routine. His father had once brought home a copy of *National Geographic*, which he had bought to get change for a pound note. Aiden had seen there his first picture of the Mediterranean coastline, a cobalt sea and salt white sand and parasol pines of deep resinous green, almost black to the shoreline. He had loved these pictures, and had kept the magazine rather guiltily under his bed and sure enough Mrs Goodman had reached underneath one day and drawn it out with her face squashed up in anticipated horror, and thighs no doubt squeezed very tight together. Aiden had stood by the window, fiddling with the net curtains awkwardly, willing her out of the room with his unexpressed spleen on the tip of his tongue, which he would have in that moment gladly swapped for a snake's tongue or a scorpion's tail, to sting her with his repressed yearning for langour and breadth. And when the chance had come, with independence and the long school holidays, he found he could take it only in moderation. He travelled, yes, he walked in foreign mountain ranges, he saw the lip of the sea on various European shores, and observed the different guises of the setting sun, but it was only travel. To have done otherwise would have required him to cast too many skins. He could not pretend to himself that if he did this, or that, or dressed differently, or changed his diet, or married, he would be any better equipped to enjoy these sweetmeats, which were never far from his mind's eye, like chocolate to a diabetic, or the alcoholic's bottle of vodka. He read a lot of classical literature, and was familiar, more familiar than one might have supposed, with the Bible, and this was typical of his covert relationship with the exotic – it came in the cunning disguise of dusty books and even, occasionally, filtered by the cool stones and cadences of the Church of England. In Alicia, deceiving, untouchable Alicia, the world of his imagination had sought him out, cocked a beckoning finger and left a trail of scent. And because she was untouchable, there was, despite her immediacy, nothing different about the experience, it was simply that it was closer to home. Goodness me, it was *at* home!

"Tell me what it is, Alicia," he said in the stern but kindly voice of patriarchs in Victorian fiction, "and then you must go. Where do you live? Is it far?" he added, in order to make it clear that he was bringing forward the information for her benefit, not his own.

She put her cup down on the table. "I live in this block of flats. It's in Hindwell. I know. It's miles. I know this mini cab driver. He'll pick me up somewhere, it's OK. I'll phone. My grandmother lives there, we share it. The man who built it got an award for it in the sixties. It's supposed to be like a Mediterranean building – white and terraces. It looks like shit now. I said to gran, I bet he went off to the Mediterranean with his prize money. She likes it, but it's not a house, not like this. I mean this is the country, really, isn't it? Did you ever live in the town?"

"This is the town."

"Oh no," she said, "it's nothing like it." She stirred her tea.

"I used to live abroad, but I don't remember. I was little then. My gran's Spanish, but she always lived here. She was a typist after the War. She got pregnant and my grandad jumped off a bridge. He was a bit funny. She did really well with my mum – that's what she says; sent her to university and everything. You know" – she looked up at Aiden – "she did languages. She did Spanish because of gran, and French. Don't know why she did French. I suppose everyone does, don't they, I mean if they're any good. Saves the school having to buy stuff in Japanese and all that."

She was about to pause, then realised that any intervention by Aiden at this point might be of an admonitory nature, so she skipped on, saying,

"She went abroad, like before I was born, conceived and that. She got a job au pairing for this snooty family in Madrid. My gran says she hated it. She wrote her these letters. It's funny, she goes on and on about how she hates children. They pushed her around and the man, he was a politician, he tried to sleep with her, and she ran away. She stopped writing for a bit. Gran said she didn't worry because she knew it was all right."

"Don't you think," said Aiden carefully, "she might be a little worried about you this evening?"

"I'm *seventeen*, for God's sake," said Alicia. "She knows I'm OK. I often stay out."

"School tomorrow," said Aiden, for the first time in his life.

"Sod that," said Alicia. "I'm trying to tell you. My gran and my mum, they got this kind of gift. Gran says it's a gift. They know things about people. Stuff that's going to happen. Premonitions. I know you won't know about that stuff, I'm just telling you, like a fact. OK? Like my gran knew when my grandad jumped off the bridge. She didn't dare tell the police to look for the body in the river, in case they thought she'd done it – you might think that – so she kept quiet, but she was right. She even knew he'd had his lunch, and he had it early, so as to drown better. Well my mum, she discovered she had the same thing. After she ran away from Spain, over the mountains, you know, like Laurie Lee, she met these sort of hippies – it was in the seventies, they were all sorts, from everywhere, I mean, and she hung around with them and then— "

"Yes?" asked Aiden quietly. He had quite accepted that this was a *récit*, an acceptable literary form, and was listening carefully.

"She joined this gang. Anarchists and stuff. I don't really understand what they wanted, but it was like that then, wasn't it? I mean everything was different, young people and things. She used to tell them when it was a good time— "

"What for?" asked Aiden, thinking of planting seasons, perhaps, or auspicious days for travel.

"Bombs."

"Oh."

"Assassinations. Hijacking." She stretched her hand out across the table. "She never *did* anything. I mean, if it was, you know, destined, it would have happened somehow wouldn't it? It was just reading the signs. Oracles and so on. I don't know. I don't think she changed anything. She sort of believed in it though. Like reading the entrails in Julius Caesar. Or the gods in *Phèdre*, like you said. It's another way of talking about what's going to happen anyway. What's for you won't go past you. Don't you think?" She waited for him. "Maybe," Aiden said, "maybe." "Good", Alicia said. "Now she was in love with this man called Etienne. That's a French name. It's what Miss Sowerden used to call Steve Marks. It used to drive him crazy. Etienne was the leader. He was Catalan, whatever that is. She told my gran – she wrote to her from prison, you know, when it was finished – she told her all about him. He's my dad."

Aiden moved his cup aside and touched his forehead with the fingers of his right hand. Taking it away, he looked at it, almost as though he expected to see blood stains, or at least cold sweat. He rubbed his eyes. Alicia reached over and touched his sleeve. He straightened himself in his chair and poured out some more tea.

"It's all right," she said reassuringly, as though talking to a child about a nasty ghoul. It's only a story. Everything that happened once is only a story . . . He's dead now. He got blown up in an aeroplane."

Aiden was well relieved to hear it. At least he wouldn't be walking in the front door at the beginning of the next episode, wearing a leather jacket and saying, "fuck the establishment" with a Spanish accent.

"My mum had me in prison. Then she got killed. They said it was suicide, but it can't have been because my gran knew. She went out there – all the way on a train on her own – I suppose she wasn't that old then, forty or so. She knew Ali, that's my mum, that she was going to die, and she said she knew it wasn't suicide. She came to fetch me," she added, rather proudly. "It was quite funny really, because Mr Alcock, he's the greengrocer in the shopping centre near us, he really liked my gran, and he had all these jail bonds for if you get arrested in Spain – just for a car crash or something, or parking, and he gave them all to my gran to try and get my mum out. But she was dead. I don't suppose it would have worked anyway. So she brought me back."

This was all so astonishing that Aiden didn't like to interrupt and say he really didn't see why these circumstances, extraordinary though they were, had brought her to his doorstep.

"And I've got it too."

"What?"

"I've got the gift."

"You've got the gift."

"Yeah. The sixth sense"

She got up from the table and went over to feel the radiator. It was warm. She slid her back down the pipes and sat crouched against the wall. She was still holding her teacup clasped in her hands.

"Last summer I hitched up to the lakes. It's really beautiful there. I only stayed two days. It was just to see what it was like. I'm going to go back. I'd see that thing on the telly, about the bank manager and this girl – she's only about seventeen or something. They keep going off there. It was crap actually, but the scenery was great. I slept in the back of this lorry in a car park in Keswick. I couldn't walk that far because I hadn't got the right shoes. That's half the key to life, really, having he right shoes. I got a lift to this place by a lake and I just wandered about all day. I had my camera. I was trying to decide what to do. 'A' levels and that. I don't know what I want to be."

"It's perhaps a little early— "

Alicia nodded. "I wish I'd been born twenty years ago. People didn't seem to worry so much then. You could go off and hang out in Katmandu. Learn about things. People lived together. It must have been amazing. All that music. Everything was beautiful. You're so lucky."

"Me?"

"Oh no. I don't suppose you did that stuff. Grass. Woodstock. Communes and things."

"Hardly," said Aiden, but he smiled.

She clenched her fists, pressed her elbows against her sides, so that Aiden thought for a moment she was about to hop around the floor like a chicken. Instead, she started to roll her shoulders, in a sort of front crawl action without the arms. She looked up smiling. "I listen to all that music. My mum had the records. Hendrix, Dylan, Morrison." Aiden remembered a particularly odious Hendrix who had passed through his hands twelve or fifteen years ago. "They believed in things. In peace, love. Changing the world. It was all new. Now, you listen to Nick Carter and his mates, they've got this band, all they play is bloody Purple Haze over and over and over again. That's ironic, isn't it? Twenty years later. Oh," she said, as if she had been being thoughtless, "you don't understand all that, do you?"

"Not really." 1970, '71. It had had no meaning for him at the time, and certainly had none now. He had been vaguely aware of a lot of pretentious talk going on in academic institutions, had marvelled at the time, at the gullibility of the student generation, believing that youth knew anything about values. Values were there to be kept, maintained. The idea of creating new ones was absurd, a contradiction in terms. It would upset the whole delicate balance of the moral economy. The world had seemed to him to be pedalling in mid air. Robert, he remembered, had fallen for a lot of it. In May '68, Aiden had been a student. He had taken his *Collins Guide to the Sea birds of Northern Europe* and gone out to the islands for a week.

"You were in the Lake District, I think," he prompted.

"Yeah. It was evening. I'd been reading my book. *Tess Of The D'Urbervilles.* Miss Booth said we had to read it in the holidays. It was good, but I'd been reading it all day, and when I finished it, I felt really empty, the way you do. I hate it when things end like that. In fact" – she looked up at him with a frown – "it makes me really angry. Like the edge of a cliff. There's just nothing. It makes your stomach hurt. Sometimes it's like a confidence trick – you fall for it, and then you feel like shit afterwards, you think things might have changed, but it's just another book. Perhaps I'll write a book one day. That goes round in circles, so people can drop it gently, or it comes to an end so slowly, no one notices. My gran says when you're old, you slow down bit by bit, like a pendulum, losing a little bit of energy every day, so gradual, you don't notice, and you lose contact with the world, ever so slowly. She says it's a gift of God, to get you used to dying. Books should be like that. Anyway, there I was, feeling bloody miserable, and thinking I couldn't possibly go back to school, because I'd read the book now, and it would be like that the whole way through, old stale stuff, you knew the end, and thinking about going off to Katmandu, except I was twenty years too late, and instead I'd have to go down the job centre and fill in a load of forms, so I could get a job on a checkout, so I could earn some money to go and buy some crappy CD at the end of the week to cheer myself up and it would be some jerk playing something that sounded like Deep Purple, like what is it, my gran says, old wine in new bottles. I hate all that. I *hate* being young now."

She blinked after a moment, and a tear appeared in the corner of each eye, and wandered slowly down her cheeks, picking a gentle path. Aiden was moved by her hopelessness. She was a stray creature in time, he thought.

She stood up and came back to the table. "I chucked the book into the lake. It was a bit a of mistake really, because I had to go and buy another one, but it felt all right. And then I saw you."

"Me?"

"I saw you on the shore of the lake. I didn't recognise you at first, I mean, I couldn't put a name to you. I thought you might have been someone off the telly, a news person on holiday, or something. Then you started walking across the lake. You were cutting off a corner to come over to me. And you said, 'Don't be afraid.' I knew it wasn't quite real, then, because that's what they always say isn't it, 'Don't be afraid', like in the nativity play. And then you said, 'follow me.' They say that too, don't they?" She held up her hands in a gesture of giving and receiving, rather like a singing instructor describing the production of the voice from the diaphragm. "Don't be afraid. Follow me."

"But," said Aiden, "I wasn't in the Lake District last summer. I was in the Dolomites actually. So it couldn't have been— "

"I *said,*" corrected Alicia, "it was you. I *saw* you. OK, so you don't know yet. But I saw you."

I saw you I saw you I saw you I saw you – it pulsed in the room, in his mind, like the throbbing technique in films, he thought, when they are about to take you back into the past. It was a convention now, but who had first decided that that would be the sign, this repeated pulse of the present, trapped, like a blood clot in a narrow artery? There was no more voice. He realised his eyes were closed, he was listening for something, which was different, altogether different to listening *to* something, it went beyond, the anticipation of the sense experience took away time, suspended all other experience. He opened his eyes. Alicia was looking at him expectantly.

"What do you think?" she said. "I thought about it for ages. I wanted to be in your class. I had to be – you'd said, 'follow me,' so I did. Do you see?"

Aiden took a big breath and pushed his shoulders up. "It is very nice of you to come and tell me Alicia. Now you must go."

"But *no*!" she said in a loud voice, a child's voice. "You can't do that. I've told you, I let you know, I passed it on. I'm *here*. You have to tell me what to do now."

"Alicia, you are tired. You have – I don't know, you imagined this. The imagination is a very powerful thing. We cannot fathom— "

"Imagination's just a word," she said. "It's your imagination."
"That's really helpful, isn't it? As though if you call it something you don't have to understand it any more. Fuck that."

"Alicia!"

"You turned me down. I came all this way to tell you, I've been in your class for three months and I didn't say anything, because I wanted to make sure it was you. It *is* you, and you tell me it's my imagination. You should be careful."

"Careful?"

"Yeah. It's a gift, a vision, If you say no— "

"I'm not denying the reality of the experience – to you— "

"Thanks." She was sulking heavily, there was a wave of anger and resentment just at the point of breaking, held back only by the faintest skein of thread. Then suddenly she relaxed. "OK, you don't believe me. You think I just made all this up. You think I'm some sort of space cadet."

"Space—?"

"Airhead. I'm not. I'm bloody intelligent actually, it's just I don't listen much. At least you didn't chuck me out."

She stood up and took her cup over to the sink, and turned on the tap. The water system gave a thump, and she washed out her cup. Leaving the tap running, she came over and fetched his, and did the same. She left them upside down on the draining board, and dried her hands on the mushroom tea towel. The casual tenderness of the gesture caught him in the throat. She came over and stood in front of him. "I'm going now."

"Alicia." He sighed, the way people do when they've taken a breath to say something, then change their minds about what they're going to say, and want another second or two to consider, so they let that one out, and start again with a new one. "Go now," he said. He didn't ask her if she wanted to use the phone. It seemed out of keeping with the annunciatory flavour of her visit, which had been more in the nature of a visitation, he thought, although he couldn't quite work out what the nuance was.

She started to pull off his jumper. "Keep that," he said.

"I'll bring it in tomorrow."

"No", he said, "Keep it. There must never be any reference to tonight. You must never tell anyone." He looked into her eyes, and she looked back and nodded slowly, and he realised he was already using his power over her, that in some way he was exploiting her fantasy, using her faith.

"I'll show you out," he said and guided her to the door.

When she was on the doorstop, she turned, and he thought for a devastating moment she was going to reach up and kiss him, but instead she said, "I took a photo."

"A photo? Of what?"

"Of you, by the lake."

Oh no, he thought, this is some ridiculous hoax. Blackmail . . .

But,"What was strange," she said, as though it proved her point all along, "was that when I had it developed, you didn't appear on the photo."

As he pulled the curtain to again, and slotted the chain into place he wondered for a second whether he had invented her. He had known there was something extraordinary about her when she had first appeared in his class at the beginning of that term. Had he merely sensed that she had some fixation, which he had certainly begun, in a very innocent way, to reciprocate? He must be very careful to be professional. She was, after all, on the hysterical side. It was a single occurrence. Almost a laying to rest. It was all psychologically quite easily understood, and yet the outward manifestation did have, she was right, a certain magical aspect, the way unexpected affinities can turn your flesh cold or stop your heart for a second, making you believe you have been touched from the outside, by a force not your own, when in fact it's just your mind playing tricks on your body.

He went back to his desk and put the essays back in his briefcase ready for the morning. He slept quickly, dreaming that the telephone was ringing and fighting to waken so that he could go and answer, and realising even as he struggled to regain consciousness that this was only a dream, a fancy, and of course the house was silent and it was night and he should let himself sleep.

The next day he made a smart entrance, crossed the room with a single stride and sat down. The class looked at him in silence. It was Thursday and he had them for the next two hours. He had decided that today he would really teach them something. He opened the text in front of him and smoothed the page. Running a lean, neat nailed finger under the lip of his collar, he began.

"Racine represents the flower of French neo-classical tragedy. We may roughly define tragedy as a serious drama in which a human is placed in circumstances beyond his control, against which he must struggle to assert his dignity and worth. At the moment in which his humanity – and we should remember that reason, the capacity to think, where the animal world may only feel, is perhaps our most human trait of all – makes him most vulnerable, he is also at his most noble. Dignity, reason, self control are stretched to the utmost limit by ungovernable factors such as emotion, heredity, fate, vice in those who surround him. These elements may be said to find their embodiment in what we shall call 'the gods', who will frustrate man's noblest efforts to defend those values he deems most precious. In Racine we find no bloody battles, no tawdry physicality. The stage is invariably bare. Unlike Shakespeare, he concentrates the entire drama in language; the strait jacket of the Alexandrine mirrors the emotional restraint of the characters – yes, Hopwell?"

"Scuse me sir, I need to be excused."

"Really Hopwell, there was plenty of time for that at break— "

"What for sir?"

"For – for being excused . . ."

"But sir I couldn't be *excused* at break, sir— "

"Oh do go along, Hopwell."

"Thank you sir."

"And don't come back. You can wait in the common room. I won't have my lessons interrupted by this – this childishness. You will have to ask one of the others afterwards."

"Yes sir."

"What – Alicia, what were we saying?"

She looked confused, and then pulled herself up in her seat. She spread her hands before her and twisted the ring on her middle finger, a slim gold band.

"You said about the characters being restrained – not showing it." She smiled, and slid back down in her chair, fixing him with interest.

"Ah. Yes, economy. Economy of language. We have before us princes and princesses, kings and queens, who live in a decorous world, untrammelled by want or disease. All traces of bestiality, if I may use such a term, have been eliminated from their lives. This is not social drama. We do not need, or desire to know what they had for breakfast, or," he paused for a little humour, "what, to speak anachronistically, they saw on the television last night. We see human intercourse at its most refined, the transactions of lofty men and women in a highly civilised environment, expressed not, as I have said, so much in action – no thrust of the sword, not so much as the touching of hands – but in the highly stylised language of the seventeenth-century French court. Into this world is introduced the alien element of Phèdre's ungovernable passion for a man whom social restraints, decency, naturalness – he is, after all, her son in law – forbid her to love. You have all read the play. Can anyone suggest to me which moment in the drama most completely summarises Racine's vision?"

As usual, there was silence.

"Come on, somebody must have an idea. Melanie?"

Melanie looked up grudgingly, folded her arms and locked her ankles together defensively under the desk. She had been taking notes as Aiden talked. She started to rummage through them visually, as though Aiden was mistaken if he believed he had provided adequate information on which to base an answer to such an inquiry. She shook her head.

"You won't find the answer there, Melanie, I'm asking you

for your reaction to the play. Which moment seems to you the most dramatic?"

"The end?"

"I see. And why do you think that, I wonder?"

She appealed by shrug to the others. Her attempted insouciance only managed to look like misery, thought Aiden. She had despair written over her face, the kind of despair you might expect to find in the face of a grieving mother after a battle has taken the life of her two sons, mingling incomprehension and utter resignation to defeat. He sighed and turned to Gareth Johnson, who could at least be expected to give a straightforward answer.

"Johnson?"

"When she's been talking to Hippolus— "

"Hippolyte— "

"Hipp— "

"Hippolyte."

"Hippo— "

"Potamus!"

Aiden turned on the voice like a snake and spat him down.

"Get out Dickson!"

"Sir— "

"Just get out. Go on – now! Take your bag with you."

Dickson got up from his desk, scraping it across the tiled floor as he did so. He banged his way out of the room. As he crossed in front of Alicia he looked down at her with a grin, but she did not notice. She had her book propped up in front of her and was running her finger down a page slowly, quite absorbed in her reading. He banged the leg of her desk noisily with his bag, a gesture which Aiden identified as the male adolescent equivalent of a flounce. He noted the unpleasant stipple and boil of the boy's chin, as though whatever hormones governed the condition of his complexion were having a thorough clear out. He ran his fingers over his own smooth underlip, regaining possession, and waited until the door had shut. He had a pleasant sensation of eradication, that the war against the messy and irrational was being splendidly waged on this side of the text at least. He beamed at the remaining seven pupils – Witt and Thurlow being absent in the service of the rugby team. Gareth

Johnson said, grinning, rather too widely for it to be entirely contingent on his inability to pronounce the word 'Hippolyte', "She goes from '*vous*' to '*tu*'."

"Good. Yes, that's an important breaking point. Anyone else? Alicia?"

She had only to lift her eyes towards him to gain his attention. Melanie, who had been about to try to redeem herself with a bright suggestion, converted her hovering arm movement into a rather, Aiden thought, implausible gesture of biting off a thread on the forearm of her blazer. We are all frail, he thought, every one of us, and in anticipation of Alicia's contribution, he smiled generously.

"At the beginning."

"Yes?"

She squinted at the text. Then back at Aiden. "It says— "

Aiden picked up a piece of chalk and went to stand by the blackboard, like a game show host who can't wait to chalk up those extra points.

"—She sits."

He smiled beatifically across the room at her. "Thank you," he said. "She sits."

The others scrummaged in the text to find the direction. Aiden held up his hand.

"Find it later, please," and he wrote in his rather baroque hand, "*Phèdre s'assied sur une chaise.*" He paused triumphantly, then went back and underlined the expression.

He placed the chalk back in the little dent where, as Miss Chambers would have said "it lived", and brushed his fingertips lightly off against each other.

"This is one of the great moments in European drama," he said, and sat back at his desk. There was a slight lilt of anticipation in the air, as more than one pupil savoured the delicious possibility that Aiden's chair might, in one of the great moments of dramatic irony known to room nine, periods two and three, Wednesday, topple backwards and land him on the floor. But no, he was safely home.

"This single gesture represents, among the sparcity of physical gestures explicitly indicated in Racine's *oeuvre*, the latent wantonness in Phèdre's character, her submission to the brutish wilfulness of the flesh. She enters, and she sits down, and in that single moment— " he looked earnestly round at their faces, trying to catch their breath with his eloquence – "her spirit weakens. Her flesh has made its demands, and has won over. Phèdre, we know, from this revealing moment on, will be crushed and devoured by the force of Venus *'toute entière à sa proie attachée'* – note the bestiality of the image."

There was, he noticed with gratification, complete silence in the room, and he told himself with a sigh of satisfaction that they had just collectively experienced one of those rare moments of union, when the petty weaknesses of adolescents, their dreadful vanity, their piety in the face of the necessary cult of *ennui* was for a moment vanquished.

He drew himself forward, with his hands clasped in front of him, in a gesture of sincerity. His Ciceronian features served him well when, in rare moments like this, he held the attention of the room, when he had actually successfully reached across the abyss which represented the gap between their view of life and his own, their concerns and fear and his, his experience and their hope, his knowledge and their indifference.

One of the boys asked whether Mr Goodman had seen the play performed. He admitted that he hadn't. "The drama of Racine is located in language and psychology", he told them. They might be interested to hear an excerpt from a recording he had acquired from the BBC. "It will give you a feeling of the cadences of the language. At the moments of highest drama the Alexandrine all but breaks under the tension of feeling. It is," he finished, taking off his glasses and setting them before him, "a most moving rendition." And of all the pupils there in room nine that morning, he wondered later that day, stepping off the train onto the platform, which, if any of them, had recognised in that slight, unconscious gesture, a sign of submission to forces beyond his control which measured no less the frailty of the human condition than Phèdre's collapse into the chair.

The secret tie which bound Aiden and Alicia was all the more precious to Aiden because it not only did not call for any modification of his usual behaviour, it made any such modification positively inadvisable. He was able to enjoy the little ironies which always arise when the outward face contradicts the state of the soul. On the surface of it he remained cool and snide, as he had always been; beneath, where the still waters run, but do not cool, he thought constantly of her. He managed to separate the Alicia before the night of her visit from the Alicia she had revealed herself to be. With the former he was able to be more distantly supercilious than ever, because, he imagined, there was no fear of her misinterpreting what was after all only the face of his caution. With the latter, he was promiscuously intimate – they walked together – often by the shores of a great lake, they laughed, sometimes even ran hand in hand, grew old and nodded by the fire, comforted and grieved. It was a fine romance, and his head spun with all these unrealised – pray never to be realised, indeed – possibilities, of which she remained totally ignorant. He became a great master of pretence, even persisting in snubbing her when they met alone, like some obsessive method actor.

Alicia watched him closely. At first she thought he was angry with her for having confided to him her vision of his destiny. But he had shown no real anger at the time, although she thought that might be a reason for heaping it on now, in what people called good measure. Maybe he was angry with her for being his angel, she thought. Maybe the idea that she knew something, had had it vouchsafed to her, concerning his future, made him dislike her. The prophet comes bearing manacles, chaining us to our destiny, determining our footsteps. It is, historically, an invidious role. She watched and waited, and studied hard at her French, and tried to please him, so that he might be convinced of her suitability for the role of hand maiden should he require one. But he never gave any sign. She could almost be sure she had seen him at the lakeside, not in the flesh, but not quite in the spirit either. It had felt a little bit like one of those farmyard sets you have when you are little, with a sticky sort of board and lots of little animals you could dispose about the landscape at will – she had selected Aiden, and placed him by the lakeside where he had been in the landscape but not of it, and it had been so unconscious and unnecessary that she had to believe it was not she who had done it, but a greater hand than hers, who had placed him there before her. She could almost believe, now, that she had heard a voice saying "Behold".

The other children accepted that she was moody and difficult. She had always been a stranger in their midst, and the easiest solution had been to elect her as a kind of queen, allowing them to worship her whilst covertly grumbling about her differences, her aloofness and unpredictability. Now she was in retreat, most often alone. She spent hours in the school library, where no one could talk to her except in a whisper. Her other teachers were amazed at the progress in her work. She began to enjoy the fact that no one meddled with her. She slipped quietly away into her own reveries as those dying a peaceful death are said to slip quietly away. Aiden presided over her existence, as certain icons will often be awarded governing powers over adolescent girls – it would not be inexact, for instance, to say that her friend Jackie's existence was presided over in much the same way by a certain young Irish actor who enjoyed widespread hero worship amongst a certain age group. Alicia vaguely grasped that Aiden was maintaining a façade, she perceived that he was not unaffected by her – although she quite failed to realise that any role to which she might have appointed him by her disclosure was, as far as he was concerned, a useful illusion on her part, which either unconsciously revealed a gratifying interest in him as, to be honest, a man, or at least put him in a position of influence over her. He was, in this, no more and no less than human. It should not be thought that he entertained any fancy of actually making her his own. He wanted no more than to luxuriate in a certain atmosphere, the existence of which was guaranteed by the simple fact of her presence in the world. In order that we might be able to speak of chastity we must be able to identify at least some degree of desire. Yes, it was there, glimmering, so we can talk of pain and pleasure and maybe even relate Aiden's position to that of the troubadours, in whom restrained passion was harnessed to function as a sort of magic charm, which they came to confuse with, or identify as, depending on the case, poetic inspiration. Or that of the knight at war, whose girded loins and lust, first raging, then, in times of danger, quieter than a monk's, protected him against error and death.

It will have been understood, no doubt, that Alicia's home life was not typical. She and her grandmother had an understanding, in fact if they had one they had a hundred. There were understandings concerning Alicia's behaviour, understandings concerning her grandmother's requirements, understandings relating to perceptions of the world outside their lodgings, which was largely understood to be made up of an unpleasant combination of soft underbellies and things nasty and brutish. And there was above all an understanding about money, which was that they hardly had any at all, and that Alicia was required to supplement her grandmother's pension and family allowance from time to time through the discreet deployment of her feminine charms.

But Alicia's activities in this domain play little part in this story. Aiden did not walk into a prepaid room one lunch break and, blinking as he came from light into darkness and, seeing her silhouetted against the heavy red curtain, say in a voice desolate with longing and repulsion "you!" Nor did she contract the *maladie de l'époque* and come to throw herself on Aiden's compassion and live as his chaste companion through the next blissful thirty years of 'A' level marking.

What happened was that Alicia grew tired of waiting and, unconsciously or not – we keep having to add this proviso now, much thanks Mr Freud – decided to precipitate a crisis, which will be reported here with the very minimum of detail. Aiden was asked by the head of the sports department, of whom he had always entertained a vigorous dislike, to officiate at the school dance for May day. This was mischievous on the part of Mr Foxton, and he was most taken aback when Aiden agreed. Aiden sat on a chair outside the dance hall and counted the tickets and was quite astonished at the licentiousness of the affair. Alicia arrived late, looking very peculiar, Aiden thought, and one of the other teachers mentioned to him in conversation that he suspected her of having smoked a marijuana joint at some point during the evening. He said he'd gone through the pockets of her coat in the cloakroom and found nothing. It's all inside her head, no doubt, he said, and Aiden pondered for a moment the idea that she could in a sense be in possession of the drug whilst it was in her blood stream even though it was not in her pockets. When all the other teachers and pupils had gone home, he volunteered to lock up. Once he had done this, he went to his own classroom, where he had left his own coat. He was struck by the strangeness of being there at night, and by the moon, stuck like a piece of translucent paper against the window, which he had never seen from here before. And underneath a desk in the far corner, Alicia lay, undressed, in the arms of the much loathed Mr Foxton, in post coital oblivion, the two of them as guilty as the day they were born, and as unconscious of their fault, being fast asleep, and as Miss Chambers later observed, stoned out of their brains. For a moment Aiden was tempted to do as King Mark had done, and creep quietly, shamefully away. Then Alicia came back to him, the Alicia of his fancy, of his private moments, and he was overcome with a violent desire to expunge the man's life, to tread him into the dust, and he raged over to where he lay, picked him up from the floor by the hair, and smashed his face against the desk, emitting, as he did so, a roar like that of an angry giant. At that moment Alicia opened her eyes and smiled sleepily, and Miss Chambers, who had come back for forgotten car keys, snapped on the light.

"You are going home?"

Aiden stopped short, counting out his notes, and looked at the girl behind the reception desk as though she had come out with some surprisingly bad language.

"No," he said. "No, I'm not. I'm going to catch a train."

"Ah," she said brightly, "you would like some information? We have all the information on our computer."

"No thank you. I have all the information." He held out his hand and took back his passport, thanking her for a pleasant stay. Very comfortable.

She watched him leave through the revolving door. When he had first booked in three days ago she had taken him for a Jehovah's Witness, with his formal clothes and austere luggage, but the absence of an American Express card, of enquiries after the location of the fax machine, or extra mineral water in the minibar, had quickly changed this initial impression. He certainly did not look like a teacher, which was what he had put down on the *fiche d'acceuil*. He looked like someone rather dangerous keeping a low profile, but as the elections were only a few months away, it seemed a bit late in the presidential term for an assassination attempt. He looked sad and imposing at once, like a dignitary at a remembrance service.

He did not have all the information, not by any means. He knew where the railway station was, roughly, and he knew he wanted to go south. He would take a night train from the Gare d'Austerlitz, and wake with the new morning on the Mediterranean, and walk down to the sea and look at the clean washed sand and listen to the cry of gulls. Then he would work his way inland. He had visited the Poussin at the Louvre. It had recently been cleaned for a special exhibition. He had been standing quietly, contemplating its sumptuous colours with slight consternation, when an opulent blonde lady who looked, he thought, like the kind of woman who some forty years previously might have been some sort of heiress, turned to him in such a way that the full weight of her heavy perfume descended on Aiden like tear gas and said in a voice deep with the kind of insight you felt couldn't have come from the pages of a book, *"très troublant, Monsieur, très troublant."* He turned back to the canvas and saw it afresh through stinging eyes.

There had been a shower around six o'clock that evening and the passing cars threw up a light spray and steamed in the evening sun. His walk took him past the bolted cages of livestock lined along the pavement of the Rue de Rivoli. A long, red-necked turkey had squeezed its head through the bars to peck thirstily at a puddle just beyond its reach, looking dangerously like someone who had done the inadvisable on an Italian train. Rabbits and geese, and a tiny baby goat huddled shoddily amongst their droppings and discarded food. A man came out from one of the shops and started loading the cages into the back of a lorry, exciting a flurry of indignant squawks from the geese. Aiden felt disgust at the sight of so much flesh, and it was disgust at the flesh itself, not sympathy with it. The manner in which the animals were presented made them look like the very tail end of an evolutionary mistake, to be shuttled off to another planet to work out their own degenerate fate, hybridising themselves into extinction. Viewed in the glorious evening sunshine, against the backdrop of lovely buildings, and the quiet river flowing smoothly to the sea, they looked, in all honesty, as though they had brought it upon themselves, like ravaged cabaret roisterers caught out in a dawn raid by the police. A listless-looking woman in gum boots was spraying the exotic foliage of the plants. Even the geraniums looked oily and exotic among the bamboo and other flora, grotesquely misplaced, deviant as a bunch of punk rockers walking the fells.

The concourse of Notre Dame was almost deserted. There were no pigeons. Perhaps they were wary of further showers. No new picture either. Employees of the Ministry of Works swilled down the pavements early each morning, so that you rose each day to the impression that it had rained in the night. Normally they left Christian's pictures, but it depended who was on duty. It was still there, its colours faded, no more than a reference to the act of painting it. But yesterday there had been a demonstration, proclaiming itself "anti-Aids" (which Aiden felt really wasn't good enough; "do you think anyone is in favour of it?" he had wanted to ask the girl who had dealt a leaflet into his hand, and which he had accepted without looking at it, like the first card in poker. But he hadn't, because she would have given him a discourse about the origins of the disease being traceable back to scientific dabblings in the Pentagon and, he thought wearily, perhaps she would have been right. But still, the flaccidness of the language depressed him.) Several young people had lain down on the pavement in corpse-like attitudes, and he had been struck by the realisation that they were too young to have seen dead bodies anywhere other than in films, so that the poses were all ones of violent death, limbs flung out, heads twisted to one side, as though they had been shot or blown up. He had wanted to go and realign them all in positions more appropriate to the cause of death proposed. Before they got up and went home, someone had gone round tracing the silhouette of each body with a piece of chalk and traces could still be seen, half washed by the spray, but just still visible, and Aiden had found himself avoiding the patches where the mock corpses had lain, as though it were sacred ground and walking over it a sacrilege, or in its secularised form, an error of taste.

terms of their enrolment [illegible] on their own rate of [illegible]. A [illegible] even to men [illegible] was [illegible] of the [illegible] with the [illegible] [illegible] of the hills.

[illegible]

Part Four

Elizabeth stood on the bridge hearing Mr Heythrop's voice dripping menacingly in her ear: "water's a popular choice" – like a sales assistant trying to help a husband choose a perfume for his wife's birthday. It was five weeks and five days since she had received the ashes from him in his tea-sodden office. A wilderness of time. For a month she had been unable to move – once the decision to leave London for a while had been made, she allowed herself the luxury of hesitation. One evening she had been discovered in the steam room of her health club, clean out on the stone floor, and Frances, convinced that Elizabeth wasn't eating properly, had insisted she come to stay in Pimlico for a week or so. She put Elizabeth to bed and brought her eggs in various forms, baked on beds of spinach, scrambled with peppers and tomato, but Elizabeth's response was listless at best. She brought her trivial magazines and books to read, satirical novels, great classics with no love scenes, a biography of Fischer-Diskau, the Mitfords, but Elizabeth just lay there, scarcely speaking, always polite, until after two days the sound of the children's laughter got her out of bed and into her clothes and a taxi, and home. She spent a day clinically shopping, without desire, except the desire for distraction, then booked her plane from a small travel agency behind Kensington High Street.

No, she thought, not water, it had to be ashes to ashes or dust, not to water, it would create a horrible sort of early-stages-of-a-packet-soup consistency. Her reason had its reasons that her heart knew nothing of. She was hot. She buckled up her handbag. Inside, her constant burden, with its canny screw top – the most reliable fastening known to man. She turned to walk back over the bridge, the way she had come, back towards the old city, wondering whether there wasn't a superstition about crossing water altogether or not at all. Perhaps you should never go half way across a bridge and turn back. She turned round quickly and caught the heel of her shoe in a pavement crack. She stumbled slightly. She seemed to be always stumbling these days. "Oh, I'm the same," Frances had said, when Elizabeth remarked on this at the airport, "I'm always going headlong over something." "I'm not," Elizabeth said, and she knew Frances wasn't really either, that it was pure solidarity. Whenever she stumbled it was not because of her feet but because of her heart. Her feet missed a beat, as though it had been a dance, but the beat came from the heart.

The entire town, including the vast, military-style cathedral, was constructed in red brick; not the iron-red brick of England but a softer, pinker variety, laid long and thin between scarcely visible skeins of mortar. The cathedral was built in the fourteenth century, on the orders of the Catholic Inquisitor, not as a gift to the townsfolk but as a defence against them, a fortress against the heresy. Its presence is not without menace. Someone had told Elizabeth its foundations lay as deep as its tower rose high, as a building reflected in water is dogged by its inverted double. It dwarfed the encircling streets of little town houses like a huge chess piece, when one of the set has had to be improvised, a peg for a king, or a candlestick for a castle. It always looks odd to me, this usurpation of housing bricks for something so colossal. It reminds me of the way an adult who has adopted a child's costume can end up creating an effect which is somehow rather sinister, like Judy Garland in the *Wizard of Oz*, or Benny Hill in school cap and pants.

Elizabeth took a seat at a pavement café overlooking the courtyard in front of the cathedral. She had passed through this town once with Mark. They had spent a night here, although she seemed to think that it had been one of those times when you fail altogether to discover the heart of a place and wonder rather balefully what all the fuss is about until someone says to you a year later, "but you cross *over* the bridge!" and you realise you spent your evening in the scrappy *banlieue* of a glorious mediaeval town.

She would look round the cathedral in a while. Just for the moment she felt a bit leaden. Maybe as grief comes nearer to term its weight increases. Maybe if she hadn't met Will she would have spent her entire life skirting the *banlieue*, never crossing the bridge into the old quarter, with its dangerous corners, mysterious smells, bursts of song and dance, its pestilence and its wild *jours de fête*. Mentally she was on a bridge between the two now, between the conception of her grief and its resolution, and it seemed it was that, and not just bereavement – missing someone, basically – that was causing her this misery. For all her apparent serenity, she *was* miserable, and there was nothing, confessor or no, I could do to help. She never said she was lost, as people often do. It was more serious than that. The world was lost to her. I clung to the association between singing and healing. If she could sing, she could heal. And she *had* sung, but for her it was a purely physical process, so that although it might have sounded fine to an unaccustomed ear it was soulless and mechanical, like the girl in the fairy story who opens her mouth to sing and croaks like a frog. In her own terms, she was croaking.

The second night, when Will came round to her house, she told him in the small hours, about losing her voice.

"I couldn't make a sound," she said.

"I shouldn't worry about that. It's normal," Will said from the windowsill, where he was smoking a cigarette and looking out at the street. His face was lit by a neon from outside, an orange mask, moulding his features.

"Normal? How can it be normal? Sometimes I just don't understand what you say."

He came over to the bed and put his arms round her neck. Sometimes, she said, she would have moments of fear, and she would believe he was going to kill her, or at least that somehow he would be the end of her.

"You'll see," he said, "it won't be forever." And he told her he couldn't stay long, not in her bed, not in the country, but in life. His time, he said, was nearly up. What time was left, they would spend together. Her voice was just a thread she would pick up one day, not lost and gone, just lost. Like the little mermaid, she had emerged from the cool, mysterious waters to find him, and it wasn't easy, though she was happy. Knowing he would leave one day was a kind of torture, every step burning her dancing feet.

It's not the immortal soul that the voice represents, it's the tragic mortal one, so that if there is a heaven she imagined it was full not of angel voices but of a deep underwater silence. She needed to recover her voice to prove that she was still alive, still mortal, not condemned to awful, silent immortality. This seemed to me a strange way of seeing things, a sort of private myth she had invented for her own healing. That, and her inability to throw away the ashes. Had she not told me that atoms were atoms, that her body was a temple, but only for the religion of the rational materialist, who said you'd better hang on to what you'd got, because it was all you were getting? It seemed to me at first that it was this creed that prevented her from parting with the last remnants of her lover, like keeping a lock of hair – even rational materialists can be sentimental. But I recognised another, quite conflicting motive. I don't think it's at all impossible for someone to have two conflicting motives for doing something. Coleridge talks about the distinction between contraries and opposites. Contraries are unrelated, opposites tend towards union. Opposites conflict, contraries don't. Elizabeth's conflicting motive was a feeling that if she consigned Will's ashes to some watery or dusty end she would be releasing him for immortality. Off, up, up and away he'd go. There is a notion that in grieving we prevent the souls of the departed from finding rest. By rest do we mean immortal life or extinction? These are all hazy questions, too vague to be remotely metaphysical, and I only raise them to account for her state of mind. Like Freud, in treating the patient who was convinced he had rats up his trousers, or whatever it was, I feel you have to give credence to the fancy in order to resolve the anguish that gives rise to it. Perhaps I'm not the person to tell her story, because I have no belief, only knowledge.

She ordered water. An elderly gentleman in a linen suit sat watching her from a nearby table as she sat with her hands clasped in front of her, gazing across at the cathedral, which seemed to glow like a clay oven in the midday heat, her face calm as plain chant, her dark secrets bundled up, as Will said, in her cupboard below the stairs. She vaguely noticed him, and was able to describe him to me afterwards. A man of seventy or so, with long white hair. When she tried to pay for her drink the waiter said that the monsieur at the other table had included it in his own bill, and she turned round to find an empty table. "You should have told me," she said to the waiter, but he shrugged and said that the man had simply gestured in leaving to say that the money for both of them was on the table.

There is something about approaching a very tall building, you know exactly the moment at which you step into its shadow, even if there is none because the sun is exactly overhead, more like its lee, perhaps, than its shadow. The Cathedral of Saint Cecilia is monstrous. Vertigo singlehandedly brings on a condition of religious awe. You enter by the south door, having climbed a broad flight of steps leading up under an exuberant Renaissance canopy, which flutters alongside the solid red-brick mass like a handkerchief from the window of a fortress. Mark and she had played a game whenever they travelled, in which one person read a description from a travel guide and missed out all the adjectives, which had to be supplied in the style of the author by the playing partner. Here, exuberant was the word.

Christian was squatting on the forecourt shading in the foliage on a tree. He had noticed her, a few minutes earlier, as she sat in the café, although her face was not particularly English, nor the short ivory skirt and lycra top. She wore pearls, though. Only English women wear pearls for everyday. Later, when he came up behind her in the cathedral, he knew by her perfume, which was a mixture of flowers and dark autumn fruits, like a luscious stain on her creamy clothes and skin. Her hair was caught back in a leather thong at the nape of her neck, then sprang over her shoulders. He started to clear his things together into his hessian bag. As he came from light into darkness and lingered a moment inside the porch, she crossed him, walking down the aisle towards the vast painting which screened off the south portion of the church, a fifteenth-century Last Judgement.

Certain buildings seem never to be aired, a last pocket of the darkness before the first day, where the *lux mundi* has not penetrated yet, bastions against the illumination of the Mediterranean world.

Saint Cecilia's is not a very successful story on the whole. She is now thought not to have been a martyr at all, but simply a wealthy woman who founded a church in a certain quarter of Rome. This is clearly rather uninteresting; the version which the founder fathers of the cathedral in Albi, and the many worshippers therein adhered to had a certain vitality, if no authenticity, to recommend it. Cecilia, according to a passion written in the sixth century, was a Christian girl of patrician rank who was betrothed to a young pagan, Valerian. On her wedding day she informed him that she had consecrated her virginity to God, and won him over to respect her vow and to be baptised. His brother Tiburtius likewise became a Christian. Eventually the two brothers were arrested and put to death as obstinate Christians, together with a man called Maximus. Then Cecilia was brought before the priest and, upon refusing an act of idolatry, she was sentenced to be stifled to death in the bathroom of her own house. The steam and heat failed to suffocate her, so a soldier was sent to behead her; he struck three ineffective blows, and she was left to linger three days before she died. Afterwards her house was turned into a church. Only since the sixteenth century has she been regarded as the patroness of musicians. The only justification for this is that the little story described above says how she "sang in her heart to God" while instruments were making music at her wedding. Now there seem to me to be an awful lot of rather dubious elements in this story – why did she go and put Valerian through the whole thing of betrothal and marriage if she'd already given up her virginity to God? Couldn't this have been seen as just a little bit naughty of Cecilia? And this bathroom? What was it about young Cecilia that made a death by this of all methods particularly appropriate? What did the bathroom become in the architectural scheme of the church? And don't we have anyone in the whole history of saints who's made a greater contribution to music than wee Cecilia, "singing in her heart"? One really feels they gave the wrong girl the job. On the other hand, I do think of Cecilia on the rare occasions I take a sauna.

It is very hard to be unselfconscious when visiting a cathedral as a tourist. Perhaps I say that as a non-believer. I once visited some really splendid Turkish baths in Budapest – art deco mosaics looming out from the steam (Cecilia, are you there?), lovely ceilings, and an atmosphere of senatorial conspiracy as elderly men huddled in the tubs to discuss affairs of state in hushed voices. But you didn't like to look too hard. The rule seemed to be if you had your own kit off, fine, you could engage whoever you wanted in a discussion on anything from the price of aubergines to the overthrow of the government, but if you were fully dressed you had to keep your eyes studiously fixed on the tiles and stained glass windows as you walked round the rim of the pool in the special issue slippers thoughtfully provided. It's a bit the same in church. You trot along with your guide book checking out the bits and pieces, stop, crane your neck, frown, finger to the page . . . ah, right, so that must be . . . back up the aisle to something you've missed, turn your back on the altar to look back at the rose window, and so on, until you hear a quiet mumble and look round to see someone praying, on their knees and somehow the sight is shocking, and it is you who have rendered it so by your blitheness and you turn away, embarrassed. You gaily drop a coin into the box and an electric candle lights up and the child at your side squeals with delight and tugs your hand for another coin, so you do it again and only notice afterwards the man who was waiting behind you to put his coin in, and who does so after you have stepped aside and there is a world of difference between your toy and his oblation. And yet even if I enter a church alone – although I love church architecture, I feel unable to relax, for even a few moments of peace and quiet and gentle contemplation smack somehow of *mauvaise foi*, I feel somehow as though I'm wearing clothes that aren't really me, and that people are looking at me and thinking, that's not really her colour, no, a mistake, I'm afraid. So whenever I visited churches with Pierre I used to find some particular feature I liked – a war memorial, a St Sebastian, a Sunday School display about little children in far off lands, and concentrate on that for a bit, then go outside and have a wander round. Pierre, on the other hand, spent mysteriously protracted lengths of time in churches. He would always come out smiling, as though he had quite by chance met a very good friend in there, but one he knew I didn't like to be reminded of, and would take my arm and squeeze it and bear me off serenely to a tea shop.

Elizabeth stood before the Last Judgement, the middle panel of which, bearing the Christ figure, had been removed in the seventeenth century to make a doorway through to another chapel, that of St Clare. (St Clare is in quite a different league, so it seems rather unfair that she should only get a chapel and Cecilia a whole whopping cathedral; Clare founded the order of the Poor Clares in Assisi under the guidance of St Francis – they practised extreme austerity, although Clare guided her sisters in the order with legendary tenderness, writing to a nun who had started a Poor Clare convent in Prague to tell her not to overdo her austerities, "for our bodies are not made of brass". I love that – she should have been canonised just for the one phrase. The Last Judgement is the work of French artists, and is divided into several bands, angels at the top, closely followed by apostles, saints and other incontestably worthy candidates, the definite "ayes", then the newly elect, still bearing their Book of Life before them, as though God might pass by at any moment and pause to look over their shoulder at what they've been doing in the holidays (would you like to do a picture of that?), and on the opposite side of the missing Christ (when I told Mr Goodman about this he said he must remember to tell his brother so he could use it as a supplement to his "Xmas takes the Christ out of Christmas" sermon) the doubtfuls, clearly about to be swilled down into everlasting darkness, and at the bottom, the definite "no's", all subject to a punishment appropriate to whichever of the seven deadly sins has been their undoing. Of these seven, sloth is absent, having been cut out with the Christ when they made the doorway, but it rather gives the impression that the artist just couldn't be fagged to paint it.

The effect of a large number of tourists inside a church is one of a group of people at a house party, who have been given a game to play, one of those where you have to find railway connections, or consequent clues to hidden treasure, and communicate with your partner without giving the game away to other couples; (this must be the rood screen, where's Dottie, she's got the pencil – and sometimes, I don't know if you played it this way, you had to attract Dottie's attention by making an animal noise, in response to which she would come scurrying over with her pencil. Animal noises might not go down too well here, but you get the idea – a large number of people weaving around the place with leaflets and books in front of them, looking pretty puzzled and worrying that other people are finding all the interesting bits.) Elizabeth, alone and aloof in the middle of all this darting about, turned her back on the Last Judgement, and went back up towards the choir, an enclosed sanctuary of flamboyant renaissance carving. Here, local artists had sculpted figurines to decorate the pedestals above the wood-carved seats, and it was not hard to imagine that these were the faces of the sculptor's acquaintance – there the butcher from the slaughterhouse by the bridge, who owed him two guineas for a carving of a pig for his counter, to his left the money changer (a look of pleasant equanimity on his face – a money lender in Occitanie was by no means a disrespected character, indeed, there was a law stating that a borrower must be at least as wealthy as the lender), and there, above the bishop's chair, surely the sculptor's mistress, gazing down with a kind of teasing benignity at the seated prelates, her face a picture of promise. Not once, but over and over again, she appeared, under the guise of different biblical characters, so that Elizabeth felt that as she walked slowly along the line of figures, the woman was hitching her skirts up and skipping behind the pillars to assume her next position, like a sort of ecclesiastical Aunt Sally, where a hole is left for a face and you pay a penny to fit your head to the more or less appropriate lower half. There was a feeling of laughter here, one in the eye for the slack-bodied clergy who sat about and watched the sinewy sculptor at work, waiting for the bell for prayers, when the workman would down tools and go off for a drink and the prelate could sniff up close to the lovely female figure, only half liberated from the wood, and would recognise her features with a guilty start.

As Elizabeth was standing looking up at the woman as Judith, Christian sketched her face in profile from a distance of thirty yards, where he was leaning back against a pillar with the sole of his left shoe propped against the stone. A man in black robes with a cord around his waist came and pointed to a notice requiring visitors to the cathedral to be appropriately dressed, and glanced down at Christian's shorts. Christian calmly extended one leg for the clergyman to examine at closer quarters, shin, calf, etcetera as though the man had unjustly pronounced him unclean and the priest actually recoiled and hissed at him, like a startled cat. Christian tore the page from his notebook, slipped it into the priest's girdle and walked out into the daylight.

2

Elizabeth dropped a coin into the box for the maintenance of the buildings, and bought a postcard of the Last Judgement. She looked relieved as she emerged, and began to walk quickly down the steps. Christian watched her cross the road in front of the cathedral and turn into one of the cobbled side streets of the old town. She was easy to follow. She moved quite slowly, looking in shoe shop windows, pausing with her hand on the strap of her bag in front of window displays of the kind of clothes Christian had never looked at in his life. She turned round once, and he thought she must have felt him following her, but in fact she saw straight through him. She had a small map in her hand, and she looked up at the names of the streets, which were written in French and in Occitan. It was just past midday, and a few shops were still open, but there was a sense of impending calm, everyone making for restaurants, or for home, as though the lull before the storm, spelling danger, were due, though in fact it was a bleachingly hot day. There had been no cloud for weeks. She turned left, then, turning her map through ninety degrees and tipping her head round after it, she located the doorway in the wall which led to the cloister of a ninth-century church.

Half a minute later, Christian followed her through. He stood watching, in the shadow of the cloister. Elizabeth had walked out onto the lawn, and was looking over the edge of the central well. Among the grey and pink stones, she gleamed, in her ivory clothes, like newly cut limestone. There were few colours – no flowers – but each one was clear in its tone, and asserted itself strangely on the eye, so recalling the scene once it had passed, you could have dabbed your brush in the green of the grass, the blue sky, the grey and pink stone, or the cream of her dress, the dark rich brown of her hair, and used it elsewhere, to paint a different picture again. Christian walked towards her. At the moment he left the shadow of the cloister and stepped out onto the grass, even though his shoes were of soft rope and canvas, she turned. Maybe she simply saw his shadow, dark green as a cypress on the grass. He hadn't thought what to say to her. He approached new situations without the slightest preparation. He seemed always to believe that speech would come to him, and it did. I never heard him say a foolish thing. His silences were never the kind you keep because you fear if you say something it will sound foolish. They were silences like long stretches of washed sand, and his thoughts moved distantly like the sea at low tide. Then he would suddenly speak, and you would be startled. Elizabeth was looking at him thoughtfully. She was half sitting on the edge of the well, her head turned away, towards him. He came up beside her and looked down the well, then up at her face. She was smiling at him very slightly, or more as though she were smiling at a thought which had occurred to her about him.

"When I was little," Christian said, "I found twelve stones, each one different. About this size." He made a circle with finger and thumb. "I came here and dropped each one down. I was only allowed to drop one an hour. I had to wait for the bell." He nodded up at the bell tower on the corner of the cloister. "There was one for each year of my life."

"What did it mean?" Elizabeth moved her bag down onto the ground and he came and leaned against the stone next to her, his back to the well, and his arms folded, his feet crossed at the ankles. He was wearing a blue shirt, the same blue as the sky. His arms were the pale brown of the stone. On his finger tips was a blush of purple chalk, the same purple as her rich autumn perfume of berries. His face was as familiar to her as if she had painted it herself, painted it into this scene, in which, however, he was entirely real and present.

He grinned and uncrossed his ankles. "I've no idea. Anything will do, really, when you're little. I'm Christian. You're Elizabeth." It was as though he were assigning them roles, rather than making an introduction. He leaned across and kissed her, just on one cheek. You would have thought they were related.

"Yes," she said. "I thought you must be. Marguerite will be pleased." It was as though they had an appointment. "Or did she tell you I was here"

"No," he said rather proudly. "I found you myself. I knew I would. I knew you'd come back."

"Back?"

"I saw you first time. Or heard you. I was – " he grinned at her, and stooped down to pick up her bag for her – "'walking in the garden in the cool of the day.' Two years ago. You were singing."

"So I was."

"Come on," he said. "Let's go now."

The meeting reminded her, in its simple peremptoriness, of that other meeting, where she had taken another entirely on trust. The difference here was that she had a choice. There was a gentleness to Christian, a calm of movement that would make you follow him not because he compelled you with a strange hypnotic charm, like the other, but because you felt he would lead you somewhere you already knew, from long ago, from the days when your world was so small that when you cried, or were frightened, it was often because you recognised something you knew, and knew could and would be dispelled if you showed your fear, made the ordinary signs to ask for help.

They walked back towards the cathedral. "I just have to finish this picture."

"Are you doing the same one?"

"I do lots."

"I only ever see one."

He stood aside as a child came scooting past on roller skates and held up his hand. The child slapped it in salutation as he passed and Christian turned to watch him for a second.

"That must be the Poussin."

"Yes. Always."

"Well, yes, it is, this morning. I've nearly done. It goes down well here. And I've been away for two years. It's kind of a way of saying I'm back."

"You haven't rung the farm?"

"No. But she's OK, isn't she?"

"Yes. She misses you. She showed me your photograph yesterday. As a child."

"So you knew who I was, just then?"

"No. I didn't recognise you. Not like that. But I recognised the picture."

"That's better," he said, and took her arm. "Much more interesting that way."

They arrived back in front of the cathedral. "I'll be really quick. Don't stand too close. You spoil my destitute image. Sit on the wall there and I'll just finish off."

He carried on drawing for a while. She watched him, and waited. "Did you send someone called Mr Goodman?"

"No"

"He turned up with your card. An Englishman. He's come from Paris. Have you been in Paris?"

"I've come from there. Is he about fifty? Stiff. Panama hat?"

"Yes."

"I've seen him. He watched me all week. Have you got a car?"

"I came in Marguerite's. Will you come back with me?"

"Is your boyfriend there?"

"Which . . .?" Of course. He meant Mark. "No." She almost laughed with relief that he hadn't meant Will, that she hadn't had to say no to that question.

He didn't look up for a while.

"The stone's too hot," she called to him. Her hands were hooked over the angle of the wall and she kicked her heels, which were bare at the back of her sandals, against the stone.

"I won't be long. It's just silly to leave it when I've spent all morning doing it."

Elizabeth was surprised how many people paused and dropped their coins. A pigeon pecked at one of the shepherd's eyes.

"How much do you earn a week?"

Christian stopped and looked up, and it seemed as though it was the first time he had ever worked it out. "Depends. In summer – about two or three hundred francs on a good day. Always enough. If I get hungry I draw. Just something small. You can't start something you won't finish. Not that anyone looks at it when you move on, but it would upset them if it was only half done. It's not the picture you get paid for. People pay to watch you do it. It looks awfully sad afterwards – sort of pointless. It just shows, original paintings – people don't want to spend money on them, because the best thing about them would be watching them be done. They feel they've missed out on the most interesting bit. Imagine watching Michelangelo painting the ceiling of the Sistine chapel. You'd kind of leave when he got to the end, wouldn't you?"

Elizabeth thought of the two occasions when she had seen his drawings in England. It was true that they had an air of having been abandoned, like a sandcastle, to the elements.

"I saw the Poussin in London."

"Where?"

"St Paul's, once. And Westminster Cathedral."

"Everyone goes past there."

"I don't normally, ever."

"No, well, you're different. I don't suppose you do. I had breakfast at half seven. What time is it now? We could have some lunch. I've earned it. As they say. At least, I think so. Have to tot this lot up." Another coin fell down beside him. He looked up at the retreating donor then at Elizabeth, and gave a smile, but his smile was more like a soundless laugh, it had none of the modification of a smile and the self consciousness of a proper laugh. "Pennies from heaven." He craned his neck round and squinted, slightly mockingly, she thought, at the cathedral. He moved round to another portion of the picture, skirting the edge as though the drawing had been a jigsaw he mustn't disturb. He was rubbing some shade in with the pad of his thumb, hopping round the edge of the picture like a Russian dancer.

Elizabeth looked at her watch. "Twenty to one."

"I'll be another couple of minutes. I have to finish it. It's a superstition."

"Do you do proper painting?"

He wiped his forehead with the back of his wrist, brushing his hair out of his eyes as he fished in his sack for new colour. His hands were covered in chalk. "No. I'm not much good really. It's just a knack I learned when I was hanging around in Germany once. There were some hippies outside Cologne Cathedral. I was only about fifteen. I went with Marguerite – she was visiting some vineyards on the Rhine, and she took me along. I took my bike with us on the train and I cycled all over the place. The hippies were doing this massive picture – one of those really droopy madonnas. They gave me some colouring in to do. I picked it up. It's kind of a cheapy thing to do sometimes. Some people, that guy over there, doing the oil on the easel, he always pretends to get really annoyed if people watch him working, but he really loves it, he'd be livid if no one ever stopped to look. I like it, sometimes I talk to them, let them do bits. Kids love it."

All this time, coins had been dropping his way. Elizabeth was surprised to see how difficult people found it to pay for their pleasure, even though they clearly wanted to – it wasn't the parting with the money, it was the being seen to do so. They would give the coin to a child, more often than not, and the child would run up and tinkle it down beside Christian, then run shyly back to its parents. They somehow didn't want to be caught out in frittering their money away, as though it were a kind of gambling. Even the children seemed to be aware that it was an illicit pleasure.

"OK," he said, standing up. His knees were covered in chalk of different colours. There was lots of blue. "Let's go and eat." He took her arm, and Elizabeth, half amused and half enfeebled by his fatherly air, let herself be guided across the road and down a little pedestrian street to a restaurant overlooking the river.

"We don't have to look at the cathedral from here," he said, as they climbed a wrought iron staircase, which jutted out above the water then brought them onto the terrace of a first floor restaurant. "Let's sit over there. I'm just going to wash my hands, otherwise I'll get chalk all over the tablecloth. *Salut,*" he said to the waiter, and went inside.

She chose a table under the shade of a white awning, like a mediaeval tent. The restaurant was an interruption to a huge brick wall, crenellated in parts, which ran on and on, along the river bank, so that you could walk along in company with the flowing water. The waiter handed her the menu, she asked for a bottle of water, and Christian came back. He sat opposite her on the chair closest to the river, and propped first one foot then the other on the chair beside him to tie up his shoe laces. Then he turned back in towards her.

"I've only been back a couple of days. I didn't warn her, in case I was late. It's good isn't it? She's all right?"

Elizabeth felt as though he was asking her to confirm, as though he had already said to her, some time ago, you must go, you'll really like it.

"It's lovely," she said. "I'm translating her books. I saw the editor this morning. He wants to do the whole series."

Christian was eating bread. He threw the last bit down into the water, and two mallards came skimming towards it like a pair of colliding water skiers, braking with their heels, then splashing forwards. He took another piece and broke off a second bit. All at once there seemed to be a whole family of ducks, and more, pecking at the water. He chucked the remaining portions of bread down into the river and gestured with the empty basket. The waiter cocked a comradely finger and went inside to get some more.

Looking down at the water at the scene of his creating, Christian replied, "I bet he does."

Elizabeth had chosen. She had been shaded slightly by the menu, and when she laid it down to one side of the table felt suddenly exposed, to his youthfulness, to his candour. She hadn't expected him to have a cheeky look, but he had, like a tinker boy. He was, to the eye, quite ordinary, but there was a quality – not poise, nothing learned, that warmed the edges of his presence. You felt, she said to me later, that having been perceived by him, through any one of his senses, you were somehow changed, fractionally, but for ever, a fundamental structural alteration which would modify your development for ever more. She said it was the opposite of the kind of genetic alteration that takes place when cells are exposed to radium. If radium creates mass reproduction of cells, more and more of the same, multiplying matter, Christian distilled, reduced things to their purest, most stable form. She usually resented people whose fascination was hidden – if it wasn't apparent from what they said, or how they looked, then she suspected it of being chimeric, a sort of trick of the light; and yet he was far from being a party trickster, as, in his way, Will had been. If he had just been another English boy of his build and colouring, spotted lounging by the Serpentine, or queuing outside a cinema, he would have been just one more instance of something very common. Perhaps it was her knowledge of his peregrinations that gave him a universality, so that you might almost begin to see him in other people, other examples of him in impossible circumstances, as though he were the original prototype of which there were countless incarnations.

"You've got great legs," he said, and she laughed and nearly spluttered her drink, not at his candour, but at his ordinariness, having subconsciously parried her thoughts.

Elizabeth ordered a salad and some grilled sardines. Christian just ordered a big plate of baby vegetables, which came with mayonnaise. He was a vegetarian, he explained, but they knew him here. Elizabeth noticed that the service was quite different to any she had ever known. Whether it was just an exceptional restaurant or whether, as she was inclined, almost superstitiously, to believe, there was something about Christian that inspired them, the waiters served them with a sense of their own privilege and importànce, which is, she thought later, the only real way that servility can combine with dignity.

"When I asked who you were, when I came back after Pierre died, she said you were someone who was waiting for something to happen."

"She said that?"

"And did it?"

She found herself telling him, in very few words, what had happened. She was surprised how very few words were required. She said she had once seen the child she called Tristan hovering round Christian's painting.

"If your life was a dream," he said, "you would be waiting for him" – he meant Will – "or me. Same thing. The little boy – he's the child you had, your body didn't have. Maybe he's what it takes to get better, to get back in with the world, to care about it again. Where you feel human love. Not erotic love, or love of God, spiritual love, but human love. Or perhaps," he said rather dreamily, as though it were a soothing hypothesis, "the little boy was the unmade choice, him or me. He could become either of us." His words were somehow mysterious and perfectly obvious

– true, maybe – at the same time. When he talked of himself it was not of himself as a person – this person in front of her – but as though he were a symbolic person, like a character in a Greek drama or a mystery play.

Elizabeth stared at him. "I made my choice— "

He ignored her. "I knew I'd see you again," he said, putting some of his vegetables onto her plate. He always seemed to be spreading things around him. "Here, have some of this mayonnaise with them."

"Before I saw you?" Elizabeth looked at him over the top of her glass. She was sure, somehow, that that was what he had thought.

"If you start knowing what I think," said Christian, "this will be very complicated. Yes, except I think you saw me first, even if you didn't know it was me. I saw you second, but I knew who you were."

"I do feel as though I've met you before."

He shrugged. "Of course. And no. We are very alike." She understood that he was not talking about the two of them, but about himself and Will.

"In some ways."

"Bits of us are the same. Other bits not at all. Is that right?"

"Yes."

"I thought so. Shall we not talk about that then? I don't want to upset you. Although you look fine. I'd have expected you to be strucken."

"Strucken?"

"With grief."

"Stricken."

"Yes."

"No", she said, looking down at her plate. She put her knife and fork down like a pair of oars, propped on the edges of the plate, and wiped her mouth on her napkin. She looked at it for a split second, as though she thought there might be blood, but there was just the faintest trace of her lipstick.

"You're not grief stricken. You just don't feel anything."

"Not very often."

"I expect people are always giving you this 'it will happen', stuff. You know, one day it will all come gushing out and you'll be healed. That's not true. Not in your case, I don't think. It might do. But it isn't bound to."

Music started to creep out from inside the restaurant. Christian got up and went to shut the door. She was grateful to him for this. Ever since Will had disappeared, she had been quite unable to support sentimental music. Anything that could be whispered, or crooned – that is, not obviously performed as it would be in a natural acoustic – was too close, too personal. She needed the distance provided by the knowledge that the singer was doing all the natural singing things – constriction of the diaphragm, expansion of the ribs, and so on. The waiter, bringing more water, had to open the door with his elbow, but he didn't say anything, and closed it carefully behind him as he went back to the kitchen.

"Perhaps you'll stay like this for ever."

"I'm feeling a lot better."

"You don't know what you want but you do know what you don't want."

"Yes."

He leaned across the table and said very sweetly. "Do you think you could possibly want me?"

She leaned back in her chair and laughed without fear of hurting him. He laughed too. "Just checking," he said.

"What were you checking?"

"Your condition."

"And what is it?"

"Cold. Very chilly." He took her hand and kissed the back of her wrist. Suddenly he looked quite serious. "I'm only twenty-two," he said.

"I know."

"Well, then. It won't do me any harm to wait."

Afterwards they wandered off to sit by the river. "Siesta now." Christian lay back on the grass with his head on his sack, and Elizabeth watched him as he appeared to sleep. Then she decided it didn't matter if she got her clothes a bit dusty and lay beside him. She dreamed of Tristan, playing alone on a sea shore, with a kind of martello tower in the background, daubed roughly on the sky. She woke to find Christian's hand in hers and he was smiling down on her. The river flowed without the slightest sound and there was no sound of traffic or bells or passing feet. "Not her," I said to Christian, later, when he told me about the day, although he didn't report everything, and I felt quite stern, protective of her too, perhaps because she was so much older than him, and the older need protection against the very young. At that he took his arm from round my shoulder, where he had been rubbing my back for my rheumatism, and kicked the table leg on the way out of the room. "Vincent's son," I said to myself, in that spiteful way you can with someone you really love, and resolved to keep a closer eye on him.

3

Anna's letter to Mark was a model of courtesy and kindness, expressed in an English watercolour prose that did not wound, nor disturb, but enabled him, even in this moment of his release, to comfort himself that his relief was not untinged with admiration for the woman who had been for fourteen years his wife.

It was a long letter, written on heavy, ivory coloured paper, in the black ink the colour scheme cried out for. He would not normally have found it, except he had been staying in college for a night, though term was over now. Most of the undergraduates had departed, for holidays in Greece, lovers' trysts in Budapest or Prague, desultory research funded by a bursary that would barely keep a cat in Whiskas for a month. He had been dining with friends in Park Town, by the river, and had decided not to cycle back up to the cottage at Boar's Hill. He had arrived back in college around midnight, and let himself in through the side door with his late key, wheeling his bicycle through the quad to the bottom of his staircase.

There was a note from Polly on his door, asking him to lunch in London the next weekend. She had bumbled her way through finals with a certain improvisatory flair, and would no doubt be happy with her lower second, and never think about the *Chanson de Roland* again in her life. She was living with girlfriends in Putney and they were inviting people for 11.30 on Sunday. In the afternoon, she said, they had booked two courts, and he should bring his racquet and his kit. Mark had felt immensely wearied and dispirited by the note, its tone and its contents. Polly's course ran as inevitably as the Thames, at Putney, swung north, leaving a clump of expensive suburbia for her and her friends to inhabit. They were already set well on course by the time they came up to Oxford, in the geography and peculiar vernacular of which they were already entirely secure, having brothers or cousins or sisters or parents, most often, who had taught them the idiom of Oxbridge life along with all the other ghastly idioms of the complacent classes. The *Chanson de Roland*, or troubadour poetry, all that was at best a lake to be trawled for appropriate quotations to scribble in Valentine's Day cards or letters home, to prove you wore your learning lightly, the careless insouciance of fake scholarliness. He chucked the note in the bin.

Sitting at his desk by the window which looked out of the roof of his college chapel, he felt irritated by the lunatic stare of the full moon, just one more of life's picturesque accessories he could have done without. He was wondering whether to go up north to see Anna for a bit. He hadn't seen her since Easter – no, that was wrong, she had brought some of her sixth formers up to look round another college in May, and they had had tea together and chatted amiably. There had been a feeling even then that the marriage was over, and over seemed a rather appropriate word, as though it had been no more than a game of cricket, or a season, something which came to an end which was structurally pleasing, something which drew to a close. Maybe that was why he didn't like the moon. Its existence seemed so much less satisfactory, structurally speaking. It was merely there like a light left on in a disused room all day. When the sun died, it came into its own for a while, but it was mere doodling, really, and it was mischievous and annoying of the romantic poets to have allowed it to assume a role of any importance. The moon was simply not important. The moon was the absence of the sun. He had forgotten the influence of the tides, tugging at the earth's heartstrings by day as by night.

He had meant to work. The University of Toulouse had sent him a proof of an article which Pierre had finished just before he died. Mark had checked it, and found it fanciful but touching. It radiated a feeling for the stark paradoxes of mediaeval life which had been lost in England, where Oxford and Cambridge had become the standard picture book references for it all. They wanted him to attend the summer conference this year. He was in two minds. He felt, on the one hand, that he would prefer to avoid all that area, both geographical and emotional. On the other hand, he sensed that to grasp the nettle was to harness its potent charms, that somehow to return there might help.

It was strange how since he had last seen her, Elizabeth, of whom he had always thought in terms of an image – when she was not with him, it was her image, the two dimensional picture of her, in silhouette, which had accompanied him – had come to possess his other senses too, to exist in flesh and blood, accessible by touch and smell, taste even, where before she had somehow been definable only in terms of her face, and her voice. As a child, he had always had difficulty with the idea of the senses. Because people talked so often of the sixth sense, he had assumed – and was not corrected until really quite late in adolescence – that there were indeed six senses. And when he tried to count them, he always forgot at least one, or counted another twice – it was like trying to count a litter of new born kittens. Now he had them sorted out. Hands, eyes, nose, ears, mouth. Those were the five senses. Those were the five organs by means of which he perceived the world. He believed that if he could cradle Elizabeth in the bower of his collective senses he could in some way possess her. He could even make her happy. He had worn gloves, met her by moonlight, doused the room in sweet smelling oils,. used his mouth too much, too often to speak, and not to kiss or to taste her. He had heard her song – but had he really listened? His intellect, his inclination to cast events in the light of myth, or metaphor, had been his undoing. He had always, mistakenly, assumed that intellect was the sixth sense. Now he was convinced he had been wrong. The sixth sense wasn't intellect, it was love.

He had known that night at the concert, that it was ended. He still had the diary with the inscription, "7.30, St John's, Pergolesi." It had been determined, partly – admittedly – by his own failure, that she would leave. But he felt quite sure now that what he had seen then as a dead end, an impasse, had been but a parting of the ways. He had had this to do, and she that. Will – that name, it seemed to express something of both a determination to freedom, and a future hope; and a legacy, a death. And where Will had seemed to him the incarnation of all that was wrong, and cruel, and destructive, he was now, since he had witnessed Elizabeth's grief, obliged to think again. Mark could not think of him really as Elizabeth's other lover. He *had* been, he supposed, Elizabeth's other half, the half she had been fragmented from as long as she had been with Mark. He was the half that had made her whole; there, Mark had failed. And now that he was dead . . . and now he *was* dead. There was no second clause. It was not because he had died that Mark would be worthy of Elizabeth, or that she would love him. So what could he do?

He went over to the other window, which looked down into the quad. The light was still on in the room above the buttery, across the lawn. It was in that room that he had first met Elizabeth. She had come to read him her essay on Beroul's *Tristan y Iseut*, "potion or passion". (what a bloody silly title, he thought; what was it, an op-ed article? No wonder they didn't take their education seriously. Flaubert, realist or romantic? Heine, lyricist or poet? Adolphe, cynic or martyr? Polly, Putney or Fulham? Advertising or management consultancy? The come-uppance of dualism. Tragedy or farce?) Potion. Or passion. The argument had been a straightforward one. In early versions of the myth, Tristan fell in love with Isolde because her nurse put something in their drink. No free will. No choice. They were no more responsible for their actions than a mouse who has been injected with LSD. In later versions, the potion, a word which was supposed to be etymologically linked to passion, each deriving from the root word for strength or power, wears off after three years. Technically the lovers are now released from bondage. But they still cannot renounce their love. Was that just an image for marriage, conceived in passion, pursued through habit and familiarity? It was clear that the potion was a symbol of sexual attraction, he had said to Elizabeth, in the detached and seductive way he could not help, and she had looked up from her essay and fixed him with a puzzled look and said, "Yes, but doesn't 'passion' also mean suffering?" And were Tristan and Isolde not innocent as long as they remained in ignorance of the effect of their passion on the injured King Mark, ignorant of his knowledge of their love? As long as our sin has no shadow, is it sin? If we sin at high noon, or while the moon is behind a cloud, shall we be called to account? Mark opened the window and breathed in the soft air of the city. So many questions.

The next morning he was on his way to drink coffee in the covered market. It was a hot morning, and he woke late, having learned to sleep through bells, in the way that, inversely, certain people become immune to sleeping draughts. In the porter's lodge he stopped to talk to the fellow in history, who wanted to know if he knew of a good translator. He had co-written a book with a French colleague – (he and Mark had a century – the twelfth – in common, as others have mutual friends) and the University Press now wanted to do a co-edition. Mark suggested he come to his rooms at ten and he'd give him some names. As he was about to step out into the street, the porter called his name, and waved an envelope at him, "Mr Chester! Sir!" Mark hesitated and took the letter, recognising Anna's handwriting. He had not seen it look so elegant since she had addressed their wedding invitations, because her mother had Parkinson's disease and had not been able to do it herself. Anna had learned a calligraphic hand, quickly out of a book, so that she could say to her mother, "Look, I'd like to do it, I've just learned this proper calligraphy, it would look nice maybe . . ." so that her mother could hand over the task to her as a favour, not be relieved of it by a more competent hand. Thinking of this, Mark felt something like love for his wife, but it was in fact, he thought, no more than the love you might feel for a stranger who has committed an unexpected act of kindness.

She wrote of her plans for the summer. She called him "my dear". She said that she had sought advice from a friend who was a priest, who thought that grounds could probably be found on which to seek an annulment of their marriage. She begged him not to be offended by the sterility of the language in which this was expressed. She hoped they might thereafter be free to love one another as much or as little as they chose, but that she would prefer to feel that the formal vessel of their marriage did not exceed, in capacity, the amount of active love it contained. That she would rather have a small cup that ran over than a great goblet with an inch in the bottom.

Mark folded the letter and walked down to Magdalen bridge

and from there along the river, where he stopped and read it again. He wished that he had been the one to write, or at least that he had had the courage to talk to her, even if it was better for Anna, like this, that she should be the one who pointed out that it was over. She had gone to Amsterdam. He imagined her, with a friend, exciting herself over the canals and the galleries, and giggling in the red light district, and driving rather fast on flat roads, through flat fields, and arguing with strangers about the British system of education. She had been doing these things for years, without him. Now she would do them without him and without his sanction, which would no longer be required. Another dispossession – of power, in a strange way. He wished her well. He wondered if she had ever known about Elizabeth. The marriage bond you break is not the same bond as the one you made. It has weathered and changed. Some marriages age well, others not. Is it always the finest paintings that last? Is durability a virtue? Or is it simply that the paintings that last are the only ones that we have, and the oldest, and therefore sometimes unjustly called the best? At least a butterfly does not grow old before it dies.

He went back to his rooms, and gave his colleague a name – not Elizabeth's – and cleared up his room for the summer. He cycled back to the cottage, passing the house where Edward Thomas and his wife Helen had lived, so young, and he so soon to die. He took pen and paper and wrote to Anna as she had written to him, and tried harder than he had probably ever tried in his life to say nothing that was untrue, to exaggerate nothing, to state his feelings correctly, in quality and degree. When he had done so, he felt that he had learned something from Anna. He had thought to cut some roses from the garden, because she liked roses, and he wanted somehow to celebrate her. Then he thought it would actually be an act of rather ghastly sentimentality, so he weeded the border round the roses instead, which seemed a better way, if a way had to be found, of saying thank you for his release.

Mr Goodman had come downstairs quite late – just before nine o'clock. He had been moving around in his room for a while, but I think he thought it was like a hotel – you had to surface before nine to get breakfast, and if you were too early you had to spend ages talking to the landlady instead of having your coffee in peace.

"Coffee?" I asked, breezily, hoping this approach would put wind in his sails. He didn't look all that rested. In the bright garden light his glasses looked oddly indoor, as though he should have used them only for pouring over texts in a dim, cobwebby library, while outside the rain and the early dusk fell. His face, although stern, had the makings of kindness in it, but I doubted whether he had ever had much opportunity to develop it.

"Ah, tea, please. Thank you."

I brought out the tray, and as I'd been up early, I decided to drink the coffee I'd made for him myself. There was a glorious smell of honeysuckle floating around the table, which only dipped into my range every now and then, carried, perhaps, on the fleeting wing of a butterfly. I kept picking up on it as I moved around setting out the basket of bread and the honey and cups. It was like a memory, suddenly it is there, like a blessing, and the next second is gone, a fugitive fragment, uncatchable, unbiddable, but still possible, still hovering somewhere, on the wing.

He was dressed in a pale green cotton shirt, with short sleeves, and some rather smart stone-coloured trousers. The last person I had seen wearing socks and shoes in this house was probably about eleven and had just come from her first communion. His arms were very pale, but he was basically dark skinned. It was just that he had been out of the light for so many years. I asked him a few questions about where he had come from. He had come from Paris. It was his first visit to this part of the world. The room had been quite comfortable.

"Well, you are very welcome," I said, in an excess of hospitality. "I hope you'll be able to stay for a while."

I reached over and took a sugar lump from the tin. I had trapped a fly in there earlier and it came reversing out and took off towards the honeysuckle, where it would be turned away at the gate, no doubt, by the more specifically adapted of its kind. It would need, I thought distractedly, to equip itself with horns, like Bottom, a pair of mock probosces.

"Elizabeth has taken my car to Albi. She'll be back this evening or tomorrow."

He drew a handkerchief from his pocket and wiped his brow. I realised that this genial chit chat was for him painfully intense.

"Eliot!" I said emphatically, as though with a dramatic swing of the camera in a film. She was sitting quietly watching butterflies, suddenly realised she was needed and obligingly got up and walked in under the shade of the table. By the look on his face I could see she was doing her act under the table, and rubbing her flanks sensually against his calf. I didn't mean that, I thought. He shifted slightly. I decided to leave them to it.

"If you have any washing, leave it out and it can go in with the rest," I said, and picked up my cup. I paused on my way back inside to pick a few dead petals from a hollyhock. "Lunch will be at midday. Just a salad. We tend to eat more in the evening, when it's cooler."

I left him to spend his morning alone. I tried to keep an eye out to see what he liked to do. He went back to his room after breakfast, and emerged twenty minutes later, and set off for a walk. When I went in to see if he'd left his washing out there was nothing on the bed. He had unpacked – the suitcase had been placed on top of the wardrobe. Well, at least he hadn't put it outside the door to be taken up to the attic. Perhaps he wouldn't be staying with us that long after all. Elizabeth would help. But I was already regretting our intimacy; I use the term *regret* as the French do, to hanker after something past, not to rue. (This rather changes the emphasis of the Edith Piaf song, if you think about it. "No, there is nothing I long for that is past." Rather different from, "no, I'd do all the same again." *Je te regrette* – I miss you.) Ours wasn't quite the amiable discourse of the fat one and the thin one of Pergolesi at St John's, but there was a serenity between myself and Elizabeth, and I wasn't sure that it would survive the arrival of Mr Goodman. We would keep the intimacy safe, but I could feel that it would change, thin out, to return on occasions, compressed, an intense version of its earlier, easy self, and drift away again, more like a neighbour than a friend.

That afternoon Mr Goodman's twin brother phoned.

"I'm afraid he's not around at the moment," I said. "Would you like me to ask him to call you?"

"Er, who is that?" he asked, as though he were asking a third person who I was.

"Marguerite d'Astige. You are telephoning a bed and breakfast in the south of France."

"Oh, quite." He began to gabble, remembering it was costing him.

"This is such an unfortunate business," he said. "The headmaster was really quite prepared to overlook the whole incident. The girl was just a troublemaker. No other word for it. Still, it's his choice." People always tell me things. I wish they wouldn't, but they do. I don't know what that says about me. It's not as though I have any discretion. He said that I should pass on the message that he was going over the very next day to sort out possessions. It sounded as though Mr Goodman was dead. Not my brother's keeper, I was thinking, as he sketched a line drawing of the truth, which was later filled out for me by closer acquaintance with the protagonists.

Mr Goodman ate like a little bird. I had made a chicken salad, with a rather spectacular tarragon dressing, but he didn't want any dressing, just a couple of slices of breast and some lettuce and tomato. We talked a bit about England, and about the house, and the garden. Simple things. I felt I was negotiating something very delicate, which had to be in place before Elizabeth returned. I think he approved of me. I was not hysterical, I talked in a reasonable, calm sort of way, I was a widow. My underwear didn't show through the fabric of my dress. My nails were clean. I didn't float around in a haze of aromatic oils. I knew just the type of woman he would back off a mile from. I felt a bit protective and a little bit delicate myself in his presence, as though we were two old people.

"I shall have my siesta. I advise you to do the same. It is quite impossible to do anything until four o clock. Elizabeth will be back this evening." I kept saying that, a bit like that woman who says over and over that they're going to Moscow, except there wasn't any reason to think she wouldn't come, it's just that I wished she would hurry up. I went up to my room and drew the curtains, read a couple of pages of Simenon and fell asleep. When I woke up, I combed my hair with the Spanish comb, then went down into the kitchen and from there into the garden, where I met up with Mr Goodman, who did not appear to have taken his rest, at least not in his bed. Every time I came across him I felt as though, in a photograph album, I had fallen upon a single black and white snapshot amongst the pages and pages of vibrant colour. There was something of the *memento mori* about him, the skull looming out from behind the fruit bowl.

I was in the kitchen, and could see him, with his back to me, sitting in a chair in the shade. I had told him he would find a chair in the barn underneath Christian's attic, a huge vaulted, ramshackle structure where the old wine vats now stand empty. There's still a rusty smell of old vinegar in there. I didn't go out to fetch it for him because I was rubbing in pastry at the time, so I told him precisely where he'd find something to sit on. I was alarmed, when I came out into the garden once the pie was in the oven, to see that he had unearthed Vidalou's chair.

Vidalou was a hired labourer who used to turn up every summer to do the *vendange*. He was a drunken old sod, but I had a soft spot for him. He reminded me of the character in the Robert Frost poem, the hireling who turns up long after he has ceased to be of any use, and comes back to the one place where they have always given him work, his way of coming home to die. The wonderful lines: "home is the place where, when you have to go there, They have to take you in." I love that. It will be a good subject for deathbed meditation. I am saving all really serious consideration of it until then. For the time being I just hum it as a kind of theme.

Vidalou used to come and get drunk late every summer. Pierre claimed the Albertines drooped at the very sight of him toiling up the track. He always sat on that chair in the barn in the evening and drank and drank, and it is difficult to be churlish about how much the workers drink during the *vendange*, because there is so obviously an abundant superfluity of the stuff. Two summers ago, inflamed by his intake, and no doubt by the day's sun, which seemed to have taken no note of the declining season, he picked up his chair – his, please note, though I don't know how it fell from our into his possession, these things just happen, and flung it across the room at a young couple who were sitting in the shadows, wrapped around each other, smiling. He didn't like them smiling, apparently. Ariadne had to have five stitches in her brow. Christian was unconscious for three days. The other pickers pinned Vidalou to the floor, but he wrenched himself free – he was immensely strong – and ran down the track and disappeared into the night. They say he was cursing young love at the top of his voice as he went, and the top of his voice was quite something to be reckoned with – even the lower to middling registers had a derisory, menacing tone, like a noise emitted by some demonic gargoyle. Christian recovered, of course, and left as soon as he could walk. I hadn't heard from him since. Not that he considered it my fault. He just came round a slightly different person. No one had sat on that chair since. I don't know why we didn't burn it, except that it was actually rather a lovely, carved chair and seemed too good to waste. And there was Mr Goodman, comfortably propped up in it, considering the tips of his fingers, and apparently deep in thought. I decided not to say anything, and set to weeding my border of thyme and campanula, which is beset in early summer by a nasty thing called a trefoil, a leaf just like clover, and insistent, rampaging little bulbs three inches below ground. After a bit I got sick of the sound of his silence, and a little click in his throat as he seemed, every two or three minutes, to be turning a page in his mind. He was politeness itself – which is never really enough, is it? Who wants an abstract noun hanging around the house? But he seemed comfortable, as though he believed he had received a summons, as perhaps he had.

"Miss Faulkener is a translator. You will have an academic approach to French in common."

"Really," he said sceptically. "And what does she translate?"

"Oh, all sorts, as far as I can gather." I illustrated my reply with a sudden random sort of snatching at stalks of this and that among the proper plants. "Car manuals, ferry boat brochures, a novel or two. She's translating some travel guides of mine. Today she has gone to see my editor about the production of the one I have written to this particular area. It deals largely with the Cathar heresy. I imagine," I added, having absorbed something of his own prim idiom, "that you are familiar with the story. Perhaps you would like to take Miss Faulkener around. There are a number of major sites within a day's drive from here. You might both be interested."

He ignored my suggestion with a nervous little smile of fake equanimity. "I should like to read this guide of yours. Would that be possible?"

"They're all in my study. On the left hand side of the bookcase behind the door. Help yourself."

"I thank you."

He had the strangest way of talking – although English was his mother tongue he seemed to manage to make it sound like it was something he had learned to perfection, quite recently, certainly as though he had only the scantest, and not altogether voluntary acquaintance with his mother. Perhaps that just came from years of clear enunciation in the classroom. You expected him to repeat his sentences twice over, like those people on language-learning tapes: "Michelle is enjoying her ice cream." (Pause). "Michelle is *enjoying* her ice cream." It can become rather menacing after a while. I watched him walk back into the house. I had noticed that when he moved about he was constantly aware of being on someone else's territory. It wasn't quite gaucheness, indeed it had a kind of discreet grace, but it disturbed. This is something you find quite common if you receive a lot of guests. There are certain people who have a tip toe tread – they try not to bustle or hurtle as they might, on occasion, in their own homes. It is a kind of deference, and I know what it means, but it can make one quite uncomfortable. It usually goes with not knowing how to offer to lay the table or give a hand in the garden.

He came back outside with the guide in his hand, moved the chair he had been sitting in back into the shade and opened the book with that well considered, page-smoothing sort of gesture that implies a lesson is about to be read. I was quite relieved when he settled down in silence. He had the most beautiful hands, long and graceful, like a ballet dancer's – people always talk about ballet dancer's feet, while it seems to me that what they do with their hands is equally important, and as we do not wear shoes on our hands, even more vital to get right from birth. One could never, of course, imagine Mr Goodman dancing – in fact, what a pity I didn't meet him sooner, he would have been an absolute cert for sitting out the heat and dust routine. Eliot slithered down from the roof of Christian's attic where she had been lying in the sun on her side, so that all her little pink teats were exposed. She settled in front of Mr Goodman with her two front feet placed neatly together like a pair of shoes in a tidy young lady's closet and looked at him with a very carefully veiled kind of insolence that could, had I not known her so well, have been read as perfect, all too perfect respect. It was like one of those games you play in a railway carriage when you are going to school and someone very serious-looking is sitting opposite to you. You hope to discomfort them but end up embarrassing yourself by giggling. In Eliot's case, though, practice had made perfect. Mr Goodman wasn't the kind of thing to make a cat laugh.

I hummed as I weeded, the kind of humming that indicates you want to be left alone, the vague menace of an electric fence. After a while Mr Goodman looked up and I wasn't sure if it was my humming or Eliot's staring that was disturbing him. I moved my kneeling mat to the left, shuffled along the edge of the border as though making room for someone in a pew, and continued the song in my head where it couldn't annoy. He sighed, involuntarily, it seemed, which was unusual enough to make me look up. He took off his reading glasses and tapped the book with them. "Excellent," he said, thoughtfully, "this really is quite excellent," at which I felt extremely embarrassed, and about twelve. "Most interesting."

"It is," I said, passing the buck of his praise, "an interesting area. There are very few documents, I'm afraid. If you're persecuted, you tend to circulate your beliefs verbally. The only things we have are written by the other side – the records of the inquisition. They are on the whole remarkably impartial – documentary evidence, just the witnesses' words, very lively too. A few religious texts – they used the Lord's Prayer, St John's gospel. Some other prayers we know from the records. A couple of legends. They're in the appendix."

He ignored me *again*, and went back to where he had left off. Eliot gave him a couple more seconds of contemptuous attention then padded over to rub against my legs. Then she stepped delicately on to the soil and started scraping. "Ssssh," I wanted to signal to her, "he'll hear you," but she stuck her little nose in the air and did it anyway, and with such nonchalant dignity that I quite wanted to kiss her paw with devotion. If you do these things publicly you have to develop a kind of dignity about them I suppose. Perhaps mediaeval life was rather like that, which would explain how people put up with living on top of each other as they did. This is the way I think when I am gardening. I'm not one of these people who can think deliberately, step by logical step. It has to be incidental, as though all my thoughts were little illegitimate bastards, with no title or obvious provenance.

I was aware, as I ran the little threads of root through my fingers, shaking off the excess soil, that Mr Goodman was somehow deeply affected by being here – both here in the general sense that he was staying with me, had found a haven from whatever it was that was hunting him down, and here specifically, sitting reading his book in Vidalou's chair. It became apparent, a little later, that he believed that he had been guided here by an unseen hand. I tried to point out that providence in the form of Christian, who made a point of this kind of behaviour, wasn't really providence at all, just kindly intervention. He had noticed Aiden that first afternoon as he painted outside the cathedral. He said he had been aware of him from the moment he entered the square. It is true that Christian is extraordinarily sensitive to these things. He knows when something has happened to me. He knew the night Pierre died, and arrived the next evening, having hitchhiked, without phoning, from Florence. This doesn't strike me as alarming, or supernatural in the least. Christian is perhaps a little short on the information aspect of education, but he is noticeably better educated than most in the area of "formation", of being human. He has grown into the world in a strangely individual way, it fits him, and he wears it with ease. This is so unusual for a child educated in England that I am tempted to see it as a special kind of grace in him, a gift of . . . etc. but I would not be the first to say it. So, yes to Mr Goodman's view, in a way there is something extraordinary about him – where Christian walks, the voice of God seems to make itself heard, portents and warnings fall across his path, coincidence reigns, the pathetic fallacy works. This makes writing him down, describing events which were touched by him rather difficult, because the whole issue of implausibility does start to come in to it. There is too much synchronicity. Sometimes I feel a bit like Admiral

Collingwood before the Battle of Trafalgar: "I do wish Nelson would stop *signalling*, we all *know* what we have to do!"

It is particularly difficult, telling this story, to get my retrospective right, if that is the word for perspective with hindsight. It is one of the remarkable things about the depositions made to the inquisition by the members of one particular Occitan village touched by Catharism, a whole century after the crusade was supposed to have wiped it out, that the reports betray no sense of drama. A witness will tell his story from beginning to end and then suddenly announce that the neighbour whom he has been describing was in fact a heretic, but he only uses this information as a narrator as of the point at which it occurs in the story. This is, I suppose, a very primitive way of telling stories. They say that children have no sense of suspense, nor epic storytellers either, that they will happily divulge the whole plot and then spend hours embellishing and exploring its tiny details, nothing daunted by the fact that, for instance, we all *know* that the king dies, that he hasn't just gone off to live in the forest, or that the spaceship was brought hurtling to earth with total loss of life and crucial documents, and we needn't worry our heads about whether it's going to crash into the satellite after all. It seems these witnesses had a similar approach. They gave a wealth of detail about the way a woman cooked her broth before announcing that of course she believed that God and Satan were separate beings and that the world and all matter was the work of the latter and redemption was a question of the return of the imprisoned spirit to the heavenly realm after a series of purifying reincarnations. Quite. Give us those broth ingredients any day, you may say. But I find myself in a similar situation. Knowing what I know about Mr Goodman, if I were one hundred per cent storyteller and not also a witness, should I tell you now, should I say – and that was odd/significant/telling because in fact it later turned out that . . . etc? I know there are more subtle ways of doing it. Perhaps I've really tried here and there – like the bit about the shoes in Paris, for example. Of course I don't know he thought that, but somehow, because I wasn't there, I found it easier to sympathise with him in that bit, to see him in the light of his dilemma, and of his subsequently revealed and deeply problematic personality. Now, in this bit with me in the garden and him in Mr Vidalou's chair reading my book about the heretics, I'm back with my old ignorance of him somehow, unaffected by what I later learned.

Companionable silences – I've known a few. Have you noticed how the best ones are the ones you aren't aware of at the time? Sometimes I find myself thinking I haven't said anything for a while and wonder whether the silence can justly be deemed companionable. It denotes an awareness of the other, and of their preoccupation with something outside oneself which is registered in the happy confidence that your own presence is not impinging on them but rather making their detachment more comfortable. For this to work both ways is really very rare.

The silence with Mr Goodman that afternoon was, I would say, formal, even a little stiff, but I realised after a while that this was only my own feeling, that he in fact was quite absorbed. I felt a bit like one of those children who lolls self-consciously against a teacher's desk while the teacher is trying to make head or tail of their attempts to solve an equation. If I'd tried to make a move indoors – and my pastry must be nearly rested, I kept thinking – I felt he would have bidden me stay with an admonitory hand signal, without lifting his eyes from the page. In the end I stood up rather painfully and brushed the soil off my knees.

"Are you fond of beef, Mr Goodman?" I asked, in the formal idiom of the moment. "I have a large piece in the refrigerator. I eat meat occasionally, though we didn't for years. My husband was a vegetarian."

He looked up from the page with the air of one who somehow couldn't quite place me. "Why?" He might as well have used any other one of the interrogatives, it was a rhythmic use of the word, really, independent of its meaning.

"He believed in reincarnation. He felt it wasn't fair to lop off a struggling soul when it might actually be getting somewhere. Animal or human. Not that he was in the habit of human slaughter," I added quickly, "although he was very keen on population control. At the other end, of course. Contraception and so on. The south can be very backward."

"You mean the church?"

"Yes, the south is very Catholic of course. Except in enclaves like this, and the Cevennes, you know. Huguenot country."

He paused and pursed his lips. "It appears from this – " he tapped my book "that your local heretics had similar ideas. Procreation as evil because it perpetuated the whole business of mortal existence."

"It made more and more bodies for souls to come back and occupy, yes. Usually souls that had forfeited salvation, that is release from the material world, by having sex. It's a bit of a vicious circle."

"They might have other reasons for coming back. Not just that they had— " he waved his arm, as though he were talking about a far distant country on whose location he was rather hazy – "copulated. But I find the idea attractive. A genetically doomed religion, one which wills its own extinction."

"Extinction upon victory," I corrected. "The idea is that Lucifer himself must be saved, even when the last fallen soul has been reunited with its spirit and its celestial body, which are waiting for it in the celestial realm. I don't suppose the others mix with him very much," I said lightly. "I don't expect he enjoys quite the same degree of popularity up there. Once Lucifer himself has been purified, the material world will become an irrelevance. Empty. It will probably self destruct. That was the strange thing. They talked of the material world as *'le néant'*. Nothingness. It's a very different way of seeing things."

"Not to me. Lucifer's fall, such as you describe it here—

"Not me," I said, "the myth; I don't necessarily subscribe— "

He waved me aside.

"Lucifer's fall dragged the perfect into the imperfect, trapped spirit in matter, turned order into chaos, eternal into temporal." He met my eye with what I can only describe as a beatific expression, which I don't think I've seen before, only read about, unless Christian has it sometimes, but this was a strangely, to me, malevolent version of it. "Darkness into light," he finished.

"And how do you account for Lucifer's knowledge of evil, even his ability to do it? Its existence? It's not as though he could have been a fallen angel creating an evil world unless evil had existed already – even in the form of free will."

"Ah, free will," he said with an amused smile, and it seemed to send him into an indulgent sort of reverie. I felt like a sixth former who has mentioned fox hunting during the course of an altogether more elevated discussion on political freedom or something.

"I don't like all this putting down of evil to something beyond man's control. Evil is just not being good enough. It's as simple as that. It's shortfall. I am entirely convinced that the human race is capable of achieving collective goodness – that is freedom from fear in a world that is also free. Babies aren't born good, goodness means learning sociability, accommodation, tolerance, and not just in order that you can survive yourself, but because you want other people to as well. If you reduce the world population perhaps those things do become easier to organise because there are fewer other people to accommodate, but I don't see it as a necessity. You could just as well say that more people means a greater requirement on us all to be good."

"I'm not talking about goodness, he said rather contemptuously, "I'm talking about perfection. For all."

He made it sound like getting the vote. Women too? I wanted to ask.

"Please excuse me," he said, getting to his feet. "I should like to go and shower now."

That's right, I thought, childishly, go and spruce up that infernal machine that is merely an emanation of the devil's imagination. And don't use up all the hot water. I picked up Vidalou's chair and put it back inside the barn door. "You've done enough mischief for one day," I told it, and went off to wrap the pastry round the beef.

She had decided to come to France, because in England everything she saw, heard, touched, smelled and tasted recalled Will. It was a staggering sort of insensitivity, I felt, that allowed her completely to overlook that she had last been here with Mark, who was as dust, more so than Will, to her.

It was not just the experience of, say, walking through the park, not just the memory that they had done that together; it was that each of the infinite details of the experience had the same power again, in the way that each of our cells contains the means of its own replication, so that the memory lay in deep layers, deep as a whole winter's snow. There was only one season in which she had not known him – but even spring, when it came, would not be a season whose memories she would be spared, because the anniversary of his absence would remind her of her loss. Perhaps that would be less painful than being reminded of happiness. She wondered whether in preserving her body as the perfect, soulless machine, she was not indulging in a cult which in the end would bring no kind of salvation from pain at all, for her body included her sense organs, and her sense organs brought her comparisons with other times, other places, and they all fell so far short that she was constantly reminded that the machine was soulless, that the light had gone out. Did she then blame Will for this? Had he extinguished something in her by his disappearance? No, she told herself, he had tried to spare her the fading of the light. Here the sights and sounds were different. She had never been here with him. She had been here in fact with Mark. Perhaps passion flourishes in direct proportion to the amount of time you spend thinking about someone, digging your garden, enriching the soil. Will, who had invaded her life, leaving no corner of the picture uncoloured (except that ninth month and with it, symbolically, the whole of their possible future together), had demanded, and duly received, all her attention. Her every act was inflected by his presence in her life: if he did not share her experience, or it could not be related to him afterwards, set to his peculiar music, then it had no interest. Mark fell from her like a windfall too. Love is hateful and selfish, she thought, and yet she could not stop thinking that there was nothing else.

Christian drove the car. He hardly spoke. Although in a strange way – perhaps it was because he had suggested it to her – he was a kind of mirror image of Will, his ethereal partner, she found nothing about him summoned up painful memories, not even his dusty sour shirt, or his smile. There was something of the Huck Finn about him. His skin was quite pale, from being crouched on city pavements. He wore a hat made of some kind of straw, but individual grasses were beginning to come unstuck, and poke out at odd angles where it was most battered, and give the impression it was only half finished. Christian was not shy, but he could retire for long periods, into a world to which there was no obvious door, so you had to imagine for yourself whether it was open or shut, and whether you could enter and disturb him. He drove carefully, without seeming to notice where they were going. He bit his nails from time to time.

When they were still about twenty minutes from home, he began to tell her about Ariadne. They were driving east, with the sunset behind them, and every now and then it appeared in the wing mirror, and Elizabeth had the strange impression that it was catching them up, gaining on them rapidly. As she listened she realised Christian had the storyteller's gift, irreducible to pure discourse, just as he had a magic, even of a banal nature, when he drew his transitory pictures on the ground. There was a kind of temporariness, a lack of individuality, none of the egotism and reach for posterity which characterises the personalised version, copyright and secure. She could picture him, in his transitoriness, drawing lazily in the sand while the pharisees demanded a judgment, which they might quote for evermore as precedent, cut into granite stone.

Ariadne was Christian's childhood friend. Her parents had left Paris in the sixties to found a sort of sect called the "*Compagnie des Bergers*", somewhere above Montpellier, the members of which were mostly former psychoanalysts and doctors and lawyers – real third estaters – escaping from the pressures of life in the sixteenth arrondissement. There were about thirty of them, mostly couples, with an extraordinary number of assorted children who all slept together in large, whitewashed dormitories. The children were educated by correspondence course. The girls must have been better educated than the boys, who spent much of the day out with the flock of four hundred goats, which they milked out in the pasture. In the evenings they brought the milk back to the white-stoned commune, where the girls formed strange spherical cheeses out of them, pitted like golf balls, with their bare hands. The goats were a rustic breed, whose name I've forgotten, but the work was hard, since they weren't bred for milking, so the yield was always small. The cheese was wonderful, though. It was driven up to Paris twice a week, where it was sold to delicatessens in the sixteenth arrondissement. They even had a special arrangement with the Palais Elysées.

In the late seventies the whole thing started to break up rather. The founder members were getting on in their thirties, and were developing an interest in things like marketing and information technology. They began to look up old contacts from pre-*berger* days. Splinters broke off. The first splinter started up a purified version of the original. Other, later splinters joined up with remnants from politically based communities who had abandoned their activities after ten years of agitation. Still more became esoteric spiritualists. Some of these are are no more than "harmless", ecologically-minded post-*soixante huitards*, in flight from the technocracy of the capital, who have become unwittingly involved with what might otherwise seem a rather suspect group of right wingers; the latter, on the other hand, can with good reason claim descent from the neo-facists who were attracted to the region during the 1930s – in particular to Montségur – *silence, on chante.*

The fragmentation of the student generation after 1968 is an extraordinary phenomenon. In a way Pierre was one of them, except he was not a student, but a middle-aged academic in sympathy with his students. Our move down here followed upon his disenchantment with the failure of the revolution – and it was a real revolution, I don't think we realise how serious it nearly was, nor mourn its failure with sufficient absence of sentiment – for when sentiment sets in, all hope of revival is lost. He became a Christian communist; he even joined the party, which was one of the rarer options in those days, for the party were seen to have sold out the students in their attempt to "enlarge the context", as they say. He soon gave up the card-carrying business. I regret he didn't live to see the fall of the eastern block. I can't help feeling that it would have filled him with hope for the future of Communism.

Ariadne's parents chose one of the stranger options. They settled in the Ariège valley, became members of the esoteric church – or at least her father did. I don't think they let the women in by much more than a nose. He was a pan pipe specialist, and the instrument was introduced with great success into the spiritual ritual of the (literally) underground church, exploiting that faked innocence that is peculiar to it, a sinister toothless grin of a noise if you ask me, lisping through those dank caverns, their cathedrals, to hypnotise the neophytes. He soon found himself being funded to set up a factory to produce the instrument, which was exported worldwide, and made a great deal of money. No doubt they were able to buy lots of fairy lights for the caverns from the proceeds. At this point Ariadne was sixteen, very pretty, and extremely well educated. Christian received a letter from her one day – it had been sent here and had sat on the mantelpiece for two months waiting for him – putting it on open display like that was my way of burning a candle for her. I don't know what was in the letter, but Christian set off straight away, on his horse. I had never been so moved by him as when I stood out there in the courtyard watching him saddle up Escorie, with the anger of the young against the corruption of the old bringing a new kind of rigidity to his features. But it was not a brittle rigidity. It was more like the generous give and growth of a three-year-old sapling, which has survived the first dangerous years and is no longer in fear. He rescued her and took her off to help him with the pavements. Needless to say, the takings improved no end. Unfortunately she was discovered in a bar in Munich by a modelling agency and they whisked her off for restyling and she was never quite the same again.

"She was my first girlfriend. My last, actually. The last two years, I didn't . . . I don't know, it didn't crop up. We were like juveniles, I suppose, particularly with neither of our parents ever having much of a say in anything. She was like Pippa."

"Who's Pippa?"

"She's a character in Browning. She has a genius for great emotion. She lives like a child, through her instincts. She's like an artist, except she doesn't create anything. But she has all the feelings as if she did. It just spills out all over her. We split up after the chair incident. She went off doing this modelling. I found her in Paris again. She's married some bastard film director. Adverts, not even proper films. He made her get rid of a baby last week – his. The next day he had her filming an ad for wedding dresses in the Jardins Du Luxembourg. She ran away and stayed in my flat, well, one I borrowed from this cleaning agency, for a few days. Then she went back to him."

"Shouldn't you have stopped her?"

"She wanted to go. She's chosen her life now."

"You believe that?"

"She's cracked."

"Crazy?"

"No, like a mirror. She'll always have bad luck."

"You believe that?"

"No, but she does."

"Why have you told me all this?"

He turned up the road leading to the farm. They had been retarmacking that day, and the road spat up at them as they approached the house. Christian chucked his fag end out of the window, in front of the car, and drove over it adroitly to extinguish it.

"You reminded me of her."

"But I've got nothing in common with her at all. I mean, my life isn't like that at all."

"No," he said, "I didn't say it was. I said you reminded me of her. Opposites. Hang on, here we are. You go in. Don't tell her. I'll be in in a moment."

Elizabeth came into the dining room. In her cream-coloured clothes, with dark eyes and hair, she had the sensual yet *noli me tangere* quality of a fresh printed book whose pages have not yet been cut. I was sitting at the long polished table marking in pink fluorescent pen some concerts I meant to listen to on the radio. Delius – Cello Sonata, tick, Poulenc – flute, no not again . . . I could see Mr Goodman sitting in a strangely camp attitude out in the courtyard, his legs crossed and his clasped hands dangling slightly to one side. He was looking around the garden as though he were trying to memorise or price it – the sentinel hollyhocks, bowed with thirst, the bank of cornflowers sprouting from a trough edged with white alyssum, and a cushion of golden hypericum along the edge of the house. It was all tumbling a little, slightly blowsy. Perhaps, I was thinking, he'd like to do a spot of tidying up for me. I feared, though, that he would come like time with his abhorréd shears, and cut not only the faded flower but the whole plant, and we would be left with grinning stubble, a sort of death mask of a garden, for the remainder of the season. "Thank you, Mr Goodman," I imagined myself saying with a not quite theatrical tear in my eye "You've been most thorough," and he would beam, in as far as in him lay, and dash the petals smartly from his sleeves and trousers.

I was still reeling from the impertinence of his brother's phone call. I had guessed that something was up. He had appeared in such a ghostlike way that it was obvious to me, who have observed strangers at privileged quarters over so many years, that he had left the one little drama of his life behind him, and was but a husk, which still bore the shape of whatever experience it had been that had convulsed him into action, into flight. What shocked me was the mean indiscretion of the brother – who had stressed his clerical credentials and proceeded to belie whatever Christian charity he had by scandalising over his brother's relationship – he actually called it a relationship – with a girl in his sixth form. He managed to imply that there was something not quite nice about the relationship – quite aside from the schoolmaster's frustrated libido – that it hinged on an element of black magic or soothsaying. "One church is as good as another," I was tempted to say, but I didn't, because I didn't want him to think I gave any credence to his insinuations. Later, when I found out more about Alicia, it seemed she had played almost a novelistic trick, coupling their destinies in his mind. I thought how superstition sniffs out its own – to some it sticks, to others it is water off a duck's back. Both brothers had fallen for it in their different ways.

"What are you thinking about?" She was right. I was thinking about her. She dropped her bag on an armchair and came over and sat at the next chair at the table, board-room style.

"Nothing. An inane comparison."

"More comparisons."

"Who else has been making them?"

She shook her head and looked down at the page I was marking.

"You've missed the Schumman Lieder on Friday evening."

"Do I want to hear them?"

She ran her finger down the page and I noticed her skin was much darker already. The range of graded sun creams lined up on her bathroom shelf made you feel you were walking into some kind of laboratory, and that the applications should have been made by a qualified person in a white coat. The whole process of tanning seems more complicated even than getting the yeast and sugar right in the wine, or mixing diesel with two stroke for the lawn mower, which was the nearest I ever got to any operation of a scientific nature. But she never wandered down into the garden with a bottle of lotion in her hand. When she appeared she was always ready prepared, there was no liberal splashing on of unctions in the midday sun.

"No. Schumman's off."

I hadn't planned to tell her. What's that expression? *Truth will out.* When people say that they are usually trying to justify an untimely indiscretion by presenting it as a means of pre-empting the inevitable. It's an odd way of suggesting that the precedent already exists even though it hasn't occurred yet in real time. That wasn't the case here. There was no saying she would ever have had to know. In this case, truth will out, meant just that. I had to tell her. *Plus fort que moi.*

"I had a phone call this afternoon."

"Who?"

I meant to tell her about the vicar.

"It was Mark."

The surprise must have registered deep inside her, for there were no outward vibrations at all. She seemed almost to meditate on the news, swilling it round her brain like a dubious wine. She was leaning back in the chair, legs crossed, with her hands clasped to one side. I looked out at Mr Goodman, realising that his position implied not, as I had thought, relaxation, but some kind of fiercely contained stress. But he had moved off. He was like some phantom figure on a park bench – you never saw him move from place to place, he just appeared, then disappeared, emanating here and there in isolated episodes, but with no obvious narrative linking his various apparitions.

"Why? What did he want? Why did he call here?"

"He wanted the number of a colleague of Pierre's."

"Nothing to do with . . .?"

"Nothing at all."

"He must know. Frances sees him sometimes."

"Perhaps," I suggested. "Frances will think it better not to talk of you."

We had spoken of Elizabeth, of course, but I had been impressed by his tact and kindness, by his refusal to ask me questions or to pry.

She looked doubtful.

"It's strange. When we were together, I never thought he really thought that much about it. I thought I was just a pleasure."

"Just a pleasure?"

"A luxury. Something that embellished his existence."

"Goodness. I wouldn't have put it like that."

"When he went so strange over my leaving him – I somehow thought it was because it was Will, that Will had somehow changed the nature of his feeling for me."

"Of course. He took you away, and he did the thing every man probably wants to be the one to do – he woke you up – sensually, erotically, whatever the word is."

"That is the word."

"Yes, well. It is impossible not to be in love with a man who has that erotic power – and it doesn't come just from what you do – in that sense –"

"In bed?"

"Yes. It's everywhere, all the time. As far as I remember, it is not much different from obsession of any other kind."

"I can't remember," she said dully, in that underlined fashion that puts a remark in quotations and declares it a deliberate and final falsehood.

"Anyway," I said, ploughing on, and it had been my nearest brush with the possibility of telling her to snap out of it, as though life were not after all one long continuous take and one could from time to time shout "cut!" "It was nice to talk to him." I had to speak to the back of her, my words stealing up from behind. "You know, don't you, he's divorcing his wife?" What the hell, I thought, it's only gossip to her. And then I realised that that was wrong, that I belittled him by implying that he had meant me to tell her that.

She was standing by the big mahogany dresser, and was aligning the knives and forks I had put out for the evening meal, so they looked like something in a learn to count book. How many knives are there now? She turned towards me with the last one in her hand, shook her head and turned back to place the knife at the end of the row. She looked mature and amused, in that way people do who want to indicate that they are not at all amused, and are quite possibly only ironically amused at the fact that others might find what fails to amuse them funny.

I heard someone rushing across the hall, and before I had had time to think it couldn't possibly be Mr Goodman, because it wasn't his style, he appeared in the doorway. His face was puckered with excitement, and a nervous smirk did nothing to complement those otherwise rather Grecian features. He was suddenly all alive, almost hopping from foot to foot.

"I, excuse me, there's someone in the garden. I think . . ." He looked inquiringly at Elizabeth, as though he were soliciting permission to go on. "Perhaps you could . . ."

Elizabeth looked at him for a few seconds. He stared back at her. I could feel he was intimidated by her. He referred to her as Miss Faulkener. He was thrown off balance by having nothing specific to despise in her. She came and sat back next to me and covered my hand with her own. "Christian. I met him in Albi. He's come back."

While the emotional part of me gasped and sprang me to my feet, the rational part was registering that she had said "come back", not "come home" and wondering whether that meant that she or he regarded it as a place to return to without seeing it as home, with all the extra sentiment that word contains.

I stopped in front of the mirror in the kitchen on my way out to find him. Pierre said it was a shame I was such a hopeless dancer, because my face was pure ballerina. I suppose that means I now look like an irascible dance mistress, the kind that in a few years might take up a limp and a walking stick for rapping in annoyance on the polished floor. I straightened my dress. It was a sort of turquoise seersucker, with big front pockets for sticking paintbrushes and hairpins into. I took out the Spanish comb and ran it through my hair, then fastened it back into place again. A mirror is a kindly thing, a constant companion, slowing down the ageing process, familiarising us with the little lines and imperfections that age brings. It is strangely in tune with time, unlike a photograph album, always present, always true.

Christian was walking in the vines. He had grown. I was able to approach without being seen, for the vines were taller than myself. A bit like stealing up on someone in a supermarket. The ground was caked almost white, the same colour as the stone of the house, Elizabeth's dress, the uncut pages. Discarded twigs from the last winter pruning lay trodden underfoot by the vineyard workers. The bunches of grapes were formed, miraculous miniatures, waiting for water to swell to full size, some already purple in patches, like the landscape, rich green with violet tinges, in the shadows of the hills. There were large grey clouds in the east, from the sea, so that the sky, with the sinking sun at one end and the airy cushions of grey, almost black at the other, looked like a representation of two hemispheres. You could almost imagine the four winds taking up their customary positions, to huff and to puff from their four corners of the sky. What there was of a wind was westerly, and the sky would be quite clear again by morning.

I stood at the top of the row. Christian was walking up towards me, chewing on a stalk, stopping now and then to handle a bunch of grapes, moving between the two lines almost like a dignitary inspecting a parade, pausing here, a little touch of the hand, a genial word . . . then he saw me, and waved. I went towards him with my arms outstretched, but with the palms facing downwards, as you do with a dog or a horse, offering the back of your hand to show you mean no harm; a gesture you use when little children run to you, or when you are passing down the line in a barn dance (Nottingham Fair, 1952, puddles). He took me by the wrists and kissed me.

"Where have you come from?"

"Paris. I've been all over. The grapes look good."

I thought he looked tired, and wondered if it was the two years, or the single day which had worn him.

"I hope so. Pascal isn't too optimistic."

"How were they last year?"

"It was a good year."

"Sorry," he said. "I've been away a long time, haven't I?"

I didn't ask him if he was staying. I had a feeling that if I asked the answer would be no, and if I didn't there was a chance it might be yes. We started walking back towards the house.

"And you met Elizabeth."

"Yes. I recognised her."

It hadn't even crossed my mind to wonder how they had met. It was to me quite obvious that they were two people who would find one another in a crowd. Because you know them both it is as though they have already been introduced.

"I never told you," he said putting his arm round me. "I've seen her before. The last time she was here. She was singing. You were, you know." He stretched his hands out in front of him and wiggled his fingers.

"You never mentioned it."

He looked at me in concern. "You're thin," he said.

I smiled at him, and at myself for saying it. "I'm a widow."

"So you are. But not really." He stopped and looked about him. "He's almost still here isn't he? You haven't let him disappear."

"No. I let him go. That's why, somehow, he's still here. That's how it works."

He stood aside to let me through the garden gate ahead of him and said in a piercing imitation of a Scottish accent, "You're a wise wee woman."

Then he pulled me back quickly and shut the garden gate, so we were still on the outside, waiting to go in.

"What is it?" I almost expected him to hiss "Ariadne, she's hidden in the barn again! She always does that! Let's pretend we haven't seen her!" and lead me off round by the vegetable garden and start telling me one of his sing song little stories, as though he were twelve again.

"Mr Goodman? That's him isn't it?"

"That's him. Nothing to do with you?"

"I saw him. He watched me all week. I felt like – what's his name?"

"Tadzio?"

"That's it. How'd he get here?"

"He had your card. You must have left it lying about."

"Yeah. I left it on a cafe table by mistake. I came back with Ariadne in the afternoon, but they didn't have it. I know them, so they would have kept it. Sorry."

"Well, he's very quiet." It was the best I could say, the same sort of register as "very acceptable" for socks on birthdays. I told him what the puny priest had said on the phone. Christian said "I think you should get him out of the way."

"I can't tell him to go."

"No. I'll have a think. He's a sore thumb. It's not right, to come through cheating."

"Well, I am public, I mean it's not strictly invitation only."

"Yes it is," he said, "people select themselves."

"Well he's selected himself. He has every right."

Christian pushed open the gate.

"Not like that."

"Well, he is a little heavy going. Apparently he's been involved in some scandal. He's a teacher. Something to do with a girl. I don't think we talk about it."

"Hope not," he said.

Elizabeth was crossing over to her work room. She had changed into jeans and a red tee shirt. I was surprised. She looked much younger, a bit like you imagine Greek statues must have looked in the days when they were freshly painted. She gave her subdued smile.

"I've cut up some vegetables. On the kitchen table."

"Run down to the cellar and fetch some wine, could you?"

Christian ignored me, though I knew he'd heard, and would eventually do as I asked. He was operating a sort of queuing system of priorities.

"Where are you going?"

He had this way of asking questions that made them sound like quotations from an ancient tale. Where are you going? What is your name? What ails you? Elizabeth managed to turn it back into an ordinary question.

"I'm going to write a letter to Marguerite's editor and tell him what order we're going to do the books in."

He looked up the wooden steps. "Is that where you work?"

"The room on the right, yes."

"Good. The room on the left's mine."

She was carrying a pile of books. "Here, give me those." He looked at me. "I'll get the wine in a second."

I must have been looking a bit sceptical, because he said, "Promise," and winked at me. Then he ran up the steps and opened the door of Elizabeth's room with his shoulder.

While I was waiting for the vegetables, Mr Goodman came into the kitchen. I was thinking about Mark, who had rung just an hour before they returned, and how I felt, a little, as though

I had betrayed him. I couldn't have said no to Elizabeth, refused to take her in, not cared for her. But I felt he must see it as a kind of abduction of affection. Something that had been his, that he had brought here first, had become mine.

"I'll look after that, thank you."

I jumped. I had been about to pick up a tray of glasses which I had unloaded from the dishwasher. Mr Goodman moved me aside and stooped to take it in his hands.

"Thank you. On the table in the dining room, if you don't mind." Then I turned away to deal with the potato peelings so I wouldn't have to look. He was trying to be normal, to be involved, but he was all stiff jointed, like a creature of nuts and bolts.

Christian came in with two bottles of wine. He was exuberant. He wasn't really looking at me. He was happy to be back, but I was just one of the things that set a scene in which he could be happy. He set the bottles on the kitchen table.

"Not there, in the dining room."

He picked them up again. He was just about to turn and take them through, when I saw him hesitate and blink.

"What is it?"

He looked up at me. He was biting his lips together, and they were quite white.

"Nothing. It's OK. It's gone."

Mr Goodman, who was standing behind him, moved elaborately aside.

"Sorry," said Christian, and turned round. He tucked one of the bottles under his arm and held out his hand.

"Christian."

Mr Goodman seemed suddenly to turn shy. He rubbed his hand on the front of his trousers and put it in Christian's. I thought for a moment Christian might say something to hurt him, that he hadn't been asked, that he wasn't wanted here.

"No," I thought, very hard, and probably looked sternly over at Christian, who glanced back at me, and said, "Good. 'Scuse me."

Mr Goodman followed him into the dining room. I was reminded of a performance of *The Tempest* I saw in some municipal park in England once, where the crowd kept having to follow the actors round at every change of scene. But I was wrong to worry. Christian never harms. I thought he was going to grow into one who at least had power to do so, but instead he got stuck in a kind of rut of adolescent tenderness. Or perhaps I'm transferring, and it was just that he inspired more tenderness, indiscriminately, than anyone I've ever known. He was the one you loved. He loved, too, by example. When you were near him you suddenly remembered the tune, the steps, it became as simple as breathing. I suppose it was easy for him. He was free. The only right he reserved was not to be there, not always to appear to care. He wasn't good on birthdays. I never knew what he did at Christmas, but to my knowledge he didn't observe it. So in a way his love came, you could say, cheaply. It cost him little, but I always imagined that was because his cup ran over with it. He could afford to give it away. I thought perhaps he had changed, and I knew with a mother's instinct that it was, after all, the single day and not the two years' absence that had changed him. He had lost some of that dreaminess that made people smile and draw out of his path, for fear he would wander straight into them, absorbed in his own landscape, finding his footing in the real world only by instinct and luck.

I heard him crossing the yard. He ran up the steps and into Elizabeth's room. Ten minutes later, he brought her over. She looked slightly reluctant. That first day, he still believed that if she had faith in him she could be helped. Later, he realised you simply can't have faith in someone you think might love you in that way, the hardest way, the way that has nothing to do with neighbourliness. You can reciprocate, but you can't ever believe they'll change the world for you. You recognise their frailty, you know how vulnerable they are. To love you have to renounce your special powers, come down to earth, hand back the magic stone. Or to use your special powers, you must renounce your love. This won't work, I thought. Not for him. She's too raw, deep inside, even if she looks burnished and succulent. She carried the food through for me. Christian sat opposite her, and I sat by him, and opposite Mr Goodman.

Mr Goodman had very little to say for himself. I was rather fascinated by him. I liked to watch him listen. Christian was telling a strange story about a woman he'd met in a churchyard in Stockholm, who said that she'd been sitting by the fire one autumn day when her husband, who had been dozing, smiled at her and made a movement of his hand. She had gone over to him and kissed him lightly and he had caught her hand in his and said, "You have such beautiful eyes." She was going to sit down again, when he added "azure blue," and having said it, died. "What was strange," said Christian, "was her eyes were brown."

All this time, I was watching Mr Goodman. He couldn't take his eyes off the wine bottle. He had a way of not looking the speaker in the eye as he listened which made it look as though he were listening to a recording on the radio, or to a translation coming to him over headphones. At first I wondered if he was a closet alcoholic, and was measuring how many mouthfuls were left in the bottle, what portion was due to him, and so on, but then I realised it was the label. Christian had brought up some of the special reserve with the *Et in Arcadia* labels.

I felt an odd warmth for Mr Goodman that evening. He was, as Elizabeth said, a cold fish, and rather unlovely, as cold fish are. You really did feel that if you drew your finger down his cheek the scales would come off on the tip, and that they would not be hard, as you always expect scales to be, but soft and glaucous. I had the notion you could wear him away to nothing like that, without even meaning to, because there was a husk and a skeleton missing. So no, maybe it wasn't warmth I felt, but a kind of curious pity. He was neither sensuous – a creature of life and pleasures – nor an intellectual – an arid observer, whose every attempt to engage, even on the fringes of the world, resulted in no more than melancholy, the "*Ich möchte träumen, aber sie will tanzen*" of those stern Thomas Mann characters he physically resembled. Nor was he an artist. He had nothing to create, no vision to realise. He was stuck somewhere – maybe the world has a lot of these, but you don't usually notice, because normally there's a place for them, because of the kind of world we have made. He had a painful sensitivity to the harm the world could do him, that was all. Perhaps in Christian he precisely recognised one who, as it has been said, mistakenly, of another in this story, had power to hurt and did none. It's a dangerous wager.

Christian said suddenly "I saw Arnaud in town today. You

know, the goatherd? He wants me to goat-sit for a few days. He's off to a wedding in Perpignan tomorrow. Or a funeral. I can't remember."

"All the way up the mountain?"

"They're right at the top. But I don't want to go straight off again."

Elizabeth was watching him, and turned to me as he appealed to her, for arbitration, perhaps, noting my indulgence, and measuring her own resistance to his charm by my lack of it.

"Don't rush off again. Can't you find someone else? It's a lovely place," I told Mr Goodman. "The goats are quite delightful. I spent some time up there myself," I added, "The autumn before last."

"I brought her food."

"He did," I said, "he brought me food."

Elizabeth had taken the remains of the bread out into the garden in her napkin. She came back inside, leaving the glass doors open. "They're burning the mountain," she said. "It's the night of St Jean." I turned and saw the sky flushed a pale amber to the west. So that was why he had come home. He loved the fires of Saint Jean, that burned on every mountain top from coast to coast. There was no timetable. You lit yours when you saw your neighbour's burning. The speed with which the chain ignited reflected the speed with which an idea can be passed. No faster than the speed of light, but not much slower either.

Christian turned to Mr Goodman. "Do you think," he said, as though he were asking him to go and check the time, or find a candle, "you'd be able to goat sit for me? I could send you in my place. It's not for everyone. But you might like it. Watching the flock."

Mr Goodman was sitting with his hands clasped by his mouth and his index fingers either side of his nose. ("Is a roman nose straight, like a roman road?" Christian asked me the next day.) He gave a fake little gesture of shock, rousing himself from what was more vacant than pensive mood and cocked his head in an almost flirtatious way. He was quite bewitched by Christian, although you wouldn't have thought he was his type at all. He followed him with his eyes, almost as though hoping to catch him out in a sleight of hand, the card up the sleeve, the magnetic ring sewn into his cuff. But it was a look of confidence at the same time. Here, where you least expected it, was a kind of faith. There was no reason for Mr Goodman to trust in him. Christian was never exactly a star pupil. On his school reports they said "Christian is so intelligent it renders him really very stupid", or something like that. I certainly wouldn't say he was educated.

Elizabeth had sat down at the table again. She had hardly eaten anything. She reached out for the water jug and the ice, falling into her glass, made a clinking noise like Christian's coloured chalks.

"Where is this?"

"About two hours from here. He's got this sort of little hut up a mountain. He's made a goat park round it. It's great, you can see all the way to the Mediterranean, and all the mountain peaks. It's like being on a trampoline. Someone just has to be there. He's got books and things."

He looked over at Mr Goodman, who was sorting brown bread crumbs from white around his plate. We'd had brown bread with the soup and were now eating cheese. "There isn't a telephone, though," he said, so Mr Goodman would say, "Oh that wouldn't matter at all . . ." and the deal would be clinched, which is exactly what he did.

I got up and poured wine into their glasses. "Elizabeth?"

"No thanks." She was sitting there with her fingers touching her temples, feeling the beat of her blood, maybe, with just the tips of her finger pads. "Actually, I think I'll go to bed. I don't feel very— "

Christian, rather elated with his success in engineering a temporary relocation of Mr Goodman, said, "Oh don't go yet. Won't you sing?"

There was – and it was accentuated by the last word of his sentence, by the contrast between the exhortation and its response – a rather protracted silence.

"No," said Elizabeth, "I don't really sing any more." She took her plate out into the kitchen and I could hear her doing some of the washing up.

"Don't do that," I called, but there was no answer. Christian started to get up and go and see her, but I told him to stay put. He looked crestfallen. "I upset her?"

"No, it's not you. Don't worry."

I went out into the kitchen and she was bent over the sink with her hands in the water, and tears running down her face. I put my hand on her shoulder.

"Leave that."

She couldn't wipe her face because her hands were in the sink, so she just licked at a tear as it ran past her lips.

"What is it?"

Mr Goodman came in. At least I suppose he did. He was doing his park bench bit again. "Excuse me, I er . . ." It seemed he was looking for the corkscrew. Christian was taking the easy way out and offering him more wine.

"On the hook there, by the stove."

"Thank you." He sidled out again, deliberately not looking at Elizabeth, who stood as though frozen, with her head bowed.

"It's just . . . I don't know. Christian."

"Christian?" It wasn't what I had expected.

"Nothing. He's just like you said. But . . . it doesn't help."

"He's a great healer. Can be. Like time. I know you don't want to hear that. Everyone prefers the epic to the dramatic, Hamlet to Beowolf. We want to think it's quick, cathartic. But it does take time, usually. That's why you're here. There's all the time in the world. Christian and I will look after you. And when Christian goes away again we will look after each other."

She paused, then drew her hands out of the sink. She stood there with them dripping, held well away from her shirt, over the bowl. It was a gesture I had seen in films, when the surgeon withdraws his hands from the patient's entrails. I handed her a towel. She dried her hands, and then her face and said, "I saw that little boy again. He looks like Christian, the way he is in the photo."

"You saw him where?"

"In a dream. After we had had lunch. He was playing on a beach by a martello tower."

I sighed, perhaps just a bit impatiently. I was beginning to tire of all these wistful images. There was a whiff of morbidity and decay. I wanted, all of a sudden, to think of airlines, and wipe-clean surfaces, and, yes, bright lights, not bright light, and stamp on all this rather *fin-de-siècle* atmosphere. I wanted jokes, and blaring music, and people arguing about politics. Oh hell, I thought, when this is all over I'm going to visit Cousin Jean. Cousin Jean is eighty and lives in a condominium by a west coast beach.

"Then you didn't really see him."

"No, I suppose not."

"You still think about the child?"

"Yes. I don't want to, but I do. I know I sound sickly and morbid."

"Thank heaven at least you know you do. Now off to bed."

Christian was sitting talking chirpily to Mr Goodman. I couldn't imagine what it was about, and I found, strangely, since it was his first night back, that I didn't care. Mr Goodman had taken off his glasses and was rubbing the lenses tenderly with his napkin. Elizabeth's rose, the one Pascal had handed her the day before, was wilting a little in its narrow vase. We had stripped the mildewed leaves away, to leave just the bud, which was only half open, or half shut. I changed the water and brought it into the dining room and put it on the the dresser.

"I'll clear up," Christian said.

"Yes—". Mr Goodman. Enthusiastically. Anything to get me out of the room. Christian gave me a kiss and said he'd see me in the morning.

"Can I take your car to drive him up?"

"Yes. Don't ride the clutch. Good night."

In the middle of the night I got up and checked someone had switched off the garden light. Someone had. As I looked out into the garden I heard a noise, and looked up to see a long white hand push open the shutter by its fingertips, first the left, and then the right shutter. As the right hand shutter folded back against the wall I saw him standing at the open window, his chest bare to the night, a strong white chest, with hair high up to the throat, but springing only from the breast bone. I felt chilled by the white of him in the moonlight, and those frightened, unblinking eyes that looked out into the darkness but could not see. I picked up my torch to move back inside and he heard me, and slipped quickly, with a practised, childlike stealth, back into his room, closing the window but not the shutter behind him.

Part Five

15

Robert heard Janet's breathless "yes!" and shoved hard. Ah, satisfaction! The airwaves were open.

"Hello there!" he cried jovially. "Can you hear me?"

Janet felt that for someone who was forever reminding his congregation that the line to Him up there was always open, Robert showed remarkably little faith in the ability of British Telecom to achieve the same end on their own modest scale.

"I was just ringing— " what was the precise grammatical function of that "just"? He was always saying *just*. "Oh Lord, we just want to thank You . . ." Was it an excuse for having only popped in briefly, as it were, before nipping off to pay the papers or prick the lawn? "We're just so full of Your praises, Lord . . ." Well really, if that's all, why make such a song and dance about it? Why even bother to mention it at all? We just want to stand here before you humbly and tune into your presence . . . It was only a redundant adverb, but it seemed to have become an indispensable element of extemporised prayer. Honestly, didn't they ever think the Almighty might actually appreciate a bit more *bottle* from time to time? It was like one of those birthday card messages – just to say, on this special day . . . and so on. Why? Why were people always pretending to apologise? They were always the ones who importuned the most. There was a fake bashfulness, a don't mind me-ness, which frankly got up her nose. Janet, for her own part, was always saying "frankly", as though when the highlight wasn't there she could be assumed to be being just a fraction deceitful.

"What?" (I really am rather busy).

"Well, I'm here, love, safe and sound, just thought I'd let you know."

"It's raining. I was just getting the washing in." Just? What kind of just? Only a little job? Certainly not! At that moment, yes that was what it meant – so, redundant again. Perhaps she'd write a letter to *The Times*, though they didn't get *The Times*, that was just (oh God) a manner of speech.

"Oh, not so bad here, a bit of cloud . . ."

"Can't hear you, I'm afraid, its' a bad line. I'll see when I see you."

On the way out of the phone box Robert had a little local trouble with the door arrangement, which was like something in one of those visual spatial ability tests for eleven-year-olds. Out on the street he looked at his watch – a little plastic digital thing he had found strapped to an extra large bar of white chocolate he had bought on the ferry back from France to cheer himself. Not that he was a man who timed his life with great precision. His visits to members of his congregation were haphazard. His sermons (a right ranter, was the opinion of a hitherto stalwart member of the congregation, one of the many who greatly missed the former incumbent, the Reverend Thackaray, who had married late and moved away) seemed to follow a timing system more appropriate to the kitchen than to the House of God. They came immediately after the Offertory and seemed to come out at about twenty minutes to the pound and twenty minutes over. His daily routine was a bit of a shambles, too. It was all very well to say the Lord's work was never done, Mrs Frampton remarked to one of the other ladies on the social committee, it was hardly surprising if the poor man couldn't stick to even the simplest agenda. They always referred to one another as ladies, though Janet had valiantly set up a women's group during the first month of Robert's tenure. That hadn't lasted long. By the time she had organised a programme of speakers it had renamed itself the Ladies' Circle and seemed to be well launched on a programme for the fabrication of tea cosies for the third world. She imagined Robert going on a deputation to deliver said items to some sabre-bearing tribe in deepest Africa – "my wife and her loyal team of ladies just wanted to say . . ." Poor Janet. The role of "one of our ladies" was not one she felt at home with. She couldn't imagine Peter gathering the disciples together in the week after Easter and saying, "And now for the notices: some of our valuable ladies made quite a startling discovery this morning as they went about their duties – for which thank you very much Mary and your team. You'll find this the subject of a short address in this week's newsletter." Janet fervently wished she could have been one of the early Nazarenes. A little more militancy would not have gone amiss.

2

It was a north eastern town – mildly industrial, its wealth built up in the 1870s on a shoe-manufacturing business. Aiden had once told Robert that the founder of Herring's shoes, Nathan Herring, a widower, had had a very ugly daughter – so ugly, he said, that whenever he brought a young man home to make her acquaintance, the suitor's gaze would automatically drop to the floor. "I says to myself, if they're looking at floor, let's give them summat to look at, no point wastin' what's goin' for nowt." So Nathan had founded a shoe factory, which had been opened by Queen Victoria herself. Nathan had seen Queen Victoria's ankle – when he told the story he cradled the imaginary foot in his hands as though it had been as fragile as a Wedgwood teacup – but he would recount only the fact and not the detail of the Queen's ankle. Propriety obliged. And the story had a happy ending. Lavinia, whose feet, like those of her sovereign Queen, were pretty as porcelain, married well and wealthily, and to this day the factory thrived, although the top of the range shoe was now the all leather doc marten, worn by the sons and daughters of the upper middle classes, and only shop assistants tottered round town in daintily heeled slippers.

The town looked well in June. Flowers everywhere, a clang of church bells, shops selling country craft pottery, the doctor's plaque in gleaming brass, the children streaming out of the school gates. Unfortunately, as Aiden would have been quick to point out, where things were not to be taken on the strength of faith alone, you usually needed more than four versions if you were to establish anything like a true picture of the facts.

It was half past twelve. Robert had arranged with Aiden's

landlady – who sounded like just the sort of person who would choose Aiden for a tenant – that he would pick up the key around two o' clock that afternoon. At great pains – his pain, he felt, as though she had been twisting his ear – she had explained why it would not be possible for her to find time for him before that. "I'm sure you'll understand," she had said in a way that was meant to be cutting – in fact it was pretty difficult to cut Robert, so the effect was simply that of creating a slight whistle in the air as she sharpened her knife. It was almost as though she had wondered what he was doing taking time off to run around after keys, when she, who was only a humble servant – and he at least a vassal in the Lord's army – was so frightfully busy. People always seemed to expect him to be either visiting the sick or on his knees. It was difficult not to feel that the greater part of the flock was stuck behind some turnstile of their own making called modernity. A sermon, there. Robert's forbearance was not a very flexible friend, it was a purpose-made tool, forged, by attrition, out of long habit of mind, no more the natural excrescence of a heart of gold than Aiden's high mindedness. Robert would have felt more sympathy with his brother's occupation of the moral high ground (before the Event), if he had been able to see it as a hard won victory over a lascivious epicurean streak lurking in the depths of his psyche. No, forbearance bore a very distant relationship to love, tolerance, and patience, because it was always demanded in one's dealings with those who were precisely incapable of provoking such normally accessible emotions. Reforming zeal, yes; exasperation with petty godlessness masquerading as quiet devotion (the Martha syndrome), God, yes. Too many of his loyal parishioners (and give him ninety-nine unredeemed drop-outs for each fully-prayed-up stalwart) seemed to think that access to God's direct line could be gained only by a kind of furtive phone-tapping. If any one of them had somehow got through, if illumination had come their way, he wouldn't have been able to stop himself from feeling a rather sour, Salieri-like disappointment in the randomness of God's dispensations. "We only want to give of our very best, Mr Goodman," one lady had said to him the other week. "I do not feel clapping my hands in time to the rhythm of the 'Lord of the Dance' is the best I can do. I studied at the Royal College for three years and feel I have something rather more to offer." There was a distinct absence of "unless ye become as little children" in the Church today. "God doesn't care what you wear, Mrs Frampton", he had said, when she had objected to communicants wearing jeans. "Do you really think He notices whether I wear my dog collar?" "No," she had answered rather coldly, "I expect He's too busy answering phone calls." He had preached the previous Sunday to the effect that it was only during the Industrial Revolution that idleness had supplanted pride as society's top sin. "Behold the lilies of the field," he had quoted, pausing eloquently before shuffling his notes and announcing the next hymn and Mrs Frampton had collared him afterwards for a quiet word about the state of the churchyard, which had a nasty case of ditch campion. It was all extremely trying. Anyway, he was off on sabbatical soon, and he would be glad for the er . . . change. He sometimes wondered whether it shouldn't have been he who had taken to the blackboard and Aiden to the pulpit. Mrs Frampton would have thoroughly approved of Aiden's lack of divine fire, and for himself, well, he certainly wouldn't have got himself into a mess of this sort.

In short, Robert was feeling rather below par. He had begun to think that the ecclesiastical system in Britain had been designed to cater for a society whose entire framework had since changed. The whole thing of Sunday mornings and organs and flowers and fund-raising activities was completely anachronistic. So too with the structure of services. Funerals! Weddings! Why, when he and Janet had wed over twenty years ago, they had been garlanded and barefoot (Janet's father, who had refused to attend the wedding because he disapproved of their premarital co-habitation, had called his only daughter a whore and reminded her not to leave the price on the soles of her feet, which was the nearest Robert had ever come to hitting anyone, though Aiden actually smiled.) So too, to be honest, with God. The cult of God should surely be as fluid and as susceptible to regional variation as the cult of Apollo. "We wither and flourish but Nought changeth thee," they all sang, he felt not without a certain complacency, as though they could jolly well allow the grass to grow under their feet because it wouldn't change anything in the long run. He felt they could do with a more capricious God, one who kept them on their toes more. What with him and his "More capriciousness!" and Janet with her "More bottle!" perhaps there was hope yet.

But Janet – Janet too was changing. As recently as this summer in Brittany, she had felt somehow pocket-sized, that is, he did not have to move over to accommodate her. She had in some ways been his amanuensis, she had enlightened him over the role of the social gospel in the modern world, encouraged him to go into the church, marched alongside him whilst continuing her job, threading it artfully through the cloth of their existence, a fleck or two here and there of her own preoccupations, but nothing to ruck up the smooth surface of their life as a couple, public or private. Now, at forty-eight years of age, childless and with waning energy (perhaps it was just a phase of life) she seemed to be becoming increasingly irritable, less prepared to hold her forefinger down on the knot while he painstakingly elaborated the bow, pulling and teasing to get the balance just right. She was withdrawing into a world which was of course smaller, pettier, than his own – and yet she managed at the same time to imply that she had had enough of the daily round and common task and was becoming in some way a contemplative. It was something to do with Aiden's defection – not his misdemeanour – but his action in abandoning them at the roadside that day. In rejecting their support he had undermined them, brought into question their whole approach to the resolution of social problems, which was their particular area of expertise. "You kept talking to him about Lacan and Dolto!" insisted Janet as they bumped up the ramp onto the ferry. "Why didn't you talk to him about the love of God, you great fool!" Robert had tipped his head from side to side, the tilt indicating that he was weighing up arguments on either side of a mental line – he, a reasonable chap and not opposed to a bit of dialectic from time to time. There would be other causes, other lost sheep, and goodness knows, we all need them – what reassurance can we have that we are not lost ourselves unless we are out on the hillside looking for others?

He decided to go and take in a quick pint.

"You not on duty then?" asked the barman, quite seriously,

and Robert, who was wearing his dog collar for once – perhaps with all this travelling about he was frightened of getting lost – had to point out that he was always on duty, but that unlike policemen he and his kind were allowed to imbibe on the job. Yes, even chapel. The barman thought this was a great piece of information. From such seeds can great ideas grow. Robert felt that if the man had been an eighteenth-century essayist he could not have been more delighted with the thought and that he would elaborate it, almost unconsciously, throughout the long, pint-pulling day.

As he was sitting there in the gloaming watching with satisfaction the neat comings and goings of the regulars, the pleasant ease of the barman, who was explaining to an American lady that the Citizen's Advice Bureau was home not to a revolutionary organisation who told you how to make Molotov cocktails but rather to a conscientious and hard working team of people who gave advice on how to fill out your tax form, the door opened and a young girl of about sixteen or seventeen walked in.

She was quite tall, and she hung her head slightly as she walked, though the rest of her walked well. She was wearing the uniform of Aiden's school, a dark red blazer with a little white lion on the pocket, a white shirt and long narrow dark blue skirt. Over her shoulder she wore a string bag, from out of the top of which poked a selection of books and files. Her black hair fell all to one side of her head in small coils. It was long, beyond shoulder length and when she wanted to push it aside she did not brush it back from her head, but carefully picked it up near the ends, where it clustered in a large swing of curl and placed it absently over her shoulder, putting it behind her, leaving her finger where it was, twisting the end of her hair. She was reading a letter, standing at the bar. The barman poured out a grapefruit juice and put it in front of her. She looked up.

"Thanks."

Pete leaned over the bar. "He's upstairs. All ready for you. Nice bloke. Salesman."

She carried on reading, bending over the words under the light of a faked carriage lamp, turning the flimsy pages this way and that – they seemed to be in the wrong order, or she could not make the words follow. Then she finished, and stuffed the pages back into her bag, picked up her glass and drank. At that moment she caught sight of Robert in the glass behind the bar. He was sitting on a leather seat against the wall directly behind her.

It could have been any time of day. Even morning in an English pub can seem like one hour before closing. For a moment it seemed to Robert that the neon dipped, that the synthetic fabric round the little red lamps had given up its place to stiff, dyed, eastern cottons, that the kegs on the floor really did contain ale from the hop yards of Kent, born up north in horse-drawn barges, and that this girl had stepped straight from a lithograph of Flint or Murillo, off a sea-faring vessel from the isles. Music came from the juke box by the door, but it was a slow, dreamy song, a woman singing as though alone in a room at night. She saw a long face, with quite a lot of hollows and bumps and creases, strong, wide open eyes and sharp clear nose and, softly outlined by a fair beard, a mouth she knew from somewhere else. But how could she possibly know it from somewhere else, when she had not seen the man before, unless she had seen it on someone else? But a mouth wasn't like a garment of clothing from a shop, you couldn't have more than one of them the same. It was a sensual mouth that did not seem to go with the man's general appearance. As she stared at him in the glass he bit his lip slightly nervously and then took a gulp of his pint. When he came up for air she was still staring at him and he had a little fringe of foam on his beard, matching the circular collar underneath. It was almost, he thought, as though she did not realise that he too could see her, that the trick of the mirror was not such as to render her invisible. She pushed herself back from the bar, picked her bag up off the floor and went over to the staircase. He watched her run up red-carpeted steps, her hand trailing after her along the banister rail, and her fingernails against her olivey hands were palest pink.

"Have I seen you before?" asked the barman as he ordered another half.

Robert felt that was really a bit much, as though being seen by Pete would have been a more memorable event in his life than setting eyes on Robert, if he had done, had been for Pete.

"I don't know," he said. "Have you?"

"Dunno. Not one of these telly preachers? *Songs of Praise*, all that?"

"No."

"Good job. Creepy crowd, that lot. Take over the world if we're not careful. You regulars want to watch out. Queering your pitch. That what's 'is name, Bakker fellow – they all loved him didn't they? That's television for you. Money – advertisements, it's all connected. 'Scuse my French," he added, rather confusingly.

Robert assured him that it took all sorts of people to do the Lord's work, and that things that seemed negative now would perhaps be seen in later years to have borne very real fruit.

"You can't have very real," said Pete, perhaps feeling that a point of language might gain him a surreptitious upper hand here. "Only real."

Robert handed over a five pound note.

"How right you are," he said heartily and glanced at his watch. "There was something funny about him", Pete said to a regular that evening. "He was wearing this little plastic watch."

It was half past one. Robert went out and sat under the trees in a little park opposite the pub and watched the children making their way back to school. He saw how the girls floated past him, whispering about things that were so new to them – how he envied that newness, like speculators storing up their treasure somewhere not too far, but just a little way, into the future. He realised he was quite invisible to them. And yet, he thought, I am a man, like any other. My vows have not bound me to be sexually inert. And yet this is how I am perceived. Janet was often saying things were castrating. He wished she wouldn't use the word quite so freely. Whatever horror stories you heard, he couldn't help feeling that it was an experience most particular to the male of the species, and that they therefore had prior claim over any metaphorical use of the word. He abhorred the absence of sexiness in the church, its musty smell of oasis and damp and old hymn books. Full of Grace, they said. Grace? When had he last seen anything of grace – a bridal procession, a bored bridesmaid dreamily plucking the petals from her bouquet? Perhaps, but if that was the best they could do. The girl in the pub – he could very well picture her pouring oils over the Lord's feet and wiping them away with her hair – and she wouldn't have bought it with the very encouraging profits (for which a very big thank you again, ladies) from the cake and handwork sale either. The girl's mysterious disappearance up the staircase had disturbed him. "He's upstairs, ready for you."

He collected the key from a voluble Mrs Coleman, who was eager to milk him for information about Aiden. "We were never close," she said, and Robert couldn't help feeling that she was stroking her little ginger cat rather too languidly as she said it, and wondered if that denoted regret. He felt stifled in her house, dehydrated, like her prominently placed weeping fig, which looked more like someone that had cried for a very long time and then dried up, crinkled and a bit chapped.

"I'm sorry he's had to leave though, I can't hope to be so lucky next time. What was it you said . . .?"

"He's abroad – he, er – he needed a complete rest. It was, well yes, I suppose his job, you know."

"Oh yes," said Mrs Coleman, "I know. Teachers. All this stress. We all have our cross to bear."

He felt she had been saving it up like a birthday card with a particularly appropriate theme: "for a fishing uncle" etc. He did not like the expression, it implied such an awful cheapening of the idea, as though the cross, an instrument of torture, could be substituted for a rather heavy load of shopping from Sainsbury's.

Aiden's house was in a terrace which dated from the period of the town's brief affluence as a market garden centre in the mid-eighteenth century. The façades were all neatly maintained, and Robert reflected that Aiden had lived well, and about as elegantly as it was possible to do in a suburb which had largely been given over to the *fin de siècle*, plastic high street and prefabricated car parks. The front door had been painted burgundy red. He wondered whether Aiden had done this himself. Although they had had so little to do with one another during adult life, Robert was pretty sure that his picture of Aiden was an accurate one. He couldn't see him engaged in any kind of DIY to save his life. He would have had somebody in.

He let himself in, and was surprised to notice that a light had been left on. He switched it off and put his little suitcase down next to the umbrella stand. Then it seemed a bit dark inside, so he switched it back on again. Several pairs of shoes were laid side by side on a rack next to the umbrellas. A coat on the peg above. No keys on the hook. He wondered what Aiden had done with his school keys.

He decided to do a quick tour of the house. He had stepped straight through the front door into the living room (there was a straw mat which denoted the no man's land between indoors and outdoors). The room had a high ceiling, and the walls were white. The carpet, again, a deep burgundy. On the walls, fine drawings in the manner of Augustus John, very plain, the subjects – mostly portraits from an indeterminate era. The furniture was scarce. A large, dark sofa, perhaps a little worn on the arms. Along one wall, books, from floor to ceiling. The curtains were hung from a dark gold, upholstered pole, and drew by pulling on a heavy brass weight attached to a cord. Robert opened them, and went over to look at the books.

It was a typical collection for the most part. A great deal of poetry. Classic novels, a lot of crumbling French paperbacks of a certain style, manila coloured, and fragile as parchment. Quite a few things on classical antiquity, astronomy – where did Aiden get these interests from? Essays. He imagined Aiden sitting there on the sofa during winter evenings, perhaps sipping a small glass of port and carefully turning the pages of *The Way of All Flesh*. It was a world far removed from his own illuminatory texts by retired deaconesses living in Alabama – homilies, witnesses, short prayers for a busy life. On a desk against the wall, which folded back up, and locked with a key, but was now standing open, stood a pile of essays. Robert took one from the top of the pile. "*Le coeur a ses raisons que la raison ne connaît point.* Discuss in French (no less than five hundred words. You should spend exactly one hour on this question)." Goodness, thought Robert, one hour to explain irrational behaviour, and there was a certain poignancy, a little short of irony, in the requirement to be brief.

He went into the kitchen. Everything was neat and tidy – although the washing up had been left on the draining board. Was it that Aiden had been in a hurry – or had he known he would not be returning from the holiday? Had he packed for a long absence? He had not thought to ask. He knew his brother had used a credit card in Brittany, so presumably he had not had to think very far in advance about money. The kitchen was fairly spartan – just a wooden table and four chairs, a jug next to the cooker with some kitchen implements – Aiden had surprised them one evening in Brittany by disappearing into the kitchen and preparing a meal far beyond the standard set by Janet (who had not been best pleased) of halibut poached in white wine with baby vegetables. It had taken him about twenty-five minutes and afterwards there was not a pot or a pan out of place.

He went up the stairs and tried one door – the bathroom – a free standing bath with rather elegant ball and claw feet, dark green towels and a new-looking wallpaper with broad, barely discernible lemon and yellow stripes. One towel had been hurriedly used and draped over the side of the bath. Robert picked it up and smelt it and looked at the two glass bottles, unmarked, stopped with cork, that stood between the bath taps. There was no shaving equipment. There was something feminine, not as though a woman used it, it wasn't that – what was it – nothing he could see.

"D'you want to see the bedroom now?"

His heart jumped about a foot and he dropped the glass bottle. Its oily contents washed over the floor tiles and instantly a powerful smell of orange spice bloomed in the air. The girl from the pub was standing in the doorway. She had changed into a pair of jeans, which transformed her school blouse into a different kind of garment. Round her neck she wore a thin gold chain. Her feet were bare and she was chewing faintly but rhythmically, twisting the end of her hair around her left forefinger.

Alicia had a way of pushing herself off whatever she was leaning against, as though she needed the extra impetus, like a boat leaving the harbour wall. She drifted through to the bedroom, and Robert followed stupidly in her wake. He had still said nothing.

She was sitting on the bed. The curtains were closed and a small bedside lamp cast a pool of light over the bed and part of the wall. The room was quite small. He saw Alicia's school skirt and long dark stockings over a chair. The feet of the stockings dangled over the wooden backrest and there was something about the way they hung, the way they retained the shape of her feet, that reminded him of a painting he had seen on the front of a diary, of dancers resting backstage, putting their feet up, he supposed.

She put her back against the head rest and stretched her legs out in front of her, patting a space by her feet, showing him he should sit. The bed was high off the ground, on wrought iron legs; it was not one you could pretend to sink down onto for want of anywhere better to sit. You had to hoist yourself a little, and when you were sitting on the edge, your feet no longer touched the floor. Robert had a faint memory of childhood games where there was a sort of sacred spot, usually elevated, which exercised a magic charm, a kind of immunity. Whatever you did there, you couldn't be got.

"You have to take your shoes off." Her voice was gentle, but matter of fact.

"I don't . . ."

"Go on. Or you'll mess the cover."

He slid off his shoes. When he'd finished he looked across at her. She was watching him with a smile, chewing the edge of her thumbnail.

He gave a nervous little laugh and looked down at his own clasped hands, shaking his head. Laughing at his own ridiculousness. All his bedside manner was for the sick and dying. "I really don't . . ."

"Don't say don't. Aren't you going to take your jacket off?"

A bare foot wriggled against his thigh. He reached up to lift his jacket from his shoulders. She leaned over and pulled it back for him. When it was off she dropped it off the side of the bed, and they listened to the loose change clinking out onto the carpet. She got him to take his collar off ("you look like you hurt your neck or something") and then his shirt. Underneath he wore a faded green tee shirt. He still wore his vicar-about-town jeans, so that thus divested he looked, she said, like a man. She lifted herself up onto her knees and bent forward to touch the back of his neck with her long fluting fingers. Her hair smelled of the orange spice in the bathroom. Her lips moved, barely touching, over his neck, his ears, so that he could hear her quick breath, magnified, like the sound of the sea in a shell. He sat there with his eyes closed, aware of nothing but the smell of her and the sound and feel of her breath on his skin. Somewhere, in darkness, a wall was holding back the rest of the world, everything he had ever known, lived his life by. It was a wall he could not see round or over or through and the knowledge of it there, safe and strong against whatever was not in this room, was a total reassurance, and he was not afraid. As her lips moved over his skull, where his short cropped hair touched her cheek like the coat of something, he felt her body move and heard the movement of shiny cloth, like the noise of a sheet of paper falling to the floor. Her arms came coiling round his chest and he could not help his hands, which felt for her first, and then his mouth touched her breast as something in his brain kicked into neutral and he coasted blissfully, and with the kind of cascading power that can only come from natural motion, free wheeling on the wild drive of the wind, he fell onto her body and Aiden's bachelor bed.

They lay in silence for a while, Robert staring up at the ceiling, where he noticed that Aiden had polyfilla-ed over a crack and not yet repainted the new plaster. He could not speak, not because he had lost his voice, or was dumbstruck, but because he wanted to say so many things that were not part of what he should say; it was as though there were two competing orthodoxies, and whichever he uttered first would be the one he had to swear by. Later he would discover that his body ached in a way he had never known before as a result of making love. He had so flung himself upon her and so engaged his whole body, till it sang, in the act of spilling himself into her that the cry he uttered at the moment of release, though in fact it came out as a low rasping noise, sounded in his head like a primeval roar, the kind uttered by someone who has just thrown a piano across the room in one of those superhuman feats of strength that has more to do with the mind than with matter.

She spoke in his ear. "You're his brother, aren't you?" And he remembered, or at least let pass through a crack in the wall the admission that this was his brother's house and this girl either his brother's mistress or an intruder. It didn't seem to matter very much. Outside he heard the noise of a spade ringing against stone in a nearby garden and he remembered it was still daytime and that this was the artificial light of a theatre matinee. He knew he would not move from there until darkness fell, at the earliest. He didn't answer. She turned from her side onto her front so that she could look down on him. He put out his hand and traced the lift of her buttock from the hollow dip of her spine.

"I know you are. I saw you in the pub."

"I saw you too." He felt a little bit as though he were under interrogation, in a specially closed off area of the mind – that he had to watch not only his words but his thoughts too, like the feeling you have when you doze in the afternoon and know that there is a level of alertness you cannot let yourself rise above, or the result will be crude wakefulness and the sharp bell of consciousness will ring.

He did not dare ask or even try to read in her eyes whether it had been extraordinary for her too, whether they somehow breached normality together or whether it had only been for him. He felt that although she might be, well, some kind of professional, she had the gift of the true courtesan, who takes her pleasure as well as the envelope from the dressing table. And perhaps here it had been something more than pleasure, there was a sense of her having appointed him for this role. She had taken a kind of virginity from him, certainly, though obviously he was not a novice. But there is a new kind of virginity to be taken by the first encounter to break the marriage vow, and he felt the same boyish triumph he had known the first time, when he was seventeen, mingled this time with the extra dimension which comes from knowing you have sinned and realising it was worth it, of choosing and having chosen, the choice being held in a kind of chalice of determinism, as though his own little consciousness were a liquid but the circumstances which had brought him here, held him here, and in her arms, were an indestructible vessel from which he had had no choice but to drink. He still felt slightly delirious.

She wanted to know why he had not asked her what she was doing there. "Don't you want to know?"

"Not really," he said.

"Weird. Is he coming back?"

"I don't know. What are you doing?" His voice was little and sleepy.

"Looking behind your ears. See if you're wet. My grandmother used to do that."

He didn't want to know about her grandmother. He'd find out the details later, send her home if he had to, whatever. Do his bit.

"He's my teacher."

"And you are Alicia." He said it without thinking.

She had been resting her chin on her hand, an inch or so from the pillow, so her voice had been slightly muffled. Now she jerked her head up and her voice was clear and slightly frightened, the kind of fright that finds its expression in anger.

"How d'you know my name?" She said it as though she feared his knowledge of her name could give a special witch-doctor-like power over her.

"He said it once." Not "he told me about you". Just, "he said your name", as though he had cried it out in a fever.

She let her head drop beside his on the pillow and her body seemed to slump. She was thinking about it. There was complete silence in the room, no ticking clock, no insect humming. After a moment she said, "You're not so like him. He's cool."

"Cool?" Robert repeated after her, "Aiden, cool?"

"Mr Goodman. Yeah, he's really cool. I didn't— " she gestured at the bed with a loose movement of her hand – "you know. Everyone said I did."

"I know."

"I could have. I could, I mean. He wouldn't let me."

"He didn't say that."

"What did he say then?"

"Nothing. He just said your name. Alicia."

"That's all?"

"Nothing else. He wouldn't come back. He hit the man – well, you know."

"Yes." "It was in the paper. I don't go to school much any more. Only for French. I'm nearly good enough now anyway. Sometimes I listen to the radio."

"Good enough for what?"

"To go."

"What, to France?"

"Yeah."

"Why do you want to go to France?"

"That's where he is, isn't it? I thought about it and I reckoned that's where I'd go if I were him."

Robert didn't answer. She prodded him. "Is that where he is?"

"I can't say."

"Can't say? What d'you mean? You're not allowed or you don't know?"

He sighed and lifted the edge of the bedspread so that it flipped over to cover him, marking the end of intimacy, his own undoing of it. His twin was there again, the objects in the room, the house, all seemed to flex infinitesimally, just the slightest tiny realigning pulse, as though his spirit had quietly come in and repossessed the place in the last few seconds.

She got up and picked up her shirt off the floor. "I always feel like shit afterwards, don't you?" she said glumly, and went out, just wearing her shirt, to the bathroom. He heard water running, then she came back in wearing a man's dressing gown. He presumed it was Aiden's.

"I bet I wouldn't with him."

Robert was looking for his bits of clothing among the bed clothes.

"Are you a priest or something?"

"I am."

To his relief, she did not seem to feel that raised any complications, but simply said, "I promised myself. I said if I slept with you, then you'd tell me where he was. I wouldn't have if I hadn't thought that. You've got to tell me now. It's your honour. You have to."

"Alicia – I can't. He doesn't want anyone to know. He wants to be alone for a bit."

"Why?"

"Well, because sometimes people feel they have to have a change. They need to get away and think about things."

"I could help him."

"I don't think so."

"You don't know."

"No, I don't know, but that's what I think."

"He liked me." She made it sound far superior to loving.

"Yes, I think, if he likes anybody, it's probably you. If."

She climbed back onto the bed and rummaged under the cover. "Here."

She held out his underpants. "I looked at all his clothes. His underwear. It's all white, with little air holes in."

Robert suddenly remembered. "Does he know you're here?"

"Course not. Blimey. I got in through the window in the roof. It's really easy. There was a spare set of keys by the front door. I only come here on Wednesday afternoons. That's when I'm supposed to be doing typing at the poly. Half day release. They don't care. Your bath's ready. You married?"

"Yes."

"You better have a bath then."

He stayed in the bath for five minutes or so, making plans. He would go down to the supermarket and get a load of cardboard boxes and start packing up Aiden's things, then bring the car round from the car park. In the same way as, a few minutes previously, he had not been prepared to awake, now he would not let himself adrift again. He must not think of her. Later, somewhere else, he would see her just as part of the house, like a cup he had drunk out of, a book he had picked up.

He rubbed himself dry and pulled on his clothes. He would go back into the room and kiss the top of her head and say, "that was very special," and pretend it was nothing much, keep a level head until he had time to think. He would have liked to have given her some money, but felt that would have worsened his own sin, so he decided against it. He'd have to take the keys off her. Mrs Coleman would want them. It was quite lucky he'd bumped into her really. He did wonder vaguely what, if anything he would say to Aiden. He began to hope he would stay in France for a good long time, time for Alicia to grow up and move away to somewhere anonymous, where she would never set eyes on either of them again.

But when he came back into the bedroom she was gone. He looked for her, called her name rather halfheartedly. She had left the keys on the kitchen table. In a way he was rather relieved. It had been a kind of dream. And it was already dark. He would shut up house and go to find his hotel, come back tomorrow and start packing. Only hours later did he notice, as he hung up his jacket on the hotel hanger, that Aiden's letter, with the carefully marked address of his hostess, Mme Marguerite D'Astige, was missing from the inside pocket.

Part Six

15

It was as though he had been waiting for a direction, and that direction had presented itself not just as a place to go, but as a promise of spiritual guidance, a hint of redemption. He was given a small rucksack and a map, and borrowed a couple of books from the shelves. Christian had said he would drive him up there. The mountain was in the Ariège, on the fringes of Cathar country. Aiden looked at the map, then put it into the glove box. Christian glanced across at him as they bounced down the track. He realised that Mr Goodman would rather not know where he was going.

It was difficult to know where they should start. Aiden was actually feeling surprisingly relaxed. He had said "Good morning" to Miss Faulkener with what he could himself only describe as warmth this morning. He had asked tentatively after her circumstances the previous evening, after the women had gone to bed. Christian had told him very briefly that she was depressed because her lover had died and she couldn't get back into life. "She can't sing any more, and she's got to chuck this man's ashes away." Aiden had to admit that it sounded rather miserable. He had nothing against Miss Faulkener. She was a good example of her type. He had telephoned his brother, who had been most obliging. It would be a burden off his mind to know the standing order for the rent could be cancelled. Aiden would have preferred it if Robert had been churlish and selfish about his own time, but the latest policy towards the vagrant brother was clearly one of humouring him. And praying. Oh dear, yes, they would be praying for him, importuning the deity with their earnest pleas for Aiden's safekeeping and reform.

Aiden was not himself a religious man. That is, he felt in no way bound to his God. He was fond of the old-fashioned paternal image – he thought it only appropriate that God should wear a gown, and he pictured him sweeping through the halls of heaven (lower sixth stay behind to stack the chairs) with an ermine hood of academic distinction. Recourse should be had to the highest authorities only in the case of dire emergency, and then concerning a third party – illness or moral turpitude thereof. Any problems of a personal nature were rather to be kept, as far as possible, from the authorities, so that a certain heroic discretion might be hoped to temper the seriousness of the fault. You couldn't really argue with omniscience, but volunteering to cope with the consequences of one's own disasters might surely invite a more lenient approach.

They had not gone very far, when Christian suddenly braked and started to reverse.

"Sorry," he said, "I've just got to drop these off for Marguerite." He indicated some envelopes that were lying on the dashboard. Aiden noticed a large splashy hand, as though the letters had been flicked from an inky toothbrush and only by chance fallen in a pattern that bore relation to the information intended to be conveyed, like a primitive version of the monkeys on the typewriter. As Christian turned with his arm slung over the back of Aiden's car seat, he showed the opposite profile to the one which had been facing him so far. His neck was straining slightly with the turn. Aiden noticed how in the act of reversing the driver became so much more intimately connected with the car, handling it more like an animal somehow, as though the arm stretched across for balance were there to reassure, to calm. Christian's cheek, as smooth as Aiden's own, was taut with concentration. Then they stopped abruptly and Christian pushed the letters into the box, which was attached to the wall of a house. As he turned swiftly from him, Aiden shifted slightly uncomfortably, and thought that Christian might have been aware of his scrutiny. He stretched his legs out in front of him and laid his palms on the top of his thighs in an attitude of calmness.

Christian had what for Aiden was almost an uncanny way of disregarding their age gap. The habit of the years had bred in him a tendency to see all people of Christian's age as charges, objects of his professional attention; usually tiresome; if talented, unnerving. He responded to intelligence and behaviour, not to character. It was difficult to see Christian's character anyway – he seemed to wear it as though it been given at birth and fitted him perfectly. Aiden's pupils, because he was so accustomed to observing the changes which took place in them at a distance over a matter of six or so years, seemed to slip more or less comfortably into different guises over the period of his acquaintance. There was neither distorting deference, nor insolent intimacy in his bearing. Aiden felt the roles strangely reversed, as though he were the pupil. He wished he had accepted the offer to drive, but he had never owned a car, and was not sure he could remember how to do it. He was pretty sure it wasn't like riding a bike. Anyway, cars were so different these days.

It seemed that the only possible topic of conversation was the occasion of their meeting in Paris, the meeting which in fact had never actually occurred. Aiden felt it would be unsubtle to make reference to this, for he felt so much appointed to be there that it would be like a faltering thank you for a kindness that was supposed to have been invisible, somehow suggesting that it had been imperfectly performed.

"I saw the picture you had drawn on the pavement outside Notre Dame," he said, hoping it sounded a bit like a password, an empty phrase full of meaning.

"*Et in Arcadia*?"

"Yes. *Et in Arcadia, Ego,*" he added.

"I do think," said Christian, indicating to turn left, "it's a bit of a weird picture. But I like the story. Some people think the inscription means 'Even in Arcadia there is death', as though death itself were speaking, in fact, there's an idea the woman herself represents death. And other people say it's the voice of whoever was buried in the tomb saying, 'I have too lived in Arcadia.' A sort of 'They can't take that away from me.'"

"What?"

"It's a song. Fred Astaire."

"Oh. Thank you."

The car pulled out onto a main road. For a second Aiden felt they were on the wrong side and almost lurched towards

Christian in an attempt to correct at least his own position vis à vis the hedgerow. Then he gathered his wits and tried to relax.

"This is it," Christian said, stopping the car under a tree, where a clay-red track wound up out of sight, with high rock faces dotted with broom on either side. "You follow that track. It'll take you about half an hour. It only forks once. You bear right. Cross a little bridge over a stream then follow the left hand side of the stream up. You'll see the *bergerie* when you get to the top. I'll bring the food up by the road on the other side. The track's too bumpy."

Aiden felt a bit like an elderly invalid. Christian's directions were written on the card at the bottom of the bed, and were issued to him with no expectancy of ifs or buts. He couldn't see the grand scheme – he was not allowed to know the diagnosis or prognosis. He was calmly accepting treatment, and this new state of passive dependence was one of the aspects of the cure, like lying down to receive an injection. As he started off up the track with his rucksack he found himself counting his own steps, and portmanteau phrases which had been uttered in the car bleeped in his head, undecoded. "It only forks once, *Et in Arcadia . . .*"

He felt tired and strong at once. He had thought that Marguerite's farmhouse would be the answer – but in fact it had been too cluttered somehow, he had been unable to locate the eye of the needle – perhaps it had been just that concentration was lacking. He had shifted from room to room, picking up books, unable to read, glutted with the paraphernalia of existence, even on such a gentle scale. He had not felt the same sense of gratuitousness as when he had sat on the bench looking at Notre Dame Cathedral; he could see the sense of the place: it was a home – a home, indeed, such as he had never known. A sense of passing time was registered in the visible accretions – the additions which had been made to different parts of the building over centuries, the gradual silting-up of possessions, books with strange names and dedications written in the fly leaf, in varying degrees of faded ink, handwriting changing with the decades, all composing an intractable whole which was inaccessible to him, because he had only been able to browse there, as in a quality junk shop, useless to him, for he had no acquisitive instinct. His mother had always lingered in such shops, fingering the goods, slurping up the broth of history, and eventually buying some slight trinket which she would bring home and unwrap saying, "now that's what I call craftsmanship," except it would never find a home there, and would quickly fade, like a cut flower, among the sleek fifties veneers and ready-wipe surfaces.

The pointlessness of the acquisitive instinct had never been so clear to him as now. The desire to possess was surely at the root of all human unhappiness, not because possessions brought you unhappiness, but because you had to admit that they did not bring you the happiness you thought they would, because time after time the palliative proved illusory, and you were back with your old discontent. Even if he had married Audrey it would have been the same after a year or two, maybe even a month or two, who knows. He believed now, looking back, that he had wanted her in the same way as a man may crave a painting or a car – her cardigans, the sweet, slightly penicillin smell of her lipstick, the confident draughtsmanship in her bone structure, her ready-madeness, just heat up, no extra cooking required. He was left now, far more than he would have been if they had married, if he had had all of her, with essence of Audrey, a tiny pinch of it, in his mind. Similarly with his family, his childhood, his life as a schoolmaster. They were all in there somewhere, in their concentrated form, like one of those super-concentrated washing up liquids, to be diluted, bearing a crop of a billion bubbles. It must have been the thought of Audrey that put that into his mind: she was associated for him with washing up and table laying – when he had visited her on Sunday afternoons at her mother's house, for tea, they had spent only minutes in unchaperoned company of one another – and that had been when Audrey's arms were plunged into the kitchen sink, her gaze fixed on something out in the little scrap of garden. He had had a recurring dream, after she turned him down – not passionate enough, she'd said – that she had been turned to stone, or at least into some kind of statue, with her hands forever petrified beneath the soap suds, and he could creep up behind her, if he liked, while her eyes stared out at that invisible gnome, or greenhouse, and stroke her mounded breasts unseen, unchastised, unnoticed.

He was wearing a faded grey shirt which had belonged to Marguerite's husband, and some canvas trousers supplied by Pascal. He had been embarrassed by this gesture, but she had behaved as though it was all part of her brief, like providing pillowcases and towels, and had even taken them up slightly for him. In a way, it was good to be wearing clothes that were not his own, like some kind of regulation issue – more anonymous, more secretive too, since they were in no way a statement of his own taste. Like all women, Marguerite was a tricker out of people and places, couldn't leave well alone. She had a fine enough mind, she was quick and deft in her thinking, but there was no power there, it was that distinctively female kind of intelligence which is closely related to instinct. He thought of Janet, in Brittany. They had played chess one evening, and she had made some startling and disconcerting moves. He had been quite baffled by her strategy until he realised that she was doing no more than dancing her pieces into the open spaces, as though she were playing hockey and sweeping the ball up or across the field, with the bishop shouting "switch!" to the knight, anticipating a quick run down the wing by the castle. When the game was over, he had sat looking at the board in its final position, trying to remember how each of the pieces had come to be in that particular square, in that particular relation to all the others, trying to make a three dimensional thing of it, by reintroducing the element of time, seeing the beginning and the middle in the end, collapsing it all into an organic whole, so that it would become a single thing and not a series of moves, of triumphs and errors. Janet had moved from the table and taken up a book, read a chapter, or a fragment of a chapter, turned to something else, the game quite forgotten.

Women seemed so much better adapted to the episodic nature of life, their motives for this and that quite incontingent. Perhaps it was because their bodies did all the work for them, informing their subconscious with a sense of pattern and necessity which left them free for frivolous action, which was why they were so good at the decorative arts, the pointless stitching of a piece of cloth, the ripple of a slight melody on a keyboard. They had no time for the underlying structure – when did you ever hear of a woman trying to conceive a picture of the universal meaning of life, or to explain the genealogy of world religions, the interrelatedness of things? To see heaven in a grain of sand – yes, but not in the way he, or Blake would have conceived of it, as a kind of DNA molecule containing all in one, but in the same way as a metaphor, messiest of devices, may contain by inference and allusion, not by its essence, a hint of vastness, sniffed on the wind.

It was one o'clock in the afternoon when he crossed the little stream. He had not eaten at breakfast. There was a packed lunch in his rucksack, but he decided he would push on upwards. He could eat when he got to the top. He was sweating – his brow was damp – and his hunger seemed not to affect his energy. Indeed, he seemed to grow more sprightly, and lighter as the sweat left his body and he was aware of a pleasant, empty ache in his stomach. As he climbed higher the air grew less scented and thinner. His eyes, more alert, felt brighter and, keeping the most distant point of the track constantly in view, he travelled ahead of himself in his mind, so that it preceded him, hauling his body after, his flesh and blood like a novice companion, to be waited for impatiently at each turn in the road. When he finally reached the plateau and saw the little stone-built house, with its crumbling walls ("It looks a bit like a torn off hunk of *pain campagne,*" Marguerite had said, rather vaguely) he felt he had already looked it over, that some part of him was already familiar with it and would turn to him and gesture down at the plain and the hills and the hand-sized villages and he would nod and shade his eyes so that he would not betray the fact that he had seen it all already and knew it, like a man who is introduced to his own mistress at a party, and must pretend she is a stranger to him.

The goats were dotted among the trees; grey, white, brown and black, the colour of stones on the bed of a running stream. The grey green leaves of the cork oaks were still and stiff as brushes against the sky. The lower bark had been removed so that the bottom portion of the tree looked a bit like an elderly shin protruding on the occasion, perhaps, of a paddle, from a rolled up trouser leg. A billy goat stared at him from a distance of forty or fifty yards, its head tilted a little way back, a fine, bearded head, with its two horns tipped forwards, scaled like bamboo, but curled smoothly and tapering to a rather vicious looking point. There was a strangely familiar smell. Aiden sniffed and was mysteriously reminded of school, a particular room . . .

"Sulphur", said Christian, coming up behind him. Aiden turned. He was carrying the bags with the supplies from the car to the little house. He was smiling and looked a bit crumpled, with bits of twig in his hair. He had taken off his tee shirt, and he had that adolescent thinness that makes the young martyrs look so convincingly *souffrant* in paintings, with their ribs showing and still the slightly feminine dent at the waist – which is why you don't get many Saint Peters but an awful lot of Sebastians.

"Sulphur?"

"Well, something devilish anyway. Hormones. That's Mephisto. That's why Arnaud tried to get rid of him – he smells so much. It's a gland on the top of his head – to do with attracting females. Come and see the house."

There were two rooms, a kitchen, with a table and cupboard containing a few plates and glasses, and a bedroom with a hard little bed and whitewashed walls. The walls in the kitchen were bare stone. Aiden was both impressed and shocked by the austerity. Did Arnaud live there all the year round?

"Most of the time. It's quite warm in the winter – he gets a big fire going."

"He stays here alone?"

"Yeah. Reading things. He's writing a sort of memoir about a Day in the Life of a Goatherd. It's not very typical, otherwise he wouldn't be writing it, he'd be picking his nose and shagging the goats – oh, sorry . . ." Aiden blanched slightly at this distinctly non-ecloguian portrait, because since he only had one picture of a goatherd – that of Arnaud – he had somehow to combine the two types Christian put forward in the one man, the *comme ci* and the *comme ça*, the black and the white, the sheep-shagger and the shepherd king, so to speak.

He frowned. Christian was making up the bed. He stood awkwardly and watched. Christian suggested he go and get the rest of the things from the car. They ate some bread and cheese, and Aiden immediately felt sleepy. Christian explained to him about the goats, told him their names, those he knew – Esmerelda and Helen and Eros. Neither he nor Arnaud knew how many of them there were – "but you can just tell by looking at them if they're all there, like the stars. They won't run away anyway, they can't get through the woods, it's like an enclosure." Aiden sat with his back against a rock, his head feeling slightly boiled in the sun, as Christian talked in a low peaceful voice which had the effect of an incantation.

Arnaud had been keeping goats on the mountain for seven years. The little *bergerie* had no electricity, and the water had to be fetched in huge churns every day from the spring. He made cheese from the milk, which was destined for private consumption only, since he did not have a laboratory to satisfy the standards of the lady who arrived in her white coat with clipboard and stilettos from Toulouse every three months. So he took his week's output down to market every Saturday morning, often assisted by Christian, and sold it clandestinely, darting in and out of the plane trees, joyously employing the language and artistry of the drug pusher's trade to pedal his irreproachable produce.

No one really knew where he had come from. He had a family in Belgium, a mother, at least, and had presumably arrived as part of the hippy exodus of the sixties, when half Belgium seemed abruptly to up end like a churn of milk given a sharp kick by an ill-tempered goat, pouring down France in streaks and dribbles, collecting in a particularly large puddle in the south west, where the climate and terrain were suitable for such pursuits as were most likely to cure the various malaises of modern civilisation. They lived in communes, worked hard, learned farming skills, gave birth to children whose genetic constitution was more random than that of the universe itself, splintered, bought farms, did them up, settled down, went to parent-teacher meetings in the little village schools and complained at the inclusion of sugar in the children's diets, at the emphasis on Western religion in the theological syllabus for the under-nines, or at the fact that the drawing paper was rectangular and not round.

Arnaud had been unusual in not developing along this path. Instead he had worked as an employed shepherd, in the service of a Belgian princess. *Ma princesse*! he called her, and it sounded on his lips like the term of endearment, instead of a genuine appellation. He often told Christian that shepherds and the aristocracy had a special sort of affinity. At first he simply maintained the property, mending the fences, thinning the forest, making paths and collecting honey. One day he and the princess discovered a goat skull lodged in the crook of a turkey oak, where a swarm of bees had made their home. The princess told him the story of Wancelot, who had been slaughtered by the people of Cyprus, and his head left out in the sun "to dry", she said richly, and in whose skull bees had likewise nested. From then on Wancelot became an object of veneration and the honey was eaten only by princesses of the royal house of Cyprus – those same princesses, she said, who rode postillion on wet, black stallions, wearing a black shift under their cloaks of finespun gold and purple filigree, as a mark of their mourning for the City of Jerusalem. The princess's husband – though no one ever called him the prince – spent his days trying to mend a huge Citroen DS, a kind of gangster car from the forties. Occasionally it would run, and he would bolt rapidly out of sight down the hairpin mountain bends and the princess would sigh and cross herself, scarcely daring to hope that the accident might, this time, be fatal.

One day, Marianne, whose job it was to milk the goats and make the cheese, fell ill of a disease which the princess promptly declared was consumption, and was packed off back to Belgium, where she turned her hand to making fresh cream chocolates and soon forgot about the princess and Arnaud and the goats. "What shall I do?" cried the princess in alarm. "Who shall milk my goats?" (She had forgotten, in her haste to be rid of Marianne, whom she called the "anti-muse", for fantasy stopped when she walked in the door, that the girl had been the mainstay of their livelihood and that without her they might all very well be reduced to returning to Belgium and the manufacture of truffles). Arnaud volunteered to fill the gap. "I soon discovered," he told Christian, "it was in my genes. Yes, I have a gene for making goat's cheese. These people, in their laboratories, trying to isolate the purpose of every gene – why! they have no idea, there are more oddities and obscurities in the genes of just the population of Vermont-sur-Eyles to keep them foxed for a millennium. We don't tell, eh?"

So with his goatcheese-making genes and a guide to goat

husbandry and cheesemaking he set to, and produced a fine batch of delicate roundels, placed carefully in a tray on sheets of greaseproof paper. But it was soon Saturday, and the prince – if prince he was – and even the princess looked rather dark about this, had disappeared. "He is after the *putes* in Barcelona," announced the princess wanly. "Oh, who will *sell* my cheese?" Arnaud would, but there was one problem – "I do not drive cars," he said, "I do not know how." So the princess climbed in behind the wheel herself and drove him down the mountain, lurching from one side of the road to another, while Arnaud sat in the back with the seats down, guarding the trays of cheeses against the motion of the vehicle. That first morning, she left him to it, and went off to the butcher to buy four kilos of minced rump steak for her puppies – which though already huge, were only babies, and needed, she said, a pure diet. Often her "babies" would leap on her from behind while she was bending to sniff a rose or to count eggs, and tumble her to the ground and ravish her with their wild, flapping tongues, while her shrieks could be heard from one side of the valley to the other.

When she came back at the end of the morning, the market had almost finished, but still Arnaud was pushing and wrapping and fishing for change in his little leather satchel. She counted the profits and looked him in the eye. "You," she said, "will sell my cheese next week also." After three years she let him go – he was too successful, and the flock by now too large for the pasture available on the princess's land, and he moved to a nearby cottage, and set up on his own. Every Sunday, after mass, the princess would arrive with a basket of seasonal fruits and a book, and reminisce all afternoon, over a bottle of rich Cahors wine which left a sad, slightly hairy stain at the corners of her mouth, and which Arnaud, in his devotion, would gladly have licked away himself given half a chance. Then came the new European laws, and the collapse of the princess into advanced old age and a nursing home. Arnaud gave up the greater part of his flock and kept only twelve or so goats for his black market business. The days of the white DS were over – it had been towed away by the police in Barcelona and the prince had never been sober enough to work out where it went. Now Arnaud had a little black Renault and trailer for carrying churns.

Christian looked round. He had been leaning against a rock, telling his story to the mountains beyond and the goats, and the sky. Behind him, Mr Goodman lay stretched out on the ground, his head propped against the rock. Christian went into the house and fetched a towel and gently placed it behind his head. Then he walked back down to the car and left the seventy-two-hour goatherd to dream.

2

Christian arrived back at the house in the early evening, and immediately looked for Elizabeth.

"Where is she?" he asked abruptly. I was in the kitchen talking to Rudolph Garnier, the local estate agent, who had come to tell me how much my house was worth, in an attempt to get me to sell it to a foreign client who had taken a fancy to it while flying overhead in a hot air balloon. He knew he had as much chance of success as he had of persuading me up into a hot air balloon myself, but at least we could have a nice apéritif together. Rudolph was not the category of acquaintance one felt moved to clasp to one's bosom every time he crossed the threshold, but he was amusing, and he knew perfectly well he was on a hiding to nothing. But it was "*le temps de crise*", everyone was saying, and estate agents were having to set higher temptations still to unwilling clients, in order to buy and sell property.

"Elizabeth is in her room having a rest. You remember Christian?"

Rudolph swapped his car keys into his left hand and held out his right to Christian. Christian looked at it as if he couldn't understand the gesture, as though Rudolph had forgotten to put anything into his hand before extending it. To grease his palm maybe. Perhaps he thought he should be offering him the keys to the Mercedes outside. He took his hand eventually then took it quickly away. Rudolph must have felt suspected of free masonry. Christian had no fond feeling for estate agents. He had an instinctive antagonism towards the ties of property, just as he had towards the written word, the printed page.

Civilisation, he once said to me, when he was still quite raw, was the story of man's fall from grace. We lived in an age of disease, of the knowledge of facts and not of self (he quoted the Greek inscription "Know Thyself"), of separation from nature, of alienation between men, of agonising self consciousness. But he still believed in – knew of – a second age of innocence, a new Arcadia, in fact. The new Arcadia would be one in which the shepherds no longer gawp at the tomb in dumb curiosity, but wander confidently in their pastures, knowing the tomb is there, and fearing nothing. In fact I expect cremation would be more the order of the day. Christian, it is true, knew no evil. I had never seen or heard him being cruel, although his solitary tastes had often made people shrug and give up the attempt to become close to him. He was whole in mind and body. It goes without saying that he was pretty difficult to live with. You were always tripping over his different way of seeing things and feeling clumsy, stumbling over the trip wire, with your unstable ballast of prejudices and preconceptions. But he moved on, moved away, returned, as now, and you spent most of your time scanning the horizon, longing to see him appear like Tom the Piper's son, from over the hills and far away.

"You settled him in all right?"

"He's fine. Arnaud's back the day after tomorrow. It's a funeral."

If it had been a wedding it would have been a week.

"Try not to make too much noise, darling," I called as he left the room. He had caught his little hessian satchel on the table and it had dragged after him a few inches before he disengaged it. He went out into the courtyard garden and sat on the ground. Elizabeth's window was open, her shutters half closed. He leaned back against a post that supports my overhead vine, which was already set hard with little fruits, the kind you might feed to a parrot – it seems unimaginable that they will later turn into those luscious purple droplets. He began to roll a little cigarette. But instead of lighting it, he kept turning it and plucking at the little bits of tobacco poking out at each end until he had picked it quite to pieces and had to start another one. This time he lit it, and sat there, staring up at Elizabeth's window, his arms hooked round his knees, made very small. He was wearing a short sleeved tee shirt, plain – I never saw him sport a slogan, or even anything with a pattern or a motif of any sort. His upper arms, so slender below the elbow, were surprisingly muscular. I always forgot how much manual work he did – fruit picking, labouring, general odd jobbing.

I saw Rudolph off, and came and sat at the table. There was a little bit of wind, lifting Christian's hair from his brow. He had fine brown hair that still resembled in colour and in texture the little locks I had in the envelope by my desk.

"Did she sing at all today?" he asked. She hadn't. Otherwise he might have caught the memory of her voice on the air, the sense of her. Evening is a time for scooping up the day's impressions – they are all there, suspended in the late day's light, who has walked there, with what song, what hopes, how light or heavy a tread. He looked back up at her window, his wrists balanced on his knees now, waiting. He was in one of his slow, cello moods, which were entirely real and involuntary, but loaded the air almost intolerably, so that if you cracked a pistol shot you felt the whole place would ignite and explode with a bang. He brought the weight of the world with him over the threshold. I came and laid a hand on his shoulder, crouching down beside him where he sat beside the marigolds, mixed, unintentionally, with viper's bugloss, sky blue and purple fronds among the orange buttons, which danced like musical notes in the breeze.

"Don't be sad. It's always different, every time you come back."

"No," he said, "it's always the same."

He reached out and touched my pendant with the cobalt blue stone he had found on a mountain path and set for me in a metalwork class at school. When he let it go it fell back against my breastbone, and I was surprised by its weight. It almost winded me.

"What is it then?"

He was drawing in the dust with his finger. He paused, then rubbed the whole pattern out with his shoe, and took a handful of gravel, which he poured though his fingers back onto the ground. His fingers were grazed in places; perhaps he caught them as he drew on the pavements, rubbing away on the ground. It took time for his thoughts to develop, like a photograph, and he would wait, patiently, until they were ready to be spoken. I reached out for a little hand fork and began weeding the barrel of herbs that was just within range, stabbing at it and breaking up the soil, to give the roots some breathing space. But I didn't move from where I squatted beside him, taking a long arm to the task. There was a tension in the air, not heaviness, but the feeling that something was being stretched out very very thin, to breaking point. It was as though the air might suddenly start to sing, in the way a glass does if you run your finger round it after it has just been washed.

When I looked at him again, his head was bowed almost between his knees. Then with a sigh he lifted it again. He looked round and saw me watching him. I didn't smile, I couldn't. There was nothing I could say. Christian was incapable of self delusion. Perhaps he was even saying to himself that it would be better if they never were friends. I had thought that maybe he could help her, but I didn't reckon with his having to pay a price. For him it was a kind of test, the temptation to select happiness and love. He had known love before, but it was the unconscious, playful adolescent feeling he had for Ariadne. He had never known what the French call *le manque* – absence, need, desire, lack, shortfall. *Le manque*. It sounds like a wound, or the cry of a lost animal. Modern love. *Le manque*, shame, regret, need. Elizabeth is an absence. She never really appears, and for the lack of her, someone else, more than one person, was feeling *le manque*. All such adult emotions, post fall emotions, Gesthemane fears. There is so much unexpressed love in this story, I have almost forgotten how the words go, but I will never forget the look on Christian's face before he rubbed his hand over his eyes, and came up with one of his radiant smiles, or rather the only one he had, it wasn't a range or a repertoire, it was just his smile. *Allez,* he said, and pulled me up from the ground. My marvellous boy. Who was it had a marvellous boy? Coleridge perhaps. He ended up a callow and wasted young man, died before he was of age, almost. Not my marvellous boy, not mine.

* * *

It was not quite a vision, nor a dream, but the understanding that came to him while he was up the mountain had this much in common with both, that it left him feeling that the world was in fact quite dead, and that life existed only in his mind. He sat on the grass looking west. It was about five o clock in the afternoon. He had slept for several hours, and he was in that state of false alert that awaking in an unfamiliar place can bring, whereupon little children cry and adults are unable to recognise their surroundings. When vitamin B levels are low, it provides a piercing insight into the gratuitousness of the world. His eye was led from mountain peak to mountain peak, like a stone skimming on water. The grass was hard and spiky; it felt dead to the touch. The mountains, with their strange buckled contours set for ever in stone, would never move. This was as far from the world as you could get. There were no trees. Even the chestnuts had thinned out before he had reached the hut. There was no sound of wind, not even the ringing of the goats' little bells, for they wore none. He looked at his own hands, first the palms, then the upper sides. He did not recognise them. The wrist watch on its expandable silver bracelet felt heavy and superfluous. He pulled it off and it lay on the hot ground like a little dead fish. His glasses had already been picked up by a passing buzzard who had alighted at his side while he slept and helpfully deprived him of any chance of future clear sightedness. He flew hundreds of feet above the sleeping mortal and circled thoughtfully, grazing the ground with his eyes for signs of life, then dropped the fragile frames from his beak, sending them spinning like a sycamore seed down into the river below. Aiden undid the buttons of his shirt and pulled it off, throwing it behind him, out of his line of vision. The sun was still quite hot but it did not warm his flesh, which was cold and slightly damp. He could smell sweat from under his armpits. He suddenly felt a desire to pull out the hairs on his chest, to rub his scalp clean, to bury his head in his hands so that he would see no more, and the world would not see him. "I am alone," he thought honestly, "and there is no help for me." Only his spirit was strong, bottled up under pressure inside him. At that moment, if he could have smashed open his skull and let it out he would have done. He looked up at the sky, as it turned to pinkish grey, flushed with success at another day done and had the strange feeling he was looking down into something, like a great lake, that he could fall into and tread water in the emptiness, like the men on the moon. No people. No time. The drossy world, pickled in materialism and driven by physical desire, machine-like into a never ending, extinctionless void, seemed to be sinking far below, he could almost see the mud rising to engulf it. He realised he had a raging thirst, and yet did not go towards the house to fetch water, but let his head sing from the dryness in his throat as though it had been an exquisite pleasure, and in a moment the wide eyed, floaty feeling triumphed over the parching of his throat and he overcame the need for liquid. He had found the answer. He would become an ascetic. He would breathe the thin air of the mountain tops, purified, rarified, intoxicating by its very absence, till the whole microbiological and chemical machine seized up of its own accord and his soul would be released, like a bird from captivity, and there would be no more desire, and no more disappointment, and no more feeling that the world had not been made for such as him. Alicia, his last desire, with the sand of the desert on her feet, and the scent of the spice of life and love wafting in her wake was behind him. In a single convulsive leap of the mind, he heaved at the boulder of his past, sending it crashing down the mountain into the gulf below. Aiden Goodman, forty-seven, and looking every day of it, was born again, not of the flesh, but of the Will itself, the will which says that the world with all its pain, treachery and broken dreams is not a beautiful world at all, as the engraven plaque in his mother's hallway had wanted them to believe, it was in fact the most sordid of prisons, and that for the man of the spirit there could be no greater goal than liberation from it, and no smaller price to pay than the little world itself. Alicia had glimpsed it in her vision by the lake side. He was no man of the flesh – how mad he had been, he had quite misunderstood her message – it was a greater glory that would be his, the glory of renunciation and denial. And Christian, the dear boy, the voice crying in the wilderness, than whom a greater one was still to come – could it be me, could it not be me? His stomach rumbled fiercely, a trumpeting, a veritable campanule of celebration issuing from the pit itself. All this took about three minutes, at the end of which anyone capable of appreciating a good cup of tea and giving five good reasons for the start of the French Revolution might have been tempted to declare Mr Goodman clinically mad.

35

Elizabeth's chastity of the voice was a deliberate choice, a renunciation. According to the church, there is no virtue merely in liking someone, because there is no effort of the will involved. But to love is a virtuous act, because at its best love entails a voluntary submission of one's will to that of the beloved. No wonder priests don't marry. Still, Elizabeth's inability to sing when she had been with Will had now been replaced by a higher order, a willed refusal. Had she cut her hair or refused food it would have been a manifestation of the same determination, but it would only have been an affliction of the body.

She drove with that kind of virile grace which certain women acquire behind a steering wheel, her chin a little raised, perhaps because the last person to drive the car had been taller than she, and had set the mirror accordingly. It was not sufficiently out of line to prompt her to readjust it. It seemed easier to adjust the hold of her own head. She was on her way to pick up Mr Goodman, glad to escape from the house, where Christian was silent and Marguerite over-watchful. It was like waiting for fruit to ripen, and yet she had no expectation at all of a harvest and an autumn, of that peculiar mixture of richness and melancholy which comes with the bringing to term of the year's growth.

On the previous evening they had been sitting in the drawing room – she had been reading a biography of Madame de Pompadour by Nancy Mitford, Marguerite had been mending her sewing case, and Christian had been sitting on the step where the doors opened into the courtyard, his head tipped up towards the sky, as though he were watching for a sign. Earlier in the evening, while they were making soup for supper, Elizabeth had been explaining how the whole production of the voice was a purely physical process involving the successful collaboration of diaphragm, lungs, trachea, larynx, vocal cords, nasal cavities and what was known as the buccal cavity, or mouth. Correct pose, attack (the stroke of the glottis) were essential to the emission of the voice, which should also have the additional qualities of true intonation, steadiness and beauty of tone. There was a list of things considered essential to beautiful vocal tone. Correct balance of ground tones and overtones. Freedom from constraint (Christian came into the room at this point, and settled down to chopping celery, listening to her bland recital with an ironically docile air). Forward placing of the voice. Correct use of the resonating cavities. Oh, she added, and what they call "personal perception of good tone".

"What's that?"

"Whether you can hear yourself."

So we sat in silence later on, just the noise of my thread running through the cloth, a fraction of a second briefer each time, by the length of a tiny stitch, as though time were speeding up, or being calculated in ever decreasing measures. A bat swooped in, and began to circle the room at great speed. At least, it seemed fiendishly quick, but only because it didn't slow down to negotiate the difficult bits, the table lamp, or the vase of white iris mixed with sharp-bladed gladioli. Speed was not an impediment to accuracy. I couldn't help feeling this was a useful characteristic, and that it was rather a shame it hadn't opened more doors for the bat during the course of evolution. I say that, of course, as a human being, who, because she is able to claim as one of her species' characteristics the ability to darn a cloth, chooses to consider this a skill to be grateful for. It flew in decreasing concentric circles around the table lamp, to which a variety of night insects had been attracted. Elizabeth didn't flinch, but followed its flight path around the room with her eyes, letting her book drop in her lap. It appeared finally to have left, then popped in again almost the minute it had flown out, circled once again like a circus pony, for applause, then disappeared into the night. I asked myself whether it was possible for an animal to realise it had forgotten something and come back for it.

"It was trapped," said Elizabeth. "It's extraordinary. Such control. That extra sense."

"It wasn't trapped," said Christian, looking over from the step. "It was feeding."

She had left the car at the bottom of the path and taken the steep walk upwards, the same as Mr Goodman had taken three days previously. She had on a cotton dress in a print of tiny dark blue and white flowers which was cool, if perhaps a little over decorative for the occasion of the retrieval of Mr Goodman. I would have been quite happy to leave him up there, but Elizabeth had said of course he must be fetched. Looking back, it is obvious that the dynamic of the three of us was quite intolerable for her. Christian had fallen so quiet on her, in waiting, that she already looked back on the day of their meeting at the cathedral as the highlight of their accord. Since, there had been nothing. She cannot have been unaware of Christian's feeling. He had taken one strand from their first important encounter, and walked off into the wood with it, turning one of his magical songs over and over in his mind, winding it round trees, getting further and further from the light. The attraction of Mr Goodman was that he, like her, was caged, inside his inhibitions, his sad little story, his nervous guard of his privacy and his fear of disclosure. He was a *look right, look left, look right again* sort of person. Christian just operated on a kind of radar of intuition, like the bat.

She had slept badly, with needle points of consciousness stabbing her into wakefulness every ten minutes or so, so that this morning she had been up with the dawn and the strident cock, and had spent a long time in the shower, under a punishing jet of hot water, massaging her head so that it felt whole again, not broken into its constituent bits, its various worries and fears and black holes of the imagination, as it had in the night. As she walked she was dogged by two obsessions, one the Schumann song on which she had stalled during the last singing lesson she had had with Oscar, and the other something Mark had once told her about always imagining one was walking into the mountain, not up it, which made the climb easier. The two lines of thought, the one a series of dips and rises as she traced the melody along its obsessive, nagging path, the other a clear forward march, intertwined in her mind, like a tendril of vine wrapped around a smooth, straight stick. And though she sang in her mind, or some part of her sang, like a wretched, mechanical piano, over and over again, her body was completely distanced from the process, so that all the things she had spoken of the previous evening, which made it possible to sing even when your heart was completely gone from the process, had fallen into abeyance. I know the steps, I used to insist to Pierre, I don't need to go through them. It was, as he pointed out, a particularly lame excuse.

She stopped at a sharp turn in the path and rested her basket, in which she carried a bottle of water, some bread, cheese and fruit. And wrapped in a cloth, still inside the little terracotta urn, she had Will's ashes. Each time she had tried to throw them, it had felt like now or never, so that now she had become accustomed to the idea, and was determined that every day should be her last with him. She was waiting for impulse to catch her unawares. The empty gesture was already there in her head. Sitting with her back against a rock, she forced herself to breathe deeply and regularly, to still her mind, which seemed to be slopping and swaying like a carelessly carried basin of water. She undid the buttons of her dress and peeled it down over her shoulders so that she was naked from the waist upwards. Since the first stages of her tan had been acquired lying undressed on a bed of glass under a blue light in her health club, a sort of quick seal in the pan before the gentle braising, she was already quite brown. She lay there in the sun for several minutes, fighting off the song, which would slip back in every now and then and start insidiously moulding her unconscious thoughts. In the thickets of gorse and the ferns, jays flitted with jerky movements, sending up a noise of crumpling paper.

The same morning, Mr Goodman put his few possessions back into his bag and said goodbye to Mephisto, who took the message back to the herd. Some pact was made that morning between the sun, Mephisto and Mr Goodman, but what it was I'll never know. He came down the mountain with a new resolution, and a feeling that though life would not be as long as he had once imagined, it would be deep and intense, and have a meaning. He had a fresh light in his eyes, which were more open to the heavens, as though he could see the stars by daylight and commune with them. Solitude can do this, and the mountain air, and above all, having a history to cast off. To be born again, we must have once blundered and smudged, and known despair. He felt strong and virile in his continence, no longer weak and impotent or simply lacking opportunity, but armoured with faith in his destiny, his appointment. His cup ran over, but continued to fill, like a mountain pool by a spring, and he had a feeling that whatever draughts were drunk it would continue to be so, and that this new plenitude was inexhaustible. Coming down the mountain he experienced a desire to run and jump, that wild lust for the excitement of a dance, the joy of movement itself, neither chasing nor fleeing, a crazy erratic motion, like colliding molecules exploding into gas and air. The thing about being born again is that psychology doesn't come into it. You can't say – but he wouldn't, I just can't see it, it doesn't make sense, or anything of that nature. It just is, and it happens, and people change radically. It's the result not of the chip chip chipping away of childhood, or of the advancing years, but of great thunder claps, single blows which recast the whole. It's an illusion, maybe, but it happens – the illusion is as convincing as you could ever wish for, and, like God, to all intents and purposes, entirely real.

As he came to the stream, an old man was standing on the little ford by which he had to pass. He bade him good morning, and the man, as though he had met him before, asked him where he was going, as though, indeed, he knew whence he had come.

"I'm going down to the plain," said Aiden. "I've been alone long enough. I'm going to seek company."

"You're better off up here. The air's better here, you know."

"No," said Aiden, "I have to go down now." And he went on his way, not quite rejoicing, but with the feeling that soon there would be great rejoicing, somewhere. After an hour, he sat down in the shade and rested. He slept for a few minutes, then awoke to find his head was light and skittish still, but with a kind of lightness that gave him great hope, because for all his life he had been weighted, like a child's toy that will never entirely fall over, with that little bit of lead that said, go carefully, tread warily, love nothing and no one, and suddenly it was no longer there. It was not that he intended to let rip, to behave wildly, to roar his way through the rest of life. He felt steady underneath his ripple of happiness, as though the path were straight before him, and his footsteps, though light, would be measured and calm. Above all he would be wise and thoughtful, with the simplicity of the hermit who has solved the difficult riddles and has become as a little child, full of wonderment and unencumbered by too many constructions on life. His soul was clear, uninfested by the cares and worries of the world. Up there, for the first time, he had learned how to live. He had washed his clothes in the mountain stream and hung them to dry from the rocks. There was nothing simpler now that he knew how. In the winter he could chop wood and heat wherever it was he chose to live. A few simple books, primary texts, revelations only, no dissertations. He would grow vegetables, and keep a few goats. Music? He would fashion pipes. Company? He would be a friend to all, a companion to none. Money? He would work odd days as a labourer, well, perhaps a teacher from time to time. Would he beg? He would not, though alms would not be pushed away. A jar of honey, bread in hand, maybe.

He had only been walking again for maybe half an hour when he saw something moving through the gorse, climbing up the path by which he was descending. He stopped and crouched down close to the ground. There was a rush from the undergrowth and a small animal flung itself across the path, and disappeared on the other side, for all the world as though it had been crossing a fatal thoroughfare. He got to his feet and made his way down to the place from where the animal had erupted. As he looked down the path to the point where it bent away down the mountain he saw a woman with her face tilted up to the sun, bare to the waist, her breasts full as though she were with child. A small sound rose in his throat, a stifled cry, stifled by the fact that his body had not been ready for his heart's reaction, so that his lungs and mouth were quite taken unaware by the impulse. She was dark in colouring and at first he took her for a French peasant girl, but as he approached stealthily, hoping to creep past – he dared not take a short cut to avoid the corner, the rustle in the undergrowth would frighten her awake and he would look as though he were stealing round to get a better view, when really all he wanted was to get past this bit, oh dear, it was all very awkward, very awkward indeed – he suddenly realised it was not a peasant girl at all, not the kind of simple pastoral maid he always pictured helping out British airmen who parachuted into occupied France, but Miss Faulkener, the translator, respectable, crisp, well ironed Miss Faulkener, alarmingly exposed in all her roundness. His joyous resolve, his conversion of all his petty fears and panics, the little fragile threads of care all wound into a single, indestructible cord of belief in his new kind of positive impregnability gave a little under the strain of this shock to the senses. The last occasion on which he had seen a naked woman leapt into his mind. He had wished so often that he could replay the scene on the night of the dance in room nine (French), that he could have simply snapped on the light and ordered them to their feet, in all their wretchedness (whereas it had somehow been he who had been tainted by the whole affair, in the end, not the – couple), that it was almost a temptation to stroll up to Miss Faulkener with his arms folded across his chest and wait coldly for an explanation. Then she opened her eyes and saw him standing forty yards away from her, groping for words with which to distance himself from her while his eyes looked on, making the most of his hesitation, subverting his best intentions.

She sat up and blinked at him, her eyelids sealing the compromising picture as surely as the shutter of a camera. In his grey shirt and trousers, which, from having been washed in the mountain water and hung out over rocks to dry were crumpled and shabby looking, and with his three-day beard pencilled in round lips and chin, exaggerating the hawk-like angularity of his upper face, he looked like a different sort of person altogether to the one she had last seen getting into the car with Christian. And his glasses were gone. Elizabeth got to her feet before pulling up the straps of her dress to cover herself again. She had that presence of mind which is so rare, which forestalls the panic of being discovered and rightly maintains itself in the face of inquiry, so that the ingloriousness of the eavesdropper or interloper does not get lost in the panic. She did everything slowly, even pausing to brush an insect off her upper arm before slipping the second strap of her dress up onto her shoulder.

"Good morning," she said, and paused a fraction of a second before smiling, so that it was acknowledgment and not greeting. But she had, after all, come here to fetch him, so she swallowed her indignation – besides which, she had for so many months been thinking of her body as a machine for survival, and not by means of propagation, that it did not really occur to her to feel sexually embarrassed. It was her privacy he had invaded. It was hardly an onslaught on her *pudeur*.

Mr Goodman took his handkerchief – a very present help in trouble – from his pocket. He had forgotten to remove it when he washed the trousers, so it was damp and not altogether clean. He felt for his glasses, about to polish, the better to see his way forward, when he realised they had been stolen by the hawk.

"It's a beautiful morning," she said, in her clear, rather cool voice, and the cliché seemed to sum up her indifference to it. If there was nothing better to do with a beautiful morning than close your eyes and sit against a rock, when the whole world was laid out at your feet and there was nothing you cared to go down again for, there was no point wasting any words on it. It was simply the naming of parts with a careless adjective that cost nothing, thrown in to allay suspicion. "I came to help you down," she added, for he was still looking at her blankly, as though he might be about to say he knew someone who looked astonishingly like her. He stood hovering, still at some distance from her. Was he in some kind of trance? He did look rather peculiar. Her smile faded, and as it did so, his own smile opened out, from a scowl into a wide, not very pleasant rictus of understanding.

"Take me down?"

"Back to the farmhouse. I came to give you a lift, Mr Goodman."

Aiden felt his energy return, his slightly barrelled chest inflated a little. He had been startled by her, thrown off guard, back into the past, where his nerves had ruled his behaviour. He felt angry at her for her intrusion onto his mountain. A certain lordliness came over him, and he said, "I see. Since you are here, let's walk a little. I will show you the view."

Elizabeth hesitated. She felt strangely frightened by him. He looked as though he were acting a part, with a certain demented relish, and that when he had got her where he wanted he would turn vicious and malevolent. No, she thought. He began to move towards her.

"All right," she said, and picked up her basket.

"Let me take that," – all at once he was beside her. "No," she said quickly, but his physical presence was so overpowering – he looked almost neolithic, with his beard and slightly yellowish teeth, a garden gone quickly to seed, untrimmed and untended for three whole days – that she took a step away from him and he possessed himself of the basket and turned back up the path. "Come along, come along," he said impatiently, but still smiling that awful smile of fake patience, perfected over years of sly irony, practised on those too young to counter, even, often, to appreciate it, which is cruellest of all. She found herself hurrying after him, her eyes glued to the basket, taking little running steps to catch up with him. He strode onwards and she was quickly out of breath. "Into the mountain, into the mountain," she kept thinking. He stopped and waited for her. "Could I take the basket?" It was a demand.

He looked down at it. He'd been swinging it along without thinking. "And my yoke is light!" What was it?

"Some food. A picnic. Nothing much, just some bread and fruit and things. I'll take it, thank you."

He lifted back the cloth. Two green apples, a wrapped block of cheese. Bread. A bottle of water. And wedged into the corner, a little terracotta urn. Not a pepper pot. He saw, and slipped the cloth back over, handing it back to her generously.

"Of course. By all means. Please take it."

She grasped the handle and started walking again, several feet from him, by his side.

"I have had a most interesting time. Really – most interesting." Why, he wondered, was he leading her up the path like this? Because, he answered himself with an emphatic rhetorical thrust of the head to which he was quite oblivious, he did not want to go *down* any more, he would not do what others wanted of him, he would take his own path in his own time, it was part of the new life, the life to come, they would go *up* and *then* they would go down, and he would say just when and by what path. It would be an authority of the heart, of the spirit even, not of the rule book. And what a glorious opportunity, what a gift of the gods, this simple woman, this creature of flesh at his side, this poor Phèdre, ruled by her extinguished passions, with her miserable pot of cinders, they would be rid of that, she would be – why almost a convert, he would guide her hand and in one magnificent symbolic gesture cast off the world and its craven attachment to physical matter, which was as that! – he snapped his fingers to his thoughts and Elizabeth looked sharply at him – yes, she probably thought he was mad. Well, my dear, they thought that about a lot of people I wouldn't be ashamed to be mentioned in the same breath as, chin up, I won't bite, *bonjour mes enfants*—

"Mr Goodman, please?"

He smiled and stopped abruptly, so that she almost fell over him. "Yes?"

"This is really quite exhausting, I don't quite see—

He put his fingertips together, almost like a chinaman, she thought, and said "We are going *up* the mountain. It is only a little way," and he made a v shape with his two hands still joined at the wrists, a gesture of invitation mixed with impatience. They started walking again. Elizabeth's shoe was rubbing. "And then we will *stop,* and have a *rest,* and you can have something to eat and drink" – he felt far too excited himself – "and," he unfurled his arm in the direction from which she had come, "we will go *down* the mountain again. Such a beautiful day," he said, repeating her words back at her sweetly, and starting off again at the same breakneck speed.

"The body, Miss Faulkener, is a frail vessel, and we must not let it rule our lives, we must overcome, we must press on, up—"

– into, she thought

"– the mountain, and you will see, oh what a glorious thing it is, where the air is thin and the spirit, Miss Faulkener, is free, free as a—"

"– bird?"

"– yes, *exactly,* as a bird, a noble raptor, and all these little things – his voice squeaked a little "will simply fall away from you" – he seemed to be gesturing at her blue and white dress – "you see, and all your worries and concerns and fears will be as nothing again, I promise you, you must trust in me."

He is quite mad, she thought, and I am here alone up a mountain and he is so strong, actually, he has a sort of vile authority.

"Stop," she said.

He turned on her quickly. Insubordination!

"Stop?"

She sat down. "This is a very nice little clearing. We can see everything here. I really can't go any further for now. I'm very sorry." And she started to take the things out of the basket in a calm and ordered fashion. He stood there, casting a shadow over her, looking down at her in exasperation, resisting her example. Then, with a sigh, he sat down on the ground.

For the first five minutes he didn't speak. Elizabeth cut up slices of bread and cheese and began to eat. She wasn't looking at him but she could feel he was watching her mouth move as she chewed, with disgust almost, as though she had been gorging herself on dog food.

"A slice of bread and cheese?" As she looked up at him, he looked away down the mountain, and wiped the back of his neck, where it was staining his shirt collar with sweat, with his handkerchief.

"No thank you."

She continued eating. I shall have to eat the whole lot, she thought, otherwise we'll be off again in no time. Presently he got up and wandered over to the edge of the mountain, where the ground fell away to the path many feet below, where it wound back on itself in its descent.

"Look," he said.

She looked in his general direction.

"No, no!" as though she had misunderstood the imperative, "Come and look!" He beckoned impatiently. She got to her feet and tried to walk slowly. He was staring at her with a demand in his eyes, a hypnotic stare, drawing her towards him. She came level with him and looked down. Far down below the little road swam like a water snake in the heat, bending this way and that, leading her eye to the town, just a handful's size, miles and miles from her now, unrecoverable, as though it were part of the geomorphology, encrusted in the land, sealed over, once left, so that she might have been here for hundreds of years in a single day and the world had grown old and to dust like the ashes in her bag. He had moved behind her and she turned with a gasp to see him reaching for the basket. He thrust his hand in – would it be an apple or the ashes? – and he drew out the terracotta urn.

"What are you doing?"

"What am I *doing*? Why, I am going to release you! Your burden will be light!"

"What! Stop it, you've no right, give that to me! How do you know?"

He smiled, and shook the urn, putting it to his ear as though he might be able to hear it ticking.

"Christian has told me your story. You are a privileged person, really you are, this wonderful gesture only a – stone's throw away, I could almost envy you, it is the perfect, really the perfect opportunity to cast off the old – you have no idea."

"Christian told you? *Christian*?" What courage she had had melted away from her, and she stood forlorn at the edge of the cliff. It was as if the backbone had gone out of her. Her body was weak with the little betrayal. He came and stood by her.

"Shall we?"

Christian had been restless all day. When he heard Elizabeth had gone up the mountain he went into the workshop, where Pierre's old tools were still laid out in perfect order, and found Mr Vidalou's chair. He brought it out into the garden and began to saw it into little pieces. I watched him from the kitchen. He was working methodically, with no expression on his face. He had always worked well with wood, it came naturally to him. I went out for lunch, just down the road, to see a farmer who had evicted his wife the previous month. Since his wife had been the dairy maid, he was now at a bit of a loss, and off-loaded most of his milk onto me. I turned it into yoghurt, which gives back twice in quantity what you started with. It was a satisfactory enough arrangement – or at least, like most numerical things, it satisfied itself without satisfying anyone. I got back just after two, and Christian had burned all but the legs. He was sitting by the remains of his fire, knocking two pieces of wood shaped like cricket stumps, making a ringing noise, a series of strangely musical clinks. It reminded me of the noise the frogs make at night. I always thought that if Aristophanes had heard our frogs he would not have opened his drama with anything as rasping sounding as *caracacoax*. It was somewhere between a chuckle and a bleep. It was too hot outside and I went to lie down in my room. I must have slept for about an hour, for I woke up at three. I sat at my dressing table and took the Spanish comb from my hair. I began to comb, pushing the little mirror on its swing down horizontal so I could look out at the vines. It was dry as tobacco that month. Down in the town the river ran empty, and where Christian had once leaped among his stepping stones and cheated the waters, the children could now pick their way in pin steps and not catch a drop. Then I saw him. He was standing at the top of the field, facing the house, but with his head held up into the sky. His face was white, and his arms were lifted slightly from his sides. His eyes were open, my marvellous boy, held in the grip of something I didn't recognise, as though he were fighting against something stronger than him, with different weapons, my David, his defencelessness his only strength. I had my hand still to my head, and the comb was biting into my scalp and I wanted to reach out and undo the catch on the window and shout to him to stop, that he was hurting himself but I couldn't move, I just sat there with my Spanish comb in my hand, as though I had turned to stone and my spirit, the life of me, had been lifted out. My hand slipped on the mirror, it righted itself, and I found myself looking at my own horrified face. I dashed it back down again, and tried to struggle with the clasp on the window. But when I had it open and tried to call, no sound came out, just a croak. Christian was lying collapsed on the ground, in a violent pose, aligned between two rows of vines, with his arms flung out to his sides.

Pascal carried him in his arms like a child, though they might have been brothers in age. I went to the door, hopeless, at a loss, in shock, maybe, or dumbfounded, as they used to say, my hand clapped to my mouth.

"You're bleeding," he said, as he turned his shoulder in the doorway, so that Christian went through head first, Pascal's left arm supporting his shoulders, his right locked under his knees. I put my hand to my head. "I broke my comb."

He laid Christian out on my bed. There were no visible marks, no bruises or cuts. His pulse was beating, but he was quite unconscious.

"Is he sleeping?"

Pascal sat sidesaddle on the edge of the bed. "Sort of. Like a trance."

I reached for the phone. "I'll ring Dr Balfour."

"No, not him. Get Rodin."

I was surprised. Rodin was eighty if he was a day. We had never had him to the house. He was the doctor to the farms and the outlying hills. He was good on births, marriages (the medical side) and deaths (natural). His knowledge of medicine was patchy, but he was at ease with the sick and down at heart. The aged mother of a friend of mine had lain dying for three weeks, and she knew it. "No, no," everyone said, "you'll pull through! You're not leaving us yet," and she would groan and turn her face to the wall. When the doctor came, he nodded, told them to change her sheets and read to her, and went away again. Then one day, he sat by her bed and took her hand. *"Eh bien,"* he said, stroking her hand tenderly, *"c'est la fin, n'est-ce pas?"* She squeezed his hand gratefully and died that night, happy that someone had understood.

Looking at Christian, I couldn't think he was dying, because he seemed so peaceful, he couldn't be in a state of becoming anything, he was in a state of being. There was no imminent threshold from which we need hold him back. I felt the time of his absence, wherever he was, had already been appointed, and that we could do no more than watch over him as his bark bobbed gently on the still surface of the lake. He was breathing quite peacefully, but his lips were pale.

"You don't think if we just try to wake him?"

"No," said Pascal, getting up from the bed and going towards the phone. "It's like sleepwalking. He has to come back of his own accord."

"But – what if – don't people get brain damage? It can be dangerous— "

"He'll be all right." Pascal looked down at Christian, then

leaned over and smoothed the hair back from his brow. "I should be doing that," I thought. I went and took Pascal's place by the bed. I wanted to take his hand, but didn't dare. Perhaps I was thinking of the words of my friend, who had told me the story. "And he took her hand . . ." Would Elizabeth be back soon? If she hadn't gone up the mountain, Christian would not be laid out on my bed, he would be sitting at her feet in the garden, drawing in the dust, or scrambling up the wooden staircase after the cat, or shouting with laughter as he splashed in the pool. But I was remembering him younger than he was. The last two images were lodged with me, but he no longer embodied either of them. I was doing that old, sad trick of keeping the baby clothes.

Pascal came back to the bedside. He handed me some cotton wool for my head. It was only a little wound, but it seemed to bleed rather a lot. Still, it was more hat pin than crown of thorns.

"He'll be here in half an hour. He didn't sound worried."

"Should we keep him warm?"

"It is warm. It's you. You're shivering. He went and found a cardigan and put it round my shoulders.

Dr Rodin arrived an hour later. Pascal, who had been born in the village, and probably delivered by him, met him downstairs. It was right and meet, or considered so in the neighbourhood, to offer the doctor a glass of muscat before he went up to see the patient. Pascal had rather taken over. In moments like these, a country lore, ancient knowledge of a kind whispered from one generation to the next, comes to guide those who are initiated, like the steps of a regional dance. It is folly to think you can learn the dance by learning the steps. I stayed upstairs and waited for him.

We had met before. I had known his wife, a beautiful, simple woman, from Bordeaux, the daughter of a rich *douanier*, who had borne him two impossible sons. One of them, who must have been forty by now, was a man of mystery, a painter friend of Christian's, who had taught him to ride, and was the darling of the local bourgeoisie. He was cold and grey-haired, and utterly seductive. I wondered now whether he had been an entirely good influence on Christian. Christian once told me that the local *gendarmerie* had turned up at the doctor's house one day with two skulls, male and female. They had been found at the local dump, and the police were conscientiously looking into the case. "No," said the doctor, he knew nothing about any skulls. They had better go and ask the priest. He was about to shut the door again, when his wife shouted down, *"Mais si! Ce sont ses parents!"*. The doctor was greatly indignant to be told that she had been clearing out the granary and decided they really had no further need for the family skulls, which had been kicking around in a cardboard box for twenty or thirty years. He reclaimed them and carried them off to his office, where he put them safely in a cupboard to which he alone had the key, for it was full of the kind of deadly poisons which in small doses restore the sick to health. A year later, shortly after they returned from a holiday in Egypt, the son, who was also the local dentist, rushed in one day while his father was out and demanded the key to the cupboard. He had a patient whose gums wouldn't stop bleeding, and he needed some chemical solution, and the chemist was shut. His mother shrugged and said she supposed the key to the cupboard was in the drawer by the door. He opened the cupboard, and two skulls looked out at him from the dusty interior, carefully painted in finest gold, in the manner of the Egyptian kings. "I had wondered," he told Christian, "why he kept asking me for teeth." The son thought the only odd thing was that in reconstructing his parents' smiles, he had mistakenly implanted incisors for canines and vice versa. *"Ça me gênait beaucoup,"* he said, but was otherwise remarkably unconcerned, I thought, by the possibility that his father was not quite all there. Christian loved the old man for this, almost as much as he loved his son.

The doctor sat down by the bed, and took out his handkerchief to wipe his own brow. He watched Christian breathing for a while. It looked like a vigil of some sort. Shortly, he took out a pipe, tapped it against the sole of his shoe and began to fill it. When he had lit it, he leaned forward with his forearms on his knees and smoked thoughtfully. I stood by the window, in a position to which I had withdrawn on his arrival.

"Did Pascal tell you what happened?" I asked, hoping to render the scene a little more clinical, to loose it from its peculiar, slow bond. "Christian went out into the vines. He wasn't unwell. It's not so very hot today . . ."

"It's all right," he said quietly. "He'll be all right." After half an hour, maybe more, he got up and came over to shake my hand.

"I'll be back the day after tomorrow. Just to check."

"But –" I gestured at Christian – "surely we need to get him to hospital, some proper advice— "

He touched my arm. "Now, now," he said, "he is not sick, he is only sleeping." Before I could decide whether this was irony, or reverent quotation, he had gone, leaving only the bitter, comforting smell of his pipe, nosing its way gently round the room.

Elizabeth gave several explanations, since she was honest, and knew that one wouldn't do. The obvious one was that he slipped. He lost his footing and with an undignified yelp went tumbling down the mountain – not hurling into space, as it wasn't that kind of mountain, just rolling and bumbling like an errant stone, bouncing off trees and staggering in the open spaces, till he disappeared from sight, a lost object, with not so much as a cry. There was a struggle, as she grasped his arm, a taut sinewy member, stiff with anger and triumph, as he held the urn out of her reach, taunting her with the possibility of his gesture, until she suddenly let go of him, and there was no weight, no counterbalance, and he flew from his own lack of ballast, and the urn shot up into the air and then landed, resting in a cushion of bracken only a few feet away, while he snowballed down the slope. It was a moment of apotheosis, when the mind goes blank, and afterwards she sank to the ground and put her head in her hands. In the moment when the ashes flew something had distracted her, something had *made* her let go. "It was Tristan," she said simply, as she always said it, just as she had always simply summoned Will by his name alone, in terms of a revelation. In the corner of her eye she had seen him, standing several yards from where they stood locked in their undignified tussle. He was singing, she said, and it was a magical little song, known only to himself. As Mr Goodman took his final tumble and she looked away again to follow his meteoric flight fall, she lost sight of the child, and of the ashes themselves, and the loss of both seemed to cancel each other out, so that there was no sense of loss after all, only a huge relief. Choirs of angels? No, not that, just the day and the world stretched out before her and the feeling that somewhere, somehow, without her willing it herself, it had been accomplished.

Part Seven

15

"Can you just open the fridge, there's a carton of milk – that's it, thanks." Frances was making a fish sauce. She cooked like a man. Elizabeth hadn't really cooked. She had bought ready washed salads and chicken wings in sesame sauces from expensive delicatessens. She ate very little anyway, so it had probably turned out cheaper.

"How's bachelor life?"

"Fine."

"Will Anna be OK? It won't be messy?"

"I don't think so. It's always less nice than you think it's going to be. I suppose I'll try and take a King Solomon approach. She'll keep the house."

Billy started making a noise. Not crying or shrieking, just making a noise like a buzzer that goes off to call your attention to something. "Pick him up Mark could you, there's a love. Do you mind? It must be time for *The Archers*. When I was pregnant I used to listen to it all the time. It calmed me down. I think he sort of got used to it."

Mark took the baby out of his push chair and sat him on his knee. Billy began to play with the buttons on his shirt. Mark talked over the top of his head.

"How old is he?"

"Five months."

Mark offered his finger for inspection, and Billy touched it wonderingly. Was it that he just perceived everything very slowly, or that with his new eyes he saw so much more than someone much more accustomed to the appearances of the world?

He had got Frances to ask him for dinner while Alistair was away in America. Alistair always changed the subject whenever he mentioned Elizabeth.

"She never wanted children. She said."

"Who – Anna?"

"Elizabeth."

"Ah." Frances tapped the metal spoon against the edge of the saucepan. "That'll do. I'll just turn the gas down. Do you want another drink? Or there's white wine."

She filled up his glass. Mark thought he had bowled a no-ball, but when she had sat down with her drink and taken note of the time – for the fish – she said, "She did. Want them. Or one. I'm not sure that's the same thing. Wanting one is one thing. Wanting a family is quite a different instinct."

"How do you know?"

Frances spread out her hands at the cluttered kitchen, upended teddies, a pushchair, a miniature Jasper Johns stuck to the fridge door, with the word *Mummy* written at a tenth of normal speed, full of wiggles and hesitations.

"No, how do you know she wants a child?"

"She did. With – Will."

"She told you that? For Christ's sake, she'd only known him for— "

"I know. Honestly, I can't explain how it was. She just became consumed by him. Like he'd cast a magic spell. All the worst clichés. If he'd told her to jump off the Post Office Tower she would have done it – at least if he'd done it too. He wants your tie."

"Who? Oh, I see." He poked the soft end of his tie in the baby's face, and Billy brought his hands up to try and clasp it.

"She had a phantom pregnancy."

"A *what*?"

Frances said, "Is this really what you want to talk about?"

"Yes."

"OK." She got up from the table and took her glass over to the cooker. "I'm sure this gas is leaking. We'll all die of poisoning." Billy mewed sadly and looked as though he might be about to break into a fit of protest. Frances rushed over and swapped him for the spoon. Mark took it and surrendered the baby. Frances calmed him down and put him in the little pushchair. She looked around vaguely for the spoon. "Didn't I have – oh, wonderful, thanks."

"Like *The Marquise von O*?"

"The who?"

"The story – she's pregnant and she's a virtuous widow."

"That wasn't a phantom, she got raped while she was unconscious."

"I know. That's what I mean."

Frances looked at him wryly. "Well. I suppose it was a bit like that. But she wasn't really. It was almost like a phantom phantom pregnancy. One thing, it stopped her actually getting pregnant. I think her mind thought her body was, and her body took it from there, whatever."

"I don't see. She was sick?"

"No. Not like that. It was just a kind of obsession. A sort of image with her. She said, "I feel like I'm going to have a child."

"But surely— "

"Everything stopped. You know, all her system and everything."

Frances wasn't quite sure how biologically explicit she could be with Mark. With Will she could have talked about nappies and baby vomit and waters and afterbirth for hours. Mark was not quite so frankly lascivious in his dealings with the natural world. He had a different language for it, a less immediate one. It wasn't coyness, it was just more formal, less colloquial. She imagined it would make them very different types of lover.

"God knows. You know how she is. They should use her to advertise baby wipes. All clean and fresh, as though it had never been."

"No. You make her sound boring. She's not. Just aloof."

"At the moment she is. It's almost as though she's ceased to have a personality. In limbo."

"You're sure she's not just being a dark horse?"

"Your *dame blanche*."

Mark got up and looked over the sink out at the garden. It was a riot of just one colour. A sort of greenish yellow.

Frances paused at his side. "It's not up to much, is it? Perhaps over winter I'll have a clear out."

Then she looked up at Mark's face and realised that he had gone to look out at the garden because he was trying to contain the tears in his eyes. She instinctively put her arm round his shoulder as she would have done to one of her children and instead of speaking, tried to feel what he felt. He turned round and gave her a hug, perhaps to say thank you for her concern, perhaps just to return to her what she had given him, so he would not be in her debt. Frances put a brisk end to the moment by going and wheeling the sleeping baby into the hall. She came back in and poured the sauce over the fish and slipped it in the oven.

"It was superstition. Again." Frances passed him the plates and knives and forks. "And bring the breadboard over. We'll cut it as we need it. Could you make a dressing?" She put the various bottles on the table and Mark started measuring out the oil into the bowl. "Because he told her from the start. Or so she says. I never quite know what to believe. What's fact and what's a sort of dream. That he was going to die."

"But he never said what of."

"No. It wasn't Aids, because he used to give blood, and he actually looked as fit as a fiddle right to the end. Apart from always looking hung over. Alistair and I almost thought it might have been some kind of suicide pact. With someone else. He was very strange. But he did warn her. After that she says they never talked about it."

"So how can it have been such a wonderful relationship if they never talked about anything?"

Frances looked at him with her eyebrows raised.

He flicked some mustard into the sauce. "OK. But it all just sounds a bit odd."

"But at the time it seemed quite normal, as if they were living the only life they could possibly be living. That's why it had such a short span, I suppose. It was like madness – people acting perfectly logically but on a totally loopy premise."

"What was the premise?"

"That Elizabeth could live for longer than a year – eight months, it was – with someone like him."

"Perhaps he knew that."

"You're forgetting the ashes. He really is dead."

Mark tasted the dressing. "Sugar? Honey?"

"Behind you on the shelf. And switch the oven off while you're on your feet."

"It's not – it couldn't have been some kind of horrible joke?"

"No. He wasn't somebody who would play a horrible joke. I'm afraid— "

"What?"

"He was everything Elizabeth saw in him, in a way. You mustn't think he was a monster. Or you'll never – whatever you want. Get close to her again. There's nobody like him. I was half in love with him myself. But only when he was there. When he went away you sort of forgot about him. As though he only had a physical presence."

"Elizabeth doesn't seem to feel like that about it."

"No, it doesn't look as though she does. But I think it's actually a bit of her she's mourning, not so much him as herself."

"Which bit?"

"Ah." She got up and whipped the fish out of the oven and on to the table. She stood there thinking about it. "Perhaps if you knew that you might be in with a chance . . ."

"Marguerite thinks she needs to sing."

"She's not singing at all?"

"Apparently she does in fits and starts. But it's all sterile. I'm not sure I know how that sounds. No emotion, I guess. She just does it. Gets on with it. As they say in the army."

Frances put down her knife and fork, in favour of her glass. It was one of those conversations. "When I was in Australia," she said thoughtfully, "I had my heart broken. It really does break. Or tears. And then of course it mends, if you get all the pieces back together again. While it was mending, I couldn't bear to write with a pen. I couldn't write letters, or postcards. My mother was frantic. But every time I picked up a pen I came over sentimental and cried. There was something too personal about it. Then I bought a second-hand typewriter and I couldn't stop writing. Once I was able to miss out the expressive bit, you know, the glide and punch" – she dotted an i and crossed a t on the table in front of her – "I could do it again. You take away the handwriting and it's somehow anonymous. Perhaps she'd be able to do radio recordings."

"Surely it's in the sound?"

"Yes, it is. If it's not there it's not there. What are you going to do?"

Mark reached for some salad. He didn't answer immediately, and Frances kept looking at him, not letting go of the question. She felt Mark was about to enter on the scene in some way, that he had, in the last few minutes, suddenly reconsidered his candidature.

"Where did he live? I mean, do you know his friends?"

"He lived in a derelict club behind St James. When he wasn't at Elizabeth's. He did these sculptures apparently. I don't know what. He always had white clay under his finger nails. She said they met lots of people. Whenever they went into a pub he seemed to know someone. They went to parties and things, I think. But they never saw anyone twice."

"She never thought that was strange?"

"No. And you mustn't either – he did add up, you know."

"Alistair never mentions him."

"No, well he's a man isn't he? But he wasn't a ladies' man. He was blokeish too. But Alistair's not going to sit down and tell you all about Elizabeth's lover, is he? Besides he probably only met him a couple of times, to be fair."

"When was the last time anyone saw him?"

"Around Easter. The day Billy was born. I thought it was extraordinary when she didn't come. I thought they must have gone away on holiday. I didn't find out immediately, because at first she hid away, then I was in hospital with Billy for three days. I rang and rang, left messages for her. Eventually I went round. She was listening to the Pergolesi *Stabat Mater*. Over and over again."

Mark thought of Elizabeth listening to the *Stabat Mater* over and over again. He had had the cassette in his tape machine in his car all that summer, the summer she had left. He drove very little, just trips out of Oxford and sometimes to London if he wanted to return late at night. The music had inched forward, a few bars here and there, a whole movement there, in fits and starts, never quite finishing, or finishing on such a brief note that it seemed right to let it play again from the beginning. He took their shared obsession with the piece as a good omen, knowing he could equally take it as a sad irony, and opting for the better part.

"She didn't exactly look ailing when I saw her. Did she tell you? In the bar at Paddington?"

"Yes. She had just been to collect his ashes."

"Oh God. She didn't say."

"You couldn't be expected to know. But she said you smiled when she said he was dead."

"That's nonsense! How could she possibly—?"

After that, Mark felt he had an approach, a reason for pursuing her. She had misunderstood him. There was something to put right. Whatever happened, she must not think that he had done that, it was unbearable. The misunderstanding seemed to him like a huge complication in a plot, which once unravelled would smooth the way to happy resolutions.

2 ʃ

On the following day Mark left the reading room around one o'clock and took the tube to Piccadilly. Walking past Eros, he was stopped by two Japanese girls of around sixteen or seventeen. At first he thought they wanted him to take their photograph, and he willingly held out his hand for the camera, but they giggled behind their tiny hands and waved him back towards the fountain. No, no, it was the beautiful Englishman they wanted to photograph, to send back to their friends in Japan. So Mark put on his best look, and they photographed him with his hands in his loose trouser pockets, looking sideways and smiling at the camera. They arranged him a little bit, patting and turning him like Gulliver. "Now a sad face," one of them cried, and took the camera from her friend, and while Mark was looking at the statue without having prepared for the photograph, she clicked him swiftly. Then they touched him on the arm in gratitude and bowed off into the crowd. Mark wandered on, and then caught up with them at the traffic lights, waiting to cross from the north side of Piccadilly to the south. They pushed a notebook and a pencil at him. "Your address! We will send you the photo, OK?" He wrote down the name of his college, and they squealed and then ran across the road as soon as the lights changed, waving and giggling, and then disappearing into Simpsons.

Outside the Church of St James, a large poster proclaimed a series of religious meetings to be addressed by noted evangelists from all over the world. Mark walked across the little square in front of the church where market stalls, strangely insensitive to the "den of thieves" story, he thought, were selling Arran jumpers and wooden toys fashioned in Guatemala. There was one American girl who sold jewellery which she bought herself on trips to India. She was slightly hippyish looking, with fair hair tied back from her face with a scarf, green eyes and a lovely, not altogether respectable smile. "Hi, Mark." He went over and said hello. They had got chatting when he had called in for lunch in the restaurant one day. She had told him to throw up his job and come and see the world with her, and he had tried to imagine what life would then be like. They would have seen the world and then she would have come back and opened a slightly bohemian craft shop in North Parade and he would have gone back to work on his texts and his lecturing and an eventual book and they would perhaps have been very happy.

"When are you off then Becky?"

"Autumn. Soon. You going on holiday?"

"Maybe."

"To France, I guess. Those troubadour guys again?"

"I'll see."

He picked up a gold chain and poured it from raised fingers into the palm of the opposite hand, and it fell onto his flesh with a sort of cool melting feeling. The little price tag said £7.50 and he took out his wallet and paid her for it. Becky gave a big grin and put her hands on her hips like an angry mamma in films about the deep south.

"Whose dat fo, den?"

He shrugged. "I don't know." He bounced it on the palm of his hand, then slipped it into his pocket. "Maybe I'll get lucky."

She watched him walk on and into the church, with her arms folded across her chest, shaking her head slightly and smiling. Her friend at the next stall came over and nodded across at him.

"That's him?"

"Yeah."

Her friend patted her on the shoulder and went and bought her a cup of tea from the urn in the corner.

Mark stood at the back of the church, which was quite full, and leaned his back against the wall. The preacher was in full spate. Mark was rather surprised to see that he was praying with his eyes open, whilst the congregation had their heads, for the most part, bowed. The preacher had his arms held high, like a prophet and was looking up at the ceiling in urgent appeal. "Come down upon us!" he implored. Mark left before it did.

He ate in the Café Torino, opposite the Royal Academy. Tuesday had been his Elizabeth day. They would have gone to see the Summer Exhibition and argued amiably about what was good and what wasn't and afterwards walked in the park or gone back to her flat. He supposed that because for him it had, after all, been an illicit relationship, it was natural that the individual moments should have been more important to him. Cool from the start, she had remained so, although that certainly did not preclude a great deal of tenderness, which was generously shared. He wondered whether it was possible for two people who have had a perhaps over-courtly love affair, with too much attention to gentillesse and restraint and respect, and even good humour, can ever re-enter the garden, and find passion and a flame. When she had left, and he had known she was going to leave, he had felt such despair, that all the passion he had never before admitted, had rushed into his awful emptiness and overwhelmed him. *"Douce dame, ainc ne vous dis nul jour Ma grant dolor, ainz l'ai tous jours celée."*

He turned left off Piccadilly, and right and left, and began to walk deliberately now, looking up at the buildings, until he found himself opposite a derelict façade, like a bad tooth between its more noble neighbours. The main door was at the top of a small flight of steps, behind spiked iron railings. To the left was a little gate, which was half open. Another flight of steps ran down into a basement. He went down and tried the basement door. Outside were three bags of rubbish, old cans and bits of wood, and newspapers. It opened easily. Inside it was dark, but he seemed to have come into a sort of corridor. Feeling his way along the walls, with plaster flaking under his fingertips, he edged along, until he came to a tight, steep staircase leading upwards. When he reached the ground floor there was more light, but it was a pale beige light, of city interiors, filtered through the silted panes of glass in their lead casements. Frances had said he lived in the attic. He appeared still to be in the servants' quarters. He carried on climbing upwards. Pausing on the third floor landing, a tiny space with thin carpeting and walls which were coated in thick blistering paint with a plastic sheen, for washablity, he heard the sound of a pigeon cooing from above. He ran on upwards until he got to the top floor, where the roof along the corridor was of grimy glass, placed on a metal framework, like the old greenhouses at Kew. He was in a long corridor, with a red carpet and dark walls, with doors leading off every three or four yards, presumably onto tiny, squalid bedrooms. He began to walk along, treading very quietly. The cooing of the pigeon was coming from the far end. He tried a door on his left, then a door on his right. Finding each of them locked, he moved methodically down the corridor, until he came to a door which was slightly ajar. With his right hand on the knob, and the fingers of his left barely touching the wood, he pushed it open. Inside was a dingy attic room, with a north-facing window, which was open to the noise of the traffic below, a large, disproportionately large brass bed, a table. On the table, a plaster head, a woman, on the top of which perched a single pigeon. Mark sat on the bed. It was covered in an attractive Indian cloth. An alarm clock on the floor at his feet. He picked it up. The alarm had last sounded at two thirty. It seemed a strange time for an alarm. Next to it was an ashtray, full of little filterless cigarettes, somehow inoffensive. Maybe it was the waste that made ashtrays full of filter cigarettes look so unappealing, those once resplendent, rather elegant objects ground into the ash, spent and burned away. He stared at the plaster head. It was life-size, a woman with her hair scraped back off her face so that the shape was all there, nothing shielded. He thought for a moment it could have been Elizabeth, but it was not finished. The particularities of her features had not yet emerged from the material, and it could have been any woman almost, an archetype, which no loving hand, no experienced eye had yet moulded to furnish the details of his intimately known subject.

In a way Mark had come here to look for the truth. If, he thought, he could discover something about their lives together, who he was, where he had come from, where he might perhaps have disappeared to, he would be equipped, able to understand, it would not be a part of his own life from which he was forever exiled. Not that he would ever confront her with it, or tell her he had been there. But that he would know, have experienced, a little, even just a shadow's worth of the world she had inhabited in the months after leaving him. This strange, interior world was so alien to what he had always conceived to be the spirit of Elizabeth that somehow, instead of filling him with despair, it gave him hope, for there was another Elizabeth, there was a woman more of flesh and blood than he had ever allowed her to be, with his picture of the *dame blanche* – after all, it was he, not she, who had fostered the image – who was tolerant of squalor and had lived her passion and had not been afraid of being soiled, and who, no doubt, had changed, but was there somewhere, if only he could recover her. The pigeon was still sitting immobile on the top of the woman's head, not unfriendly looking. It was as though he believed that he was the statue and the woman's head a real one, or at least that Mark might be deceived into thinking so. On the table next to the pair of them was a printed folder from a travel company, the kind tickets are issued in. Mark picked it up and opened it. It was empty. But scribbled on the back, in a barely legible, uneducated hand, was a flight number, a time and a date.

He found an empty phone box just down from the Ritz and telephoned Frances.

"When's Billy's birthday?"

Rather taken aback, she told him. "The nineteenth. Why?"

He looked at the date on the folder. The twenty-first. Three days later.

"I'll call you back this evening."

"Come round for a drink. The children'll be in bed by eight."

"Fine."

"What's up?"

"Nothing. I'll see you later."

He got on a bus heading for Hammersmith. He had a meeting back at the museum at four. It was just coming up to half two. The bus was ridiculously slow for the first twenty minutes, then all of a sudden it seemed to gain terrific speed and be winging down Kensington Gore in a manner quite inappropriate to its size and weight. He jumped off before the official stop and walked along Kensington High Street until he found the travel agency. Inside, although the building itself was a perfectly nice – to Mark – piece of nineteenth-century architecture, you might have been in a very modern sort of caravan, all plastic surfaces and swivel seats. He felt that at the end of each day the girls and their terminals might simply fold away into the walls.

"I wonder if you could confirm to me whether a friend of mine took a flight. I've lost touch with him – I know he was thinking of taking this one." He held out the piece of paper. She took it from him, and began to click the details into her computer. Then there was a pause, and she studied her screen, waiting for the information to come up. There is, he thought, a new sort of facial expression, peculiar to people waiting for a response from their machines, a sort of patient expectancy, combined with smugness, because we all know, after all, that it is not the computer, but we ourselves who get the credit, and yet there is also the feeling that we have been very clever to persuade the computer to divulge its knowledge to us, intelligent and impenetrable as it is. There is also an element of exaggerated concentration.

"Sorry," she said, "can you give me that again?"

He showed her the piece of paper again.

This time she typed it in very slowly. She waited again, looking rather puzzled.

"It's really odd," she said. She leaned over to the girl at the next terminal.

"That's British Airways to India, isn't it?"

"Yeah. Once a day."

The girl looked at her screen again, then back at Mark.

"You got the date right and everything?"

"This is what I've got."

She span round on her chair and went to pick up a brochure. She flicked through it until she got to the page.

"That's right. There should have been one. Only I can't find it on my computer. It's just blank. It should be a whole page of records, like, who was on the flight, return dates of the passengers. There's nothing there."

Mark looked down at the top of her computer. "It's not the computer," she said glumly.

"No," Mark said. "It's odd though."

"Yes. It is odd." She said *odd* as though it were a rather obscure word, which she had not used for a few years but remembered from an English essay at school.

"Hang on," she said, "We can check it by his name. What's his name?"

"Who?"

"Your friend's name."

"Oh." There was a silence. Then he said, "Will," but he said it very quietly, realising that it was quite ridiculous not to know his friend's name, and suddenly feeling cheap and sly.

"Who?"

He made something up. The girl kindly checked the lists, and came up with nothing. She was disappointed. Mark was just turning to leave. "Take a brochure," she said.

He smiled at her. "I don't want to go to India."

"Where d'you want to go then? Balearics, Canaries, weekend break to a Euro capital? Caribbean? Greece?"

He held out his hand. "Give me the one on Greece."

"Mainland or Islands?"

"Islands."

"Hotel or self catering chalet?"

"Hotel."

"Exclusive or tourist. That means quiet or noisy?"

"Quiet."

She went and selected a brochure from the racks.

"That'll do you. Ring me when you've decided. You look like you could do with a break."

When Mark had left the shop her friend turned to her.

"You always say that."

"What?"

"They could do with a break."

"Well, it's true. I believe it. A holiday's a wonderful thing," she said stoutly, and flashed another smile at an elderly couple who had just popped their heads around the door.

The travel agency was close to Elizabeth's flat. There was a bench on a patch of green opposite where she lived, and he sat down wearily on it, and watched her house in the certainty that she was not there. It was a kind of luxury. There was the clematis he had given her for her birthday one year, clutching at the trellis by the door for dear, parched life, and the brass letter box through which he had occasionally slipped an elegant little note, accompanying a newspaper article which might amuse her, or a postcard specially chosen according to the theme of the moment. He felt ashamed of his inquiries, ashamed to have pretended Will was his friend, and yet glad he had done it. He had learned something about himself. He had not learned what he had had no right to ask. Frances had said he added up. A man who added up would not tell the woman he loved that he was dying, and book a flight to another continent simply in order to get away, particularly not at a travel agency just around the corner from her flat. If he had taken the flight, it did not mean he had not spoken the truth. If he was to win her back – he still thought in the idiom of his fancy, now expired, that she was a lady whose hand he must win – he should do so without taking from her the life she had had with another man, to which she had had every right. If he loved her, that was only fair. He took a notebook from his pocket, and wrote impulsively across the page, "Elizabeth, when you find this I will have come to find you. I love you. Mark." Then he strode across the road before he had time to think and slipped it through the letter box.

Frances and Mark were sitting in her kitchen again, drinking coffee. Mark kept looking at his watch.

"What is it," said Frances, "have you got a plane to catch or something?"

After his meeting at the museum, Mark had bought himself a small holdall, tooth brush, toothpaste and razor, a shirt, a pair of shorts and some jeans, as all his things were in Oxford. His passport was in his briefcase in his car, because he had meant to renew his reader's card, and had brought it for identity.

"A boat. At twelve thirty."

"Good Lord. Where to?"

"Dieppe."

"You're going to find her?"

"I'll try. I'm not going to abduct her. But I love her. I have to try."

Frances thought for a while. "You're right. Of course you have to try. Be very gentle with her. She may not want to see you. Be calm with her. Well, you know anyway."

Mark looked thoughtful. "I don't want to shock her. I'm not

going to leap out at her or anything. It's just – there's so much waste, I never showed her – and now— "

"Now you're a single man."

He gave her his knockout smile. He had had his hair cut that afternoon, and had changed when he arrived at Frances's into his new jeans, a lovely pale washed out blue, the colour of his eyes. She envied Elizabeth a little. Upstairs the baby was crying. "Scuse me a minute."

"Can I come up too?"

"Of course. Tiptoe."

They went and looked in on Billy, who stopped crying as soon as he saw them and began to sing a little song to himself, delighting in their company. Mark went over and pulled aside the Barbar curtain and looked out into the street. It was just still light. The leaves on the trees outside were a washed out lime yellow, the pavements dusty and grey, as though they bore all the tiredness of the weary feet that had walked there.

Frances came over and stood by him, showing Billy the world. "Beautiful world," she sang to him in a little voice, her lips touching his warm, little scalp, "Billy's beautiful world," and the baby pointed at it, and turned to them for their reaction, like a conductor giving the orchestra to the audience after the music has died and they have risen to their feet to applaud.

A few miles out of Newhaven, the bar opened, and Mark put down his book and went to buy a beer. There didn't seem any point in trying to sleep. There was an all night hotel just outside Dieppe, where he could stop for a few hours if he needed to, and get some rest. The bar was only half lit. People bought their drinks and then retired into the shadows. There were bodies everywhere. It was the cheap crossing, and most of the passengers were under twenty-five. It was a windy night, and the boat was pitching. With the dimmed lighting and the sprawling bodies, it felt as though they had been cast on the seas like convicts, for a distant destination on some luxurious vessel which had fallen into disuse, disgraced perhaps, so that all the facilities were now redundant, and would perhaps shortly be re-invented for different purposes; someone would take charge of them all and organise a meeting of the elders in the games room, and the drinks dispensers would be put to making hot water for washing in, the baby room converted into a makeshift ward for the sick.

There was an announcement, which he got the second time. "Would the passenger travelling to Montbasson, near Toulouse – c/o Marguerite d'Astige, please report to the Information desk." Immediately he thought of Elizabeth. Something dreadful had happened to her, and they had phoned Frances. Frances was saying, don't go, turn back, stop!

"There was an announcement," he said to the man behind the desk.

"Sorry?"

"An announcement. About Madame d'Astige." It seemed terribly complicated to explain what they had expressed so succinctly over the speakers, as though the idea, with all its dreadful possibilities, had ballooned, and couldn't be got back into the box it had arrived in.

"It's OK," said a girl at his side. "It's me. I lost my ticket. Left it in the loo. I was being sick actually. Lucky I had the address on it."

She was a sort of eastern beauty. He thought perhaps he had never seen almond shaped eyes before. It was always nice to run up against a cliché and discover why it had become so.

"But *I'm* going there."

"OK, OK. What is it? A closed shop or something? You been before?"

"Yes," he said emphatically, as though only one of them could go, and he needed to assert his own priority.

"Nice, then, is it?" She was chatty, like an assistant at a hairdresser's.

"Yes," he said and laughed. "It's very nice. I'm sorry. You must admit it's a coincidence. Us both on the same boat."

"I suppose. I don't really count coincidences. You can spend your whole life just harping on about that."

Alicia was like Christian. Where she walked, thunderbolts dropped from the sky, portents appeared written in the sand, coincidences leapt from the page.

"Would you like a drink?"

"No thanks. I feel bloody sick, actually. I've never been on a boat before. Except in the park, you know." She lifted her elbows from her sides and did a rowing action. She came and sat with him in the bar.

"What time does it get there?"

He looked at his watch. "About three hours' time, I think. They slow it down overnight."

"Oh. Then what happens?"

"Then the people who have cars get back in them and drive away, and the people who are on the train get on the train."

"Oh."

"Haven't you got a ticket?"

She opened her bag and took out the slip of paper stapled to cardboard. "Yeah. That's it."

He looked at the ticket. "Toulouse?"

"Yeah. It's miles isn't it. I hate trains."

"Oh dear. It'll take a day."

"It's funny," she said, "I kind of did it on impulse. Now I'm getting there I want to sort of slow down."

"Are you going to stay with friends? Do you know the lady? Marguerite?"

She thought about it for a minute. Then she shook her head. "No. But a friend of mine's there."

"Not—?"

"Not what?"

"A girl?"

She made her eyes very wide, as though she were telling the frightening bit of a story to a child, exaggerating and defusing the fear in a single gesture.

"No," she whispered loudly, "It's a *man*."

"Oh. Are you feeling better now?"

"A bit."

"I'm going to get another drink. You want one?"

"Please. A coke."

He went off and came back with the drinks. She looked up at him. She looked quite exhausted.

"I got them to put some rum in it. Is that all right?"

She stirred the drink with a long stick of plastic, then removed it and sucked it dry. Then she pushed it between the edge of the seat and the wall. "God," she said, "that's so ugly."

An announcement was made in French about safety procedures. They must have forgotten to do it at the beginning. It wasn't very encouraging. The girl said, "What are they saying?"

"That if the boat sinks you have to run for it."

She sank back in her seat. "I did French at school. I thought I was quite good, but I don't understand a bloody word."

"They'll do it in English in a minute. You won't understand that either."

A pinched voice came over the loudspeaker system. It sounded like someone doing a take off of the Queen's Christmas speech. The girl laughed and sat forward with her elbows on the table.

"What's your name?"

He was ridiculously charmed by her lack of conversational guile. He was so sick of talking to pretentious young undergraduates, with their airy fascination for the abstract. It was nice when someone just asked you your name.

"Mark Chester."

She stuck her hand out. "Mine's Alicia."

He shook her hand with amusement. "No, honestly," she said, "you have to get used to it. They do that in France. Or they do this." She leaned over the table and took his face between her hands and turned it first one way – and kissed him, then the other – and kissed him again. Then she let him go, but her fingers were slow to move from his face, so he felt them brush across his skin as she lifted them away.

"Even if, you know, there hadn't been that mix up, I'd have sat with you anyway. You were the best looking bloke on the boat. My grandmother says you should always go for a pretty face. She says you can tell a man's character in his face."

"I have a very good character," he assured her.

"Me too. I just do all the wrong things with it."

When the boat landed they were both asleep. He shook her gently. "Alicia." She woke with a little cry of fright. "Oh, it's you."

"We have to get off the boat now. I'm sorry to wake you. Unless you want to go back again?"

She gave him a sleepy grin. "What's the other choice?"

"You come down to the car deck with me and I give you a lift. All the way."

"With your good character?"

"With my good character."

"What a life," she said and picked up her duffle bag. "Let's go."

Alicia slept for the first few hours. Mark, full of his purpose, drove without feeling any tiredness. For the first hour or so he followed a long line of cars from the ferry. Then he stopped and drank some coffee, and watched all the people who had been behind him pass by. When he got back in the car, Alicia was still asleep. She was so fast asleep that her head was almost invisible, sunk down onto her chest. There was something deflated about her, the way she occupied, in sleep, so little space. He drove three times round the roundabout, for luck, and then took the *toutes directions* sign, which generally meant, don't think you can beat the system – do it our way.

He took the Pergolesi tape out of its box, and put it on. Alicia opened her eyes, but didn't speak immediately. She looked out of the window. Then she asked, "Where are we?"

"Near Tours. We get on the motorway soon. You've been asleep for ages."

"I know," she said. "I hate it, the way people think just because you were asleep you didn't know, or didn't do it on purpose. I've been asleep for four hours and twenty minutes. No flies on me, mate."

Mark said, "Shall I switch this off? Do you like it?"

"What is it?"

"Pergolesi. *Stabat Mater*."

"What's that mean?"

"It means, his mother was standing there."

"What like the Beatles, 'An' I saw her standing there'?"

"No. At the foot of the cross."

"What's she saying?"

"She saw him in torment, for our sins, her sweet son, dying in desolation, as he gave up his spirit. Something like that."

"Bloody hell. Switch it off. No wonder you look so miserable."

"I look miserable?"

"Yeah. All moony. Dead dog."

"Dead dog?"

"Well, you know, melancholic. If you're going to see a girl, I'd cheer up a bit. Not so heavy."

She was quiet for a bit, and Mark thought over what she had said. She was right. He had been feeling all momentous and "my love-ish". He had sunk into a state of morbidity about Elizabeth. He couldn't expect her to respond to that. He needed to come to her with something new.

"Can we have some lunch, do you think? I haven't got much money, but we could get a burger or something."

"We could get off the motorway altogether. We could have a proper lunch, in an *auberge*."

"Like aubergine?"

"No. An inn."

"Oh right. No, I don't think so. I can't think in places like that. Too much other stuff going on. You know, the way it's supposed to be – this is so French!" she said in a mimicking voice, holding a fake glass of wine to her lips. "Sod that. I want to think. I want to tell you something. You a good listener?"

"Not always," said Mark, "but I could try."

It was a long time since he had eaten a burger. He was surprised to find it was really rather good. Alicia showed him you had to push the straw through the hole in the top of your coke gently, otherwise it all came out all over the table.

"I've made this bloody great mistake," she said.

"Oh dear. Is it too late?"

"No. Tell me what you think. I knew this man, at my school, my French teacher. He's tall, dark, looks like an actor. An actor being a teacher."

"What do you mean?"

"I mean he's really good looking. That's what people mean when they say someone looks like an actor, don't they? They mean, they look normal, but in real life they wouldn't be that good looking. I really fancied him. You know, other blokes, always buying you drinks, flirting and that. He was different. Shy. Cross. Distant."

"Sounds great."

"Yeah, well, it makes you wonder, doesn't it? The things you can go for. I had this crush on him. I kept dreaming about him. I wanted him to touch me. Stop him being so bloody distant. I thought it was like a fairy story. If I did it with him, he'd come to life.

"He would have had to have been alive first, I'd have thought," said Mark, "otherwise it wouldn't have been much fun."

"You know what I mean. I got him to have me in his class. I'd had this sort of weird experience, when I was in the lake district last summer – a year ago. I thought I saw him. Well, it could have been a cloud, really. You know, when you're a bit stoned. I thought if I had him, everything would change."

"What did you want to change?"

"I dunno. I think I just wanted to get out of my life. Home and all that. I thought he was like a prince, or a knight or something. Mediaeval stuff. Anyway, I'm quite good at French actually, and he let me come in his class. Normally it's just the best pupils. But he let me in. We were doing Racine. You heard of him?"

Mark said, yes, he had.

"It's weird isn't it? *Phèdre* and that. I liked it. I'd never thought of it before. The idea you couldn't, you know, just do it when you felt like it. I began to think it was like me and him. I was sure he thought about me too."

Mark looked at Alicia. "Thought about you?"

She looked down at herself, as though she'd dribbled. "You know. Wanted to— "

"Oh, right."

"Don't interrupt. It's not a comedy. So I went round to his house. I made up this story about my mum, how she was involved with these terrorists in Spain and France, you know, on the border there. I was quite surprised, because I was a bit hazy about the geography on that side, but when I got home I found I'd got it exactly right. That was quite funny, really. The point of the story was, my mum had the gift."

"Did she?"

"Not that one, anyway. I said she was psychic. That she'd advised them on all their campaigns, when it would be a good time to plant bombs and stuff. He believed it all, you could tell.

I even said she'd had me in prison, and my gran had to come and fetch me because she committed suicide."

"Why?"

"Dunno. Could have been postnatal depression, I suppose. God, that's weird isn't it?"

"Which bit?"

"Well, you and me, here we are talking. We both thought it was real for a second. It's only a story."

"Maybe it did happen. Just not to you."

"I'd be psychic, then? To know?"

Mark pinched a bit of her burger, which she'd left. "Just a coincidence."

"Yeah. Anyway, he was quite nice about it really. Very serious, of course. I thought after that he'd ask me to stay, you know, but he didn't. He showed me the door."

"That was probably the right thing to do."

"No. No it wasn't. That way, it made it last. I kept on and on thinking about it. How I could get him. I was completely obsessed. I followed him everywhere. I worked really hard at lessons so he'd like me more. I completely forgot why I was doing it. I forgot about him, in a funny sort of way. It was like a cult. I didn't do anything else. Everything sort of stopped except that. Then I got stoned at a party at school and did it with the sports teacher on the floor of the French room, and he came in and found us and bashed the man's head against a table, and we all got found out."

Her story was so dense and quick and to the point, it was rather refreshing, rather like a newspaper report, but with all the missing intonation and feeling put back in.

"What happened?"

"I was on probation. I was allowed to go to some classes, until autumn term – this next one. Then I'm going to a polytechnic. I never went to his classes any more. The other teacher left. I didn't mind that. He was no good. I wanted to talk to Mr Goodman – that's his name – but he shut himself away the whole time. Honestly, you'd have thought he didn't exist. It was like he didn't have any contact with anyone, or anything. I saw him in the school hall, sometimes, but you never saw him going from anywhere, or coming from anywhere, he was just there, and you couldn't speak to him, and then he wasn't. It was terrible. I stopped eating. My gran said you could have posted me in one of those cardboard rolls. I started seeing men, just to get the money."

Mark said, "What do you mean, seeing men?"

"You know."

"Oh."

"And then he disappeared. Just left. After half term, he didn't come back. I nearly went mad."

"What for? Why did you want him?"

"You know. It's just like that sometimes. You get a notion. My gran calls them notions. It's like thinking you can't possibly live normally unless you have a certain thing. In fact, you could just do it differently, and the need would go away, but you can't see that at the time."

"Sometimes," said Mark, "you really do need it."

"Want it."

He hesitated, then said, "Yes. OK. Want it."

"So," she went on emphatically, "I was making plans to try and find him. I never knew what I'd say to him. I was always thinking I just had to be where he was, and everything else would follow. But that's not right. Even then, you have to know what you want."

"You think so?"

"Oh yes," she said, "it's obvious. Too much trusting to luck. I can see that now."

"So what did you do?"

"I screwed his twin brother."

"Goodness," said Mark. It was grand old verbal narrative at its best. Every time you were about to nod off, bang! out came another disaster, another twist in the story, and you were jolted back to attention.

"He came up to clear his stuff away, pay the phone bill, all that. I saw him in the pub. He was wearing a dog collar."

Mark started. Was the man perverted? A client with special needs?

"You know," she said, "a vicar."

Mark burst out laughing. Alicia did too.

"Shut up laughing," she said, "I said it wasn't a bloody comedy."

Mark drank his second coffee. He'd ordered two.

"Why didn't you just get a double one? Twice as big?"

"Because it's not as strong as two little ones."

"Oh good," she said, "isn't it great when there's an answer like that? I'm really glad I met you."

"What about the vicar?"

"Oh God yes, well –" She leaned forward towards him, tapping with the wrapped up sugar on the table top. "I knew he must be his brother, you see, because he just looked like him. I thought at first it was like one of those plays, you know, where one person plays both brothers, and he keeps having to rush round the back of the stage and come on in a different costume and say, 'Good Lord, I almost bumped into my brother!' "

"A comedy of errors."

"That's it, yeah. You do English too?"

"No," said Mark, "but you pick things up in life too."

"Ah. I'll have to watch out for that." She grinned at him. "I knew he must be going to the house, so I went there as soon as I finished . . . and waited for him. I was terrified I might have missed him, but he turned up."

"And?"

"I told you. I screwed him."

"Oh, yes, you did mention it."

"It was, actually, not very nice at all," said Alicia, slowing down. "I thought it might be, you know, like the next best thing. To him, I mean. But it wasn't. It was just bloody sad. When I realised that, I thought, oh, it's just a stepping stone. I had a piece of luck— "

"A stroke of luck— "

"Yeah, a stroke of luck. I found out his address. This place we're going. And I said, oh, well, that was just so I could get to the next bit you see?"

"Yes."

"Everything stopped being for itself, it was just a way of getting to him. Even things that had nothing to do with him. Like, oh I don't know, who you wanted to win in some football match, or what record you put on at a party. Then I decided to come to

France. I'd find him, and I'd tell him everything. How I felt about it, how he was kind of messing up my life. Show him what a huge deal it was. How important it was. Perhaps he'd know what to do. So, I set all that up. The night before last, before the boat, I was in London, with these friends. I was sleeping on their floor, on my way down. Well," she smiled a bit sheepishly, "s'posed to be on the floor. And I had this dream. I killed him."

"You killed him?"

"Don't keep saying what I say. It's a waste. Yes. I can't remember how. I just did. It was all over. He was gone. It was wonderful, actually. I felt great. I stopped thinking I was some kind of slug, you know, that I wouldn't get better, or perfect, or whatever, till I was with him. I was OK again, normal. That was quite strange, really, because I hadn't thought of it like that before at all. Then I woke up and he was still alive, and I thought, oh sod it, I've still got to go and see him. Anyway, I'd bought the ticket at Victoria. And there's something else."

"What?"

"Don't keep saying what and things. Don't you think I'm going to tell you? Trust me!" she said, ridiculing the expression with a long face. Then she sat back. "I think I'm pregnant."

"What? Oh shit, sorry. Who from?"

"Well," she said, considering carefully, although she had obviously already done that, this was for him. "It has to be the vicar, really." Just for that one sentence, Mark wished someone could overhear them. "There's no one else it could be. You know, you're so worried about getting a disease, you forget they're to stop you getting pregnant. So I thought, well, he's a vicar, I'm not going to exactly catch the bloody black death, now, am I? So I got pregnant, instead. I think I thought somehow, you couldn't, with a vicar. The sort of opposite of Mary and Joseph, you know.

"How long ago was this? How pregnant are you?"

"Oh. Only a few days."

"A few days? Then how do you know?"

"I just feel it. Someone told me, you just know when it happens. I knew."

"What are you going to do about it?"

"I don't know. I don't suppose I'll tell him – you know who. I mean, it's half as though it's his baby, isn't it?"

"Why? Because it's his brother's?"

"Yeah. He'll be an uncle."

"You're going to have it?"

"Oh yeah, I should think so. I think that would be quite nice, don't you?"

"Well, it's a question of what's best for both of you."

"I shouldn't think he'd care much. In fact I couldn't possibly tell him. He's married, and all that. But I'd like a baby. I wouldn't be irresponsible. I'd look after it. I've done so much other stuff already. Yeah. I think I'll do that now."

"I meant best for the baby."

"I'd be bloody good for a baby, I can tell you that now. I'm great with babies."

They set off again, and Alicia put on a tape of Mark's. "What's that?"

"Brahms. Violin Concerto."

"Bloody hell. Another one. Don't play her that either. Haven't you got anything, you know, a bit cheery?"

Mark had to admit he hadn't.

"Well it's time you did."

"Alicia?"

"Mm? Sorry. I was nearly asleep again. You must be knackered. What?"

"I don't think you should come with me to this place."

There was a silence. Then Alicia said "Why?"

"You're just satisfying some ridiculous morbid curiosity. You don't want to go. You're just seeing something through to the end when it doesn't need to be. Sometimes it's like that. Like when someone dies. Or someone you love leaves you. You think it's going to last a life time, you want it to, even, you don't want to forget, and then one day you wake up and you think, to hell with this, I want to do something else now. The real problem is, you're pregnant."

"Well," she said slowly, "I might not be." He looked at her sharply. "You made that up?"

"No. It's a hunch. What I want maybe."

"How old are you?"

"Seventeen."

Seventeen. Seventeen years ago, he had been in his mid-twenties. All he had learned since then, with all that time for learning . . . He wasn't sure he knew as much as Alicia knew. Who was he to tell her she was too young to have a child? Perhaps she would have forgotten less than him.

"But you're right. I felt it was something I had to do. Come here. Even when I realised I didn't want to, I kept on going, because I thought it was something – you know, written in the stars, like the song says."

Mark thought about it. She was right, in a way. "For me, maybe," he said.

"What?"

"Maybe you had to come for me?"

"But . . . it's not like that, is it, between you and me? I mean OK, you're gorgeous and everything, but you've got this girl, haven't you? I really hope that works out."

"I didn't mean it like that. Not quite. Though – " he looked across at her, "you're really lovely. Honestly."

"We could be friends?"

"Sure."

She drew her knees towards her. She had taken her shoes off and her toes were curled over the edge of the seat, like birds' claws. She leaned over and said in a very small voice in his ear, "Afterwards?"

He smiled at her. "Afterwards?"

"Friends, afterwards."

Mark took one hand off the driving wheel and reached over and took hers and brought it to his lips.

"Just once? For luck?" She held her index finger and thumb a little distance apart and looked at him appealingly, as if to say, just a tiny bit of love. Just this much?

Part Eight

15

As it turned out, Alicia could have come with Mark. She would never have run into Mr Goodman, because Mr Goodman never returned. Even I don't know what happened to him. It never occurred to any of us that he might be dead. Maybe he's teaching English in a school near you. Tall, slightly stooped. The odd anxious mannerism involving a handkerchief? That's him. Don't be too hard on him now. He took a nasty tumble. Being a cautious fellow, he had his wallet and his passport with him. You can never be too careful, he must have thought to himself. Perhaps that's a lesson he's learned now. You can, precisely, be that bit too careful.

So Mark fetched Alicia from the *auberge* – aubergine, she said – where he had left her, the other side of Toulouse, and brought her to me, because he was taking Elizabeth away. Pascal still can't take his eyes off her, though Felix is nearly three now. He doesn't look much like Mr Goodman, but he looks very much like Albertine. Albertine, conceived that summer, born next spring, was proof against any blight.

There was, perhaps, still a trace of that melancholy – more a nostalgia for nostalgia than the thing itself, which made them call their daughter after the roses. And in a way it was well chosen, though they could never agree afterwards who thought of it first. Elizabeth called her Bertie. She was a down-to-earth child, with a comical side to her nature. Mark always called her Albertine.

When Elizabeth got home that evening, after her harrowing day in the hands of Mr Goodman, the house was in a state of hush and quiet. She showed me her empty handbag.

"You mean—?"

"That's it. Oh, and I'm afraid Mr Goodman fell down the mountain."

"Oh dear," I said, not really paying much attention. "No yelps or screams?"

"Not a peep."

"Christian's sick."

"Sick?"

"Well, he's not sick exactly." I told her what happened, and what the doctor had said.

"Well, then," she said, "we'll just have to wait for him."

She never thought for a moment Christian wouldn't recover. I was the only one with little faith.

On the third day, in the morning, she and I were sitting at the table in the garden drinking coffee. It was still only eight o'clock. Pascal had done the night watch. Elizabeth had said that even if she wasn't worried about Christian, it was a good thing to keep watch over your friends.

"Like singing to a sleeping baby."

I raised my eyebrows, that being the quickest way of formulating a rather complex question.

"Yes," she said, and laid one of her hands on mine. "Very soon. It's all right now."

"You've got ink on your fingers," I said, "and a knot in your hair."

Her face looked a little bit tired, but in a good way. The holding-it-together lines had dropped, leaving tiny creases here and there, and she had a new look. Her face was un made-up.

"I'll just run upstairs. When is Doctor Rodin coming?"

"This afternoon. He said Christian would probably want to go out for a walk. I must say, he's very confident."

"I'll go and see. Where's Pascal? Is he still up there?"

"No. He's gone to check the roses." It had become a sort of general expression, like seeing a man about a dog. She went inside, through the dining room and upstairs to the room where we had laid Christian, and where he had been sleeping, continuously, for the last forty hours. I don't know why they always say three days. It's not really three days at all, it just involves three days, the day it happens, the day you wait, not knowing, and the day it's all all right again. She went into his room. The sheet was thrown back off the bed. He had leapt up in a hurry, with a bound, not a stagger. The window had been open in the night, and she went and looked out.

"Elizabeth!" He was down in the vines.

She waved at him. "You're up."

I heard him coming through the garden gate. He was dressed only in a pair of shorts. He looked perhaps a little pale. Even a little older, maybe.

"Christian?"

He came over and hugged me, and yawned. Elizabeth was looking down from the window.

"You OK now?"

"Yes," she said. "I'm much better. You too?"

"I'm fine," he said. If there had been the slightest tremor of a line around his mouth, a faint attempt at joviality, I wouldn't have believed him, I would have thought maybe it had failed, that it had been too strong for him. But he said it so lightly, and yet sincerely, with no extra layers, no hear-me-if-you-will, that's it, no morbidity, that I thought he might actually have forgotten. Do you think a sacrifice is still worth something if the person who makes it forgets? Perhaps it's worth even more.

Christian said, "There's someone here for you. At the gate."

"For me?" Elizabeth looked across. "I can't see . . ."

"Look sharp," I said, "Get moving. Look lively. He might not wait for ever."

"Certainly not," Mark said, "you're quite late enough as it is."

There are some moments in life you can never repossess. Maybe they are the moments which were never yours in the first place, but because you were not merely a casual spectator, because you too, caught a fragment of their emotion – even if it's only a shadow's worth – you are unable to embellish. Honesty interposes, the baldest report, the simple phrases of a revelation, and revelations not only blind you, they stun you, so that you can never, thereafter, tell it any way but one.

Mark looked up at her. She was leaning out of the window. It really is only the simplest questions you have to ask.